~THE~

CANDY SHOP
WAR

ARCADE CATASTROPHE

Also by Brandon Mull:

~THE~
CANDY SHOP
WAR

ARCADE CATASTROPHE

Brandon Mull

Aladdin

New York   London   Toronto   Sydney   New Delhi

For Tiff and Ty, magical candy and arcade prizes!

ALADDIN

An imprint of Simon & Schuster Children's Publishing Division

1230 Avenue of the Americas, New York, NY 10020

First Aladdin paperback edition June 2014

Text copyright © 2007 by Creative Concepts LC

Cover illustration copyright © 2014 by Nigel Quarless

Interior illustrations copyright © 2014 by Nigel Quarless

All rights reserved, including the right of reproduction in whole or in part in any form.

ALADDIN is a trademark of Simon & Schuster, Inc., and related logo
is a registered trademark of Simon & Schuster, Inc.

For information about special discounts for bulk purchases, please contact
Simon & Schuster Special Sales at 1-866-506-1949 or business@simonandschuster.com.

The Simon & Schuster Speakers Bureau can bring authors to your live event.

For more information or to book an event contact the Simon & Schuster Speakers Bureau
at 1-866-248-3049 or visit our website at www.simonspeakers.com.

Cover designed by Jessica Handelman

The text of this book was set in Adobe Garamond.

Manufactured in the United States of America 0218 OFF

6 8 10 9 7

This book has been cataloged with the Library of Congress.

ISBN 978-1-4814-1120-2

CONTENTS

CONTENTS

LATE ONE NIGHT

Roman lay still in the darkness, his covers up to his neck. The hall light had gone out five minutes ago. He heard no murmurs of conversation. Only the whir of the air conditioner interrupted the silence.

He could probably get started, but it would be safer to wait a few more minutes. In the dark, with nothing to do, waiting was hard. Seconds passed like minutes, and minutes dragged like hours. Roman kept losing the staring contest with the digital numbers of his clock as he willed the time to advance.

Bored or not, he chose to wait. If his parents caught him breaking curfew, he would get grounded for even longer. He had almost survived the week. He had not left the house except with family, and he had gone to bed by ten o'clock every night. Once in bed, he was not allowed to have his light on, which meant no reading comics and no drawing.

Ten o'clock might not sound early to some people, but it was summer vacation, and even during the school year, Roman usually stayed up until at least midnight. In the summer he was often awake until well after that.

Now that the end of his punishment was near, it would be tragic to get caught breaking the rules. So far, each night after going to bed, once the house became still, he had clicked on a flashlight under his blankets. Twice he had heard footsteps in the hall as his mother or father came to check on him, and both times he had switched off the light well before his door had inched open.

The air conditioner stopped blowing cool air through the vent high on the wall. The house was quiet. It was probably safe. If he heard somebody coming, he would just be quick.

Roman clicked on his flashlight. Made of shiny metal, it was long and heavy, with a strong bulb. The bright beam provided more than enough light for reading comic books. He had checked how much of that light escaped when he kept the powerful flashlight under the covers. From outside his room, a person practically had to lie down and stare under the door to see any sign of it.

Roman retrieved his drawing pad and colored pencils from under his bed. He had no new comics, and he was feeling in a creative mood. He flipped past pictures of battleships, dinosaurs, superheroes, and burning buildings. The current image in progress involved three skaters diving out of the way as a monster truck crashed through a brick wall. It was more than halfway done.

He was trying to decide what insignia to put on the most prominent skateboard when he heard distinct tapping at his window. Roman reflexively switched off his flashlight and laid his head down, hiding the drawing pad beneath his chest. He held his breath. The gentle tapping repeated insistently. As the fear of discovery faded, Roman began to wonder who was at his window.

Since his bedroom was on the second floor, this was especially strange.

Roman peeked out from under his covers. The glow of street-lights backlit the figure outside his window enough to confirm that it was a person. There was no way one of his parents was out there on the narrow apron of roof. It had to be one of his friends.

None of his friends had ever visited him like this. What if it was a burglar or somebody shady? But would robbers tap persistently to announce their presence? The figure at the window waved and gently tapped again.

Otherwise the house remained quiet. Roman crawled out of bed, crossed to the window, and clicked on his flashlight. The bright beam revealed Marisa, squinting and holding up a hand to shield her eyes.

He switched off the light. What was Marisa doing on his roof? She knew he was grounded. This could get him busted for life!

He unlocked the window and slid it up, grateful that he was in a T-shirt and shorts. When he was feeling hot, Roman sometimes stripped down to his underwear to sleep.

"Hey, Rome," Marisa whispered, carefully crouching through the window.

"Hi, Risa," Roman whispered back, glancing nervously at his door. He heard no hint of his parents stirring. "How'd you get on my roof?"

"I have my ways," she said with a mysterious smile. "You're almost done being grounded, right?"

"Unless my parents catch you here," Roman said.

"I won't stay long," she promised. "I just wanted to show you something." She held out her hand. The back was stamped with a blue fighter jet.

"You got it," Roman said, impressed.

"Chris helped me," Marisa replied. "Rome, he was right. It's better than you could guess. Way better. It's like a passport into the coolest club ever."

"I know that much," Roman said. "What kind of club? He would never tell us."

She shook her head. "I can't. I promised. You'll understand when you get yours."

Roman huffed darkly. "Right. Risa, I'm done. That's how I got busted in the first place. My parents would destroy me if I went back to that arcade. Besides, I already blew all my money. It wasn't enough."

"You have to go back," Risa insisted. "Chris and I will put up the money."

"What?"

"The jet stamp comes with perks. I've got some spare money now. You're part of the way there, Rome. Only two jets are left. You have to finish what you started."

"I don't know," he said.

"Other people are catching on. Those two jets won't stay available forever. You need to win one."

Roman shook his head. "Whether or not I use my own money, I'm not supposed to go to Arcadeland again."

"That's why I came," Marisa said. "I knew you'd think twice before coming back. I get that you're not supposed to, but you have to do it. Trust me. It's worth the risk."

Roman heard the floor creak out in the hall. Chills raced through him. Marisa shot him a worried look. "Go," he whispered urgently.

"Come to the arcade Saturday morning," she whispered back, lunging toward the window. "Use any excuse. Just come."

Marisa dove out the window as the handle of his bedroom door turned softly. Facing the door, Roman winced. There was no time to get back in bed. Not that it would matter. The crash of Marisa slamming onto the roof would give them away.

Except he heard no crash. Not even a creak. Switching off his flashlight, Roman rolled it across the carpeted floor toward his dresser. The door eased open. His dad peeked in. Roman didn't move, like a wild animal trying to blend with its surroundings. The dark offered some cover, but light from the hall spilled across his empty bed. After a brief pause, the door opened wider.

"Roman?" Dad asked.

"I'm here," Roman said weakly.

His dad stepped into the room, admitting more light as the door opened all the way. "Why's your window open?"

"I was hot," Roman invented desperately, trying to act calm. Although it seemed physically impossible, somehow Marisa had still made no noise. "I was bored."

His dad crossed to the window and looked out. Roman's stomach clenched with worry. How would his dad react when he saw Marisa out there?

But his dad turned away from the window as if he had seen nothing. "You weren't thinking of climbing out there?"

"What? No way! I'm grounded. Besides, there's no way down." There really wasn't. Not without a ladder. Had Marisa brought a ladder?

"Climbing onto roofs in the dark is a good way to break your neck."

"I know. I was just stir-crazy. I wanted some air."

His dad nodded. "All right. I guess I can understand that.

You're supposed to be in bed, you know, but at least your light was off."

"I wasn't reading or anything," Roman said. "Just restless."

"I get why you're restless. I'm sure this has felt like a long week. Still, a punishment is no good unless it gets enforced. Hang in there."

"I will," Roman said. He walked over to shut the window. Glancing out as casually as possible, he caught no glimpse of Marisa. After closing the window, Roman returned to his bed.

Roman's dad walked to the door. "Get some sleep."

"I will. Good night."

"Night."

The door closed, leaving the room dark aside from the soft light coming from the face of Roman's digital clock and the diffused light seeping through the window. Roman waited quietly, letting the minutes pass.

How had Marisa escaped? How had she done it so quietly? He could only imagine that she had dived off the roof. Which meant that Marisa might currently be sprawled on his driveway with a broken neck.

If she had been willing to climb to his window in the middle of the night, the jet club must really be cool. Chris had insisted that earning the stamp was worth it, and apparently Risa agreed. Roman gripped his covers tightly. Risa had even offered to give him money so he could keep earning tickets.

So far Roman had spent all of his personal savings earning prize tickets—more than four hundred dollars. The money had come from the little safe on his dresser, the one with the words *PRIVATE FUND* printed across the back. The money belonged to him, but, except for minor purchases, he was only supposed to spend it with permission. For more than a week before he was grounded, Roman had turned twenties into tokens until he had nothing left. When his parents had caught him, Arcadeland had been forbidden, and his week as an inmate had begun.

Could he really go back there? Chris had promised that the jet stamp would change his life, and Risa was backing him up.

The house remained quiet. After retrieving his flashlight, Roman crept to the window and opened it. He stepped out onto the roof, the shingles creaking noisily. Again he wondered how Marisa had stayed so silent.

Clicking on the flashlight, he scanned the empty driveway, finding no paralyzed bodies. "Marisa?" he whispered loudly. "Risa? You out there?"

There came no reply.

Roman climbed back into his room, stashed the flashlight, put his drawing pad and pencils away, and then returned to bed. With his mind so full of worries and questions, there was no longer any need to draw.

He had blown his savings at an arcade. No huge deal, right? He was only a kid. There would be plenty of time to earn more.

Still, it was all the money he had saved for his entire life, and he had made his parents angry by sneakily spending it. All to earn a cheesy stamp. The jet stamp had to include amazing perks, or else why would it be worth so many tickets?

Chris was a smart kid, and he had remained adamant. He had insisted that the rewards of the stamp were way cooler than a free lifetime supply of Arcadeland tokens, tons better than free lifetime Arcadeland food and drinks. Chris had promised that Roman would thank him forever. Now Risa too.

Roman pressed his cheek into his pillow. He had no savings left. He had gotten grounded for a week of his precious summer vacation. But if Marisa and Chris would put up the money for him to keep earning tickets, Roman knew he had to go back to Arcadeland.

CHAPTER ONE

DEAD MAN'S RUN

Straddling his bike, Nate stared down the long slope. He had heard older kids call it Dead Man's Run. The name seemed appropriate. Rutted by tires and rainfall, the dirt track wound down a steep hillside, skirting sheer edges much of the way. From his current vantage point, some stretches of the path seemed to drop almost vertically. The idea of walking down Dead Man's Run made him uncomfortable, let alone riding a bike.

"Look at her go," Pigeon murmured. Hair buzzed to a uniform bristle, he stood beside Nate, clutching the handlebars of a shabby bike.

Protected by a helmet, elbow pads, knee pads, and gloves, Summer raced fearlessly down the trail on a rusty mountain bike. She reached a long, straight, steep portion of the trail that swooped directly into a banked turn. They had scouted the path beforehand, and Nate knew that a fairly high cliff was hidden just beyond the bend.

Crouching forward, Summer pedaled hard down the slope, gaining way too much speed. There was no chance of making the turn.

Instead, Summer used the angled bank as a ramp, hitting it straight on at full speed and then launching into the air.

Once airborne, she kicked away from her bike, sailing higher and farther than the laws of physics should have allowed as the bike tumbled out of view. Her gliding trajectory was possible only thanks to the Moon Rock in her mouth. The candy reduced the effect of gravity on her, although it did not entirely erase the pull, as was proved when Summer gradually curved out of view.

"Think she'll be okay?" Lindy asked.

"We'll know in a minute," Pigeon said, holding up his walkie-talkie. He pressed the talk button. "How does she look?"

"She won't make it all the way to me," Trevor replied. "She'll clear most of the slope. What a jump! She's waiting to bite, cutting it close. Okay, she froze just in time. She did it perfectly, just before hitting the ground. Still frozen. Still frozen. Now she's down. She's fine. Over."

"Let us know when she reaches you."

"Will do."

Nate was glad to hear that Summer had timed her bite right. Earlier in the summer, through accidental experimentation, they had discovered that biting a Moon Rock temporarily froze you in space, no matter how fast or slow you were moving at the time. The knowledge came in handy. Even with reduced gravity, if you fell a long way, you could eventually build up enough speed to really hurt yourself.

The experience of biting a Moon Rock was not comfortable—it felt like a jolt of electricity, made your ears ring, and left you temporarily dizzy. But your body suffered no lasting damage from the sudden stop, and the results were very reliable. The knowledge that biting a Moon Rock served as instant brakes had allowed them to attempt some risky stunts with the candy. You had to make sure to bite only when close to the ground, because after you unfroze, all the antigravity effects of the Moon Rock would be gone and you would fall like normal.

"She'll probably win," Lindy said.

Nate stared at the redhead. Less than a year ago, Lindy had been an aging magician named Belinda White. She had originated the formula for Moon Rocks and several other magical treats. Mr. Stott had raided her notes and learned to replicate many of her creations, adding them to his growing menu of supernatural candy.

But Lindy retained no memory of her previous life. At the same time as she had sipped water from the Fountain of Youth, she had also unknowingly consumed a Clean Slate—a potent confection of her own design that had completely erased her identity. She currently lived with Mr. Stott, who had adopted her after John Dart had provided the necessary paperwork. She had joined Nate and his friends for most of their fifth-grade year and now routinely spent time with them during the summer. They called themselves the Blue Falcons, and they regularly experimented with magical candy.

"Don't count us out," Pigeon said. "Ironhides might still prove to be the best candy for downhill racing. Summer fell a long way, but I'll fall faster."

"Hopefully I won't fall at all," Nate added.

The walkie-talkie crackled. "She made it to me. Just over one minute."

"That'll be hard to beat," Pigeon conceded.

"We'll see." Nate pulled out a stick of Peak Performance gum. Unlike Pigeon and Summer, who had bought junky secondhand bikes for this contest, he was riding his own bike. To be safe, he had on elbow pads and a helmet, but he expected that the heightened state of awareness and coordination provided by Peak Performance would allow him to make it down without any mishaps.

He put the gum in his mouth and started chewing. It was hard to feel the effects of Peak Performance unless you were in motion. He had used the gum on many occasions, and it had never failed him. "Tell Trevor to start the stopwatch," Nate said.

"Ready with the time?" Pigeon asked into the walkie-talkie.

"Just a second," came the reply. "Okay, I'm ready."

"On your mark," Pigeon said into the walkie-talkie. "Get set. Go!"

Nate started down Dead Man's Run. It still looked freaky, but now that he was moving, he had an instinctive sense for where to guide his bike. Subtleties of balance and momentum that he had never perceived suddenly felt like second nature. He pedaled hard but resisted going as fast as he could. He could sense the limits of what he could handle without losing control.

With the wind in his face, Nate rode as he had never imagined possible. He let his rear wheel slide as he rounded tight corners. He took jumps to avoid rocky patches. When the way was straight, he tucked forward, zooming with suicidal confidence, only to hit the brakes and fishtail around a hairpin corner. Dirt sprayed. Rocks tumbled. His stomach lurched as he jumped to a lower portion of the trail, shortening a switchback.

He knew he should be terrified. Without Peak Performance, he would have wrecked his bike a dozen times. Yet somehow he managed to enjoy the exhilaration rather than fear the danger.

The exertion did not tire him. Chewing Peak Performance meant you could run at a full sprint without ever feeling winded. Maximum effort seemed like no big deal for as long as the magic lasted.

Trevor and Summer came into view. Trevor was quite a bit taller than her now, having gained a few inches during the school year. The way was getting less steep, so Nate pedaled with everything he had, skidding to a stop after he passed Trevor.

"A minute twenty-one," Trevor reported.

"What did Summer get?" Nate asked.

"A minute six," Trevor replied. "You looked awesome coming down, though. I wish I had it on video!"

"It felt pretty awesome," Nate admitted, disappointed that he had come in second. Still, coming in fifteen seconds behind somebody who had glided most of the way down the mountain wasn't too bad. And unlike Summer, he hadn't trashed his bike in the process. Now the only question was whether Pigeon would put him in last place.

Trevor relayed the exact time through the walkie-talkie.

"Pretty quick," Lindy replied. "Pigeon is ready to go. Is the timer set?"

"Ready when you are," Trevor responded.

"Great. Ready, set, go!"

Trevor tapped his stopwatch.

Nate looked up the hill. The contours of the landscape currently hid the top of the trail from sight. The brush on the hill was golden brown in response to the dry summer weather, interrupted by jutting rocks, patches of dirt, and an occasional oak tree. Evening was fading. They had timed their contest carefully, hoping the hillside would be deserted by sunset, since most bystanders would have had questions about a girl flying hundreds of yards through the air. So far, nobody had disturbed them.

Pigeon was sucking on an Ironhide as he came down the hill. The jawbreaker would prevent his skin from tearing and his bones from breaking. It made him no stronger or faster, but while the candy lasted, it would be just about impossible for him to get injured.

When Pigeon first came into view, he had clearly already fallen. The Ironhide did not prevent him from getting dirty, nor did it prevent his clothes from ripping and accumulating prickers from the weeds.

Of the five friends, Pigeon was the least confident on a bike. It showed. He took a corner too fast and plowed into a small boulder, catapulting over the handlebars and landing in a cloud of dust and sliding rocks. He was on his feet instantly, scrambling up the trail to retrieve his bike.

Back astride the bike, he reached the steep run where Summer had left the trail by jumping off the banked turn. Pigeon hit the same ramp at a high velocity, but instead of floating a ridiculous distance through the air, he demonstrated what gravity was supposed to do when somebody rode a bike off a cliff.

Losing his forward momentum, he fell with increasing speed before slamming into a cluster of jagged rocks, his husky body tumbling and cartwheeling, arms and legs flailing loosely. The rusty bike crumpled on impact and bounced along beside him. It was the kind of spine-crushing accident that should have been fatal. Even knowing that Pigeon was sucking on an Ironhide, Nate found himself wringing his hands.

Once Pigeon stopped somersaulting and sliding, he got up. He hustled to the bike, but the front tire was shaped like a taco and the frame was bent or maybe broken. Turning, Pigeon raced recklessly toward them on foot, falling twice as he jumped off small ledges.

Panting and sweaty, his clothes torn and dusty, Pigeon reached Trevor and flopped to the ground. Although he seemed exhausted, there was no blood on him.

"One minute, fifty-three seconds," Trevor reported.

"Last place?" Pigeon wheezed.

"You had the best crash," Summer consoled.

"Did it hurt?" Nate wondered.

Pigeon sat up. "No. It freaked me out, though. I thought I was dead for a second there."

"Here comes Lindy," Trevor announced.

Nate turned to watch. She was using Peak Performance and riding her own bike, just as he had. He wondered if her magic eye would give her an advantage.

Lindy had been missing an eye when Mr. Stott took over as her guardian, but a powerful magician named Mozag had provided a replacement. The glass eye looked perfectly real but could see better than a normal human eye. With her replacement eye, Lindy could see in the dark, zoom in on distant objects like a telescope, and even recognize different temperatures.

Whether the eye was helping or not, Lindy came tearing down the hillside like a professional stuntwoman with a death wish. Nate wondered if he had looked that good while taking wild jumps and careening around corners. She skidded to a stop near the others with impressive precision.

"What a rush," she said with a huge grin.

"You were cruising," Trevor complimented. "You should have had me time you."

Lindy shook her head. "Three contestants, one for each candy." She looked down at Pigeon, who was still sitting in the dirt. "You look like you were hit by a train."

Pigeon gave a weak smile. "Welcome to my life. Not only did I come in last, I'm also the most tired and filthy."

"I wasn't timed," Lindy said. "Let's say you beat me."

"I don't need your pity," Pigeon said, getting to his feet. "You looked just as fast as Nate."

Trevor stuffed his stopwatch and walkie-talkie into a backpack. "Moon Rocks definitely won as the fastest way down the mountain."

"I thought they would," Lindy reminded everyone. "But Peak Performance wasn't far behind."

"And my bike wasn't totaled," Nate chimed in.

Lindy nodded thoughtfully. "If we could mix Peak Performance with an Ironhide and a sturdy bike . . ."

"Can't risk mixing candies," Pigeon said. "Instead of a combined effect, you might get something unexpected. Like your head bursting apart."

"I said 'if,'" Lindy pointed out. "*If* we could find a safe way to mix the candies, great skill and much riskier jumps might combine to have a chance."

"I lost a lot of time going back for the bike when I crashed," Pigeon said. "And I'm a lousy sprinter."

"I could have hit the jump a little better," Summer said. "I could probably shave a few more seconds off my time."

"If we were mixing," Nate said, "Peak Performance and Moon Rocks would probably beat Peak Performance and Ironhides."

"It's all speculation," Pigeon complained. "We can't test it out."

"It can still be fun to speculate," Lindy said.

Pigeon shrugged.

Trevor elbowed Nate and jerked his head in the direction opposite from the hillside. Nate looked where Trevor had indicated and saw a pair of blocky men in suits walking toward them.

"Am I seeing double?" Nate asked.

"There are two of them," Lindy confirmed. "And yes, they look almost identical. They must be twins. One has a small mark on his neck. It could be mistaken for a mole from a distance, but it's actually a tiny tattoo of a rosebud."

The men evidently saw the kids looking because one of them waved. The pair strode directly toward them. Both men had dark hair, and binoculars hung from their necks. Nate waved back. "What do you think they want?" he murmured.

"They don't have bikes," Trevor noted. "They're not dressed for hiking."

"They have binoculars," Summer observed. "Were they spying on us?"

"I knew we shouldn't have used the candy in such a public place," Pigeon groaned. "Without white fudge clouding people's minds, it was only a matter of time before we got caught."

"This isn't a very public place," Nate said. "We're practically in the wilderness. And it's late. We were keeping watch."

"Apparently not well enough," Pigeon said. "Do we make a run for it? You guys could use your bikes. Summer and I can use Moon Rocks."

"What if they're just bird-watchers?" Trevor said.

"In suits?" Summer replied doubtfully. "Here? Now? They look like government guys."

"They look really similar," Lindy said. "Maybe they're clones."

"We should start moving away from them," Nate said. "We don't need to run. We can just act like we're heading home. If they chase us, then we can start using candy."

"Sounds good to me," Trevor seconded.

They turned and started marching away from Dead Man's Run

in a direction that would let them avoid the men in suits. Nate, Trevor, and Lindy walked their bikes so that Pigeon and Summer could keep pace.

"A moment of your time," one of the men called.

Nate looked back. One of the men had his hands cupped around his mouth. The other was waving both hands over his head.

Nate stopped walking. "We need to get home," he called.

"We have a mutual friend," the man called back. "John Dart."

Nate exchanged glances with his friends. They hadn't heard from John in months.

"What do you think they want?" Pigeon asked.

"They could be faking," Trevor warned. "They could be bad guys."

"What do you want?" Nate hollered.

"Just a few words," the man called back. "We know all about you. John is in trouble. We're all on the same side."

Nate looked to his friends again.

"If they found us here," Summer said, "they'll find us again."

"Might as well get it over with," Pigeon said.

"Stay ready for trouble," Nate warned before raising his voice. "All right. Let's talk."

Reversing his direction, Nate led the others toward the heavyset men. The duo waited patiently as the kids approached. Their dark gray suits had faint pinstripes. The blue handkerchiefs peeking from their breast pockets matched their neckties. Both suits looked worn and a little rumpled. The men had stocky necks and wide builds, and both wore large black shoes. Their blunt faces were not handsome, with heavy eyebrows and fleshy lips. Weighty rings adorned each thick-fingered hand.

Nate stopped about five yards from the men. "Who are you guys?"

"We work with John Dart," said the man on the left. His deep voice was slightly hoarse. He enunciated each word clearly.

"That isn't an answer," Summer pointed out.

The other man shrugged. "I'm Ziggy Battiato, and this is my brother Victor."

"You've been watching us?" Nate asked.

"You've been sloppy," Victor replied. "We've tailed you for three days. We know where each of you lives. We see you frequenting the Sweet Tooth Ice Cream and Candy Shoppe. We've seen you using magical enhancers out in the open."

"We're careful," Pigeon protested.

"You take some rudimentary precautions," Ziggy allowed. "But anyone intent on learning your secrets would have little trouble."

"John is missing," Victor said. "When did you last see him?"

Nate held out a hand for the others to keep silent. "How do we know you're not bad guys using us for information on him?"

"We haven't tranquilized you," Ziggy said, opening his coat enough to flash a pistol.

"We're here to help," Victor said steadily.

"What can it hurt?" Lindy said. "It's been some time. We last saw him in March. March twelfth."

Nate glanced at her. For somebody who had forgotten her identity, she sometimes had an uncanny memory.

Ziggy gave a nod. "Makes sense. He didn't want to interfere in your lives more than necessary. John went missing a month ago. He was last seen not far from here. But you never heard from him? No final message?"

Nate shook his head. "Nothing since March."

Ziggy and Victor shared a look. Victor faced the kids. "John would be angry with us for asking, but would you be willing to help us find him?"

"Yes," Nate said. "As long as you're really his friends."

Ziggy gave Nate a measuring stare. "Good answer. You're smart to be cautious." He held out a business card. Nate accepted it.

Ziggy and Victor Battiato

PROBLEM SOLVERS   REASONABLE RATES

"You kids spend time with Sebastian Stott," Victor said. "Let him have a look at that card. If we check out, come to Schwendiman's All-You-Can-Eat Buffet tomorrow at noon. We'll talk more then."

CHAPTER TWO

ADVICE

Nate and the others accompanied Lindy home to the Sweet Tooth Ice Cream and Candy Shoppe. She lived with Mr. Stott in the apartment above the store. By the time they arrived it was almost dark.

The shop had recently closed, but Lindy had a key. The interior looked much the same as when Mrs. White had run the business. Tables and chairs with chrome legs were arranged on a black and white checkerboard floor. A vast assortment of candy both familiar and exotic crowded the shelves behind the long, L-shaped counter. None of the magical candy was on display. All supernatural treats were stored in the back.

Lindy led the way to the stairs and up to the apartment. She opened the door and called, "Dad!"

Sebastian Stott came into view, wearing a tweed jacket with patches on the elbows. Underneath his coat was a blue T-shirt with a picture of a frowning stick figure. The words *FEED ME* were printed beneath. Mr. Stott's neatly trimmed beard had two thick, dark streaks interrupting the silver. His eyebrows were a bit unruly. Despite his age, he was robust, with a hearty voice and searching eyes.

"Hello, Lindy," Mr. Stott greeted with grandfatherly warmth. He looked at the others. "I wasn't expecting all of you. How did the experiment go?"

"Moon Rocks won," Summer said. "Peak Performance took second, Ironhides third."

"Hard to beat jumping down a mountain," Mr. Stott said. "Is everyone all right?"

"We had some visitors," Nate said, handing over the business card. "They said they know John Dart. I guess he's missing."

Mr. Stott studied the card. He held it up to a light and squinted at it from varying distances. Then he gave the kids a long stare. "The Battiato brothers have quite a reputation."

"Are they on our side?" Trevor asked.

"They're certainly on John's side," Mr. Stott answered. "All magicians are a little wary of their kind."

"They're policemen like John?" Nate asked. "Policemen for magicians?"

"That's how they see it," Mr. Stott said. "Not all such operatives wield their authority as responsibly as others. I could tell you some stories. But yes, the Battiatos work for Mozag. I've never met them, but this card bears markings that confirm their legitimacy. What did they want?"

"They want us to help them find John," Summer said.

Mr. Stott nodded vaguely. "I had heard that John went missing."

"You heard?" Pigeon exclaimed. "Why didn't you tell us?"

"I didn't want to upset you," Mr. Stott replied. "And frankly, I didn't want you involved. It isn't safe. These thugs should be ashamed for asking children to do their dirty work."

Nate raised his eyebrows. "We've had some experience."

"I seem to remember other people making use of us in the past," Summer added.

Mr. Stott cleared his throat uncomfortably, his eyes flicking to Lindy. "That was then. You were already involved, and it was an emergency."

"If John is missing, that sounds like an emergency to me," Pigeon said.

"John dealt fairly with us," Mr. Stott acknowledged. "I wish him no harm. Quite the contrary, I would help if I could."

"We know," Trevor said. "You can't leave your lairs. It's either this store, your house, or your ice cream truck."

"I'm more limited than most magicians," Mr. Stott said. "I don't have servants or engineered apprentices. I'm trying to keep it simple. I make delicious treats, both regular and enchanted. I tend my store. And I try to keep an eye on you kids."

"We owe John," Nate said. "Without him, we would never have survived Mrs. White." He tried not to let his eyes stray to Lindy. She had heard them discuss Mrs. White before. She knew that Mrs. White had owned this store. But Lindy had no idea that she used to be Mrs. White. In her mind, she was simply Lindy Stott, an adopted orphan with no clear memories of her life before Mr. Stott took her in.

"He put everything right for us after all the craziness," Summer said. "He and Mozag."

"John would not want you kids involved," Mr. Stott asserted.

"That doesn't mean he doesn't need our help," Nate countered.

"Or that he wouldn't be grateful," Trevor added.

Mr. Stott sighed. "Before he disappeared, John warned me that something big was going on locally."

"You never told us," Pigeon accused.

"Of course not," Mr. Stott said. "Any such information would only have tickled your curiosity."

"What is it?" Summer asked.

"He never specified," Mr. Stott replied. "He was investigating. He just wanted me to stay alert and to keep you kids away from Walnut Hills."

"How were you supposed to do that?" Trevor asked. "Walnut Hills is the next town over. We live right next door."

"If you haven't noticed how I've kept you away," Mr. Stott said, "then I'm doing my job correctly. I've done my best to suggest excursions here in Colson, or to the west of town, and to discourage any activities that might take you east into Walnut Hills."

"My mom shops at the Walnut Hills Mall all the time," Pigeon said. "Should I warn her?"

Mr. Stott shrugged. "I have no idea what the danger entails."

"We should at least hear what the Battiatos have to say," Nate proposed. "Partly in case we can help John, partly so we can learn more about the threat."

"I agree," Lindy said. "We can't turn our backs on John. He's like an uncle."

Mr. Stott scratched his beard uncomfortably. "If the Battiatos contacted you, they are here to draw you in. These men are professionals. If you speak with them, you'll end up wanting to work with them."

"If it really means helping John, I already want to work with them," Nate said. "Without him, I would be stuck as an old man."

"The Battiatos are legitimate," Mr. Stott said reluctantly. "But you could become embroiled in something very precarious. Think about it before you rush in. If somebody got the best of John, that person spells serious trouble."

"If somebody got the best of John," Pigeon remarked, "we're probably already in major trouble. Lots of people in town almost had their lives ruined by Mrs. White last year, and they had no idea. I don't want to get blindsided. I'd rather be able to put up a fight."

"Where did they want to meet?" Mr. Stott wondered.

"Schwendiman's All-You-Can-Eat," Lindy said.

"That's practically in Walnut Hills!" Mr. Stott protested.

"Lots of Colson is practically in Walnut Hills," Summer pointed out. "That happens when you share a border."

"I don't like it," Mr. Stott said. "Why can't they come here?"

"Wouldn't they worry about entering the lair of a magician?" Pigeon asked.

"They already set up the meeting," Nate said. "We don't have another way to contact them. Besides, Schwendiman's is usually crowded. It isn't like they're luring us away to some remote place."

"I'm not worried about them harming you directly," Mr. Stott said. "I'm worried about them getting you involved in a potentially hazardous situation."

"We don't even know what they want yet," Lindy observed.

"I prefer it that way," Mr. Stott said. "I try to be open-minded. I let you kids use magical candy more than many would consider prudent. But you don't want to get involved with magical enforcers. The best of them have poor life expectancies."

"We get that it could be risky," Nate insisted. "We don't want to do this for fun. We're worried about John. And if something fishy is going on right beside us in Walnut Hills, we'd be smart to learn whatever information the Battiatos can share."

Mr. Stott shrugged. "I expressed my concerns. I can't stop you kids from going. I'm directly responsible only for Lindy."

"Can I go?" Lindy pleaded.

"Not all of you need to hear their proposal," Mr. Stott said. He took Lindy by the hand. "Knowing what I know, I would be a poor father if I let you consort with the Battiato brothers. If your friends insist on meeting with them, they can fill us in later."

"That's so unfair!" Lindy fumed. "I'm the one who spotted the tiny rosebud on Ziggy!"

"What?" Mr. Stott asked.

"It's a way to tell them apart," Pigeon said.

Mr. Stott looked at Nate. "Will you be going?"

"I just wanted to make sure they weren't bad guys," Nate said. "I get that something dangerous is probably going on, but if it might help John, I'll be at that meeting."

Mr. Stott gave a nod. "Keep your guard up. Make no promises or commitments. Don't answer any questions they have no business asking."

"We'll be careful," Summer promised.

Mr. Stott faced Lindy. "Your friends will tell you all about it."

"What if I go anyway?" Lindy asked defiantly.

"Then you will reap the consequences," Mr. Stott said. "Tomorrow I want you here with me until your friends come to share what they have learned."

* * * * *

Pigeon checked the hour as he approached his front door. It was later than the time he had told his Aunt Rhonda to expect him. Fortunately, his parents were away on an anniversary retreat, and Aunt Rhonda was not nearly as fussy as his mother.

Hurrying through the door, Pigeon raced up to his room. He wanted to get rid of his tattered clothes before his aunt saw him.

"Is that you, Paul?" Aunt Rhonda called.

"Yes!" he replied. "Just a second. I have to use the bathroom."

He had worn old clothes, knowing they would probably get mangled. He hurriedly changed into a more presentable outfit, then pulled a shoe box out from under his bed. It contained a modest rock collection, along with his supply of Brain Feed. He scooped some pebbles of Brain Feed into his pocket, replaced the shoe box, and hustled downstairs.

Aunt Rhonda leaned against the kitchen counter perusing a gossip magazine. She looked up as Pigeon entered. "Just because it stays light forever this time of year doesn't mean the clocks stop ticking. Your sisters are already in bed."

"Sorry, I was riding bikes with my friends. I'll do better tomorrow."

Aunt Rhonda shrugged. "I am the oldest in your mom's family. The oldest has to deal with all sorts of extra hassles. There should be some perks."

Pigeon grinned. "Do you mind if I go outside to see Diego?"

"Go ahead. But then get ready for bed afterward."

"Deal."

As Pigeon headed out the back door, his Labrador padded over to him, then paused, looking up expectantly. Mr. Stott had fiddled with his Brain Feed recipe over the past several months, trying to increase the duration of the effect. No animal had received close to the quantities Diego had consumed. Not only had the heightened intelligence and capacity for speech granted by the kibbles started lasting longer, a permanent increase in intelligence was gradually becoming evident. Even without the Brain Feed, Diego had become a better companion than ever and could now reliably respond to a wide variety of commands.

Pigeon cupped some Brain Feed in his palm and dumped the bits of food on the patio. Diego gobbled up all traces in no time.

"Much better," Diego sighed. "I can tell something is off when I don't have the Brain Feed. As soon as I eat, my memories return with sharper clarity. It's as if I remember the dream better after awakening."

"Mr. Stott thinks eventually the effect could become permanent," Pigeon said.

"Wouldn't that be nice? No more sleepwalking through most of my life. Aren't you up a little late?"

"We had an eventful day."

Diego sat up attentively. "Tell me about it."

"John Dart might be in trouble. Looks like we have some new bad guys in town."

"I'm here if you need me."

"We might," Pigeon admitted. "We were at Mr. Stott's tonight. He's worried about us getting involved. Honestly, so am I. We were in over our heads last time."

"How did you hear about the trouble?"

"Some friends of John tracked us down. They're magical police, like him."

"Who are the bad guys? What do they want?"

"We're not sure yet," Pigeon replied. "We'll get details tomorrow."

"Do you *want* details?"

Pigeon sat down, placing his elbow on his knee and his chin on his hand. "I'm not sure. What if we end up trying to deal with another Mrs. White?"

Diego shook his coat. "Not a cheerful thought. Speaking of our former archenemy, how is Lindy?"

Pigeon gave a neutral shrug. "She's sad that Mr. Stott doesn't want her meeting with the magical police."

"They know about her," Diego said.

"Probably. Mozag and John Dart know, so I expect these guys do as well. I just think Mr. Stott is worried what bad magicians might do if they find out about her."

"Like try to bring her memory back?"

"I don't know," Pigeon said. "Mr. Stott examined the recipe for the Clean Slate. He says making one is really difficult. He doesn't think he could do it. But he assured us that the effects of the Clean Slate should be permanent. He was worried for a while that mixing the Clean Slate with water from the Fountain of Youth could have weakened the magic. Different types of magic don't always blend well. But after studying the issue, he determined that the effects of the Clean Slate would actually be strengthened by the changes induced by the fountain."

"So nobody can bring her memory back," Diego verified.

"As far as we can tell," Pigeon said. "Of course, the other worry is that deep down Lindy is naturally evil. It might only be a matter of time before she heads down a dark path again."

"The old nature-versus-nurture argument," Diego said. "Hopefully Belinda turned evil because of the way she was raised. Her behavior might have been influenced by bad examples or difficult circumstances."

"Mr. Stott has searched," Pigeon said, "but he hasn't learned much about her younger days."

"You're worried about her," Diego said. "You like her."

"I like her a lot. Am I nuts? She's cute and really fun to hang out with. Most kids don't think a lot before they speak. She's different. She listens and she's smart. She might not have her memories, but she has a quick mind and an adult vocabulary. That can be hard to find."

"You have an unusual mind yourself," Diego said. "In some ways, you're older than your years. It must make you lonely sometimes."

"None of my friends are dumb," Pigeon hurriedly clarified. "But kids like Lindy are pretty impossible to find. It's just weird to like her so much when she used to be a dangerous, magical old lady. She could have killed us! Part of me is always nervous she's going to turn psychotic."

"Considering who she used to be, that is probably a healthy concern."

Pigeon rubbed Diego's head, then scratched behind his neck. "I'm glad I have you to talk with."

"I'm not called *man's best friend* for nothing," Diego replied. "That feels wonderful. Can you scratch a little lower? Mmmm, that's the spot."

"What should I do about the meeting tomorrow?"

"With the magical cops?"

Pigeon nodded.

"You're already involved," Diego said. "You might as well go learn the specifics."

"I was afraid you might say that."

CHAPTER THREE

THE BATTIATO BROTHERS

Schwendiman's All-You-Can-Eat Buffet stood in the parking lot of a strip mall near a pet shop, a frozen yogurt franchise, and a grocery store. Nate, Trevor, Summer, and Pigeon stashed their bikes before walking around to the front. Nate found the Battiato twins waiting just beyond the door, dressed in suits, their expressions neutral.

One of the brothers consulted a heavy wristwatch. "Right on time. If anything, thirty seconds early."

"Ziggy appreciates punctuality," Victor said.

Ziggy straightened his suit coat. "It's considerate."

"We're all here," Victor told the hostess, a young brunette with some purple in her hair.

The restaurant was fairly busy. Diners milled about, selecting food from counters protected by sneeze guards. Much of the food was kept warm in steam trays. The waitress guided the Battiatos to a padded booth that curved two-thirds of the way around a table. It looked just the right size for a party of six.

Knowing he would head to the buffet later, Nate had eaten a small breakfast. The sight of all the food had his stomach rumbling.

Ziggy motioned for the kids to scoot in. Victor sat at one end of the curved bench, Ziggy at the other.

"Have you eaten here before?" the hostess asked.

"Not this particular establishment," Victor said. "But believe me, we know the drill."

"Fair enough," she said. "Enjoy your meal."

"Food first?" Ziggy asked generally.

"Sure," Trevor seconded.

"I could eat," Nate said.

Victor and Ziggy stood up in unison. Ziggy rolled his head in a slow circle, making his neck pop. Victor noisily cracked his knuckles, surveying the restaurant stoically.

Ziggy nodded at Victor. "It's showtime."

Nate bit his lip to stifle a laugh.

Nate and the others followed Victor and Ziggy over to the food counters. Pigeon collected a chilled plate and began putting lettuce onto it.

"What are you doing?" Nate asked him.

"I've come here before," Pigeon said. "I guess salad first is a habit."

"No parents today," Nate reminded his friend. "You can get anything."

Shrugging, Pigeon added croutons and some ranch dressing, then grabbed a roll and a couple of squares of butter. "I don't mind salad. I'll get other stuff later."

Nate filled his first plate with fries and tater tots, putting plenty of ketchup and ranch on the side. He had to look around for a moment to find the forks and napkins. Then he returned to the table.

Ziggy stood beside the table, his pair of plates heaped with hot wings, thinly sliced prime rib, and lamb skewers. He chuckled as Nate slid down the bench next to Pigeon. "Rookie mistake."

"What?" Nate asked, glancing over at the husky man.

"You're loading up on fries," Ziggy said. "Your friend has salad and bread. That's all filler. Like soda. You have to save room for the good stuff."

Victor approached the table, his plates heavy with meat. He stood aside so Pigeon could enter the booth next to Summer. Once the four kids were seated, Ziggy and Victor took their places at the ends.

Ziggy stared across at Victor's plates. "I missed the bacon-wrapped turkey."

"Which is why I brought enough for both of us," Victor replied, giving some to his brother. "I told you not to rush. A good general surveys his battlefield."

"I found good grub," Ziggy said, trading plates with his brother.

"You guys take this pretty seriously," Nate commented.

"This is our domain," Ziggy said, indicating the room with his fork. "We were made for this."

"Welcome to the big show," Victor said, taking a large bite of prime rib.

"Not bad," Ziggy said, licking his lips.

"Why don't you get started so I can find out?" Victor complained.

"Wait," Trevor asked, brow furrowed, "why does he have to start for you to find out?"

"And why did you guys switch plates?" Summer wondered.

"That's an observant question," Ziggy said, stabbing a chunk of bacon-wrapped turkey with his fork. He deposited the greasy morsel into his mouth.

Victor nodded appreciatively, then dabbed his lips with a napkin. "Our enemies know, so you can as well. Ziggy and I share an unusual connection. I taste only what he tastes and I smell only what he smells. The food I eat nourishes me, but he gets all the sensations."

"Vice versa for me," Ziggy said. "If I want to try the wings, Victor has to eat them."

"Weird," Pigeon said. "What about sight and hearing?"

"Thankfully we see and hear for ourselves," Victor said. "Otherwise it would be complicated. We sometimes get brief glimpses of what the other sees or hears. Flashes."

"But you can't smell or taste for yourselves," Pigeon said.

"Not a bit," Ziggy said.

"It's no picnic when he uses the restroom," Victor confided.

"Hey," Ziggy complained, waving his hands. "We're trying to eat here!"

Nate had a tough time resisting the urge to laugh. He tried not to make eye contact with Summer, Trevor, or Pigeon; based on their muffled giggles, he figured it would only make him erupt.

Pigeon was the first to recover. "What about touch?" he asked.

"We feel pressure for ourselves," Victor said, "but pain is like odors. The other guy senses it."

"If I get injured," Ziggy said, "my body suffers the damage, but he feels the pain."

"Takes most of the fun out of punching him," Victor remarked.

"We can also share certain physical attributes," Ziggy said. "It's hard to explain, easier to demonstrate. You'll catch on."

"We digress," Victor said, taking a bite from a sparerib drenched in barbecue sauce. "The main event is being neglected."

"Sorry," Ziggy said. "Let's take care of business. We'll talk after."

Both men plowed into their food, making the meat promptly disappear. They didn't eat messily, but they didn't waste much time, either. Skewers and bones were piled neatly. Nate wasn't halfway through his fries before Victor and Ziggy were returning to the food counters.

"Those guys can eat," Summer said.

"I feel bad for the owner," Trevor said. "I have a feeling the Battiatos usually get more than they pay for at places like this."

The brothers came back loaded up with Chinese food, including stir fry, pot stickers, egg rolls, and orange chicken. "Not much seafood," Victor commented as they sat. "Too bad."

"I saw some decent Italian," Ziggy replied, switching plates with his brother.

"You don't want the Italian in a joint like this," Victor scolded.

"I'll do meatballs and lasagna anywhere," Ziggy replied.

They attacked their food vigorously. When the plates were empty, they stared at each other. "Feeling warmed up?" Victor asked.

"Chicken-fried steak?" Ziggy asked.

"You read my mind," Victor responded.

Having finished all the fries he wanted, Nate got up to hunt for other food. By the time he returned, Ziggy and Victor were already back in their seats and efficiently devouring more grub with no sign of slowing. Ziggy rose so Nate could scoot in.

The Battiatos finished their sixth plates before Nate completed his meal. Their later plates were less similar as each man pursued his preferences. Nate had to push to finish his last sparerib. After the fries and a crowded meal plate, he was getting pretty full.

Ziggy patted him on the back. "You already feeling it?"

Nate nodded.

"You're not sweating yet," Ziggy said. "You've got to go until the food sweat hits. That's how you know you did it right."

"Who wants dessert?" Victor asked, rising.

"Me," Pigeon said, scooting out of the booth.

"Know what you want?" Victor asked, placing a large hand on Pigeon's shoulder.

Pigeon shrugged. "Not yet."

Victor gave a nod. "When in doubt, follow the big guy. He'll lead you to the good stuff."

Nate went to find some dessert as well. In the end he settled on a slice of chocolate mousse pie and a lemon meringue tart. Victor and Ziggy returned to the table with abundant treats. Victor went heavy on sponge cake smothered in vanilla custard, while Ziggy had constructed a towering hot fudge sundae.

"Should we talk about why we're here?" Nate asked, taking a bite of pie.

Victor held up a spoon. "All in due time. I prefer not to divide my attention."

After Nate finished his desserts, he felt ready to burst. He probably should have left some of the lemon tart on the plate, but it had tasted too delicious to stop. Pigeon looked equally overfed, his posture awkward, a smudge of pudding at the corner of his mouth. Summer pointed out the pudding and he wiped it off.

Ziggy and Victor appeared satisfied. Both men had finished their plates first, then sat watching the kids in contented silence.

"Is everyone full?" Ziggy asked.

"I couldn't eat another bite," Trevor said.

"Thanks for lunch," Summer added.

"Our pleasure," Victor said.

"So, who took John?" Nate asked.

"We have the same question," Victor replied.

"What do you know?" Pigeon asked.

"Our suspicions center on Arcadeland," Ziggy said.

"The new arcade in Walnut Hills?" Trevor asked.

"Have you been there?" Victor wondered.

"Not yet," Trevor said. "It only opened last month. It's supposed to be awesome."

"It's certainly eye catching," Victor said. "We're not dealing with amateurs. Arcadeland was at the heart of John's investigation. We haven't figured out who owns it, but the arcade is almost certainly a magician's lair."

"Which means we can't enter," Ziggy added. "Not unless we want a fight. Anybody who has been magically altered would trip a number of alarms. And nobody wants to confront a magician in his lair, especially going in blind."

"Is this why you need us?" Trevor asked.

Victor gave a nod. "We need information. Eyes on the inside. The arcade isn't safe, but during the normal hours of operation it shouldn't pose serious danger to the average customer, especially if you keep your guard up."

"We need to learn what's going on," Ziggy said. "We're not even sure what kind of racket they're running. Ideally we'd like to identify the owner."

"Would I trip the magical alarms?" Nate wondered. "Magic aged me prematurely."

"Only if you were still an old man," Victor replied. "Now that you have been restored to your original state, you should read the same as any ordinary kid."

"What about Lindy?" Pigeon asked. "Do you know about her?"

"We know her story," Victor acknowledged. "She is definitely in an altered state and would surely trip magical warning signals. Whoever founded this arcade is not one of the good guys. Letting the mystery magician learn Lindy's secret could be dangerous for her."

"Dangerous for all of us," Nate clarified. "If she somehow got her memory back, Belinda would become a major threat. I saw a possible future where she was taking over the town, and that was just the first step of a bigger plan."

"You have to keep Lindy away from Arcadeland," Ziggy agreed. "I expect that Stott understands this."

"He wouldn't even let Lindy come here today," Pigeon said.

Victor nodded as if this were expected. "You four need to help reinforce his efforts to keep her out of Walnut Hills."

"Can we bring magical candy into the arcade?" Nate asked.

"You can and you should," Victor said. "I don't expect this venture to be overly dangerous, but if things go wrong, it could get messy fast. You need to be ready to make an escape. Having edible enhancers shouldn't trigger any alarms. In fact, you should even be able to use them without setting off alarms, since you'll have been invited into the lair."

"Invited?" Summer asked.

"The invitation is implied with a public area," Ziggy said. "Same with the retail portion of the Sweet Tooth Ice Cream and Candy Shoppe. The magician gives up some control over the environment upon granting public access."

"What are we looking for?" Pigeon wondered.

"We have some cheap digital cameras for you," Victor said. "Take pictures like you're horsing around, but try to get the employees in the background. Look for unusual games. Talk to any kids who seem like regulars. Keep your ears open. Take note of anything fishy."

Ziggy pulled out a fat wad of bills and began peeling off twenties. "Play lots of games. We'll start you out with five hundred dollars. We have plenty more if you need it."

Nate noticed Trevor gazing at the cash with wide eyes. "All for video games?"

"Whatever games you wish," Victor said. "Sample a wide variety. Keep an eye out for any oddities."

"I might enjoy this mission," Nate said, glancing from Victor to Ziggy.

"Don't get too excited," Ziggy said. "Something crooked is going on at Arcadeland. If you have some fun along the way, no problem, but don't forget the place is a trap. Keep in mind what Belinda White did with her candy shop. Don't eat anything, and if a game seems to have strange effects, be an observer, not a participant."

"We'll be right outside," Victor promised. "John would have our heads if anything happened to you kids."

"Deadly lair or not, we'll be there right away if you need us," Ziggy assured them. "You in?"

Nate and his friends exchanged small nods. Nate held out his hand for the money. "We're in."

CHAPTER FOUR

ARCADELAND

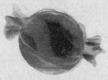

Half a block from Arcadeland, on the opposite side of the street, Summer and Pigeon ducked into an alley. Both of them looked up. The buildings on either side rose three stories tall.

"No fire escapes," Pigeon said.

"We'll have to use Moon Rocks," Summer answered, leading them farther down the alley. She looked back toward the street. Almost two hours had passed since they had left Schwendiman's All-You-Can-Eat Buffet. The sun was not directly overhead, so most of the alley was in shadow. Anyone in the cars driving by on Canal Street would have only a brief glimpse into the alleyway.

"Acceptable risk?" Pigeon asked.

"Nobody was nearby on the sidewalk," Summer said. "If we hurry we should be fine."

Pigeon glanced up. "Several windows."

Summer indicated a vertical path up the wall. "We'll be hard to see from a window if we stay along this line. People would practically have to lean out to get a view of us."

"We do need a good vantage point," Pigeon conceded.

Summer popped a Moon Rock into her mouth, feeling the familiar lightening of her frame. Pigeon did likewise. Summer jumped toward one side of the alley, soaring gently, then kicked off the side of a building, gaining altitude as she crossed to the far side. She kicked off the wall again, gliding higher.

Glancing down, she saw Pigeon staring up at her. She was already high, but she reminded herself that with the Moon Rock, to fall would be no big deal. Two more sharp kicks and she reached the top of one of the buildings.

Summer eased her light body over the edge to stand on the roof, then watched as Pigeon tried to follow her. He was kicking off the walls too straight-on, gaining only a little height every time he crossed from one side to the other. She almost called out some advice, then realized it would probably only embarrass him without improving his technique.

After springing back and forth more than fifteen times, Pigeon reached the top of the building. "Should I spit it out?" he asked.

"No point in wasting it," Summer said. "Just be careful not to float off the roof and cause a scene."

"Right."

They gingerly moved to the part of the roof overlooking Canal Street and Arcadeland. The arcade was much larger than Summer had expected. Neon fireworks burst in jerky patterns beside the flashy sign. Not only was the main building huge, but two miniature golf courses wrapped around it. There were batting cages on the near side and a twisty go-kart track on the far side. A tall chain-link fence enclosed the entire complex.

"Looks fun," Pigeon said.

Summer noticed that Pigeon was raising his head higher than necessary as he surveyed Arcadeland, making himself too visible from the street. "Stay low," she cautioned.

"Right."

Summer spotted Nate and Trevor on the far side of the street, trying to look casual as they scanned the rooftops. She lifted her head a little and waved. Nate saw her and gave a small salute. He and Trevor mounted their bikes, then rode over to the Arcadeland parking lot. She watched them deposit their bikes at the large bike rack before disappearing inside the building.

Pigeon shifted beside her. "I keep trying to tell myself they got the dangerous job, not the fun one."

"Are you believing it?"

"Not really."

"Me neither," Summer sighed. "But at least we had an excuse to climb a building. Nate was right that we'd be crazy to all go in together. This way, if something goes wrong, they can't catch us all at once."

"Think anything will happen?"

"Probably not. But better safe than sorry."

Summer studied Arcadeland. It seemed popular. There were cars in the parking lot and plenty of bikes at the bike rack. Two of the batting cages were in use, and several groups roamed the miniature golf courses, putting on artificial turf surrounded by miniature monuments. She saw the Leaning Tower of Pisa, the Taj Mahal, the Eiffel Tower, the Sphinx, Big Ben, Mount Rushmore, and others that she recognized but couldn't name.

Summer leaned toward Pigeon. "What's the name of that building in Russia with the colorful, onion-shaped domes?"

"In the West we call it St. Basil's Cathedral," he replied. "There's a rumor that the architect who designed it was blinded by Ivan the Terrible to prevent him from duplicating his efforts elsewhere."

"How do you know all this stuff?"

He shrugged. "I just like to read about history."

As the minutes dragged by, Summer felt her patience wearing thin. People made their way around the miniature golf courses. A trickle of customers entered and exited the front doors.

Summer tried to spot the Battiato brothers. Supposedly they were close by, but she hadn't seen them since leaving the buffet. She studied the parked vehicles in the area and scanned up and down the sidewalks, but she detected no sign of the beefy twins.

"What the . . . ?" Pigeon suddenly blurted.

"What?" Summer asked, glancing at him to see where he was looking.

"Do you see those two kids across the way?"

"Which kids?"

"The two near the batting cages, just outside the Arcadeland fence."

"A boy and a girl."

"Right."

"What about them?"

"Well, I barely saw it, but when they came out from behind that building next to Arcadeland, they were like ten feet off the ground. They glided to a landing on the pavement."

"Like they had Moon Rocks?"

"Or something."

Summer studied them as best she could. The girl had longish brown hair and tan skin. The boy had messy blond hair. They were looking around as if to make sure they were unobserved. Summer was about to comment that they were acting suspicious when the two kids jumped over the Arcadeland fence with a single smooth leap. The side of the batting cages would have shielded them from onlookers inside Arcadeland. But Summer saw the furtive act perfectly.

"Arcadeland must be handing out magic candy," Summer guessed.

"What do we do?" Pigeon asked.

"Those two probably know a lot about what's going on here."

"Do we go down there?"

Summer frowned. "We need information if we're going to help John. We shouldn't risk letting them get away without finding out more about them."

Pigeon gave a nod. "Then we better hurry."

* * * * *

Nate paused beside Trevor after entering Arcadeland. He had never been inside such a vast arcade before. Beyond the tiled lobby he could see traditional standing video games, driving games, shooting games, plus diverse games where a player could win tickets.

"This place is big," Trevor murmured.

"Let's check it out," Nate said.

For the first few minutes, Nate and Trevor roamed the aisles of games, surveying the different ways to spend tokens. Some of the shooting games looked really cool. One let two players hunt dinosaurs together. Another offered the chance to roam a zombie-infested mansion armed with machine guns. A third turned the player into the gunner atop an armored vehicle that prowled around a battlefield.

Trevor seemed extra interested in the racing games. You could ride a motorcycle that you turned by rocking it from side to side. A long row of car racing games used steering wheels to put the player in the driver's seat. Most featured exotic courses. Some of them were apparently set in the future. One unusual racing game allowed the player to pedal a bike that powered a one-man airship.

Nate didn't spend a lot of time on the traditional video games. There were some slick fighting games, and a few classic games like Gauntlet, Donkey Kong, and Pac-Man. But he could play games like that at home.

Most of the arcade was devoted to games that allowed the player to win tickets. Nate found Skee-Ball, basketball, and Whac-A-Mole. Some of the games seemed like pure chance, where you spun a big prize wheel or pressed a button to drop a ball onto a spinning platform riddled with holes.

On one side of the arcade they found a coin-operated shooting gallery depicting a scene from the Old West, with lots of little targets spaced around the area. They paused to watch people shooting. One target made the mannequin at the piano start playing. Another made the spittoon rattle. A third made an owl flap its wings and spin its head around.

"Let's get some tokens," Trevor suggested.

Nate led the way to a token machine. He inserted a twenty, and coins came clinking out like he'd won a jackpot. "Is this enough for now?" Nate asked.

"Do one more for me," Trevor said. "They want us to be thorough—that'll take some money."

Nate fed the machine a second twenty and let Trevor collect the tokens. While Trevor scooped them out, Nate scanned the room.

There were people around, but the arcade wasn't packed. He supposed it probably got more crowded in the evenings and on weekends.

"Where do you want to start?" Trevor asked.

"Too many choices—it's hard to pick."

"Do you want to win tickets?"

"I don't know," Nate said. "Let's see what prizes they have."

They wandered over to the redemption counter, where various items were on display alongside the quantity of tickets required to claim them. The prizes ranged from cheap little army men and gummy bracelets for 5 tickets up to sound systems and guitars for 15,000.

"This is such a rip-off," Trevor said. "The cheap things are junk, and you could buy the cool stuff for so much less than it would cost to earn all those tickets."

"Earning the tickets is supposed to be fun," Nate said. "I think they have the prizes as sort of a bonus."

Trevor folded his arms and leaned against the glass counter. "I don't know. If I put in all the effort to win 10,000 tickets, I'd want something better than a neon clock."

"You could get two mini foosball tables," Nate pointed out.

"Exactly," Trevor said. "How long do you think that mini foosball table would stay fun?"

"You can be like me, and just go for the bouncy balls. Let's see . . . the little ones are 25 tickets, medium are 50, and the bigger ones are 100. Cheap *and* fun."

"If you say so."

"You're welcome to give your tickets to me," Nate said.

"I could probably find a prize if I had to," Trevor hedged. "Maybe that glow-in-the-dark yo-yo."

"Hours of fun," Nate said. "Want to shoot some hoops?"

"We can shoot hoops for free," Trevor mentioned. "At the park. At our school."

"Right, but on a normal court it isn't timed, the balls don't automatically keep coming, nothing keeps score, and you don't get tickets at the end. Besides, we're not really paying for it."

"Okay, I'm in."

They walked over to the row of basketball shooting games against the wall. Most had mini basketballs. A couple at the end were larger, with full-sized balls and a longer distance to the hoop.

Only one person was currently playing—a skinny kid with dark hair who looked to be about their age. He was on one of the smaller machines. As the timer ticked down, he sank one ball after another, most of them swishes. After releasing each shot, he snatched another ball before the previous one had dropped. Taking no time to aim, he kept shooting with mechanical regularity. The infrequent missed shots didn't rattle him, although occasionally an inbound shot would collide with a ball still bouncing on the rim.

For the last thirty seconds, the hoop slid farther away, awarding three points instead of two for each basket made. After the hoop retreated, the kid missed only twice even though he was still shooting about as fast as Nate could imagine. At the buzzer, his score was 105. The machine started expelling a long ribbon of tickets, which joined other strips of tickets coiled at his feet.

"That was amazing," Nate said loudly.

The kid looked over. "I've been practicing."

"Can you shoot like that every time?" Trevor asked.

The kid shrugged. "Mostly. You guys want to have a competition?"

Nate didn't feel very eager. He doubted he could sink half as many baskets in the same amount of time. "What sort of competition?"

The kid smiled. "Whoever sinks the most baskets keeps all the tickets." He looked down at the tangled ribbons of tickets by his feet.

"We don't have any tickets," Trevor said. "We might only earn a few."

"Then you don't have much to lose," the kid replied.

"Sure," Nate said, taking out a token.

Trevor claimed a machine on one side of the kid, Nate on the other. Nate and Trevor inserted their tokens. The kid swiped what looked like a credit card through a card reader above the token slot.

"What's that?" Nate asked.

The kid held up the card. "If you're going to play a lot, you can buy a card from the counter and use it instead of tokens."

"Seems easier."

"It is. You guys ready?"

"Ready," Trevor said.

Nate punched the start button. Basketballs rolled his way. The hoop wasn't too far away, but he missed his first shot. The second shot clanged off the rim. The third went in. He tried not to notice the kid beside him shooting balls twice as fast and hardly missing. Nate kept shooting, missing plenty.

Just as Nate started sinking shots with regularity, the hoop slid back for the three-point finale. Nate made only one shot at that distance. His final score was 27. The machine rewarded him by spitting out three tickets.

Nate looked over to see that Trevor had scored 33. The other kid had tallied 101. His machine was gushing tickets again.

"How many tickets are coming out?" Nate asked.

"You get fifty for breaking a hundred," the kid replied. "The record today is at 114. I put it there. If you break that, the jackpot is 300. They reset the record to 80 every morning."

"How many tickets do you have?" Nate asked.

"Right now, around eleven hundred. Plus your three. And his four."

Nate tore off his three tickets and handed them over. "Why so many tickets?" he asked. "What are you saving up for?"

The kid suddenly looked a little shifty. "I don't know. One of the big prizes, I guess."

"Like what?" Trevor wondered. "The guitar?"

"Something like that," the kid replied vaguely. "You guys want to try me again?"

"Why risk all your tickets?" Nate asked.

The kid shrugged. "It isn't much of a risk, and I get a few extra. Plus I get bored shooting alone."

"I'll try again," Nate said.

"Sure," Trevor agreed.

Nate shot faster this time. He felt like he had a better feel for it. By the end he had scored 36. Trevor scored 41. The kid had 108.

Nate tore off his four tickets and handed them over.

"You're not letting him steal your tickets?" asked a voice from behind.

Nate turned. A kid in a Giants cap stood beside a girl with dark hair. They looked about his age. Maybe a little older.

"I knew I'd probably lose," Nate explained.

The hat kid laughed. "Definitely, not probably. Nobody beats Roman."

Nate looked over. "Is that your name? I'm Nate."

"Trevor," Trevor added from the other side.

Roman nodded at them.

"How many are you up to?" the hat kid asked Roman.

"Low forties," he replied.

"Low forties?" Trevor asked. "You have over a thousand tickets."

"He means more than forty thousand," the girl said.

"Forty *thousand*?" Nate exclaimed. "Are you compulsive or something? Like one of those gamblers who can't quit?"

After glaring at the girl, the hat kid turned to Nate. "He's not addicted. He's just really good. Something you wouldn't know about."

"How good are you?" Nate shot back, feeling insulted. "You on the arcade basketball pro tour?"

"I'm better than you," the hat kid replied. "Look, you should get lost, we need to talk to Roman."

Nate knew he should be focused on reconnaissance, but the rudeness was too blatant to ignore. "How about you beat me at basketball first? One game. You on one side, Roman on the other."

The hat kid chuckled. "I don't need four tickets."

"I have more than nineteen dollars in tokens. Whoever wins gets them along with my tickets. If I win, I get Roman's tickets and whatever you can offer."

The hat kid glanced at Roman, who shrugged.

"Okay," the hat kid said. He produced a card like the one Roman was using. "There's more than a hundred dollars in tokens on here. You beat me, you keep it. If Roman beats me, I'll buy him lunch."

"Deal," Nate said, pulling out a stick of Peak Performance gum and putting it in his mouth.

"You in too?" the hat kid asked Trevor.

Trevor raised both hands. "I'll just watch."

The hat kid walked to the game beside Nate and swiped his card.

"What's your name?" Nate asked.

"Chris," he said, "but you can call me daddy."

"We'll see," Nate said, inserting a token.

"You guys ready?" Roman asked.

They all hit their start buttons.

Nate grabbed his first ball. The hoop looked enormous, and incredibly close. He began shooting rapidly, never bobbling when he grabbed a new ball, never waiting for the previous shot to drop before grabbing another. He realized he could do it faster if he alternated shots between his left and right hand, but decided that his unending string of swishes was conspicuous enough.

As the hoop retracted to the three-point distance, Nate kept making shots while it was in motion. He continued to drain one after another for three points each. When the buzzer sounded, he had not missed a single shot. He hadn't even touched the rim. Chris had scored 92. Roman had earned 109. Nate had 140.

A siren went off as tickets unspooled from all three basketball machines. After the tickets stopped for Chris and Roman, Nate's kept coming.

"I don't believe it," Roman said in awe. "Were you scamming me?"

"How'd you do that?" Chris accused.

"Didn't seem hard, daddy," Nate said, suppressing a smile. "The hoop is close. How'd you miss so many?"

Chris scowled.

"I'm not sure 'daddy' suits you," Nate went on. "Maybe granddaddy?"

"What's your best all-time score?" Chris asked Roman.

"A hundred and seventeen. Yours?"

"One-ten. How'd this joker shoot 140?"

"Maybe grandmommy?" Nate tried.

"I was watching," the girl said. "He was really fast, and he never missed. Not once."

"Let me see your hand," Chris said, stepping close and grabbing Nate by the wrist. He apparently didn't find what he was looking for, so he checked the other hand. Nate didn't resist the inspection.

"Anything?" the girl asked.

"Nothing," Chris replied, peering at Nate intently. "Where are you from, Nate?"

Nate grinned. "My dad owns the company that makes these."

"Really?" Roman asked.

"No," Nate said. "I was just in the zone at the right time. I live over in Colson."

The tickets had stopped unreeling.

Nate glanced down. "How many tickets were supposed to pay out for breaking the record?"

"Three hundred," Roman said.

"It stopped around 230," Nate said. He hadn't been paying direct attention, but his instincts told him he was right. He had learned to trust his instincts while chewing Peak Performance.

"They'll refill it," Chris said. "Risa, see if you can find Todd."

"Yes, master," the girl replied, rolling her eyes.

"Are you guys going to pay up?" Trevor asked.

Chris looked reluctant, his lips pressed together. "That's only fair, I guess. You might have been conning us, Nate, but you definitely won." Chris handed over his token card.

"Bad luck for me," Roman said. "My tickets are yours. More than a thousand. That was incredible."

Glancing off to one side, Nate saw Summer and Pigeon

approaching. They walked up to Trevor. Pigeon seemed to pay abnormal attention to Chris.

"Hey, guys," Summer said brightly. "What are you up to?"

"Scamming us out of buckets of tokens," Chris said. "Tell you what, Nate, how about you give me a chance to win my card back, double or nothing. We use the bigger machines with the full-sized balls. I like those better. If I lose, I'll give you a card with exactly $100 in tokens on it."

"What are you, a millionaire?" Nate asked.

"I made some pretty good money recently," Chris replied. "What do you say?"

"My shooting wasn't a fluke," Nate said.

"One-forty can't be a fluke," Chris acknowledged. "It's too high. It's ridiculous. Still, give me a chance to win my card back on the bigger machines. I want to try."

Nate knew the Peak Performance gum would last at least another ten minutes. "Sure, why not?"

Risa returned with a man who was presumably Todd. In his thirties, he wore black jeans and a dark T-shirt promoting a band Nate had never heard of. He had a wiry build and smelled faintly of cheese puffs. His green hair was styled into a faux hawk. One forearm sported a tattoo of a dark angel holding a pair of swords rendered in blue, purple, and black. Under his other arm he clutched a large wheel of tickets.

"Whoa!" Todd said. "A hundred and forty? Nobody has put up a score like that since we opened." He focused on Nate, who still stood in front of the machine. "You did this?"

"I was in the zone," Nate said simply.

"You should be in the newspaper," Todd said. "That is just a killer score. You should see if there's a pro league for these things. Seriously, you'd be a superstar."

"I don't know about that," Nate replied, hoping he wasn't blushing. He felt a little guilty since his performance was due to magic gum rather than his own skill.

"I hear it didn't pay out all 300," Todd said.

"Yeah," Nate replied. "I think it stopped short."

"That's why I'm here," Todd said, crouching in front of the machine. Using some sort of key, he opened it up. "Yep, empty as my girlfriend's head."

"How's it going, Todd?" Chris asked.

"Good, Chris," Todd replied. He loaded the wheel of tickets into the machine and closed it. More tickets began streaming out. "Did this guy take you to school?"

"He destroyed us," Chris said.

"I was wondering when somebody would toast one of you," Todd said. "Goes to show you, can't get too cocky. There's always somebody better." Placing his hands on his hips, Todd stared at the score. "One-forty. They should pay out a thousand for a score like that. Party on."

Todd strolled away.

Chris nodded toward the bigger machines.

"We're just playing for you to get your card back," Nate clarified. "I keep these tickets."

"It's Roman who cares about tickets," Chris said. "But there's only two of the big machines. Just you and me, playing for cards."

"I'll gather your tickets, Nate," Trevor offered.

"We'll help," Summer said, giving Nate a funny look. He wasn't sure how to read her expression. Did she think it was wrong for him to scam Chris again using Peak Performance?

Summer, Trevor, and Pigeon had been engaged in a huddled

conversation while Todd resupplied the ticket dispenser. Nate wondered what had lured Summer and Pigeon out of hiding. There didn't seem to be any emergency.

Nate went and stood next to Chris. These bigger machines required two tokens. Nate pushed them in, Chris swiped his card, they hit the start buttons, and Nate started shooting. The balls were bigger, the hoop farther away, but it seemed just as easy as the other game. Working quickly, Nate hit swish after swish, the ball touching nothing but net. Hoping to avoid looking supernatural, he forced himself to miss three shots. When the buzzer sounded, he had beaten Chris by almost fifty points.

"Another new record," Chris said, glancing from the scoreboard to Nate. He looked stunned and frustrated. "I practice a lot, and I shot fairly well just now. You scored way higher than I've ever shot. I guess I owe you another card."

"It's okay," Nate said. "Don't worry about it."

"No, Nate, I can afford it," Chris said. "I asked for a rematch, and you owned me. How many times did he miss?"

"Three," Risa said. "He was shooting fast."

"These pay 500 when you break the record," Chris said. "You're well on your way."

"To what?" Nate asked.

Chris studied him curiously. "You're an interesting guy." He bent over and tore off the ribbon of tickets dangling from his machine. "My tickets weren't part of the deal. I'll donate them to Roman." He handed the tickets to his friend. "I'll be right back."

Tickets continued to flow from Nate's basketball game. "How do I manage all of these tickets?" Nate asked Roman.

"You feed them into machines that count them," Roman said.

"They print out a receipt. Or the ticket counters can store them on a card."

"You really have over forty thousand?" Nate asked.

"Pretty much," Roman said, avoiding eye contact. "I may have slipped back to just under forty."

Was he hiding something? "Do any of the prizes cost that much?" Nate wondered.

"Not many," Roman said. "I mostly earn the tickets for fun."

"I can't believe you shot like that twice in a row," Risa said to Nate. "Can you do it every time?"

"Depends," Nate said. "On a good day I could probably keep repeating. It's weird. I'm either really coordinated or pretty average. Not a lot of middle ground."

"But you were messing with me when we first played," Roman said. "Setting us up."

"Maybe a little," Nate replied.

Chris came back and handed Nate a card. "You earned it. And no offense, but I'm never playing basketball against you again. Roman, we should talk."

"Later," Roman said to Nate.

Nate nodded at him, feeling a little bad for taking his tickets.

Chris, Roman, and Risa walked away together.

Summer, Pigeon, and Trevor approached carrying a bunch of tickets. Trevor and Summer had theirs bundled neatly. Pigeon's were in tangled disarray, with several loose ribbons dragging.

"You just met some very interesting people," Summer said. "We need to talk."

CHAPTER FIVE

TICKETS

Nate, Summer, Trevor, and Pigeon found an empty room clearly used for private parties. A pair of long, orange tables with adjacent benches filled much of the space. A discarded cake box sat on a counter, full of crumpled napkins and plastic cups. Small, colorful shapes flecked the white wallpaper, giving the impression of confetti.

Trevor closed the door, and they gathered at the end of one of the tables, two on each side. They knelt on the benches and hunched over the table so they could keep their heads together and talk low.

"What's the story?" Nate asked.

"That guy you beat both times at basketball," Summer began.

"Chris," Nate supplied.

"He can jump like he's sucking on Moon Rocks. Same with the girl."

"Risa," Trevor offered.

"We saw them arrive," Pigeon said. "They came into Arcadeland by jumping the fence when they thought nobody was looking. And I mean jumping it. One leap."

"We came to warn you," Summer said. "We thought they would be good people to watch."

"We figure they must be getting magic candy from here," Pigeon said.

"Chris was acting strange," Nate said. "Like he had a secret. Or like he suspected I had one. He was tough to read."

"He and Roman were awesome at basketball," Trevor said. "They've definitely had some practice."

Nate met eyes with Trevor. "Chris and Risa seemed to be helping Roman. They were wondering how many tickets he had earned."

"You think they use tickets to buy magic candy?" Trevor asked.

"We know something out of the ordinary is going on here," Nate said.

"The tickets sound like a good place to start," Pigeon said.

"Roman has almost forty thousand tickets," Nate said. "And he's still working hard to earn more. Should we go see if any prizes are worth that much?"

The others agreed. Nate led the way over to the redemption counter, where Todd was accepting tickets from a couple of young girls in exchange for plastic rings.

"That longboard is 10,000," Summer reported.

"The little jukebox is 20,000," Pigeon said, eyes roving the shelves. "I don't see anything for more than that."

"Hey, Todd?" Nate asked.

"Yeah?" he answered.

"What prize costs the most tickets?"

Todd winced as if thinking and rubbed the tattoo on his forearm.

He eyed the shelves. "Jukebox is one of the highest ticket items. Works fairly well. I'm sort of an audiophile, and it sounds decent."

"Is it the highest?" Nate pursued.

Leaning one hand on the glass counter that held all the cheaper items, Todd gave Nate a measuring stare. Then he glanced down at the cabinet. "There are some pretty expensive stamps toward the back."

Nate crouched and examined the contents of the glass counter. Looking past the finger puppets, the suckers, the army men, the spider rings, the tiny bouncy balls, and the other items marked at 50 tickets or less, Nate saw two small signs proclaiming a value of 40,000, and a second pair marked 50,000. Behind the signs were four inkpads—one with a simple image of a submarine stenciled on the cover, one with a racecar, one with a fighter jet, and one with a tank. Beside each inkpad rested a stamp.

"Fifty thousand?" Nate asked.

Todd nodded. "We don't generally draw attention to them. Most people who notice think they're mismarked."

"Inkpads?" Summer asked. "Like for stamps?"

"The pads aren't for sale," Todd explained. "Just the stamps. Forty thousand for the sub or the racecar. Fifty thousand for the tank or the jet."

"For 50,000 tickets I get to stamp a tank on my hand?" Trevor deadpanned.

"More than once," Todd replied. "It could potentially amount to a lifetime supply. But only four people get to win each stamp."

"Are all the stamps available?" Nate asked.

Todd shook his head slightly. "Two of the jet slots are gone. One tank slot is gone. No racecar slots are taken yet. One sub slot is gone.

I happen to know there are plenty of people currently working to win the empty slots."

"Why?" Pigeon asked.

"I'm not allowed to fully explain," Todd said. "Earning the stamp is sort of like getting into a club. The details are only for those who succeed. Are you guys here to redeem any of those tickets?"

Nate realized that they were all holding a lot of tickets. "No, later. We were just weighing our options."

Todd looked at Nate. "Keep shooting baskets how you were, and you'll be able to afford anything on display." He drummed his hands on the counter. "Have fun. I need to check on some things in the back."

Nate and his friends walked away.

"Should we get a receipt for all of these tickets?" Summer asked.

"Beats carrying them around," Trevor said.

It took some time to feed all the ribbons of tickets into the machines. In the end they got a receipt for over two thousand.

"That's a lot of bouncy balls," Trevor said.

"I might be aiming higher than bouncy balls," Nate replied. "Let's get out of here. We need to talk in private."

* * * * *

Their favorite location for secret Blue Falcon meetings was the Nest, a secluded hollow enclosed by trees and shrubs at the creek below Monroe Circle, the street where Nate, Trevor, and Pigeon lived. They were pedaling in that direction when a white van pulled over to the side of the road ahead of them. Ziggy got out and helped them load their bikes inside.

"Why do I feel like I'm being kidnapped?" Trevor asked.

"Because a pair of large men we've hardly met just piled us into their nondescript vehicle," Pigeon replied.

The roomy van had space for the bikes behind the two rows of benches where the kids sat. Victor was driving while Ziggy rode shotgun.

"Where are we going?" Nate asked.

"Nowhere definite," Victor replied. "We'll just drive and talk. We want to go over everything while it's fresh in your minds."

"Did you snap any pictures?" Ziggy asked.

"I forgot," Trevor said.

"I snuck a few," Pigeon said. "I didn't aim the shots, but I got one of the employees, along with some interesting customers."

Pigeon held up a digital camera, an image of Todd on the screen. Ziggy accepted the camera and studied the picture.

"I don't know this clown," he said. "Might just be an ordinary deadbeat." Ziggy started paging through other images. Pigeon leaned forward to narrate.

"That's Chris," Pigeon said. "He's one of the kids we think might be involved with the secret side of Arcadeland. Summer and I saw him float over a fence. He didn't have a hat on at the time."

"They're already recruiting?" Victor asked.

"Seems that way," Nate said. "You can earn stamps for forty or fifty thousand tickets. It's a lifetime supply. The stamps are by far the most expensive prizes, and they're kind of hidden. After I used Peak Performance to enhance my basketball score, Chris checked my hand. I bet he was looking for a stamp. I think the stamp gives access to whatever these guys are handing out."

"You mentioned different prices," Ziggy said. "Are there different stamps?"

Summer explained about the four different stamps, and how each stamp was limited to four people. She told how some slots were already gone.

"That girl, Risa, was also floating," Pigeon narrated as Ziggy looked at a new image. "And that guy is named Roman."

"He'll probably be a new recruit soon," Trevor said. "The other two were encouraging him to win tickets."

"Seems evident that trading tickets for stamps gets kids into the inner circle," Victor said.

"Do you want us to earn a stamp?" Nate asked.

Victor pulled the van into the parking lot of a large home improvement store and claimed a spot far from the entrance. Empty parking spaces surrounded them. He turned to look Nate in the eye. "If you kids acquire those stamps, you'll expose yourselves to some serious danger. I can't guarantee that we could protect you."

"Do you have enough information now to help John?" Pigeon asked.

"We've found the start of a trail," Ziggy said. "Victor and I can't go in there and trade tickets for stamps, but we can track down the kids Pigeon photographed and look into this Todd character."

"What if we go after the stamps?" Summer asked. "Could it make a difference?"

Victor and Ziggy shared a glance. "You want the truth?" Victor asked. "It would move the investigation forward much faster. The people running this operation have been extremely careful not to expose themselves. Those stamps probably lead straight to whoever is behind all of this."

"But the information would come at a price," Ziggy said.

"The magician behind this operation is clearly powerful and

secretive," Victor said. "If you become involved directly, it might not be easy to walk away."

"We could get sucked into some serious danger," Nate said.

"At best it will be dangerous," Ziggy said. "At worst you could get killed."

"Do we know whether John is alive?" Pigeon asked in a small voice.

"We're not certain," Ziggy replied. "We hope so."

"If you're considering direct involvement," Victor said, "you deserve to know all we do. This situation is bigger than John Dart going missing. John learned something and called in Mozag."

"Your boss," Trevor said.

"Arguably the most powerful living magician," Ziggy said. "He almost never gets involved directly in an investigation. He's too valuable. He runs things from a distance."

"But he came when John called," Victor said. "And Mozag disappeared along with him."

"Mozag is missing too?" Nate exclaimed.

"Which tells us a lot," Victor said. "Away from his permanent lair, Mozag was vulnerable, but still, any magician who can subdue Mozag is wielding some serious power. And any situation that would lure Mozag into the field had to have catastrophic potential."

"Then we could be in danger whether we help or not," Nate summarized. "If we do nothing, whoever is running Arcadeland could still become a threat to us."

"The country could be in danger," Ziggy said. "Maybe the world."

"Mozag didn't get involved directly with Mrs. White," Victor pointed out. "But he came for this."

"He and John were captured at the same time?" Trevor asked.

"Far as we know," Ziggy said.

"Does Mozag have other agents who can help?" Pigeon wondered. "Are you guys here alone?"

"There are some others who could lend assistance," Victor said. "Frankly, with John out of play, we were the best operatives available. This is a delicate situation. The knowledge that Mozag polices the magical community keeps a lot of shady characters in check."

"You don't want it known that he's missing," Nate said.

Ziggy raised his eyebrows. "All we need is for every crooked magician with a scheme and a few lackeys to find out that right now is the best opportunity in decades to risk some mischief. One major crisis is bad enough."

"We want to help," Summer said.

Victor sighed. "Bottom line? You're kids. I don't want to put on the heavy pressure. We could use your assistance, but we don't require it. You now know the situation. Take some time to think it through. Talk things over with Sebastian Stott. We'll back whatever choice you make."

"Mozag saved me from being trapped as an old man," Nate said. "John saved me too. They both spend their lives protecting us all from maniacs with magical powers. I have to help them. I'll win one of those stamps. I'll find out what's going on."

"Shouldn't we talk to Mr. Stott first?" Pigeon asked.

"We should," Nate said. "We could use whatever support he can offer. But whatever we decide to do, it won't hurt to start winning some tickets."

"You mean tonight?" Summer asked.

"I mean right now."

* * * * *

Nate returned to Arcadeland with Trevor and Summer. Pigeon had left to go talk things over with Mr. Stott. It was later in the afternoon, and the arcade was more crowded. Ziggy and Victor waited outside in the van as backup.

Scanning the room, Nate spotted Roman over at the shooting gallery, hunched over the counter with his cheek against a rifle. Nate crossed to him. Summer and Trevor followed but hung back.

"Do you ever go home?" Nate asked.

"You're here too," Roman replied, one eye shut as he prepared to shoot.

"Sick of basketball?"

"Some hotshot made the record unreachable today," Roman replied. "And yes, I eventually get sick of it. Basketball is probably where I can average the most tickets per turn, but it gets old after I play it for too long."

"How are the tickets for this game?" Nate asked.

Roman stopped aiming and looked up. "Not bad if you know the tricks."

"What tricks?"

Roman hesitated for a moment. "Most people aim at the close stuff. They want to see the guy play the piano. They want to make the cow skull shake. They want the bottles behind the bar to spin. But the saloon has two windows."

"Right," Nate said. Outside one window four buzzards were circling in and out of view, each with a tiny target attached. A small train went by the other window, as if in the distance, an engine pulling four cars. Each train car had a target. The train moved fairly quickly, coming into view every fifteen seconds.

"The vultures don't do much when you hit them. You just hear a faint squawk and the target lights up. The train does even less. The target lights up. That's it. You get ten shots each turn. If you hit all four vultures on your turn, you get 25 tickets. If you hit all four train cars, you also earn 25. Those targets aren't easy to hit, but if you get good, you can pick up 50 tickets per turn without much trouble. Using any other strategy, you're lucky to get 10."

"Thanks for the tips."

Roman glanced back at Trevor and Summer. "I haven't seen you guys around before today. You plan to hang out here much?"

"I like it here," Nate said. "It's the best arcade I've seen. I want one of those stamps."

"Stamps?" Roman asked, trying much too hard to sound casual.

"Aren't you after a stamp?"

"Why would I want a stamp?"

Nate shrugged. "They're the most expensive prizes, and you keep working hard to earn more tickets even though you have a ton."

Roman shook his head. "Chris and Risa are getting sloppy. They were so careful not to let anything slip before they had theirs."

"Which one are you after?" Nate asked. "Jet, tank, racecar, or sub?"

"Which do you want?"

"I'm not sure," Nate replied honestly. "That's why I'm bugging you."

Roman seemed like he wanted to end the conversation. "I want a jet. My friends have jets, so I want one."

"What's the big deal?" Nate pursued. "Why work so hard for the stamps?"

"I don't know," Roman replied, glancing around to make sure

nobody was eavesdropping. "Chris and Risa aren't allowed to tell me. They just assure me it's amazing. It better be. I've blown all my money on tickets."

"Only two jet slots left, right?" Nate asked.

"I've gotten good at earning tickets," Roman said. "I should have enough for one of them by tomorrow."

"Are other kids after stamps?" Nate wondered.

"People are catching on," Roman said. "You better hurry if you want one. The way you shoot a basketball, you could probably get there if you try."

"You want the third jet stamp," Nate said. "Is anybody after the fourth?"

"Nobody we care about," Roman said. He glanced at Trevor and Summer. "Just don't try to take both slots ahead of me. Chris and Risa would hate you for it, and so would I."

"We don't want to beat you," Nate said. "Besides, you're too far along. We couldn't catch up even if we went nonstop. But my friends might go after other stamps. Who knows?"

"Hold on a second," Roman said. "You're wrecking my concentration. Let me finish up."

"Go ahead."

Nate watched as Roman lit up the buzzards and the train cars.

"The vultures are tricky," Roman said. "You have to pay attention to the differences, make sure you hit one of each. Hitting the same one four times doesn't do it."

His last shot was at the train. Nothing lit up.

"You missed?" Nate asked.

"I'd already hit everything with the first nine," Roman explained. He paused as if debating whether to say more. "Look, other people helped me, so I'll help you. There are two bonus shots that are almost impossible. They aren't marked. One is through the window of the engine. It's worth a hundred tickets. I know it exists, because I've hit it twice. The other is a tiny star that shines behind the vultures for barely a second every two minutes. I've never hit it, but I saw Risa do it. You can only hit it while it's lit. Supposedly if you hit all eight far targets plus the two bonus shots on a single turn, you get some kind of mega bonus."

"Has anyone done it?" Nate asked.

"Nope."

"Then how do you know it's possible?" Nate asked.

"Chris found out somehow after he got his stamp," Roman said. "He was the first person to earn one."

Nate glanced over his shoulder, taking in the assortment of games spaced around the floor. "What game gives the biggest pay-out?"

"Shooting Stars," Roman answered. "But playing is like buying a lottery ticket. The lights all move around in crazy patterns, and you have to get the ten red ones to line up in the middle by freezing them at the perfect time. They move too fast to win with skill. People get tickets off of it, but you'll average more on games like basket-ball where skill makes a bigger difference. A lot of those redemption games are basically gambling for kids."

"Redemption games?"

"The kind that pay out redeemable tickets. Arcade lingo. Look, I better get going."

"You're not sticking around?" Nate asked.

Roman shook his head. "I'll come back in the morning when the high scores are reset. My parents don't want me here, so I shouldn't hang around all day. I have to be sneaky, make up excuses for where I've been. By the way, if you come in the morning, raise the records slowly. If you set the basketball record too high on the first try, we'll all earn fewer tickets for the rest of the day. Beat the records little by little and you cash in more."

"You have this down to a science."

Roman chuckled. "It has sort of been my summer job."

"A summer job where you lose all your money."

Roman snorted. "Exactly. That stamp better be cool. Later."

He gathered his tickets and left.

Summer walked up to Nate. "Good info. We could overhear most of it. I didn't want to interrupt. He seemed willing to talk to you."

"I'm not sure how to read him," Nate said. "He isn't super friendly, but he's been pretty helpful."

Trevor clapped his hands together and rubbed them. "If we're here for tickets, we should get started."

"Should we use the gum?" Summer asked.

They had each set out that morning with two sticks of Peak Performance gum. Nate had used one of his, but Pigeon had given up his two before they separated, so Nate now had three.

"Might as well," Nate said, pulling out a stick of gum.

Trevor and Summer did likewise.

"We should make the most of it," Nate instructed. "Split up, play fast. Try not to wait in line. We'll only get the full effect for fifteen minutes or so."

"The effect will get weaker the more gum we use," Summer mentioned.

"True," Nate said. "Mr. Stott has been trying to make the effect more stable, but the results still shrink the more sticks you chew. Do the trickiest stuff first."

"Where are you going to start?" Summer asked Trevor.

"I want to break Nate's basketball record."

"I'll stay here and nail targets," Nate said.

"I'll go try Shooting Stars," Summer said.

"There might not be enough skill to it," Nate warned. "It could be all luck."

Summer shrugged. "I'll find out soon enough." She stuck the gum in her mouth. "I've always liked the games where you have to stop the lights in the right spot."

Nate put the stick in his mouth and started chewing. He had given his tokens to Trevor. Summer had one of his cards with token credits. He had the other. He swiped it and picked up the rifle Roman had been using.

Nate aimed through the window at the circling vultures. The targets seemed absurdly easy to hit. On his first turn, he practiced aiming for different parts of the targets, and found that his rifle shot slightly down and to the left from where he aimed. It wasn't mis-aligned enough to miss when pointed at the center of a target, but might be enough to mess up the tiny winking star and the engine window shot.

On his next turn, Nate lit up the four buzzards and the four train cars with casual effort. Then he waited for the star and shot when it appeared. The pinprick of light briefly glared red, which it had not done before, convincing him that he had hit it.

The next time the train came by the other window, Nate sighted barely up and to the right of the engine window. When he squeezed the trigger, every target in the shooting gallery flashed. The piano guy started playing, the raccoon peeked out of the honey pot, the bottles spun, the pans clattered, the rattlesnake rattled, the turtle flipped over, the bear trap snapped shut, and all the other movable elements came to life in a burst of motion, light, and sound.

A siren was wailing. Tickets were unspooling. Evidently Chris had been right about a bonus for hitting all ten targets on a single turn.

A man came up to Nate and clapped him on the shoulder. The man had dark, neatly carved sideburns that widened as they got lower. He wore tinted glasses, western boots, blue jeans, and a button-down cowboy shirt with banjoes embroidered on the front. "How'd you know to do that, son?" he murmured, almost making it an accusation.

"I heard a rumor."

"Who taught you to shoot like that?"

"I was raised by mountain lions."

The man gave him skeptical look, followed by a slow smile. "You got a name?"

"Nate."

"I'm Cleon. You just won a whole mess of tickets. Saving up for anything special?"

"Maybe."

Another siren went off over by the basketball hoops. Cleon turned to face the pulsing light. "Basketball? That record was up in outer space today!"

A new siren went off in the middle of the game floor. Cleon's jaw dropped. "You've got to be ribbing me! Shooting Stars too?"

"What's going on?" Nate asked, trying to act confused.

"A storm of big winners," Cleon said. "Uncanny. Have we been hacked or something? What exactly did you shoot?"

"All the far targets."

"Including . . . ?"

"The buzzards, the train cars, the star, and the engine window."

Cleon slapped Nate on the shoulder. "You should have 2,500 tickets coming your way. I'll be back to make sure they all pay out. We've got a plague of winners all of a sudden."

Cleon walked away toward the Shooting Stars machine. Nate waited as the endless strand of tickets emerged from the dispenser. He grabbed the long ribbon and started folding. A modest crowd had gathered to watch the tickets pay out.

By the time the machine had quit, Nate had a sense that all of the tickets were there. He regretted having to wait for them to unspool, since he knew the duration of the Peak Performance gum was limited.

Cleon returned and opened up the ticket dispenser. "There are still some left on the reel," he announced. "This model only holds 4,000 at a time, so it must have been fairly full when you started. Congratulations." He closed up the machine and strode away.

Tickets in hand, Nate went to find Summer. As he moved across the floor, the siren went off at the larger basketball game. Trevor had beaten his other record.

Nate found Summer feeding tickets into the counting machine. "I won in three tries," she said. "The pattern is complicated but not impossible. Five thousand tickets!"

"That's crazy," Nate said. "Why waste time counting tickets? Peak Performance doesn't last long."

"I have a ton of tickets to drag around," she said. "Lots of people crowded to see when I won. Won't I be sort of obvious if I keep winning huge?"

"Who cares? We're not breaking any rules. Did the jackpot lower after you won?"

"No. It stayed the same."

"Take my tickets. I want to try before my gum wears off."

Nate handed over his shooting gallery winnings and hurried to the Shooting Stars machine. A grid composed of hundreds of tiny bulbs twinkled impressively. Each bulb was either white, red, or off. The white lights swirled and cascaded in complex patterns. Among the white lights, ten red lights zipped through the pattern like hyperactive fireflies.

A horizontal line of ten bulbs in the middle of the grid was enclosed by a red rectangle. The rules explained that if you could freeze the display with the ten bulbs lit, you won a hundred tickets. If you could pause the grid while the ten center bulbs were red, you won the jackpot.

Even with his perceptions enhanced by Peak Performance gum, Nate could see that the center bulbs only glowed simultaneously for the briefest instant. And it would require patience, because all of the reds only gathered there roughly once per minute.

The young woman currently playing hit the button to pause the lights and trapped four white ones in the center rectangle. The machine gave her eight tickets.

When she stepped aside, Nate approached the machine. It required two tokens to play. Nate swiped his card. He watched the flashing pattern of lights, finger poised above the button that would halt them.

The reds were about to synchronize. He would have to get it just right. When he hit the button, all ten red bulbs froze, but there was a single bulb outside the rectangle. He realized that there was an infinitesimal delay between the pressing of the button and the stopping of the bulbs.

Nate swiped his card again and waited. Freezing white lights in the rectangle would be simple. But getting all the reds would be tough even with Peak Performance. He would have to hit the button a tiny bit early.

He saw the reds approaching. He hit the button, trapping ten red bulbs inside the rectangle. Sirens shrieked and lights flashed. Two ribbons of tickets began unreeling.

Cleon hurried over. "You again?" he asked, lowering his tinted glasses just enough to stare at Nate directly. "What is going on?"

"Quick reflexes?" Nate tried.

Cleon stepped close. Nate could smell his cologne. "You know we have security cameras? We'll review your every move."

"I'm glad," Nate said. "You'll see that I won fair and square."

"Maybe," Cleon said, hands on his hips. "But whatever trick you and your friends have discovered, you shouldn't flaunt it so blatantly. We have lots of games here. It's a fun place. But you're here chasing something, and that is no game to us, you read me?"

Nate assumed he was referring to the stamps. "Will the machine deliver all my tickets?"

"It will this time," Cleon replied. "This monster holds two reels of eight thousand each. But we'll be shutting down Shooting Stars for the night for maintenance. Same with the shooting gallery. You might consider making an exit."

Nate scrunched his eyebrows. "Are you throwing me out?"

Cleon shrugged. "I'm not going to haul you over and chuck you out the door, but the way I see it, you've already passed the point when you should have walked away. Might be about time to run."

Cleon sauntered off. He returned as the tickets finished streaming out. Cleon shut down the machine, unplugged it, and hung an OUT OF ORDER sign. Nate met up with Summer and Trevor at the ticket tallying machine.

"All of these games seem super easy," Trevor said. "I broke the record on the football one as well."

"I won a couple more of the light games," Summer said. "Smaller jackpots."

"Has Cleon talked to you?" Nate asked.

"The guy with the sideburns?" Summer asked.

"He seemed suspicious of me," Trevor said.

"Me too," Nate said. "He basically told me to beat it."

"Did you have to go win the biggest jackpot in the place right after me?" Summer asked.

"We've all been winning jackpots like it's easy," Nate said.

"It was easy," Trevor muttered.

"But it shouldn't be," Nate replied. "We've drawn enough attention. Let's save the rest of our gum and try again tomorrow."

Nate was feeding his tickets into a machine. It speedily sucked up the long strips. He noted that they went in much more quickly than the other machines spat them out.

"Is it safe to come back here?" Trevor asked in a low voice. "Might have been dumb to win so much so quickly."

"We know these guys can be dangerous," Summer added.

"We'll need to come ready for trouble," Nate said. "But no way am I quitting the hunt for one of those stamps."

CHAPTER SIX

LINDY

Pigeon sat across from Mr. Stott in a back room of the candy shop, spooning mouthfuls of chocolate sludge out of a mug. Mr. Stott had invented the rich concoction, which was essentially chocolate milk with loads of chocolate and not enough milk. Though it was too sugary for some people's taste, Pigeon loved to overdose on the potent treat.

"They're there now?" Mr. Stott asked.

"That was the plan," Pigeon said after swallowing. "Nate wanted to start earning tickets. I know him. He's already determined to win a stamp. Once he sets his mind on something, he's hard to stop."

Mr. Stott nodded. "That can be a good quality, depending on the situation."

Pigeon took another bite of the concentrated mixture. He had already related what the Battiato brothers had told them, and had also summarized the events of the day. "Are we making a mistake?"

Mr. Stott sighed. "You're certainly out of your depth. The

Battiatos are probably in over their heads too. If this enemy overpowered Mozag, there is likely little any of us can do."

"Wasn't Mozag exposed?" Pigeon asked. "He was far from home, and magicians are vulnerable outside of their lairs."

"I know Mozag has at least one portable lair," Mr. Stott said. "A motor home, I believe. And his Cubs hat functions as a limited lair as well. A magician of his caliber is never defenseless. Still, you're right that he would have been much more vulnerable here than at home."

"Do you know any magicians powerful enough to get both John and Mozag?"

Mr. Stott shrugged. "I could make guesses. Few magicians advertise their abilities. Because of the many rivalries in the magical community, it's wise to keep your talents hidden. Without knowing what skills you possess, an enemy will be less eager to pick a fight. And in the event of a confrontation, if your capabilities are unknown, you keep the element of surprise on your side."

"So it would be hard to guess who we're facing," Pigeon said.

"There would be no accuracy in guessing without more information."

"Should we walk away?" Pigeon asked. "Should we leave this to the Battiatos?"

"It's complicated," Mr. Stott replied, shifting uncomfortably. "I may not love garnering attention from the magical police, but the service they provide our community is invaluable. We can't lose Mozag. Who knows how many villains would come out of hiding? The process of finding a magician to take his place would cause serious contention, which would only add to the chaos. I'm not sure whether anyone really could replace him."

"So we need to solve this?" Pigeon said.

"The need is great. There must be a terrible scheme in motion if Mozag got personally involved. Out of our depth or not, we might be harmed more by inaction than by involvement."

Pigeon licked his spoon. "We need to give it a shot?"

Mr. Stott held a finger to his lips and glanced toward the door. He rose, crossed silently to the door, and opened it, revealing Lindy in a suspicious pose.

"Give what a shot?" Lindy asked without shame.

Mr. Stott scowled deeply, his bushy eyebrows crowding together. "How long have you been there?"

"No time at all," Lindy replied. "Long enough to hear what Pigeon just asked. How do you always know when I'm listening?"

"Every magician has his secrets," Mr. Stott replied. "Run along while Pigeon and I finish our conversation. He has some private concerns."

"I know exactly what concerns him," Lindy said. "I don't need to eavesdrop to figure that out. He met with the Battiatos today, and it's getting messy."

"This is none of your business, young lady," Mr. Stott insisted.

Lindy glared at him incredulously. "But all of my friends are involved! What's my defect? Why can't I help?"

"Your defect is that I'm your father," Mr. Stott answered. "It might not seem fair, but this situation is too hazardous for me to let my daughter participate."

"Oh, right," Lindy complained. "What a great protector. You'll send all the kids in the neighborhood into harm's way, just not me."

"I'm not sending anybody anywhere," Mr. Stott replied calmly. "I am not Pigeon's guardian. I have no authority over him. He came to me for advice. Should I turn him away?"

"Maybe not," Lindy said. "But do you have to give him magical candy? Isn't that encouraging him?"

"If I feel the candy might help protect him, I'm willing to provide some."

Lindy looked to Pigeon. "What's going on, Pidge? I want to help."

Pigeon locked eyes with Mr. Stott. The warning there was unmistakable. "Sorry, Lindy. Your dad is your dad."

"Is he?" she replied harshly. "Then why don't I remember him? Why do we hardly know each other?" She faced Mr. Stott, her expression livid. "I'm not asking to go to an edgy rock concert. I'm not asking to hang out with druggies. I'm asking for something good! I just want to help. If you won't let me go with them, at least fill me in on what's happening!"

"I know you too well," Mr. Stott said. "If you had details, you wouldn't be able to resist. This is for your own good, honey. Call me the worst parent ever, but my first priority is keeping you safe."

"While putting everybody else in danger?" Lindy challenged.

"I have my reasons," Mr. Stott said, getting frustrated. "This isn't safe for anybody, but you would be in even greater danger than the others."

"Because I'm stupider?" Lindy blurted. "Because I'm less capable?"

Mr. Stott turned to Pigeon. "I'm sorry, Pigeon. I'm afraid we'll have to continue this discussion at another opportunity."

Lindy backed out the door. "My mistake, Dad. Don't let me disturb your little powwow with my friend. I don't want to mess things up for Pigeon. I just wanted to help. It's bad enough to be useless. I'd hate to also be problematic. I'll find something that suits me better. Maybe I'll go upstairs and stare at the wall."

She closed the door briskly. After a moment of silence, Mr. Stott went and peeked to make sure she was gone.

"You understand why I can't let her in on this," Mr. Stott said.

"The Battiatos agreed," Pigeon replied. "We don't know who we're up against. If our enemies figured out Lindy's identity, she really could be in serious trouble."

"Even if her memories remain truly irretrievable, once her identity leaks, she will become a target. Some magicians might want revenge. Others may aspire to enlist her. None of the consequences would be good for her—or for us." Mr. Stott frowned. "I don't relish keeping your activities from her. She's already curious enough about where she came from without adding new secrets to the mix."

"She thinks you adopted her," Pigeon said.

Mr. Stott held up a finger. "Which is not a lie. I have adopted her. She also believes her parents are long dead, which is probably true. I told her she had an accident and lost her memory, which is generally true, although I've concealed some key details. I told her that John placed her with me because, as a magician, I was better suited to handle a unique case like hers than most parents would be. Also true."

"Does she keep asking about the details?" Pigeon asked.

"I try not to lie outright," Mr. Stott said. "I told her that even John knew little about her origin. I told her I'm not sure if she'll ever regain her lost memories. I maintain that I know virtually nothing about her past—which is mostly accurate, by the way. I knew little about the magician Belinda White. But I do know that she became our Lindy, which information I withhold."

Pigeon scraped the last of the chocolate sludge from his mug. "Everything is so complicated."

Mr. Stott harrumphed. "Life gets that way."

"You think we should go undercover and try to take these guys down?" Pigeon asked.

"That would be the noble and brave thing to do," Mr. Stott said. "It might even be the wisest thing to do, considering all the trouble that might come unless this magician is stopped. But don't forget that being noble and brave is one of the most proven ways to die young."

"I'll try to keep that in mind," Pigeon replied.

* * * * *

Pigeon lay in bed trying to remember how to fall asleep. Sometimes it was so easy—you just closed your eyes and relaxed, and the rest took care of itself. That was not the case tonight. No position seemed comfortable. No trick could stop his mind from worrying about what new dangers the morning would bring.

Nate had called earlier. Apparently they had caused quite a stir by using Peak Performance to dominate the arcade games. Nate and the others had stopped by the candy shop after Pigeon had left, and Mr. Stott had essentially given his blessing for them to keep trying to infiltrate the arcade by winning tickets.

Pigeon rolled to his other side, curling his knees and bundling his covers, hoping to find a perfect position that would finally let him slip off to sleep and leave his stresses behind. He was supposed to go to Arcadeland tomorrow with the others and keep winning tickets. Nate had basically been thrown out today for that very thing! How did he expect tomorrow to be any different?

The door to his bedroom nudged open. Was Aunt Rhonda checking on him? No, it was Diego.

"Hey, boy," Pigeon said softly. "What are you doing in here?" The Labrador normally slept in his own house out back. Maybe Aunt Rhonda had left a door ajar.

"Lindy opened a window," the dog replied.

"You're talking," Pigeon said.

"Lindy brought Brain Feed. She's waiting on the back patio."

"She wants to talk?" Pigeon asked.

"She seems a little upset," Diego replied.

Suddenly Pigeon wished he had played possum when Diego entered. The uncomfortable exchange between Lindy and Mr. Stott had been bad enough. He didn't want to try to manage her curiosity on his own.

"Can you tell her I'm sleeping?" Pigeon asked halfheartedly.

"She ordered me to wake you," Diego said.

"All right," Pigeon relented. He got out of bed and put on some slippers. His plaid pajamas looked sort of goofy, so he grabbed a robe from his closet and slid his arms into the loose sleeves. "Do I look okay?"

"I'm a bad judge," Diego said. "Dogs don't require artificial coverings."

"That didn't stop Mom from dressing you as a cowboy for Halloween."

"Don't remind me."

Pigeon led Diego to the back door.

"Stupid hat," Diego muttered.

"Sorry I brought it up," Pigeon said.

"And that bandanna! Cruel and unusual."

They crept out to the patio.

Lindy stepped out of the shadows. "Hi, Pidge."

"You're out late," Pigeon said.

"I snuck away," Lindy replied. "I needed to talk to somebody."

"What's wrong?"

"Where did I come from, Pigeon?" Lindy asked. "Who am I really?"

"How should I know?"

Lindy wrung her hands. "Somebody must know something! Everyone acts like my origin is some big mystery. I have a feeling there's more to it than people are telling me."

Pigeon tried to collect his thoughts. She was wasting no time in taking the conversation exactly to the subject he most wanted to avoid. "We didn't meet you until after we defeated Mrs. White." At least that was true in a sense. She looked like she expected him to elaborate. "None of us knew much about your past. One of the guys who worked for Mrs. White made it clear that you had no family. John picked Mr. Stott to watch over you because he thought he would take good care of you and could accept your mysterious background. We all care about you, Lindy."

"I know you care," Lindy said. "I don't doubt that. Dad is just so protective lately. He has let me do some crazy things with you guys, but he seems extra worried about me trying to help John. Maybe he's just being cautious, but it started me thinking. It makes me wonder if he knows more than he's telling me."

Pigeon licked his lips. His fingers felt fidgety. "I don't know anything."

"I'm sure you're not supposed to spill any secrets," Lindy said. "But we're friends, right?"

"Of course."

Her voice became more sincere. It sounded like she might cry. "I'm having a hard time, Pidge. A really hard time. Can you imagine having no memories of yourself? Of the person you call Dad? Of any friends or family? I can't shake the suspicion that you all know more than you're saying. It's there in certain looks you give each other. I know you guys think you're protecting me from something, but it's making me crazy. I need somebody to be straight with me."

Pigeon felt unsure how to respond. He had no right to give her the information she wanted. Knowledge of her past could end up harming her. It could harm everyone.

"Everybody clams up when I talk like this," Lindy said. "I don't push the issue too often. At first I felt too off balance to really worry about it. I just wanted to fit in. But lately it has been gnawing at me. When Dad banned me from helping you guys, he forced me to really confront the issue. Let me tell you my guess. I'm worried . . ." She put her hands up to her face, as if hesitant to utter the next words. She finally whispered them: "I'm worried that my parents were bad guys. Evil magicians, maybe, working with Mrs. White. And John Dart had to lock them away. Or maybe they got killed? I was devastated, so somebody erased my memory. Then John felt guilty and brought me to live with Mr. Stott."

Pigeon felt tense. She expected a response. He felt like the truth must be written all over his face. Her guess wasn't too far off—except her parents weren't the evil magicians. She was. What had Mr. Stott said about handling these inquiries? He tried to respond without blatantly lying.

"I don't know anything about your parents," Pigeon said. "As far as I know, they might have been really good people. Maybe they were hexed by bad magicians or something. Maybe Mrs. White kept them prisoner. Maybe they weren't magical at all."

"Maybe some big spell killed my parents and wiped my memory

at the same time," Lindy said. "Somebody threw a magic bagel of power at us and I lost my family."

"Not all magic is edible," Pigeon pointed out.

"Do you get why I'm freaked?" Lindy asked. "If my real parents were good people, why all the secrecy? They must have been bad. It must be a dirty secret. Maybe I hated them. Maybe I loved them. I might never know. Am I supposed to believe that I lost my memory and nobody knows how it happened or where I came from? Seriously? What happened before I turned up in that candy shop with you, Nate, Summer, and John? My life didn't start at that moment. What happened before?"

"What did John tell you?"

"Dad and John both told me that I lost my memory by accident. They told me no magic can restore it. They claimed not to understand the spell. They said they never knew my parents, but they're certain that I have no living relatives. My first memories from the candy shop are hazy. Everything was so new and unfamiliar. I felt deeply confused. I hardly heard what anyone was saying. It was as if in that instant, fully conscious, I had just been born."

"If Mr. Stott can't explain what happened," Pigeon said, "I don't have a prayer."

"Does it have to do with Mrs. White?" Lindy asked. "The lady who owned the candy shop before Dad? Was I her prisoner? Her helper? I know she was a big villain."

"John and Mr. Stott defeated her," Pigeon said. "We helped. Nate especially. She went away. She won't be back."

"Did Mrs. White do something to my parents?" Lindy asked. "I mean, my first memories are at her candy shop."

"I don't know, Lindy," Pigeon said, terrified by how close her questions came to revealing the truth. "I'd never met you before that day. I don't know much about what Mrs. White was doing, except that she was trying to take over the town with her magic. I was a captive there myself. Have you considered that there might not be any big conspiracy to hide your past? Maybe nobody can answer your questions because nobody knows?"

After staring at Pigeon searchingly, Lindy sighed. "It stinks getting left out. I want to help John. I want to help you guys."

"We don't even understand what's going on yet," Pigeon said.

"What do you know?"

Pigeon paused. How much should he say? Anything?

"Have you ever felt left out, Pigeon?" Lindy asked.

"All the time," he confessed. "I mean, I used to feel like that all the time. Before I became friends with Summer, Trevor, and Nate."

"That's how I'm feeling," Lindy said. "I'm wondering if I have any real friends."

She *was* his friend. He couldn't tell her where she came from. Shouldn't he tell her something? Making her feel friendless and desperate might be worse than telling her that she used to be a psychotic, murderous magician.

"You can win tickets at Arcadeland," Pigeon finally said. "That new arcade in Walnut Hills."

"You just blew my mind," Lindy said dryly. "Why haven't I heard about this on the news? How have they covered this up?"

"There's more," Pigeon said uncomfortably. "You use the tickets to buy prizes. The most expensive prizes are four hand stamps that grant membership into four different clubs. We think the kids in the clubs can get magic candy like Mr. Stott makes. We're not positive about anything. We have no idea who runs

Arcadeland. We're not even sure about the clubs. But we're investigating."

"You're trying to earn tickets to join the clubs?" Lindy asked. "So you can find out what's really going on?"

"Pretty much," Pigeon replied, worried that he had said too much.

"I could help," Lindy said, her eyes lighting up. "You need help earning tickets."

"Lindy, no," Pigeon said. "Please. Your dad would kill me if I got you involved. I trusted you by telling you. Don't betray that by getting us busted."

"He won't know," she promised. "I'll be sneaky."

"It could be extra dangerous for you," Pigeon said, his mind racing. "We don't know where you came from, but we suspect your origins must be magical. I mean, your memory was wiped, and we found you at Mrs. White's. Nobody wants you exposed to magical bad guys."

Lindy regarded Pigeon thoughtfully. "You guys are going there tomorrow?"

"Right when it opens at nine," Pigeon said.

"Don't stress," Lindy said with resignation. "I won't crash the party." She reached out and rubbed Pigeon's shoulder. "Thanks for trusting me. I appreciate it. I won't let you down."

"Okay. Sorry I couldn't be more helpful."

"You were great. I should go. You need your rest."

"Good night, Lindy."

"Good night."

CHAPTER SEVEN

ODD HOURS

Hunched over a rifle at the shooting gallery, Nate chewed his fourth stick of Peak Performance gum since entering the arcade. When the doors had opened at nine, he, Trevor, Summer, and Pigeon had wasted no time getting started.

By his third consecutive stick of Peak Performance, Nate could feel the effects waning. The light games were getting tougher to freeze at the right time, and he could no longer break the high scores on basketball, Skee-Ball, or the football tossing game. But if he took his time, he could still hit all ten of the far targets at the shooting gallery.

The arcade workers had made some adjustments since last night. Shooting Stars remained out of order, as was a high-paying game where the player spun a huge wheel. The shooting gallery jackpot for the ten far targets had been reduced to 250 tickets. When the ten farthest targets were hit, sirens no longer indicated that anything unusual had happened. Nate saw the lack of attention as a good thing, although he lamented losing the huge payout. Still, 250 tickets remained very attractive when you could claim them every turn.

Nate was sighting through the window at the star when a hand came down on the back of his neck. He accidentally pulled the trigger and missed the shot. Disgruntled, he looked up to find Roman standing over him.

"You're swimming in tickets," Roman said.

Nate had won the shooting game nine times in a row, which meant 2250 tickets were currently snarled around him on the ground. "I got a hot tip about the gallery."

"You have a weird way of thanking me," Roman said. "It's barely ten and the records are all worse than yesterday. Didn't you hear what I told you?"

"We upped them little by little," Nate assured him. "We started right when they opened. We never beat the basketball records by more than three points. We usually only won by one or two."

"They're already so high!" Roman complained. "You would have had to raise them every try."

"It happened pretty quickly," Nate admitted. "A few of us were working at it."

Roman shook his head, clearly frustrated. "My day is shot. Without records to beat, earning tickets will be a pain. How many have you won this morning?"

Nate hesitated to answer. "Lots. Over 8,000."

"In an hour?"

"I had a hot streak."

Roman shook his head, trying not to let his irritation show. "You've obviously got the shooting gallery figured out. Did you snag the jackpot?"

"Yesterday."

"Unbelievable."

"They reset the prize. It pays 250 now if you hit all the far targets on one turn."

"What was the prize yesterday?"

"Twenty-five hundred."

Roman made a low whistle. "You're raking them in faster than anyone I've seen."

"It's going all right," Nate said.

Roman sighed. "Congrats. I better go start playing. Tomorrow I'll make sure to come when the doors open." He walked off.

Nate could tell Roman wasn't happy, and he felt a little bad about it. He knew Roman was excited to earn a stamp, and the process would be slower while the records stayed high. But in a way they were doing him a favor. Roman didn't know what he was getting himself into. The perks that came with the stamp would be cool, but there would be strings attached. Bad people were running this arcade. People who had taken down John Dart. The deeper Roman got involved, the greater the danger he would face.

Nate settled back in and started shooting targets again. He hit all of the far targets three times in succession before somebody cleared their throat behind him. Nate looked up, recognizing Cleon.

"You couldn't resist?"

"We're not cheating," Nate replied. "We have the same right to play as anyone else. You guys set the rules. It's not our fault if we're good."

"Gather your tickets," Cleon said. "The director wants to have a chat."

"Are we in a movie?"

"The director of the arcade, smart guy."

"Why does the director get to chat with me?" Nate resisted. "Is he a police officer? Are you? Am I under arrest for winning tickets?"

Cleon leaned closer. "You're in her arcade. You're on her property. If you wish to continue playing here, you'll have a talk with her."

Cleon awaited a response. If this would provide a chance to meet the person running the arcade, Nate supposed he should play along. It might give him the knowledge the Battiatos needed. Then again, he might end up disappearing just like John and Mozag.

Nate noticed Pigeon watching him from not too far off. Trevor was observing from across the room. His friends could call in the Battiatos if he disappeared. Besides, who knew what Cleon might do if Nate tried to run? The man currently had the air of a disgruntled bouncer.

"I'll come," Nate said, collecting his tickets.

"Good choice," Cleon replied, kneeling to help.

* * * * *

Trevor watched Cleon lead Nate away from the shooting gallery. He kept one hand in his pocket, fingering the Shock Bits hidden inside. At the first sign of any struggle, he was ready to spit out his gum and replace it with the electrifying candy.

Summer walked up to Nate and Cleon with a camera and blatantly snapped a picture of them together. Shaking his head slightly, Cleon gave her an amused smirk as he walked past her. She returned his attention with an innocent grin. Trevor thought it was a smart move. With Cleon knowing she had photographic evidence, he would think twice before letting Nate come to harm.

Nate seemed to go along willingly. Trevor followed until they passed through a nondescript door marked EMPLOYEES ONLY.

Pigeon came up beside him. "What should we do?"

"I want the Battiatos ready to move," Trevor said. "You have the other walkie-talkie?"

"Yeah."

"Keep an eye on that door. Call if anything happens. And watch my tickets."

"Got it."

Trevor handed over his tickets to Pigeon. Summer approached as Trevor headed to the door.

"You're telling them?" she asked.

Trevor nodded. "Help Pidge keep watch."

On his way out, Trevor noticed a girl staring at him. She looked to be in her older teens or early twenties. Her light brown hair was pulled back in a simple ponytail. She wore a blue Arcadeland work apron and was sweeping debris into a dustpan attached to a pole. Her glance moved past him as Trevor returned the eye contact. She had a slight build—fairly short and quite slender.

Trevor ignored her until he reached the doors to the outside. As he pushed through, he glanced over and saw her watching him again.

Only after reaching the Arcadeland parking lot did Trevor realize that he wasn't sure where the Battiatos could be found. He scanned the lot for a white van, then tried the street, but saw neither a van nor any sign of the husky twins.

Trevor crossed the mostly vacant parking lot to the street. Gazing up and down the sidewalk, Trevor saw plenty of vehicles, but no van and no twins. He started paying more attention to the surrounding rooftops and businesses. Where were they? Could they see him?

A plain white van pulled around a corner a couple of blocks down the street. Trevor watched as it pulled over to the side of the road. It was still well over a block away. They were probably worried about being spotted by Arcadeland employees.

Trevor walked briskly to the van. When he arrived, the side door opened and he climbed inside.

Ziggy sat at the wheel. Victor had opened the door.

"Trouble?" Victor asked.

"Cleon took Nate through a door marked for employees," Trevor explained.

"Did Nate go willingly?" Ziggy asked.

"Seemed like it," Trevor said. "Summer and Pigeon are still watching the door. Pigeon has a walkie-talkie." Trevor held up his.

"I wonder what they're up to?" Victor mused.

"They noticed the kids earning tickets too easily," Ziggy said simply. "These guys are players. No player likes getting played."

"This could help us," Victor replied, his large fist bumping against his forehead. "Nate could learn something."

"The kid could be in trouble," Ziggy said.

"We need to be ready to act," Victor said.

"I'm worried about him," Trevor said.

Ziggy and Victor gazed at each other.

"Should we get ready?" Ziggy asked.

"Sure, just in case," Victor replied.

"My turn, right?"

"Your turn."

Victor bowed his head. He started to sag. His coat was fitting looser. Trevor watched Victor's hand transform, the fingers getting subtly shorter and slimmer while the back of the hand expanded slightly, swelling with fat.

When Victor raised his head, Trevor gasped. Victor's cheeks drooped flabbily. His eyelids seemed heavier, the creases around his mouth more pronounced. Blubbery jowls dangled unhealthily. Despite his looking fatter and older, his clothes seemed baggy, as if he had shrunk. Victor had wilted from robust to sickly in a matter of seconds.

"That's the stuff," Ziggy said from the driver's seat, his voice heartier. He turned and gave Trevor a cocky smile. His face appeared more chiseled and masculine. Not only did he look younger, but his neck bulged with muscle, new veins suddenly prominent. He loosened his tie, apparently trying to accommodate his thicker build.

"You good?" Victor asked, his voice a bit wheezy.

"That's plenty," Ziggy answered. "Any more and I'll pop the seams on this suit."

"What just happened?" Trevor asked. He had an idea, but he wanted confirmation.

"Victor loaned me some of his vitality," Ziggy said. "I gained a few inches in height, a bunch of muscle, more endurance—the works. Sometimes one really strong guy is preferable to a pair of pretty strong guys."

"It leaves me feeling wiped out," Victor said. "Not completely worthless, but certainly worth less."

"We take turns," Ziggy explained. "He got to be superhuman last time."

"It's the only fair way," Victor said.

"This is in case we need to take action?" Trevor asked.

"You're catching on," Ziggy said with a wink. "I kind of hope Pigeon calls."

"No you don't," Victor said. "It would mean Nate is in trouble."

"I don't mean the kid any harm," Ziggy apologized. "You know how it is, Vic. I itch to be in motion. I feel like a sports car in the slow lane. I want to run, climb, maybe knock some heads together."

"Patience," Victor said. "Nate might be acquiring important intelligence. We wait for the call."

* * * * *

Cleon escorted Nate to an office, opened the door, and stepped aside. Nate entered. The door closed behind him. Cleon had not followed him in.

An Asian woman sat behind a large desk, typing on a laptop. The office was nothing fancy. A bulletin board on one wall displayed shift schedules along with some charts and graphs. Piles of paperwork cluttered the desk, spread among a few knickknacks, including a tiny hula girl and a fancy snow globe. Two chairs were positioned in front of the desk, facing the woman.

"Are you the director?" Nate asked.

She held up one finger, eyes down, still typing briskly with one hand. Her fingers rattled against the keyboard so quickly that Nate wondered if she might be typing nonsense. Then she looked up, stood, and smiled. Her hair was short and tidy. She was fairly tall. She wore a blouse with a blazer over it.

"I'm Katie Sung," she said professionally, extending a hand to Nate over the desk.

Nate stepped forward and shook it. Her skin felt cool, her grip limp. He noticed that her nails were short.

"I'm Nate."

"Nathan Sutter," she agreed. "Have a seat." She indicated one of the chairs.

Surprised and perplexed that she knew his full name, Nate sat down. "You own this place?"

"I wish," she said, her smile widening. She sat. "I'm the director here, appointed by the owner."

"Am I under arrest?"

"A peculiar question. Should you be under arrest?"

"Not unless it's illegal to be good at arcade games."

Her smile faltered. She brushed her fingertips together. "Uncommonly good. Your friends too. Supernaturally good. Are you chewing gum?"

Nate froze mid-chew. Busted.

"Did I say something to upset you?" she pressed.

"I just felt like I was back in school for a minute. My teacher last year wasn't a fan of gum chewing."

"You were in fifth grade?"

"Yep."

"I don't mind the habit," Katie said. "Not unless it allows kids to sink hundreds of free throws in a row."

"Performance-enhancing gum?" Nate asked, trying to sound incredulous.

Katie settled back in her chair. "You tell me."

Nate shrugged. "Sounds ridiculous."

"As ridiculous as hitting the ten toughest targets in the shooting gallery over and over again? As ridiculous as winning the Shooting Stars jackpot at will?"

Nate rubbed the wooden arms of his chair. "Is this arcade for losers only?"

"We don't mind winners, Nate. We like winners. Actually, we adore winners. But we prefer winners to use their natural abilities."

"Felt natural to me."

Katie closed her laptop. "Why are you here, Nate? You and your three friends. What are you after?"

"You could probably guess."

"You won nearly ten thousand tickets in just over an hour. Humor me."

Nate folded his hands. "If you don't want people to go after your stamps, don't offer them as prizes."

"And why would you want a stamp?"

"Because I'm curious. Anything worth so many tickets must be amazing."

"Indeed," she said. "Enough prattle. I know who you are, Nate. I know you were involved with Belinda White, and you're now involved with Sebastian Stott. Did he send you to spy on us?"

"Belinda who? Sebastian what?"

"Don't play dumb. You've insulted us enough by taking our tickets."

"Mr. Stott would rather I wasn't here. He thinks you guys might be dangerous."

Katie leaned forward. "And what do you think?"

Nate knew he could be in trouble if he didn't play this right. He grinned. "I think I like magic candy. And I think you might have some."

"Magic what?"

"Exactly."

Showing a hint of a smile, Katie regarded Nate silently for a moment. "I don't know what sort of operation Sebastian is running, but this isn't a game."

Nate snorted. "You have games all over the place."

"We have games, yes. We know games. This isn't one."

"You're recruiting."

She gave no answer.

"I've been through this before," Nate said. "Different magician, same drill. Don't you want good people? The best? What's wrong with me and my friends doing our best to win?"

"We're not eager for candidates with divided allegiances," Katie said.

"Is that another way of saying you don't want anyone with experience? With proven skills?"

"We don't want to draw too much attention," she said. "Your antics out there have to stop. It's one thing for us to know how you're scoring so well. It's quite another for the general public to start catching on."

"If you don't want us putting on a show, you could just give us each a stamp. Or just give us the tickets."

Her eyes flashed. "You want easy tickets?"

"We want tickets. You want us to stop winning so many. I'm thinking up possible solutions."

Her demeanor predatory, the director stood and leaned forward, her palms on her desk. "Nathan, you tell me the truth or this will not end well for you. Did you break in here and steal tickets last night?"

The accusation startled him. "No." He didn't have to lie.

Her eyes narrowed. "Where were you last night?"

"At home, mostly. After I left here I didn't come back until this morning."

"You realize that we have cameras. We know exactly how many tickets you four have earned."

"Are you missing some tickets?"

She kept staring at him like she suspected he was hiding something. "No."

"That Cleon guy doesn't seem very—"

"I'm not worried about our employees," Katie snapped. She sat down. "Let's get back to you and your friends. The stamps must be earned. Giving away tickets would defeat part of our purpose. We're looking for a certain kind of person. We don't want to disrupt our little contest."

"But you don't want us winning so many tickets in front of your customers."

"You're catching on."

"But we need tons of tickets quickly in order to get the stamps."

Katie fingered her slim gold necklace. "Quite the dilemma."

"Even if there were such a thing as magical candy that would make winning easy, I don't see any rules against it."

"It's hard to post rules against the impossible. Some rules are quietly understood and are therefore quietly enforced."

Nate stretched his legs and stared at the floor. The carpet was not particularly nice. "Are you threatening us?"

"Are you taking advantage of us?"

"I want a stamp. If you try to ban us, we could get pretty loud about it. We could make a much bigger scene than by winning lots of tickets."

Katie gave Nate a challenging look. "Now are you threatening me?"

"Only if you discriminate against us. I just want a chance to win like everybody else."

"But you're not like everybody else. We can't afford the attention."

Nate nodded. "How about a compromise? If you can't give the tickets away, but you don't want us earning them in front of everybody, why not open up early for us? Give us a few hours before the crowds arrive. Just a few hours each day, until we earn enough."

Katie considered him. "Five to eight?"

"All the machines open. No point in limiting us if we're working in secret."

"I have no desire to prolong the process."

"We'll already be pretty limited. Other people will be able to play twelve hours per day. We'd only have a quarter of that time."

"Once I start agreeing to your terms, you can stop selling."

"Right," Nate said, a little embarrassed. "Five to eight would work. We'll stay away otherwise. You can reset our records after we go."

"We have a side door."

"We'll be sneaky," Nate assured her. "Nobody will know."

"They better not," Katie said. "Word of this gets around, the deal is off."

"We're good with secrets."

"Okay. Tomorrow at five in the morning."

"Thanks," Nate said.

Her eyebrows lifted. "Don't thank me yet. Once you earn a stamp, you become part of us. We make sure of that. We can't have outsiders interfering. You might be getting more than you bargained for."

"I'll take my chances," Nate said, trying to act confident even though the warning concerned him.

"Don't make trouble for us," Katie warned sternly. "Don't try to mess with us. Do this right, and you might end up more satisfied than you can guess."

Katie started shuffling some papers. While her eyes were averted, Nate removed the small digital camera from his pocket. He held it on his lap. He had not yet seen Katie in the arcade. She might not be the owner, but she must be part of the inner circle. A description would be worth little. Same with her name, since it could easily be fake. But a photo might prove useful to Ziggy and Victor.

"I have high hopes," Nate said.

She stood. "Anything else?"

Nate rose, holding the camera near the side of his waist, attempting to be subtle. He tried to keep it pointed at her. Should he risk taking a shot? Her eyes were on him again. "I think I'm good."

"Did you want a picture?"

Nate froze. He hadn't snapped a shot yet. "My friends and I are big on recon," he explained sheepishly, holding up the camera.

"We have cameras too. We've noticed you taking photographs. Might as well get a good one." She came around the side of her desk and smiled, one hand on her hip.

Nate aimed a shot and snapped it. "Thanks. Although the pose takes the mystery out of it."

"Well, I doubt the low angle together with the poor aim would have been very flattering. I do have my pride."

"See you tomorrow."

Her smile changed. "I doubt you'll see me, but I'll be watching."

CHAPTER EIGHT
STAMPS

"We believe her true name is Suyin Chen," Victor said, staring at the image on the digital camera. "You were right to feel nervous. She's a ComKin—a Combat Kinetic."

Nate leaned against the inner wall of the van. Ziggy was currently driving away from Arcadeland along with Trevor, Summer, and Pigeon. When Nate first saw Victor, the man had looked terrible, but then he and Ziggy had evened things out, so now he was back to normal.

"A ComKin. Which means what?" Pigeon asked.

"You remember the dwarf?" Ziggy asked.

"The one working for Mrs. White," Summer said. "He was a Kinetic. He could store up energy, then release it all at once."

"A mighty throw," Victor said. "A tremendous jump. A devastating punch. The dwarf was dangerous, but in bursts. His energy was volatile. ComKins have learned to harness a similar ability in a different way. They store up a larger reservoir of kinetic energy, and, instead of unleashing it in a single burst, they release it in a focused stream that can go on for minutes."

"They're usually trained in a variety of fighting techniques," Ziggy said. "Martial arts, wrestling, boxing—you name it. They're a pain in every sense of the word."

"Do you know what magician Suyin works with?" Summer asked.

"Yusiv in Poland, right?" Victor checked.

Ziggy nodded. "And Kwan in Singapore. And Villaroel in Peru. Anyone else?"

"That nut on that island? The one who loves water?"

"Right. I forgot about him."

"Don't you guys have a computer to run her name through?" Trevor asked.

Victor tapped his temple. "We keep our data in here. We're all frequently briefed. Pictures, bios, mission reports. Magicians mistrust technology."

"Suyin Chen has gone by other names than Katie Sung," Ziggy said. "She's a mercenary, taking jobs contract by contract. She could be working for anyone."

"Not *anyone*," Victor corrected. "She's expensive."

"We already know her employer is well funded," Ziggy reminded him.

"True," Victor replied. "Did you kids learn anything else?"

"I'm concerned about their nachos," Pigeon said.

Ziggy rubbed his belly sympathetically. "You need me to find a restroom?"

"Not because I ate them," Pigeon explained. "I noticed lots of people buying them. Who stops by an arcade in the morning for nachos to go? I saw seven or eight people. And several more eating them there."

"Could you get us a sample?" Victor asked.

"I meant to," Pigeon said. "Then Nate returned, and it seemed more important to come talk to you guys right away."

"Think they'll be on sale in the morning?" Ziggy asked.

"When they open early for us?" Nate said doubtfully. "I wouldn't hold my breath."

"Don't worry about it," Victor said. "I'll find somebody to buy us a sample."

"We did background checks on those kids you met," Ziggy mentioned. "Roman Cruz, Marisa Fuentes, and Chris Hughes. On paper they're good kids from regular families. Excellent students. Some minor discipline issues with Chris, but no criminal history."

"We'll learn plenty more about them if we earn stamps together," Nate said.

"How is the hunt progressing?" Victor asked.

"Together we're almost to 45,000," Pigeon said.

"By tomorrow we'll easily have enough for a stamp if we combine our winnings," Trevor noted.

"We should get somebody a stamp as soon as possible," Summer asserted.

"Nate should get a jet stamp," Pigeon said. "Those are the closest to running out, and he's already getting to know those kids. They're expecting him."

"It would be good to have one of us on the inside," Trevor agreed. "Who knows what might already be going on? The rest of us could keep earning tickets. Maybe one of us can join each club."

"That's ambitious," Victor said dubiously. "Having all of you in clubs would increase the risk, and it might not yield more info than we'd get from a single insider."

"It'll let us watch out for each other," Summer argued. "Besides, who knows what opportunities might be available to kids with different stamps?"

"Valid points," Ziggy approved.

"Will you guys drive us?" Trevor asked.

"You need to be there by five in the morning?" Ziggy asked. "Absolutely. I love starting early. We'll bring bagels."

"We should meet around four-thirty," Victor said. "I'm not as enthusiastic as Ziggy about early starts, but you ought to arrive on time. We'll meet at the bottom of Monroe."

"Early to bed, early to rise," Ziggy said.

"Early or late, sleep is sleep," Victor grunted.

* * * * *

When Pigeon got home, he found an ice cream truck parked down the street from his house. The faded blue vehicle had the words Candy Wagon emblazoned on the side. He immediately recognized it as Mr. Stott's.

Pigeon rushed over to the truck. Mr. Stott had never waited at his house before. Pigeon found the magician sitting behind the wheel.

"What's wrong?" Pigeon asked.

"Come inside."

Pigeon climbed into the passenger seat.

"Would you like a treat?" Mr. Stott asked.

"I'm all right."

"Have you seen Lindy?"

Pigeon paused. Mr. Stott was her guardian. He deserved honest answers. "She came to my house last night."

"I knew she left last night. She returned in the small hours of the morning. We had an argument about her leaving. She made it clear that if I would not grant permission, she would do whatever she wanted. I made it clear that such behavior was unacceptable. She ran off again afterward. She hasn't come home. I've been looking for her for hours."

"I haven't seen Lindy today," Pigeon said honestly. "She was pretty worked up when she came to visit me. She probably just needs to blow off some steam."

Mr. Stott rubbed his beard. "I'm worried about her. And a little concerned about the rest of us. As much as I have grown to care for Lindy, we must not forget who she used to be."

"Right."

"I can't find her anywhere. I worry she may have gotten into trouble."

"I'll keep an eye out," Pigeon said. "If she shows up, I'll call."

"Could you tell the other kids to be on the lookout?" Mr. Stott asked.

"Sure," Pigeon said. "I'll get in touch with them right away."

"How are things at the arcade?"

"Nate has almost enough tickets to join one of the clubs. One of the women working there is Suyin Chen. She's going by the name of Katie Sung."

Mr. Stott looked startled. "I know of Suyin Chen. She's a dangerous woman. You don't want to fight her. If circumstances ever lead to a physical confrontation, run, and don't look back."

"That's my basic plan with any confrontation," Pigeon replied.

"Smart lad. Still no clue who owns Arcadeland?"

"Not yet. We're hoping Nate might find out if he earns a stamp."

"All right." Mr. Stott caressed the steering wheel. "You kids take care. I'm working on a new batch of Peak Performance gum. You four are using it up at an alarming rate."

"Sorry," Pigeon said.

Mr. Stott waved away the apology. "It's for a good cause. I wish I could make the effect stay at full potency with consecutive uses. Moon Rocks work every time, regardless of the quantity consumed. Brain Feed seems to work better when administered often. But not Peak Performance."

"It's working fine," Pigeon encouraged. "We're cleaning up on tickets."

"I'm glad. Stay prepared for trouble. And watch for Lindy."

"Will do," Pigeon pledged. He climbed down from the ice cream truck and watched as it drove away, not playing any music.

* * * * *

The next morning, Todd looked tired when he admitted Nate and his friends through the side door. Todd and Cleon were the only visible employees. They supervised as Nate, Summer, Trevor, and Pigeon dominated game after game. Attractions like Shooting Stars paid lots of tickets but also gobbled time, since all of the tickets had to pay out before another turn could be taken. Having the arcade to themselves allowed Nate and his friends to move around aggressively, playing other games while tickets spooled out after a big score. It was only a matter of minutes before Nate had enough tickets to claim a stamp.

Todd went behind the redemption counter when Nate approached.

"Finally going to cash in some tickets?" Todd asked.

"One jet stamp, please."

Todd covered his mouth and chuckled. "You only started playing here a couple days ago and you're already taking the big prize. Talk about some serious skills. Let's count your tickets."

Nate handed over four cards and Todd scanned them.

"You have almost two thousand tickets to spare," Todd said. "Nice work. Your extra tickets are on this card. I assume you'll want it for your friends?"

"Yeah, we worked together."

Todd handed the card back to Nate. "No rules against pooling your tickets." Todd crouched and removed the jet stamp from under the counter. He handed it to Nate. "Last one."

"Last one?" Nate furrowed his brow. Roman must have finished up yesterday after all. "Who took the second to last?"

"I can't share that with you," Todd said. "It was claimed yesterday evening. You're welcome to ask around. Or you can find out when your first stamp gets applied. The other Jets will be there."

"When it gets applied?" Nate wondered.

"You earned the stamp itself. The ink comes later. Come back at ten this morning, we'll get you hooked up. Then you'll learn what your prize really means."

Pocketing his jet stamp, Nate turned to rejoin his friends. They gathered around him, and he dug it out of his pocket.

"Doesn't look like much," Trevor said.

"The stamp itself probably isn't valuable," Pigeon speculated. "It's like a ticket."

"I'm supposed to come back at ten to get the stamp applied," Nate said. "I guess I'll find out more then." He held up a card. "This has about two thousand tickets. We should start earning more."

Pigeon had a knack for hitting the Shooting Stars jackpot on every try; Trevor kept claiming the grand prize on Wheel of Destiny; Summer worked some of the other games where the player had to freeze lights; and Nate methodically upped the record on basketball. Todd and Cleon watched in disbelief, replacing rolls of tickets as needed.

The flood of tickets slowed as the kids moved into their fourth, fifth, and sixth sticks of Peak Performance. Cleon and Todd stopped having to refill ticket dispensers quite as regularly. Pigeon remained able to freeze Shooting Stars for the jackpot longer than the others, but when his average fell below once every twenty tries, he moved on.

As Peak Performance elevated their abilities less and less, they migrated to the shooting gallery and the basketball game. They could no longer beat any records, but they could hit preset benchmarks to earn reasonable payouts.

By the time Cleon announced that he and Todd needed to close up to prepare to open the arcade to the public, the four kids had accumulated more than 75,000 tickets. They gathered near the redemption counter to confer.

"Who gets the next stamp?" Nate asked.

"We should buy a tank," Pigeon said. "It costs more tickets than the racecar or the submarine, so it might be more important."

"I could do the tank," Summer offered.

"Fine with me," Trevor said. "I like the look of the racecar."

"Does that make me the submarine?" Pigeon asked.

"Do you mind?" Summer checked.

"Not really," Pigeon replied. "We don't even know what the stamps mean."

"Can we buy another stamp?" Summer called.

Todd hustled over. "Which one?"

"I want a tank," Summer said.

"Nice choice," Todd said, handing over the stamp. "Two tanks left. You can come by at eleven to get it applied." He slapped his hands on the counter. "All set?"

"Thanks," Summer said.

"Great," Todd replied. "Beat it for now. We have to get ready to open up for the mere mortals."

"We're mortals," Nate said.

Todd squinted and waggled his hand, suggesting that Nate's statement was iffy. "Maybe part of the time. Not so much when you're chewing that gum. Hey, I don't blame you. I miss the days when those kinds of enhancements worked on me. Enjoy it while you can. You get older every day."

Nate knew that a lot of the magic produced by magicians worked better on young people, which was why they recruited kids. But he hadn't wondered much about what happened to those kids once they grew up. He wanted to ask follow-up questions, but Cleon was shooing them toward the door. "This plan only works if you leave when you're supposed to go. We'll be here tomorrow. We'll be rooting for you to finish your stamp quest so we can get some proper sleep."

Pigeon led the way out the side door. Heavy morning traffic clogged Canal Street. At five the street had been quiet—now it was bumper to bumper. They walked down the sidewalk for three blocks, then turned up a side street to the find the white van waiting as promised.

"Earn many tickets?" Victor asked as the kids entered.

"Two stamps and a bunch of extras to put toward tomorrow," Pigeon replied.

"It was almost too easy," Summer said.

"Peak Performance takes the challenge out of it," Trevor said. "We're lucky they didn't stop us from using it."

"They want resourceful people," Nate said. "They just didn't want us showing off in front of other customers."

"Watch yourselves," Victor cautioned. "If they know you have magical enhancers, they know you're involved with another magician. I can't imagine they'll be quick to trust you."

"Do you think they're setting us up?" Pigeon asked.

"One way or another, I'm sure they are," Ziggy said.

"John needs us," Nate said. "I have a meeting at ten. Summer at eleven. It might be risky, but at least we'll finally get a chance to learn more about what's going on. Hopefully it's not too late to help our friends."

CHAPTER NINE

JETS

Nate felt nervous as he approached the redemption counter ten minutes early. He tried to persuade himself that he wasn't as alone as he felt. Trevor, Summer, and Pigeon were stationed nearby with Shock Bits, Flame Outs, and other candy. The Battiatos waited right outside, ready to charge to the rescue.

Nate had debated over whether to bring any magical candy to the meeting. In the end, he decided that since the arcade employees seemed to already suspect he had been using magical candy, it couldn't hurt to have some on him in case of an emergency. He had two doses of Shock Bits, two Moon Rocks, and a Frost Bite. He would have liked to have brought a Sweet Tooth, but none of Mrs. White's remained, and Mr. Stott had failed when he had tried to replicate them.

A trio of teenagers stood at the glass counter choosing prizes. Nate didn't recognize the woman helping them. A hand clamped down on his shoulder from behind.

"You're early," Cleon said. His hair and sideburns looked more styled than they had this morning. His shirt had a glossy sheen and rhinestone buttons.

"Better than late," Nate replied.

"Let's head on back."

Nate followed Cleon through a different EMPLOYEES ONLY door than he had used on his previous visit behind the scenes at Arcadeland. Soon they moved along a cramped, concrete hallway crowded with pipes and electrical equipment.

"So this is where the magic happens," Nate said.

"Trust me, kid," Cleon replied. "The magic around here isn't in the plumbing or the wiring."

They stopped in front of a wooden door.

"Here we are," Cleon said. "Be polite. This is no joke. You brought the stamp?"

Nate held it up.

Cleon opened the door, revealing a plain room where a lone man sat at a bare table. He had black, wild hair, either gelled or greasy, and a thin beard that traced his jawline and circled his lips. His face was creased enough that Nate wondered whether he dyed his hair to hide his gray. The man wore white gloves and a loose coat fancifully embroidered with many colors.

"Can I get you anything?" Cleon asked respectfully.

The man waved him away, then indicated the only other chair in the room to Nate. Cleon closed the door, and Nate sat facing the man across the flimsy table.

"I understand you won a jet stamp," the man said in a syrupy voice.

"That's right," Nathan said cautiously.

The man leaned forward, extending a gloved hand. "We haven't been introduced. I'm Jonas White."

"Nate. Nathan Sutter." Nate shook his hand.

"Rhymes with *stutter*. You may have known my sister. Belinda?"

Nate was unsure how to reply. "You're related to Belinda White?"

"Only by blood."

"She opened that candy shop in Colson," Nate said, hoping his voice sounded neutral.

"And then mysteriously vanished. I can tell you're tense, Nate. You should be. I've spoken with a source close to the incident. You were involved. Another magician took possession of the candy shop—Sebastian Stott. Are you working for him?"

"I know him," Nate said. "He's given me some candy. I don't work for him."

"Good to hear," Jonas said. "Whether or not you're telling the truth, if I let you keep that stamp, you'll work for me."

"I thought I owned the stamp."

"Let me rephrase," Jonas amended. "If I grant access to the ink that will make that stamp mean something, you will work for me."

"Doing what?"

"I'm a treasure hunter, Nate, and I could use some help."

"What kind of treasure?"

"Not water from the Fountain of Youth," Jonas assured him. "That well has run dry, at least around these parts. No, I'm looking for an older, more significant prize. Have you heard of the mage Iwa Iza?"

"No."

"Unsurprising. He lived ages ago. His people are no more. His language went extinct long before Europeans discovered this continent. But he left a unique treasure behind."

"What is it?"

"The details are vague. But the prowess of Iwa Iza is renowned among magicians. He used his power to protect his people and the natural world they admired. A few of his inimitable creations have survived, but his masterwork was called Uweya, and it is hidden somewhere in this area."

"Uweya?"

"That may not even be the correct pronunciation," Jonas said. "The language is lost. I can offer no translation. But I'm here to follow some clues that might lead us to Iwa Iza's masterpiece. Many have sought Uweya. Hanaver Mills was involved in the hunt. Success eluded him, but he searched here for years, which is why he hid his water from the Fountain of Youth in this vicinity. I gleaned some insights from his failures, and from the fruitless efforts of many others. I am finally closing in on my prize. Would you like to become involved?"

"Sounds interesting," Nate said. He hoped he didn't seem too eager.

"More than interesting," Jonas promised. "The hunt will be challenging, frightening, astonishing, and perhaps even deadly. It will provide a once-in-a-lifetime chance to experience the miraculous. The relics of Iwa Iza are among our most potent talismans of protection and healing, guarded alongside other wonders by the Unseen Magi. By all accounts, Uweya should surpass his other creations in splendor and power."

"You want Uweya so you can help people?" Nate asked, trying not to sound doubtful.

"Iwa Iza devoted his life to uplifting his followers and protecting the natural world. Uweya is allegedly his crowning achievement. Yet it does no good while lost."

Nate folded his arms. "What exactly am I agreeing to do?"

"To become one of my Jets," Jonas said, producing a pad of ink in a wooden case. "The power of the stamp should remain in full effect for two days. Over the third day, the enchantment will dwindle to nothing. I will stamp you once for making the purchase with your tickets. Renewing the stamp depends on my receiving your cooperation. If you do not wish to join the club, I will offer a jet stamp to another and deny you access to the ink."

"I'll be the last to join?" Nate checked.

"You would complete the club. Each club will have four members."

"That's a lot of kids," Nate said.

Jonas shrugged. "There will be multiple stages to finding Uweya. The clubs will compete against each other. You'll learn the details later. The winning club will have the honor of retrieving Uweya."

"You'll accept me if I commit?" Nate asked.

"You worry that I would deny you because of your involvement with Belinda. I am bound to my sister by blood, but she is no friend of mine. I was always much fonder of my other sister, Camilla. Belinda's disappearance helped spawn this opportunity for me. She was also pursuing Uweya. Acquiring water from the Fountain of Youth was merely a step along that path. By foiling her, Nate, you aided me immeasurably."

Nate frowned. Something was off. Why was Jonas making this so easy? "You mentioned you were worried I might be involved with other magicians. If I helped stop Belinda, doesn't that make me a potential threat?"

Jonas laughed, tapping the side of the inkpad with one finger. "If I can't handle the hazards posed by a child, I should pack up and go home. Don't overestimate yourself. I'll grant that you're probably more capable than many others your age. I need capable people to find this treasure. It will not be simple. It is quite possible that all of my clubs will fail and I will have to start again from scratch. You let me worry about the threat you pose. I'll take measures to protect my interests. All you really need to know is that I'm willing to accept the risks if you're willing to work with me."

Nate considered the insultingly frank response. Jonas White's open attitude made Nate hungry for information. He felt tempted to ask about Mozag and John Dart, but worried it would push the magician too far. If he worked for Jonas, he would sooner or later end up in a position to learn about his captured friends. "All right. I'll be a Jet."

"Just like *West Side Story!*" Jonas gushed. "Hand over the stamp and hold out your hand."

Nate obeyed. Jonas pressed the stamp against the inkpad, then stamped the back of Nate's hand. Tingles rushed up his arm and spread across his body.

"Welcome to the team." Jonas grinned.

Nate looked at the simple jet insignia on his hand. Something had changed, but he couldn't quite recognize the difference.

"Try to fly," Jonas prompted.

Nate stood, and his feet rose off the floor. He levitated a few feet into the air. He hovered, looking down at Jonas in surprise. It felt as natural as walking. He swerved to the left, then back to the right. Deciding where to go felt as simple as commanding his arms to move or his fingers to grasp. The force suspending him in the air existed throughout his body but seemed centered in his chest. Nate slowly dropped back to the ground.

"Ever experience anything like it?" Jonas asked.

"No," Nate replied.

"I can't tell you I'm surprised," Jonas chuckled. "I'm a perfectionist. Are you a perfectionist, Nate?"

"I try to do good work," Nate said. "I like to win."

"I didn't think so," Jonas said smugly. "Most people refer to perfectionism much too casually. Being a perfectionist has advantages and drawbacks. My enhancers are not exceptionally diverse. Lesser magicians have broader catalogs. But my creations work unusually well for an uncommon amount of time. For example, real flight is a very difficult enhancement to produce. As a Jet, you will benefit from my thoroughness."

"It feels amazing," Nate said, impressed by the new ability. "I've had dreams about flying. Sometimes it's like swimming clumsily through the air. Other times I can zoom around however I want. This feels like my best dreams."

"Wait until you try it outside," Jonas said. "I can imagine nothing more exhilarating. Makes me wish I were young enough to use it. A word of caution: You have the ability to fly, but your body is no stronger than usual. In a car, you have a metal shell to protect you in a crash. A motorcyclist has much less protection. Think of yourself as a flying motorcyclist."

"I could really get hurt," Nate realized.

"There are limits to how fast you can fly," Jonas said. "But you can go plenty fast enough to get killed."

"I'll try to keep that in mind," Nate replied.

"Take care not to use any other magic while the stamp is in

effect," Jonas cautioned. "The magic involved with flight is delicate. Attempting to mix in other magic could prove disastrous."

"Good to know."

"You're not new to magical enhancers," Jonas said. "That could work either for or against you. Don't take any of this lightly. To seal our agreement, the day after tomorrow you must bring me an inanimate object to which you feel a strong attachment."

"Like what?"

"A stuffed animal. A book. A trophy. A photograph. I have the ability to measure your attachment to the item. If you comply, I will restamp you every other day. If the connection between you and the object isn't strong enough, you will not get restamped."

"Will you keep the object?"

"For as long as our association lasts."

"Do I need to bring something every time I get stamped?"

"Just next time," Jonas said. "Are you ready to meet your fellow Jets? Together you are the first complete group of four."

"Sure," Nate said, knowing that he had met all of them already.

Jonas rose and crossed to the far door. He moved slowly, as if ill or arthritic. When he opened the door, three kids came through— Chris, Risa, and Lindy.

Nate gaped in surprise at his friend. "Lindy?" His gaze darted to Jonas and back to Lindy. She might appear young, but surely Jonas had recognized his sister! What had transpired between them? What had he told her?

Lindy smiled sheepishly. "I hoped it would be one of you guys. I was worried Roman would beat you."

"Thanks a lot, Nate," Chris grunted, shaking his head.

Glaring, Risa took an angry step toward Nate. "Did you shut

out Roman on purpose? He's been working so hard for this! He even helped you! He thought you'd make a good teammate."

"Lindy was never part of the plan," Nate explained hastily, hoping they would believe him. "She acted alone. She wasn't even supposed to come to the arcade! Todd wouldn't reveal who had the third stamp. I assumed it was Roman. I didn't even know that Lindy was trying for a stamp."

"I don't really care how it happened," Chris said. "Together, you two stole his stamp."

"Now, now," Jonas chided. "This is a competition. Nobody has a claim on any stamp until they earn the tickets and trade for one. Chris, your friend Roman came close, but these two finished ahead of him. There are other stamps he can choose from."

"How'd she earn the tickets?" Risa grumbled. "I've never seen her playing at Arcadeland."

"She won't talk about it," Chris said.

"Perhaps she accomplished the task more cleverly than you," Jonas replied serenely. "Do you imagine that I owe you an explanation? Some days I wish that children had no tongues. Life would be less wearisome if the power of speech were withheld for the first forty years. How Lindy succeeded is not your concern. With four members, your club is complete. If you wish to remain Jets, learn to get along. If not, feel free to join the rest of humanity in their mediocrity."

"I didn't mean to offend you," Chris backpedaled.

"Which makes it so much more offensive," Jonas yawned. "The four clubs will soon compete against each other. The winners will keep their stamps. The losers won't. Before you know it, Roman and others will try to take your stamps away. I'll be interested to see how your foursome measures up."

Chris folded his arms and stared at the ground. Risa glowered. But they kept quiet.

Nate glanced at Lindy. She and Jonas were not acknowledging each other as more than new acquaintances. Either she didn't know they were siblings or she was doing a good job covering it up. Surely he knew? And if he knew, he probably would have told her, right? But Nate couldn't ask about it in front of her, in case she didn't know. And he supposed there was a small chance that Jonas didn't know either. Maybe they hadn't been together much as children.

Jonas pointed at Nate. "He just received his stamp. Lindy got hers last night, when I refreshed Chris and Risa. I'll restamp you all again the morning after next. Come at nine. Until then, I suggest you train together. You have the ability to fly, but practice will be required to fly well and to work as a team. Any questions?"

Nate couldn't think of any questions not involving Mozag or John Dart.

"A friendly reminder," Jonas continued. "If you tell any prospective candidates about what the stamps can do, you will lose all privileges and your slot will be filled by another. You have no right to let magical secrets spill into the nonmagical world. Don't test me. I'll know. I have many ways of gathering information. Keep your abilities private. That is all."

Jonas shuffled over to his chair and sat.

"Come on," Chris said. "I'll show you where we practice."

"One more thing, Nate," Jonas said. "You'll want to avoid my nacho cheese. It has a numbing effect on the ability to use and perceive magic. Old family recipe. The people at my concession counter know to keep it away from my candidates. They'll use other cheese for you. But don't try any if a family member brings some home."

"Family member?" Nate asked.

"You should encourage your family to sample it," Jonas said. "The cheese will simplify things for you, free you up to pursue your new opportunities." He waved a casual hand. "Dismissed."

Nate followed the others out of the room. They passed through a break room with a few vending machines, a sink, a microwave, some cupboards, and a few tables. One employee sat reading a hiking magazine. Another nibbled at a burrito.

Beyond the room they passed into a hall. Nate walked beside Lindy. "Are you all right?" he muttered.

"I'm fine," Lindy said.

"Your dad has been worried," Nate told her.

She winced a little. "I slept in one of the little tunnels at the Monument Park playground. It wasn't comfortable. I'll go home tonight. Not much he can do now."

"Except ground you forever," Nate pointed out.

"It's hard to ground somebody who can fly," Lindy said.

They reached a door that led directly outside. The far side of the door held an EMPLOYEES ONLY sign. Across the patio, a group of teenagers were putting at a hole designed to look like Stonehenge.

"You ran away from home?" Risa asked Lindy.

"Maybe," Lindy said.

"Lindy hasn't been very talkative," Chris told Nate.

"She's probably not sure whether she can trust you," Nate replied. "Which is probably smart."

Chris shrugged. "Like I care. Instead of one team of four, maybe we can be two teams of two."

"Fine with me," Lindy said.

"You heard Mr. White," Risa said. "If we don't work together, the other teams will beat us and we'll lose our stamps. We need to make the best of this."

"Then let's go," Chris said.

"Wait," Nate said. "My friends know I just received my stamp."

"So?" Risa asked.

"We watch out for each other," Nate said. "If I don't come back, they might freak out. Let me go tell them that I'm okay, then I'll catch up."

"We'll catch up," Lindy added. "You guys can go ahead. I'll show him the way."

"Fine, but don't slip up and spill any secrets," Chris said. "Mr. White is serious about keeping this quiet."

"Believe me, I get it," Nate replied. "See you soon."

Chris and Risa walked away. Nate and Lindy started looping around Arcadeland toward one of the regular entrances. Before they reached the doors, Nate checked that Chris and Risa were out of sight, then pulled Lindy to a halt.

"So what happened?" he asked.

Lindy glanced around. "Nobody included me, so I included myself."

"How did you win 50,000 tickets so quickly?"

"Who says I won them?"

Nate hit his forehead with the heel of his hand. "Katie Sung asked me about stolen tickets."

"You talked to her too?"

"She let you get away with it?"

Lindy leaned against the wall. "She was mad. After I traded for the stamp, they brought me to her. She told me how their cameras never showed me winning a single ticket. She told me seven rolls of 8,000 tickets had been stolen the night before."

"You stole them?"

"I didn't admit it. Not to her. I told her maybe I was wearing a disguise when I was here playing. I told her I was tricky."

"But you stole them."

Lindy looked Nate in the eye. "You know I see differently from most people."

"Right."

"I can usually see through walls and floors, at least for a ways. But a lot of Arcadeland is shielded from my sight. I don't know if they used magic or special materials, but I can't see underground here, and I can't see certain areas of the building."

"Okay," Nate said.

"It made me curious. After Pigeon told me about Arcadeland, I came and checked it out."

"Pigeon told you?" Nate cried.

She nodded. "I didn't try to enter the arcade. I just roamed the outside of the building. I noticed that the storage room where they keep their prize tickets wasn't shielded from my sight. I thought it meant that whatever was behind the shielded walls and floors must be pretty important."

"Because you would think they would protect their prize tickets," Nate said. "Makes sense. Maybe John Dart or Mozag are behind some of those walls."

"The thought had occurred to me. Anyhow, after talking to Pigeon, I realized that those tickets were the key to getting a stamp, and the stamps were the key to gathering information."

"He told you that?" Nate exclaimed.

"Keep it down," Lindy scolded, glancing around. "Yes, he told me after I guilted him by explaining how left out I was feeling."

"You took advantage of him."

"Just his kindness. I really do like him, largely because of his kindness."

"Go on."

"I know where Dad keeps the Mirror Mints that Mrs. White left behind. He guards them pretty carefully because he hasn't figured out how to produce more, even though he has her notes on the subject. Anyhow, the storeroom with the tickets had a full-length mirror. I went through a mirror near Arcadeland. When I came out into the storeroom, I heard an alarm go off. Somehow they had detected me. I worked quickly. Getting the tickets out was simple. I brought them in through one mirror and took them out through the other."

"Smooth," Nate complimented. "Fifty-six thousand tickets."

"They were heavy. I unwound them and ripped them apart so it would look like I'd won them at lots of different games. But they knew I hadn't because I never showed up on their cameras. The security at Arcadeland isn't just for show. They pay attention."

"Not well enough."

Lindy giggled. "Katie was upset. I think she was embarrassed that a kid stole tickets that she should have protected. Thankfully, Mr. White intervened."

"What did he do?" Nate asked, still wondering whether Jonas had revealed her true identity.

"He interviewed me. He told me he didn't mind that I stole the tickets. He just wanted to know how. I told him about the Mirror Mints. He thought I was resourceful. He told me that in his opinion I had earned the tickets because getting them was difficult and I got away clean. Of course, he mentioned that he would be removing all mirrors from the more private portions of his arcade. But he let me keep the stamp!"

"I'm impressed," Nate said honestly.

"You guys should have involved me from the start. I thought we Blue Falcons were supposed to stick together."

"True," Nate said. "But we didn't want to disrespect Mr. Stott."

"I know. I didn't want to either. But with John and Mozag in trouble, I felt like I needed to help. I knew I could contribute."

"What do you think about Jonas White?" Nate asked, trying not to give the question special significance.

"I wondered if he might be related to Mrs. White who owned the candy shop," Lindy said. "I mean, they're both magicians, and he set up his arcade so close to where she set up her shop. I didn't ask, though. I was worried it might seem suspicious."

"He's her brother," Nate said, figuring she would find out eventually. "He knows I was around when Mrs. White went missing. He mentioned it. But he didn't make a big deal about it. I guess he wasn't very close to her."

"He gave me the benefit of the doubt too," Lindy said. "He knew about Mr. Stott. Jonas connected me to him after I mentioned the Mirror Mints. But Jonas didn't seem overly concerned that I live with him."

"He must be pretty confident about his plan," Nate speculated.

"Or his security," Lindy said.

"Well, Lindy, I feel a little bad about shutting out Roman, but I'm glad there's at least one Jet I can trust."

She smiled. "I'm glad you got the stamp ahead of him. Spying is bad enough without also feeling lonely."

Nate nodded toward the doors. "Should we go talk to the others?"

"Sure."

They walked together through the doors and quickly found Trevor loitering, his eyes on an EMPLOYEES ONLY door. Trevor signaled Pigeon, who hurried over.

"Lindy!" Pigeon cried. "Where have you been? Mr. Stott is so worried."

"I'm sorry, Pidge. I couldn't handle being ordered to keep out of this. I'm a Jet now."

"What?" he exclaimed.

"She got the third stamp, I got the fourth," Nate explained. "Long story, and we can't talk long. Is Summer already in there?"

"You just missed her," Trevor said.

"She's going to meet the owner of Arcadeland, Jonas White. He's Mrs. White's brother."

Pigeon gasped. "Is he here for revenge?"

Nate forced himself not to look at Lindy. "Doesn't seem that way. He wasn't very friendly with his sister. But he's here for a purpose. I can't say too much. We're supposed to go practice with Chris and Risa."

"Practice what?" Trevor pressed.

"I'm not allowed to explain," Nate said. "You'll find out soon. Earn the stamps, then you'll see."

"You really won't say?" Trevor asked, looking a little wounded.

"Just to be safe," Nate continued in a loud whisper. "Jonas set some firm rules about what we can tell others. I'm in no hurry to break them—not yet, and especially not here. Let me see. What *can* I say? Summer and I won't be much help with tickets tomorrow."

Trevor looked even more perplexed. "You can't come?"

Nate leaned closer. Pigeon leaned in too. Nate lowered his voice more. "I can't risk mixing magic. Remember how we suspected the stamps would lead to candy? The stamps *are* the candy. They last about two days."

Pigeon and Trevor looked sober as they digested the information.

"Summer will be taking off to practice too?" Pigeon asked.

"I guess," Nate said. "Still, can't hurt to keep an eye on her. Hey, I've got to go. The others are waiting for us. I don't want to make them suspicious."

Trevor nodded. "Okay, get out of here. We'll pass on what info we have."

"When will we see you?" Pigeon asked, eyes on Lindy.

"Tell my dad I'll be home tonight," Lindy said. "Tell him I need him to be understanding."

"I'll tell him," Pigeon promised.

"We'll talk later," Nate told Trevor. "This will make more sense after you get your stamp."

"I hope so," Trevor replied.

Nate and Lindy backed away, then headed for the door.

CHAPTER TEN

TRAINING

The training facility turned out to be a few blocks away inside a warehouse Jonas White had rented. Unimpressive on the outside except for its size, the facility contained many surprises inside. An assortment of gymnastics equipment filled one corner of the cavernous room, including parallel bars, a pommel horse, vaulting boards and tables, trampolines of diverse sizes, balance beams of different heights, mats for tumbling, climbing ropes, and a wide pit full of foam cubes. An indoor pool, built partially above ground and encircled by a wooden deck, dominated another corner of the room. A third quadrant held sporting equipment, including weight sets and punching bags, and featured multiple basketball hoops and a miniature soccer goal. The last corner of the huge warehouse was devoted to fighting, with a large wrestling mat and a full boxing ring. Along the walls hung gear for fencing, boxing, wrestling, and martial arts.

"Are we prepping for the Olympics?" Nate asked as he and Lindy entered. His voice echoed slightly in the vast space.

"I couldn't believe it either," Lindy replied. "It's all for us."

"Just the Jets?"

"All four clubs," Chris answered, soaring down from above the entrance with Risa. "The other kids don't come here much. I expect more will show once their clubs fill up."

"We're free to fly in here," Risa said. "We don't risk it much outside, except at night."

"It's pretty awesome," Lindy told Nate.

"I'm excited to go for it," Nate said. Ever since hovering in the room with Jonas White, he had let the ability lie dormant, all the while aware that the potential resided within him.

"Watch your speed," Chris cautioned. "It takes some room to stop or turn. If you're not careful, you'll get flattened against a wall."

Nate willed himself into the air, and up he went. It took no more effort than for a healthy person at rest to start running. The sensation was quite different than with Moon Rocks. Using Moon Rocks, he jumped, and physics controlled his trajectory until he collided with something. Now, he could swerve in any direction as desired.

The tall ceiling in the warehouse allowed Nate to soar high above the floor. The height bothered him a little, but Moon Rocks had helped train him not to freak out in lofty places. He picked up some speed, swooping down, then curved back up. As he changed direction at a greater speed than before, he felt what Chris had meant about turning. Nate could will himself to turn, but his speed limited how sharply. It was like turning while on a bike—the higher the speed, the more gradual the turn needed to be.

Nate also practiced speeding up and stopping. Again, like with his bike, he needed some space to accelerate and decelerate. Nate found that if he turned as he stopped, he could kill his momentum more effectively.

Air whooshed by as Nate soared around the room making lazy figure eights. The sensation was by far the most exhilarating he had ever felt. He extended one arm ahead of himself, partly because it felt natural, partly in case he needed to ward off a collision. As he practiced turning more sharply at higher speeds, he felt g-forces straining his body, like when rounding a curve on a fast roller coaster.

Lindy, Chris, and Risa glided through the air around him. Lindy was the most tentative, Risa the most aggressive, swooshing along within inches of the walls, ceiling, and floor.

"You're catching on fast," Chris commented, soaring alongside Nate.

"Now that I'm doing it, flying feels pretty natural," Nate said.

Chris grinned. He slowed, and Nate came to a stop beside him, fifteen feet above the floor. "Risa and I have talked about the same thing. It feels like we had this power all along, and Mr. White just woke it up."

"Have you had flying dreams?" Nate asked.

"Sure."

"It's sort of like that's how I got my practice."

"Just wait," Chris said. "Risa and I have had flying dreams practically nonstop since all of this started. Once I woke up pressed to the ceiling in my room."

"How long ago did you get your stamp?"

"More than two weeks. I had been hanging around the arcade a lot, and Todd drew my attention to the stamps. After I earned one, I told Risa and Roman they had to get their own. She earned hers quickly, but Roman got grounded, and then you guys showed up."

"I really am sorry about him missing a jet stamp," Nate said.

"I believe you," Chris said hesitantly. "I'm not looking forward to competing against Roman. He's going to be mad, and the kid knows how to win."

"Some of my friends will be against us too," Nate said. "Should keep things interesting."

"Check it out," Chris said, pointing.

Risa was inserting poles into sockets around the room in the walls, ceiling, and floor. Each pole held a ring.

"What's with the rings?" Nate asked.

"Training exercise," Chris said. "It's one thing to fly, and another to do stuff while you're flying. The rings are good practice. I also like playing catch. When you're flying around, it's harder than you might guess."

"Is this what you guys do mostly?" Nate asked. "Fly around in here? Train and stuff?"

"Mostly," Chris replied. "Mr. White has sent us on a couple of errands lately. We get something for him, and he pays us well."

"Pays you with what?"

"Money."

"Right. Are you stealing stuff?"

"Sort of," Chris admitted. "But he isn't going to keep it. We're just borrowing things he needs for his treasure hunt. He promised to return it all in the end."

Nate remembered Mrs. White sending them to "borrow" items for her. She had sometimes pretended they were recovering family heirlooms. "What have you gotten?"

"A book from a museum near Sacramento," Chris said.

"Sacramento? That's pretty far."

"Not so far when you're flying," Chris explained. "We can get up to around a hundred miles per hour in the open sky. We went at night, of course. We had night vision goggles. You'd be surprised how easily you can nab stuff when you can fly. We set off some alarms, but none of the guards or police had a chance. "

"What else have you taken?" Nate probed.

"An old doll from a mansion near San Anselmo, in Marin County."

"A doll?"

"An ancient one like you might see at a museum. It was made of wood and carved all weird."

"Native American?"

"Probably. We didn't study it. We just snatched it. Mr. White will give it back later. We left $10,000 as a rental fee."

"They rented it to you?" Nate asked.

"We didn't ask permission. Mr. White paid us a bunch, too, since it wasn't directly part of the treasure hunt. We were helping with his preparations."

"Think we'll get more of those assignments?" Nate wondered.

"I don't know," Chris said. "The last two times it came as a surprise."

Risa glided over to them, handing Nate a short wooden baton.

"What's this?" Nate asked.

"Use it to collect the rings," she said. "They're clamped loosely to the poles. They'll pop off with a little force. See how quickly you can round them up."

Nate rubbed his hands together. "Are you going to time me?"

Producing a stopwatch, Risa gave a nod. "Let's get started."

* * * * *

When Summer entered the training facility with a short, freckly kid, Nate was playing catch with the three other Jets. They used a black, undersized football. Risa could throw and catch almost as well as Chris, but Lindy was practically hopeless, catching fewer than one in ten of the balls thrown her way.

Nate hardly dropped any. It had not taken him long to learn to anticipate the trajectory of the ball and to get into position for just about any throw that came near him. He loved when the football was a little ahead of him and he could accelerate to come alongside it, then pluck the ball out of the air almost as if it were standing still. Once he glanced off the wall fairly hard, missing a catch, and once he narrowly avoided colliding with the floor, swooping up just in time, the toes of his shoes grazing blue gymnastics mats.

"Wow," Summer called from the floor of the facility. "I've never seen a flock of kids before!"

Nate, Chris, Risa, and Lindy landed near Summer and her companion.

"Hi, Derek," Chris said. "I see you found a friend."

"Two Tanks are better than one," Derek replied.

"You're a Jet, Lindy?" Summer asked in surprise.

"I worked at it on my own," Lindy explained.

Risa looked around. "I have a feeling this place will start getting busy."

"Todd told me that a lot of kids are getting close to enough tickets for a stamp," Derek said. "You guys playing catch?" He held up his hands for the ball.

Risa handed it over.

"Go long," Derek said.

Chris and Risa streaked toward the far corner of the room. Derek made an amazing throw, the ball streaking up toward the far corner of the huge warehouse with hardly any arc. Chris reached to make the catch, but the ball slapped off his hands and into the wall. Risa curved down and caught the football before it struck the floor.

Nate looked at Derek with new respect. He doubted whether the strongest NFL quarterback could have thrown the ball so hard. "I guess being a Tank makes you stronger?"

Summer leaned close to him. "It's like an Ironhide, plus you weigh more, plus you're stronger. And it lasts for two days."

"How strong?" Nate asked.

Summer shrugged. "Try to push me."

Nate placed a hand on each of Summer's shoulders and shoved. Instead of her moving, he pushed himself away, as if he had shoved a wall. Summer smirked.

"You look the same," Nate said, surprised.

"I didn't get bigger," Summer said. "But I weigh a lot more, and I'm scary strong."

"How strong?" Nate repeated.

"Fly up to the ceiling."

Nate turned and started to soar upward. A hand gripped his ankle with painful tightness, and his upward progress stopped. He put everything he had into flying up, but didn't go anywhere.

He glanced back at Summer. "So you can hold me down. But I'm not sure I could carry your weight even if you weren't a Tank."

"Are you calling me chubby?" Summer accused.

"No," Nate said. "I'm just not sure how much extra weight I can carry while flying."

Derek walked over holding a barbell. "Two 45-pound plates on each side," he said. "Plus the bar weighs 45. That's a total of 225."

135

He tossed the barbell to Summer, who caught it easily. She lifted it over her head. "This isn't bad," she reported. "Kind of heavy. I could do more." She set it down.

Nate bent and tried to pick it up. The barbell felt fused to the floor. He couldn't lift it at all, although he could roll it back and forth.

Nate straightened, looking at Derek. "Can you lift a car?"

"The back end of a small one. But that feels really heavy. With Summer helping we might be able to lift a small one completely off the ground."

"So you're not strong like a superhero," Nate clarified.

"Not really," Derek said. "But we can take punishment like a superhero. Still, I'm not a big kid, but it would probably take the strongest man alive to challenge me at arm wrestling."

"I'm impressed," Nate said. "Do you guys shoot cannonballs, too?"

"Do you launch air-to-surface missiles?" Summer countered.

Nate shook his head. "I wish we were a little more durable. We have to be careful flying or we could really get hurt."

"You better be careful if you go up against the Tanks," Derek warned with a smile. "You might get hurt that way, too."

* * * * *

Parked near an office supply store, Vincent, Ziggy, Trevor, and Pigeon huddled together in the white van. Trevor and Pigeon munched on the donuts Ziggy had provided.

"Jonas White?" Vincent said. "He normally keeps to the shadows. Not a lot is known about him. I suppose we should have kept him higher on our suspect list. After all, his sister was here last year. But he has never been known to partner with his sister, and although we suspect that he's powerful, he has stayed inactive for decades."

"Sometimes guys like him bide their time," Ziggy said. "They're powerful, but they've learned patience. They marshal their resources and wait for a big score. Remember Vadik Baskov?"

Victor snorted. "Good point."

"What did he do?" Pigeon wondered.

"He stole the Hope Diamond," Victor said.

"From the Smithsonian?" Pigeon exclaimed.

"This was before the Smithsonian had it," Ziggy said.

"We returned it to the rightful owner," Victor added.

"How long have you guys been doing this?" Trevor wondered.

"Almost a century," Ziggy replied.

"We're straying off topic," Victor said.

"Right," Ziggy said. "Jonas White. What else did you learn?"

"Nate told us that the stamps themselves have power," Trevor said. "He was worried about sharing details."

"Summer seemed nervous too," Pigeon said. "She came by briefly after she finished with Jonas. She said he was planning a treasure hunt."

"Treasure hunt?" Victor repeated. "What could he be after?"

"That's a question for Mozag," Ziggy replied. "I'm not sure what a magician might want around here."

"What else do you guys know about Jonas White?" Pigeon asked.

"Almost nothing," Victor said. "Again, it would be nice to ask Mozag. I know that Jonas White has been around since long before our time, which means he's no featherweight. I'm not sure where he comes from or what his specialties might be."

"We looked into the nachos," Ziggy said. "They've magically tampered with the cheese. We're not experts at magical formulas, but we think the cheese is like the white fudge from John's report on Belinda White. The cheese is addictive and numbs the ability of those who eat it to perceive the supernatural."

"We think it might also be designed to reactivate any old white fudge addictions," Victor added. "We'll confirm more as we continue to monitor the situation. Certainly stay away from it."

"We will," Trevor said. "And we'll let you know more after we earn our stamps tomorrow."

"Careful about that," Ziggy warned. "Jonas White is recruiting. He'll have ways of binding you to him. He won't want you sharing info with us."

"If all else fails, come to my house in the middle of the night," Pigeon said. "I'll talk to you."

"I hope so," Victor sighed.

* * * * *

Nate and Lindy flew beside each other through the night sky. Staying well above the rooftops, Nate doubted whether people on the ground could possibly identify them as anything more than small, quick shadows against the moon and stars. The cool night air swished against him. It felt exhilarating not to be limited by a ceiling or walls. If he wanted, he could soar up to where the air would become thin and freezing.

Nate didn't try anything too fancy because he didn't want to lose track of Lindy in the darkness. He had promised to stand by her when she returned home.

They glided down to the back of the candy shop, careful to land lightly. While practicing at the training facility, Nate had landed without much caution a couple of times, and it had felt like jumping from a moving vehicle.

The candy shop was closed. Lindy used a key to enter through the back door. She flipped a light switch. A moment after the lights came on, Mr. Stott hurried into the room. He looked from Nate to Lindy, his posture and expression showing his relief. He straightened up and tried to sound stern. "Where have you been, young lady?"

"I was the first to get a stamp," she said uncertainly, showing the back of her hand. "I'm a Jet. I can fly."

Although clearly surprised and upset, Mr. Stott was trying to keep calm. "I was very worried about you."

"Then maybe you should have let me help," Lindy said. "I wasn't going to let my friends go into danger without me. I wasn't going to ignore John Dart and Mozag."

Mr. Stott rubbed his face. "This places me in a difficult position, Lindy."

"I'm a Jet too," Nate said. "We found out who owns Arcadeland."

"Who?"

"Jonas White."

Mr. Stott blanched. "Mrs. White's brother?"

Nate nodded.

"Oh, dear," Mr. Stott said. He started pacing. "This is . . . this is . . ." He stopped pacing and held out his arms. "Lindy, come here."

Lindy crossed to Mr. Stott, who enfolded her in a fierce hug.

"I'm sorry, Dad," Lindy said, her voice choked with emotion.

"I know," Mr. Stott said. "I placed you in a tough position. It's hard when I make a rule that conflicts with what you feel is right. I know you didn't disobey me casually."

"I didn't," she said.

"I'm glad that you're all right," Mr. Stott said. Ending the hug, he placed his hands on her shoulders and looked her in the eyes. "You realize that you're in great danger."

"All of us are," she replied.

"We'll talk more later," Mr. Stott said. "Go wash up. I need to have some words with Nate in private."

"How much trouble am I in?" Lindy asked hesitantly.

"I should be the least of your worries," Mr. Stott said. "You're now involved in something truly perilous. I can't undo what you have done. But I'll do my best to help you."

She gave a nod and glanced at Nate. "Thanks for coming with me."

"Sure," he said.

She flew over to the stairway and glided up out of sight. Mr. Stott followed her with his eyes. He waited until he heard the door to their apartment open and close, then motioned for Nate to follow him to his private office.

Mr. Stott closed the door and stood near Nate, speaking in a low voice. "How long do the stamps last?"

"At least two days," Nate said. "Then I guess the power starts to fade."

"You have real flight?" Mr. Stott asked. "Like Peter Pan? Like Superman?"

"Yeah," Nate said.

"Does it tire you?"

"No, not at all," Nate realized. "Less than walking. I mean, you have to focus. If you crash you can get hurt, so you do have to concentrate. But I've been flying most of the day, and my body isn't tired at all."

"Very potent magic," Mr. Stott said. "I doubt I could devise such an enhancement if I spent the rest of my days slaving on the project." His expression changed, becoming more concerned. "What has he told her?"

"Nothing," Nate said. "I'm not even sure if he knows."

"How could he not know?" Mr. Stott fretted. He folded his arms. "I suppose it's possible. Maybe so much time has passed. One sibling could be considerably older than the other. Or they might have been separated in their youth. But I suspect he must know. What is he after?"

"We're not supposed to tell," Nate said. "He's on a treasure hunt. Some great thingamajig made by a guy called Iwa Iza."

"Interesting," Mr. Stott said, stretching the word out. "He's looking for Uweya."

"That's the word he used," Nate said. "What is it?"

Mr. Stott gave a slow shrug, raising his hands vaguely. "A legend. Iwa Iza was a great mage who lived long, long ago. His creations interacted with the environment. He allegedly made a bowl that could summon a tornado, and a drum that could cause an earthquake. His greatest creation, Uweya, is shrouded in mystery. I know of it, but I know little about it. I'm not sure anyone does."

"Jonas must know something," Nate said.

"He is certainly behaving as though Uweya were more than a myth," Mr. Stott agreed. "I'll start researching the subject. Quietly, of course."

"What do we do about Lindy?" Nate asked.

Mr. Stott shook his head sadly. "Our options are limited. We could let the Battiatos take her away. They would have to imprison her. I expect such a course would destroy any chance of her being rehabilitated and living a normal life. Otherwise, with her in your stamp club and Jonas aware of her, we would just need to ride this out and see where it goes."

"She seems loyal to us," Nate said.

"Jonas could have a plan to turn her," Mr. Stott said. "I don't think he can undo the Clean Slate, but what do I know? I would have considered the flight enhancement he gave you virtually impossible. Would you mind if I studied the ink?"

"Go ahead," Nate said.

Mr. Stott stared at the back of Nate's hand. He examined it with a magnifying glass. He sniffed it. He rubbed it with a few cloths of different textures. "Interesting. I suppose I can do further studies on Lindy. Have you learned anything about John Dart?"

"There are many rooms at Arcadeland that Lindy can't see. We haven't had much chance to investigate. Mr. Stott, you wouldn't turn Lindy over to the Battiatos?"

"No, not while she remains loyal to us. I'm glad you're in this Jet club with her. You need to keep an eye on her, Nate. If you have any misgivings . . ."

"You'll be the first to know," Nate assured him. "I like the new Lindy, but I'd rather throw her in jail for the rest of her life than have Belinda White back."

CHAPTER ELEVEN

SIMULCRIST

By the following afternoon, the training facility had begun to feel crowded. Roman had joined the Tanks, Trevor had earned his racecar stamp, and, after receiving his submarine stamp, Pigeon showed up with a pretty blonde named Mindy. Nate and Summer had helped their friends earn tickets that morning, although the great majority were won by Trevor and Pigeon using Peak Performance.

While the other Jets took a water break, Nate hung out near the ceiling, watching as Summer, Roman, and Derek brutalized punching bags. Pigeon and his new teammate were in the pool. Since they hadn't surfaced for half an hour but still swam around like dolphins, they could obviously breathe underwater. Lacking fellow club members, Trevor zipped around the warehouse at astonishing speeds, trying out various activities alone. Nate was most impressed when Trevor grabbed a football and threw a long bomb to himself.

As Nate tried to assess how the Jets would fare against the other clubs, he had to admit that both the Tanks and the Racers intimidated him. If the Jets could stay in the sky, nobody would be able to touch them. But the speed of the Racers and the strength of the Tanks would be problematic on the ground or in confined areas.

The Subs didn't seem like much of a threat, unless an assignment had to be carried out underwater. Which probably meant that part of the treasure hunt would involve getting wet, or else why would Jonas have created sub stamps in the first place?

Before any of the other clubs had arrived, Nate and his teammates had experimented with how much weight they could carry while flying. The incident when Summer kept him grounded had left Nate concerned. He discovered that holding a 30-pound dumbbell in each hand was pretty close to his limit. The exertion required to fly with that much weight felt like an uphill sprint, and his stability became erratic. Twenty-pound dumbbells required effort but weren't too bad, especially over short distances. He had hardly noticed any difficulty when carrying tens.

Chris had theorized that exerting themselves by carrying heavy weights might eventually allow them to handle higher maximum loads. Nate thought it was worth a try, but he suggested they shouldn't reveal their weakness by doing it in front of the other clubs. The rest of the Jets had agreed.

Roman had pointedly avoided acknowledging Chris, Risa, or Nate all afternoon. Nate had caught him staring a few times, but Roman had repeatedly averted his gaze. For the most part, he kept his head down and focused on training with Summer and Derek.

"Nate!" Chris called. "U-turn!"

Chris was flying his way clutching a long jump rope. Nate held up his hands and tried to mentally brace himself. He had come up with this idea earlier in the afternoon, and they had practiced it for the last hour.

Without slowing, Chris tossed one end of the rope to Nate, who caught it and focused on holding steady. Chris was doing his best to turn sharply, so Nate never pulled against his full weight, but the force was still almost enough to jerk the rope from his hands. Unable to remain completely stable, Nate hung on and managed to help Chris slingshot around in a much tighter turn than would have otherwise been possible.

"Good one!" Risa called. "That might have been the best yet!"

Chris flew over to hover near Nate. "Not bad."

"You caught me daydreaming," Nate replied. "Maybe the trick is to not pay attention. Hey, do you think we should talk to Roman?"

"I don't know," Risa said, drawing near with Lindy. "He's avoided us ever since we let him know the Jet stamps were gone."

"He was kind of a jerk," Chris said. "It made me feel a little better about him getting left out."

"If we're going to compete with him, we should try to clear the air," Nate said. "Those Tanks are strong. We don't want him hating us more than necessary. You guys are friends, right?"

"We know each other pretty well," Chris said.

"He and I have been friends since we were little," Risa said.

"Then Nate's right," Lindy agreed. "You should talk to him."

Risa sighed unenthusiastically, but nodded.

Nate led the way down to where Roman was throwing a large medicine ball in a triangle with Summer and Derek. In their hands the bulky exercise tool might have weighed no more than a basketball. The Tanks paused as the Jets approached.

"Hi, Rome," Risa said.

"Hey, guys," Roman replied without much warmth. "What do you want?"

"We just hope there are no hard feelings about the jet stamps," Chris said. "Nobody was trying to exclude you."

"I know," Roman said. "Summer told me how Lindy was earning stamps on her own. Nate didn't know. It might have been a lucky break for me. Being a Tank feels really good. Even if I had the chance, I don't think I'd switch."

"I assumed it was you who had taken the second-to-last jet stamp," Nate explained.

Roman waved away the comment. "I get it. I don't blame you or Lindy. You and Summer and your other friends worked together to win tickets. If Chris and Risa had done that for me, I would have had my stamp days ago."

"We weren't sure if it was allowed," Risa said uncomfortably.

"We had to train," Chris said. "We gave you money."

"You did," Roman said. "It's okay, I understand, I don't hate you guys. I appreciate the money you shared. But things have definitely changed. We're on different teams. It'll be fun to beat you."

"I guess that's the idea," Chris said, hands on his hips. "Good luck."

"Keep doing that trick with the ropes," Derek said. "I bet you guys could join Cirque du Soleil."

"It's not cool like medicine balls," Nate fired back. "I thought they stopped making those things in 1905."

Risa held up her hands like a peacemaker. "We don't need to get nasty."

"You guys do your thing, we'll do ours," Chris said. "Have fun on the ground." He soared up into the air, spinning as he curved first left, then right, flying with impressive speed and precision.

Nate and the others followed suit, leaving the Tanks to stare up at them.

* * * * *

Under a pale moon, Nate, Trevor, Summer, Lindy, and Pigeon met behind the candy shop. It had been a hot day, and the night was warm.

"Sorry we couldn't really talk earlier," Summer said. "The other Tanks are really getting into the rivalry between the clubs."

"Mindy is too," Pigeon said.

"Everybody will," Nate predicted. "But we need to remember our real purpose."

"How do you like being a Sub?" Summer asked Pigeon.

"It's pretty amazing when I'm in the water. I can breathe it just like air. And swimming feels like flying. We might not move as fast as the Jets, but we can move way faster than a normal swimmer. I bet we could outswim sharks."

"Anything else?" Trevor wondered. "Is it just that you swim well and breathe water?"

"There are little things," Pigeon said. "I can feel where objects are positioned in the water around me without looking. Like an extra sense. And when I'm underwater, I feel a little stronger than normal. If you guys have to go against us in the water, you'll be in trouble. Out of the water, the sub stamp doesn't make much difference. Mindy is a competitive swimmer, so she's in heaven."

"What about you, Trevor?" Nate asked.

"I can be normal, like now, or I can go into an altered state where everything around me slows down. I call it race mode. I can slip in and out of it whenever I want. It's really weird. It feels like I'm moving at normal speed, but everything else is three or four times slower. I'm sure that to you guys, it must look like I'm pretty fast."

"That's an understatement," Lindy said.

"Any other benefits?" Pigeon asked.

Trevor shook his head. "I have an extra gear, a second altered state, where things get three or four times slower again. I still feel like I'm moving at normal speed, but it wears me out quickly. I can only stay in it for around thirty seconds."

"Which would feel like three seconds or so to everybody else," Pigeon calculated.

Trevor nodded. "Jonas told me that my body is reinforced to handle the stresses of high speeds. I guess that's an extra perk."

"Does the first altered state wear you out?" Summer asked.

"A little," Trevor replied. "I can handle race mode for much longer than the fastest state before needing a rest, though."

"We've all got impressive powers," Nate said. "It could come in handy when we need to turn on Jonas."

"The only downside is we can't use any candy without risking side effects," Pigeon said.

"I know," Nate replied. "I wish I could use Peak Performance while flying. The result would be amazing."

"Can you imagine?" Lindy gushed. "That would be so cool."

"Even without other enhancements," Pigeon said, "we have a good mix of powers. And they seem to be really stable."

Trevor picked up a pebble and started tossing it from one hand to the other. "What do you guys think about Jonas asking us to bring him something we treasure?"

"I'm not sure," Summer said.

"Must be for some kind of magic," Pigeon guessed.

"Are you guys going to do it?" Trevor wondered.

"Looks like we have to if we want to stay undercover," Lindy said.

"I don't love the idea," Pigeon said. "Especially since I don't know what he's going to do with my jacket."

"You're bringing your leather jacket?" Summer asked. There was no doubting what jacket he meant. The studded leather jacket looked like something a tough biker would wear.

Pigeon shrugged. "I really like it, even though I never wear it anymore. I could tell most kids at school thought I looked like a poser."

"You shouldn't let other kids get to you like that," Summer said. "They'd get used to it."

"It just wasn't worth it to me," Pigeon said. "Besides, it's summer now. I wouldn't be using it anyways."

"I wish we knew what Jonas plans to do with our stuff," Trevor grumbled.

"I wish I knew what he did with John and Mozag," Lindy said. "Unless we hand over something, we might never find out."

"It's true," Nate said. "Our main goal is to find where they're holding John and Mozag and to bust them out. We'll probably have to take some risks to do it. You guys can decide for yourselves, but I'm planning to bring something to Jonas. Everyone keep alert. We need to start making more progress." He stretched. "I'm getting tired. I'm about ready to call it a night."

"Wait," Trevor said, chucking his pebble into the bushes. "I need some help. It's my mom's birthday tomorrow. I've been so busy with all of this that I haven't gotten her a present. What should I do? I'm going to get the look if I don't have anything for her!"

"Coupon book," Nate said without hesitation. "Works every time. They're easy to make, and they cost practically nothing. Make coupons for a free hug, a free kiss—stuff she'll like. Make some to sweep the floor, wash the dishes, walk the dog, whatever makes sense. Your mom will be really happy, and the best part is she'll probably lose the coupons and forget about them. My mom has never actually used more than one or two."

"Good call," Trevor said.

"Beware, though," Pigeon inserted. "I tried it and my mom kept the coupons in a special place. She used every single one. I began to suspect she made photocopies or something. They just kept coming."

Summer giggled. "Counterfeit coupons."

"It wasn't the worst, but it added up to lots of chores," Pigeon said. "Make sure you put down stuff that you're willing to do."

Trevor looked thoughtful. "My mom is definitely the type who would love them but lose track of them. I'm going to try it."

"Good luck," Summer said. "We better get home."

* * * * *

Later that night, Pigeon and Diego crept into their front yard through the side gate. Pigeon winced when it clattered shut. After a few tense moments, the house remained dark and quiet.

"Do you smell anyone spying on us?" Pigeon asked.

"No," Diego replied. "But I can smell that you're nervous."

"I don't want my aunt to catch me," he replied. "And I don't want Jonas White to notice me sneaking info to his enemies."

"Far as I can tell, we're all clear."

Pigeon saw the white van parked down the street, lights off. He trotted there with Diego at his side. The door opened and Pigeon climbed in. Diego entered as well.

"No lights came on when you opened the door," Pigeon noticed.

"We made a few modifications," Ziggy replied.

"Thanks for coming," Victor said. "Learn anything new?"

Pigeon explained about their new powers and how they worked. He told how Jonas White wanted each of them to hand over a special item in order to continue in their respective clubs.

"That will come to no good," Ziggy said. "A magician would use such an item to establish some form of connection with you."

"If the item is handed over voluntarily, the potency would increase," Victor noted.

"Did you learn why he's here?" Ziggy asked. "What he's after?"

"He wants a treasure made by a guy called Iwa Iza."

"Iwa Iza?" Ziggy exclaimed.

"Do you know much about him?"

Ziggy shook his head and made a befuddled gesture. "He's a figure from history books. He lived, what, two thousand years ago?"

"At least," Victor said.

"I guess he made something called Uweya," Pigeon said.

"Never heard of it," Victor said.

"Me neither," Ziggy grumbled. "But we have access to books. We'll look into it."

"Anything else?" Victor asked.

"Jonas made it clear that we had better not work against him,"

Pigeon said. "He threatened me if I showed my magic to anyone who didn't know about it."

"No magician wants to broadcast the existence of magic," Ziggy said.

"And no magician with an agenda would smile at disloyalty," Victor added. "Pigeon, after you hand over your special item, we should probably limit contact to emergencies. He may be able to watch you."

"You've given us some terrific leads, kid," Ziggy said. "Keep watching him. Try not to get into hot water. If you do, let us know."

"We prepped some items for you," Victor said, holding out his palm. In it rested five buttons. "Share these with your friends. Keep one on you, and we should be able to track you. If you get into the kind of trouble where you need us to come immediately, break it."

"Thanks," Pigeon said.

"These too," Ziggy said, handing over a wooden box. Inside Pigeon found six sleek pistols. "Tranquilizer guns. Custom-made, top of the line. Very accurate and high-powered for pistols. Each holds six darts. Semiautomatic. There are several spare darts in the box. Share them, and don't hesitate to use them in emergencies."

"This is great," Pigeon said.

"Do you have anything for dogs?" Diego asked. "Magic collar? Body armor?"

"The dog can talk," Ziggy said.

"Brain Feed," Pigeon explained. "Mr. Stott makes it. Diego is definitely on our side."

"Sorry, pooch," Victor said, scratching Diego behind the ears. "We're all out of doggie gear."

"I won't hold it against you," Diego said. "Especially if you keep scratching."

"You two should beat it," Ziggy suggested. "The longer you stay near us, the more danger you're in. Jonas White will be keeping tabs on you, one way or another."

"Thanks for the gear," Pigeon said. "You think we can take these guys down?"

"We had better," Victor said. "For all our sakes."

* * * * *

Nate had decided on Zombie Nightmare Apocalypse IV as his special object. He had considered some trophies, a sock monkey that used to share his bed, and a few of the Zelda games. But in the end, the overall mayhem and general replay value of ZNA IV had won out.

He waited next to Lindy near an EMPLOYEES ONLY door. Chris and Risa had yet to show up.

"You brought a stuffed flamingo?" Nate asked.

She held it up. The toy had more expression than Nate would expect on a bird. "It was the first thing Mr. Stott got for me," Lindy explained. "I don't have many favorite possessions. I hope I'm attached enough to it. I guess we'll find out. You brought a video game?"

"Yeah," Nate said. "I really like it. There are so many different ways to take out the zombies. You can win each level using lots of different strategies."

"I don't get video games," Lindy admitted. "Wouldn't you rather actually go do something than just pretend on a screen?"

"Where am I going to actually fight zombies?"

"Is that something you'd want to do?"

"Not in real life. But in a video game it rules. That's the point. You can do crazy stuff, but nobody actually gets hurt."

"Hey, guys," Chris said, walking up with Risa. "What's up?"

"Cleon told us to wait here," Lindy said.

"Fair warning," Risa muttered. "This part will be a little creepy."

"What do you mean?" Nate asked.

"We can't explain," Chris replied. "You'll see."

"Have you had any flying dreams yet?" Risa asked.

"I did," Lindy said. "I was up in the clouds."

"I had a good one last night," Risa said. "I was in a canyon in the desert, rescuing frogs."

"Rescuing frogs?" Chris chuckled.

"I don't know," Risa replied defensively. "It was a dream. They were stuck up on these cliffs and I had to put them in a lake."

"Were they slimy?" Lindy asked.

"Not really. They were cute."

"That's the worst dream ever," Chris said.

"I haven't had one yet," Nate said. "A flying dream. At least not that I remember. Not since I've actually flown, I mean."

The EMPLOYEES ONLY door opened and Cleon waved the four of them inside. He led them through some industrial halls to a different room than last time. He opened a door and extended an arm, inviting the kids inside.

Nate entered, then froze, staring at himself and Lindy rendered as life-sized wax figures. The wax sculptures flanked a desk where Jonas White sat waiting.

"Come inside," Jonas invited. "Have you ever viewed yourselves in three dimensions? Most people have not. Chris and Marisa had a chance on another occasion. Today Nate and Lindy get a turn."

Nate approached his wax duplicate. It was exactly his height, and it wore the same outfit he had sported the last time he conversed with Jonas. He walked around it, getting a view from all sides. Lindy scrutinized her wax twin as well. Chris and Risa shared an amused look.

"What do you think?" Jonas asked.

"We should mass-produce these," Nate said, tentatively touching the wax cheek. "I bet the ladies would love one."

"Sadly, our plans do not involve placing your likeness in houses across the country," Jonas said.

"Why did you make these?" Lindy asked.

"Every magician has his specialties," Jonas said humbly. "I am a Simulcrist."

"A what now?" Nate asked.

"A simulacrum is a representation of something," Jonas explained. "A scarecrow, for example, is a simulacrum of a man used to frighten birds. These wax figures are simulacra of you two."

"You made them?" Lindy asked.

Jonas held up a hand and affectionately considered his fingers. "I do have that talent, but alas, I lack the speed to have created these lifelike sculptures on such short notice. My apprentices produced them. They have a remarkable aptitude for working with wax. Nate, Lindy, the two of you will be the latest addition to my collection."

"Why?" Nate probed.

"Do you suspect that my reasons are more than purely aesthetic?" Jonas asked. "If so, you would be correct. As a Simulcrist, I wish to establish a connection between you and your simulacrum. This connection will allow me to exact retribution should you elect to betray me."

"Like a voodoo doll?" Nate asked.

"In theory, I suppose," Jonas said. "Although there is no voodoo involved. I'm honestly not sure whether voodoo actually works."

"But this does?" Lindy asked.

"Most assuredly," Jonas said. "These simulacra will help ensure that you work with me, not against me. I have entrusted you with powerful enhancers. If you serve me faithfully, the simulacra will never be used to harm you. In fact, they can be used to help you. But if you choose not to serve me honorably—well, you should probably surrender your positions as Jets now and save all of us considerable unpleasantness."

"This is why you need the items?" Nate asked.

"Nothing gets by you," Jonas sneered. "The items will help establish the desired connection between you and your simulacrum. What have you brought me?"

Nate held up his video game. "Zombie Nightmare Apocalypse IV."

"May I handle it?" Jonas asked.

Nate handed it over. Jonas closed his eyes, clutching it firmly. "I have sensed stronger connections, but this will suffice."

"How do I know you'll give it back?" Nate asked.

Jonas grinned. "I've been around a long time. If I kept every simulacrum I made, I'd need to store them in a football stadium. Once you have loyally served your purpose, your game will be returned, the connection between you and your simulacrum will be severed, and the simulacrum will be recycled."

"Could I keep mine as a souvenir?" Nate tried.

"We could discuss the possibility when the time comes," Jonas said. "I assume you intend to proceed? If either of you finds this arrangement unacceptable, our relationship ends here."

Nate found it totally unacceptable. But if he walked away, how would he ever find John and Mozag? He glanced over at Lindy, who stared back at him uncertainly.

"Just do it," Chris said. "We did. It's no big deal. Are you really going to walk away from flying after all that work earning the stamp?"

"What can you do to us with the simulacrum?" Nate inquired.

"All sorts of thing," Jonas said slowly. "The magicians who pioneered the manufacture of simulacra did so to help people. Simulacra were principally used to reduce pain or alleviate the symptoms of certain illnesses. Years of experimentation have shown that simulacra can be quite versatile. In addition to simulcry, I have also studied acupuncture for decades. The combination can produce some fascinating results."

"You could hurt us?" Nate said.

Jonas grinned like a hangman who loved his job. "I could certainly harm you, yes. Inflicting pain is only one of my options. I could kill you. I could lower your inhibitions. I could make you thirsty. I could make you dizzy. I could create rushes of pleasure that would leave you pleading for more. Or I could simply cure your back pain."

"That's a lot of power to hand over to a stranger," Lindy said.

"So is the power of flight," Jonas argued. "So are the secrets I will share with you once the treasure hunt begins. The simulacra merely bring our shared risks into balance."

Nate hated the idea of giving an enemy so much power over him. Even if he was smart and careful, it could end very badly. He wondered whether John would do it for him? He was pretty sure the answer was yes.

"All right," Nate said. "But you had better keep your word."

Jonas rubbed the video game between his hands. "If I failed

to keep my promise as explained, the connection would weaken considerably. Of course, if you neglect to honor your end of the agreement, I will be within my rights to exact whatever revenge I deem appropriate."

"Okay," Lindy said. "I'll do it too."

Jonas accepted the pink flamingo. He held it pensively for a moment. "This will do." He rose carefully. "Congratulations on becoming the newest additions to my waxworks. Now, who would like to refresh their stamps?"

CHAPTER TWELVE

THE HERMIT

After the weekend, Todd and Cleon showed up at the training facility unannounced. Nate and the Jets were playing catch using baseball mitts when the two men entered. The appearance marked the first time any Arcadeland employee had visited the facility.

All activity came to a halt. The four clubs were now all filled. A large girl had joined the Tanks, three girls had joined the Racers, and two boys had joined the Subs. Even so, demand for the stamps supposedly continued. None of the stamps were on display as prizes anymore, but Nate had heard that a couple of kids had already been turned away from attempting to claim some.

Todd motioned for the clubs to gather to him. The Jets swooped down, arriving before all but the Racers. The Subs got there last, totally dry despite having come from the pool.

"You've all heard about the treasure hunt," Cleon announced. "The first phase is about to begin. It'll pit the Jets against the Subs, with the competition beginning at sundown."

"What about us?" Roman asked.

"Tanks and Racers have to sit this one out," Todd said. "You'll get your chance next time. If the Tanks or Racers interfere in this phase, they risk disqualification."

"We'd lose our stamps?" Trevor checked.

"At least," Cleon said. "If you're going to believe anything I tell you, believe this: you don't want Mr. White mad at you. Make him proud instead. Life can be sweet when he's pleased."

"What are we doing?" Nate asked.

Cleon pointed to Nate as if he had asked the right question. "The Jets or the Subs must secure an item called the Gate from a secretive wanderer known as the Hermit. The Hermit is notoriously difficult to find, but Mr. White has already taken care of that for you. The Hermit currently resides aboard the USS *Striker*, a destroyer mothballed after World War II."

"Mothballed?" Risa asked.

"Warships held in reserve," Pigeon said. "They're equipped for service but not in use. Many eventually get sold as scrap."

"Nice job, professor," Cleon said. "The *Striker* can be found on one of the waterways adjacent to the San Francisco Bay, not too far from here. I brought a map for each of the two clubs involved."

Pigeon collected the map for the Subs, and Chris took the map for the Jets.

"This assignment may take some finesse," Todd said. "The Hermit's a wily old dude. He won't give up the Gate easily. He has been known to bargain when cornered. He'll probably try to flee. If he gets away, it will be a major annoyance to find him again. In that case, both clubs will lose their stamps."

"What does the Gate look like?" Lindy wondered.

"We're unsure," Cleon said. "From sketchy descriptions, we assume it will be a model of a gate. Should be small enough to carry."

"Tell the Hermit you want the Gate to Uweya," Todd advised. "He'll know what you're after."

"We know he has it with him?" Lindy asked.

"The Hermit moves around a lot," Cleon said. "But he keeps his treasures close. Either he'll have it on him or he'll know where to find it."

Todd held up a small drawstring bag. "Each club will get some of this to help you. It's called Finder's Dust. Just sprinkle it in the air, and the particles will be drawn to any magical items in the vicinity."

"The effect has limits," Cleon clarified. "It'll find objects in a small room, but it won't travel down the street and around the corner. Use a little at a time, focusing on suspicious areas."

"The club that brings the Gate into Arcadeland wins the competition," Todd said. "It doesn't matter who does what along the way. We don't care who works the hardest, who finds the Gate, or who snatches it. All we care about is who brings it to us. The losers will surrender their stamps to the winners."

"These rules give the Jets an unfair advantage," Pigeon said. "There's no river near Arcadeland."

"We've explained the task," Cleon said. "The rest is up to you. Meet here at sundown. You'll depart once it's dark."

"Wait," Pigeon complained. "If we leave from here, the Jets will easily beat us to the ship. That will give them an even bigger advantage."

Todd shrugged. "Mr. White made the rules. You Subs are quick in the water. If I were you, I'd start looking for the nearest waterways that link to your destination. You guys have the rest of the day to prepare."

"I recommend searching the lockers in here," Cleon said. "You're welcome to take any gear you find. Just bring it back."

He and Cleon left the room.

"I wanted to take on the Jets," Roman complained loudly.

"The target is a ship out on the water," Summer said. "Jets and Subs probably make the most sense."

"I guess we'll get our chance," Roman said.

"Unless the Racers beat you first," Trevor said.

"We should plan," Chris said, looking at the map.

The different clubs started moving away from one another. Nate conferred with the other Jets, but the planning didn't impress him. Basically, they would fly to the place on the map and see what happened, adapting as necessary.

Nate glided over to where the Subs were getting back into the water. "Hey, Pidge."

Drew, another of the Subs, paused beside Pigeon, his eyes on Nate. Pigeon pointed to the pool. "Go ahead. Let me talk to Nate for a second."

Drew obeyed reluctantly. Nate stood near Pigeon, and they spoke with their voices lowered.

"Do you want me to throw it?" Pigeon murmured. "I could sabotage us."

"No," Nate said, somewhat surprised by the offer. "I was thinking we should both just do our best to win. I'm not sure it matters which of us stays in."

"It could matter a lot," Pigeon replied quietly. "I'm good at planning, but you're more clutch in emergencies. Plus, there are two of us on the Jets. Wouldn't it make more sense to keep you and Lindy involved?"

"Might make more sense to get her uninvolved," Nate said. "We still don't know if Jonas recognized her, or what he's planning if he did."

"I'm not sure she's any safer either way," Pigeon said. "If Jonas knows her secret, whether or not she's in one of his clubs probably won't matter. Look, I won't try hard to blow it for the Subs, but I won't go out of my way to win, either. Although it would be kind of fun to fly."

"We probably shouldn't talk for too long," Nate said.

"Right. We might not get a chance to chat more before sunset. Good luck."

"You too. Be careful. We don't know much about what we're up against." Nate flew away to rejoin the Jets, and Pigeon dove into the water.

* * * * *

As he soared away from the training center, Nate debated whether to switch on his night vision. Below him, the world had been simplified into a grid of lights. The Jets flew well above the ground, hopefully high enough to avoid attention from people down below. Their black clothing helped them blend with the night sky. They all wore protective helmets, elbow pads, and knee pads.

Nate had brought the tranquilizer pistol that Pigeon had passed along from the Battiatos. Lindy had hers as well. Although the helmets were equipped for night vision, the moon was probably bright enough to help them get the job done. Besides, Lindy flew beside Nate, and he knew that she could see in the dark much better than any night vision device.

As planned, they flew to the freeway, then followed the opposing streams of headlights and taillights toward the first junction. Freeways would lead them most of the way to the desired inlet. Chris held the map.

Chris kept increasing their speed until they were moving faster than the cars below. The air remained warm after an uncomfortably hot day. It washed over Nate like a gale as he sped forward. Even at such a high speed, flying caused him no physical exhaustion.

After a few freeway junctions, they left the busy roads behind and flew toward a dark expanse of water. Silver moonlight reflected gently off the surface in places. Thanks to the moon, the *Striker* was not difficult to see, floating alone on the water as it had for years.

The Jets gathered a few hundred feet above the destroyer to confer. Although the waterway was wide, shore lights remained visible beyond the water on both sides.

"Seems quiet," Chris said.

"I guess he's not in a band," Nate said.

Lindy rolled her eyes. "I don't see any light."

"Hopefully he's asleep," Risa replied.

"How long before the Subs get here?" Lindy wondered.

"We were hauling and we didn't get lost," Chris said. "Even if they found a ride to the nearest water, we've got to be like an hour ahead of them."

"We can't get too cocky," Nate said. "They move through the water almost like how we fly. They might get here faster than we expect."

"Not sooner than half an hour," Chris said firmly.

"I want to be gone before they arrive," Lindy said.

"Wouldn't that be nice?" Nate said. "It's a big boat."

"If the Hermit doesn't want to be found, it could take all night," Chris said. "We should get started."

"Chris and Risa should wait here," Nate suggested.

"No way," Chris said. "It'll take twice as long to find him without us."

"Think about it," Nate argued. "Somebody needs to keep watch for the Subs. Also, somebody needs to be ready in case the Hermit tries to slip away. If he escapes, we're all in huge trouble."

"Maybe Risa and Lindy should stay here," Chris negotiated. "You and I can go in after him." Chris held up a pair of handcuffs he had brought from the training facility.

"Lindy is really good at finding people," Nate said. "I don't mean she's lucky, I mean she has an eerie gift." They hadn't told Chris and Risa about Lindy's eye. Until Nate knew he could trust them, he wanted to keep that secret advantage private. He hoped he could bluff his way through this without a full explanation.

"And I guess she feels most comfortable working with you," Chris said.

"Yeah," Lindy agreed. "Is that okay?"

"Keeping watch isn't a weak job," Nate assured them. "If we flush him out, you guys will be more likely to catch him than we will."

"Fine, go," Chris said. "You're wasting time."

"You have handcuffs?" Nate asked Lindy.

She nodded. "You have pepper spray?"

"It's supposed to be strong enough for a bear," Nate said. "Hikers carry it."

Lindy led the way down to the ship, diving steeply before alighting on the deck. Nate landed beside her.

"Know where he is?" Nate asked.

Lindy scanned the ship, then nodded. "Follow me."

She walked quietly to a door, opened it, and Nate followed her through into the darkness beyond. He paused to switch on his night vision, illuminating the hallway in greenish hues. Nate had a flashlight, but he knew that relying on the night vision would give him a better chance of surprising the Hermit.

Lindy levitated a few inches off the ground. Nate followed her lead—it would enable them to move silently. They drifted along the narrow hall. The ship creaked and groaned around them—low, slow sounds. The interior of the ship smelled like old metal and mildew. Lindy led the way down a stairway. Nate hovered close to the stairs, slanting down through the still air.

Partway down the next hall, Lindy paused and waited for Nate to drift close. She put her lips to his ear and whispered, "He's up here on the right."

Nate nodded that he understood. He pulled out a canister of pepper spray and made sure it was ready to fire.

Lindy looked at him with wide eyes, her face green because of the night vision. He could see her fear. He felt it himself.

Who were they about to confront? They knew he was called the Hermit. They knew he might try to run. But what if he decided to fight? In the close confines within the ship, flying wouldn't offer much advantage.

Nate pantomimed a pistol.

Lindy produced her tranquilizer gun.

Nate put his lips beside her ear. "Our first choice isn't to put him to sleep, but if things get dangerous, let him have it."

She gave him a thumbs-up to show her understanding. She still looked scared.

Nate took the lead, his toes inches above the floor. He glided down the corridor like a ghost. Lindy stayed close behind. Pulling alongside Nate, Lindy gestured toward a particular doorway, then let him reclaim the lead.

Pepper spray ready, Nate peered through the open doorway.

A man stood in the center of the room.

Stripped to the waist, he wore tattered jean shorts and had pale skin. His head was completely bald, but his ashen body was covered by sparse black hairs so bristly that they almost looked like short quills. The hairs were thickest on the front of his legs, the back of his arms, and atop his shoulders. He had a small, upturned nose with nostrils that almost faced forward. Fleshy webbing spanned his fingers and toes.

"Who are you two?" he asked in a scholarly voice with a faint British accent. "You came directly to my room."

The sight of the man had made Nate gasp quietly. The calm, controlled voice did not match his strange appearance. The man made no threatening movement.

"Are you the Hermit?" Nate asked.

"Would it help if I told you no?" the man said dryly.

"Probably not," Nate admitted.

"You're floating," the Hermit said.

"Yep." Nate kept the pepper spray ready.

"I'm not dreaming, am I?" the Hermit checked.

"No. We're here."

"What do you want?" the Hermit asked.

"The Gate," Nate said.

"The Gate? What Gate?"

"The Gate to Uweya," Nate said.

The Hermit said nothing. Then he blinked. It was not a normal blink. It was like a clear film flowing over his eyeballs and then retracting.

"You can float," the Hermit said. "You know about the Gate. You trespassed with impunity. You found me without searching. Who sent you?"

"Does it matter?" Nate asked.

"You want to take one of my most prized possessions," the Hermit said. "I want to know who sent you. You've both been enhanced. The girl has a very impressive eye. Top-notch work. Who?"

"Jonas White," Lindy said.

The Hermit laughed without cheer. "A fellow Simulcrist, of course, of course. I recently thought I felt someone reaching out for me. Just for a moment. I decided I must have imagined it. Shame on me—I probably should have left immediately." He grasped a metallic figure eight that dangled from a length of twine around his neck. "He can glimpse me, perhaps, but no matter his power, he can't touch me."

"That protects you?" Lindy asked.

"From simulcry? Absolutely. Do your worst; I'm immune."

"We don't want to hurt you," Nate said.

"Of course not," the Hermit scoffed. "You just want to sneak into my home, threaten me with a caustic substance, and take something that belongs to me, on behalf of an enemy."

"We don't really work for Jonas," Nate insisted. "He captured some friends of ours. We just need to get close to him so we can rescue them. We'd be happy to give you back the Gate once we find our friends."

The Hermit laughed mockingly. "You think giving this Simulcrist the Gate will help your friends? If you can't stop Jonas White now, how will you stop him once he becomes the most powerful person in the world?"

"What do you mean?" Nate asked.

"It's the Gate to Uweya!" the Hermit said, as if that explained everything.

Nate had no response.

"You don't even know what he's looking for," the Hermit realized.

"We just want to help our friends," Lindy said.

"Uweya is the most powerful simulacrum ever devised," the Hermit said. "If the legends are true, it can influence the entire world!"

"Are you searching for it?" Nate asked.

"Do I look like I'm on an expedition?" the Hermit asked. "I've resided here for years."

"If you're a Simulcrist, why haven't you gone after it?" Nate challenged.

"It would require more than the Gate," the Hermit said. "Uweya? Me? No thank you. Not at present. Perhaps not ever. Although I rest much easier knowing that I have the Gate and no one else does."

"We need the Gate," Nate said. "Others are coming. We're going to get it. Don't make this difficult."

"That's too bad about your friends," the Hermit sympathized. "I wish nobody any harm. Actually, I wish nobody anything. I just want to be left alone. Is that too much to ask?"

"People are coming," Nate stressed. "Give us the Gate and you can leave quietly. We don't want to harass you."

"Yes you do!" the Hermit replied sharply. "You are here to harass me. You are here to steal from me. This conversation is over. Tell Jonas White that he has a new enemy."

"Don't make this harder than—" Nate began.

The Hermit picked up a yellowed sheet of parchment and poked three fingers through it. As he did so, with a shriek of metal, the wall behind him tore open, forming a much larger hole of the exact same shape. Casting the parchment aside, the hermit snatched a green backpack, shrugging it on as he dove through the misshapen hole and out of the ship.

Soaring forward, her body horizontal, Lindy streaked out through the hole. Nate paused to pick up the parchment. Tearing the hole in the parchment wider, he watched the hole in the wall expand to match. Nate dropped the parchment and followed Lindy through the widened gap.

Outside, Chris and Risa were flying after Lindy, who glided away from the *Striker*, roughly thirty feet above the water. She veered away from the nearest shore, pointing down as if tracking unseen prey. Nate accelerated and caught up to Chris.

"Does she really see him?" Chris asked.

"I trust her," Nate replied. "She has a sixth sense for these things."

"I have night vision, and I don't see a thing," Risa said.

"Exactly," Nate said. "Either Lindy has him, or we're out of luck."

They had caught up to Lindy. She continued to stare down at the impenetrable water. She was flying well below top speed, but fast enough to suggest that the Hermit could swim at an abnormal pace.

"He has to surface eventually," Chris said.

"I'm not sure," Nate replied. "He didn't look entirely human. He had webbed feet and hands."

"He's a merman?" Risa asked.

"I don't know," Nate said. "Some of the people who hang out with magicians have modifications. They're called engineered apprentices. I've met some strange ones, including a guy full of disgusting jelly. The Hermit might be one of those, but I'm not really sure."

"You've been doing this for a while?" Chris asked.

"I've had some experiences," Nate answered vaguely.

They continued to fly away from the ship. As they neared the center of the waterway, the Hermit surfaced. He held up a small box, opened the lid, and then got out of the way as it rapidly unfolded, inexplicably expanding into a twenty-foot sailboat. The vessel looked old-fashioned, with a single, triangular sail that hung from a slanted mast, rising from the front of the craft to the back.

"What?" Chris exclaimed. "Where'd that come from?"

"I don't know," Nate replied.

"Pigeon's here," Lindy called. "That's why the Hermit surfaced. The Subs were closing in from all sides."

The Hermit boarded the vessel and rummaged in his backpack. Nate suspected the Gate was in the backpack. He swooped down as the Hermit withdrew a small model identical to his sailboat. Arms outstretched, Nate closed in as the Hermit blew on the model's sail. The mast of the twenty-foot vessel creaked as the sail suddenly filled with wind, propelling the craft briskly forward. Due to the sudden motion, Nate missed his target and pulled up to reassess the situation.

The Hermit moved the rudder of the tiny model, and the larger vessel swerved dramatically. One of the Subs came flying out of the water like a trained dolphin. He had been aiming for the Hermit, but when the sailboat changed direction, he arced harmlessly though the air over part of the stern and plunged back below the surface.

The Hermit continued to blow the sail of his tiny model. The sail of his actual boat strained the mast as the vessel skimmed over the water. Nate and the other Jets had to fly at a good pace to keep up.

Nate glided closer to the others, thirty or forty feet above the bulging sail. "The little model controls the boat," he said.

"Uh, yeah," Lindy replied. "I noticed."

"We want his backpack?" Chris asked.

"That's my best guess," Nate said. "It was all he took from the *Striker*."

Another Sub, Mindy, surged out of the water. The Hermit swiveled the sail of the model sailboat, and the actual boom lurched sideways, batting the girl away. She splashed back into the water. The sight of the impact made Nathan flinch—the boom had clubbed her hard.

"Should we go help her?" Nate asked.

"I see a Sub on the way," Lindy said. She brandished her tranquilizer pistol. "Is it time for this?"

"Probably," Nate said. "I guess we can wake him up if the Gate isn't in the backpack."

Lindy dove down nearer to the boat, keeping well away from the boom. Nate darted down to fly beside her. She took aim and fired twice.

Howling, the hermit turned the sailboat sharply. Setting aside his model boat, he opened a weathered bin on the deck and retrieved a compound bow. As the Hermit hastily nocked an arrow, Lindy veered up and left, Nate up and right. Climbing as quickly as possible, Nate saw the Hermit release the arrow, but he couldn't follow where it went. Looking urgently at the other Jets, Nate saw that nobody had been hit.

But the Hermit did not stop shooting. He fired arrow after arrow. The fourth took Risa through the thigh.

All four of the Jets broke off the pursuit and climbed straight up. Once high enough to feel safe from further arrows, they huddled together in the night sky. Risa grimaced in pain.

"Take her back," Nate told Chris.

He looked pale, but nodded. "What about the Hermit?"

"We'll keep after him," Nate promised. "But Risa needs a doctor."

"Do I take her to a hospital?" Chris asked.

Nate shook his head. "Try Jonas White first. Some of these magicians have healing abilities. Even if he can't fix her, he'll know what to do."

"You okay?" Lindy asked, a hand on Risa's shoulder.

"It hurts," Risa replied bravely through gritted teeth.

"Go," Nate said. "Hurry."

Chris took Risa's hand. "Can you fly?"

She gave a quick nod.

The two of them accelerated rapidly, racing back toward Walnut Hills.

"Think she'll be okay?" Lindy asked.

"I don't know," Nate said. "Hopefully the arrow didn't hit an artery or something. One thing is for sure—this isn't a game. That Sub who got swatted found that out as well."

"Do we keep after him?" Lindy asked.

"I think so," Nate said. "But we need to keep our distance. He's playing for keeps."

"I hit him with at least one dart," Lindy said. "I saw it connect."

"I hope it takes effect soon," Nate replied.

The sailboat had moved away while they talked. Nate led the way down toward it again. Before long he came close enough to see the Hermit on the deck, blowing on the sail of the model. The compound bow remained close at hand.

The Hermit showed no sign of dropping unconscious. Perhaps Lindy had missed after all. Or maybe he was immune.

Nate felt unsure how to proceed. He wanted to claim the Gate so he could stay close to Jonas White and rescue John and Mozag. But he didn't want to get himself or Lindy killed by an arrow. How would that benefit anyone?

Lindy flew near to Nate. "Two Subs closing in," she informed him.

One of the Subs shot up from the water and onto the deck of the sailboat. Nate recognized him as Drew. Instead of leaping at the Hermit, he had simply come aboard. Crouched and completely dry, he remained half the length of the vessel away from the Hermit.

"Get off my boat," the Hermit warned. "Stop pursuing me. I won't ask twice."

Edging forward, Drew produced a truncheon that looked like a miniature baseball bat. Nate had toyed with some similar truncheons at the training facility.

Setting aside the model sailboat, the Hermit grasped his bow in one hand and an arrow in the other. Drew dove over the side of the boat at the same time as Pigeon burst out of the water from behind the Hermit. As the Hermit swiveled to face the new threat, Pigeon ignored him, lunging instead for the model sailboat. The Hermit had barely set his arrow to the string when Pigeon brought both hands down on the intricate model. The actual sailboat buckled and shattered, catapulting the Hermit into the water.

"Way to go, Pidge!" Nate shouted. "What's going on now?" he called to Lindy.

"The Hermit is heading straight for the nearest shore," Lindy replied. "He has the backpack. He dropped the bow to swim better. Pigeon and Drew are after him. He keeps fending them off with his hands and feet."

Lindy flew along, pointing down at the water, and Nate followed unquestioningly. He got his pepper spray ready. The shore drew steadily closer.

"Pigeon and Drew keep harassing him," Lindy reported. "The Hermit is fighting as much as he's swimming. He still has his backpack."

They reached the shore and the Hermit emerged from the water with Pigeon and Drew in close pursuit. But they didn't stay close for long. On land, the Hermit was at least twice as fast as the two boys. He dashed away into a stand of trees. The Subs stayed after him, but they lost ground with every stride.

Lindy flew over the treetops, still pointing down at the Hermit as she had while over the water. "He's fast," she told Nate. "Some of the undergrowth is pretty dense, but he just charges right through it."

At the far side of the trees, the Hermit sprinted into a field. Lindy looked over at Nate expectantly.

"Let him gain a little more distance," Nate said. "I don't want the Subs catching up. We're going to win today."

They tracked him across the field, over some rough terrain, and into a field beyond. "The Subs gave up," Lindy said, looking back. "They're returning to the water."

Nate swooped down. The Hermit's speed might seem impressive to somebody chasing him on the ground, but Nate could have flown circles around him. Once he came too close to miss, Nate discharged the pepper spray. The Hermit collapsed, writhing and shrieking.

Nate and Lindy landed a few yards away from their quarry. Back arched, tendons standing out, the Hermit rocked from side to side, making strangled sounds.

"We have more," Nate warned. "Don't make us use it."

Still in agony, the Hermit waved a hand. "No more! No more. My skin is very sensitive."

Seeing how pathetic the Hermit now looked, and hearing the anguish in his voice, Nate felt a little guilty for spraying him. "You shot our friend," Nate said.

"Only after you chased and shot me," the Hermit countered, his voice strained, his legs twitching. "How dare you blame me?"

"We need the Gate," Nate said.

Scowling, the Hermit sat up and jerked open his backpack.

"No tricks," Nate said, holding out the pepper spray.

The Hermit held up a box, his lips quivering with pain and anger. "This is not the Gate," he explained. "Nor is it a trick. You'll find the Gate in here."

Wincing and clutching his shoulder, the Hermit rose to his knees. He peeled open the box, and it promptly unfolded into a large barn made of dark wood. Nate took a step back, staring at the impossible structure.

"How do you do that?" Lindy asked.

"I have my secrets," the Hermit said. "Same as any magician."

"I need to tell you something," Nate said. "Will you listen?"

The Hermit sneered. "Long as you're holding that attack spray, I'm all ears."

"You don't want Jonas White to have the Gate," Nate said.

"Of course I don't," the Hermit said. "But thanks for rubbing it in."

"Neither do we," Nate pledged earnestly. "I'm serious. He kidnapped our friends. We're only helping him until we can rescue them. I don't want him to find Uweya."

"Handing over the Gate will move him a major step toward that end," the Hermit cautioned.

"We're taking it for now," Nate said firmly. "But we don't want it permanently. Before this is over, I'm going to take it back from Jonas, and then I'll return it to you."

With one eye squinted more than the other, the Hermit regarded Nate. "Then you're playing a dangerous game, boy. Jonas White is a magician of no small talent. He's made a simulacrum of you, I can see that plain as sunrise. Crossing him won't be as easy as you suppose."

Nate shrugged. "I'm not expecting it to be easy. But I'm going to do it. And I want to return the Gate to you afterward. We're only taking it to help our friends."

The Hermit sighed. "Much as I despise what you're doing, I hear no falsehood in your words." He extended an arm. "Travel that way some miles, and you'll find three hills of nearly equal height. For the next fortnight, I'll be in a cave on the north side of the farthest."

"Fortnight?" Nate asked.

"Two weeks," Lindy supplied.

"Bring back the Gate, and I'll no longer count you an enemy," the Hermit said. "But don't fail. If Jonas gets his hands on Uweya, not much else will matter."

"I'll do my best," Nate said.

"Want to really do your best?" the Hermit asked. "Let me go. Tell Jonas I got away. I'll run. I'll take the Gate beyond his reach."

"He has other helpers," Nate said. "And he found some way to track you. I have to do this."

The Hermit bowed his head. "Into the barn, then. You'll find the Gate in a trunk in the loft."

"Lindy," Nate said, "go get it. I'll watch him."

The Hermit frowned. "You should both go. You may need to help each other. It's quite heavy."

"Then you come too," Nate said.

"I can't enter," the Hermit insisted. "If I go inside, the barn could collapse."

"If we leave you out here, I'm sure it will collapse," Nate replied. "With us in it."

The Hermit folded his arms.

"I hit you with a dart," Lindy said. "I see it in your back."

"I felt the sedative in my system," the Hermit replied. "I'm good at countering such things. The burning spray? Not so much. Nothing has hurt me like that in a great while."

"We could tell," Nate said. "Lindy, I'll watch him. Use the Finder's Dust."

"I'll be right back," Lindy said, flying off.

Nate watched the Hermit steadily until she returned. The Hermit seemed fidgety and displeased, but he made no aggressive move.

"Wasn't hard to find," Lindy said. "It's kind of heavy. Not more than I could manage."

"Solid stone," the Hermit said.

She held a rectangular block of light-colored stone the size of a hardcover book. Set into the stone was an elaborate gate locked with a crossbar on either side.

"What do we do with it?" Nate asked.

"Burn me if you wish," the Hermit replied, "but I honestly hope you never find out. Sadly, I fear Jonas White already knows."

CHAPTER THIRTEEN

PRISONERS

Pigeon cruised through the water like no creature under the sea. He didn't need to kick his feet or stroke with his hands. The effort never tired him. His inexplicable propulsion seemed much like the flying he saw the Jets do, except it worked only in the water.

The temperature felt perfect, neither too warm nor too cold. In the open water, he could reach impressive speeds that were impossible in the close confines of the training center pool. The water was too dark for him to see anything, but he could feel for miles using a sense that seemed a blend of touch, sight, and hearing. He could feel the surface of the water above, the ground below, the shorelines at either side, and the multitude of fish and plants around him. He could sense the wreckage of the sailboat and the bulky presence of the *Striker* in the distance, and he could clearly discern the three other Subs around him.

"Do we try to head them off?" Drew asked. "Maybe we can steal the Gate from them last minute, just before they enter Arcadeland."

Speaking underwater felt just as natural as speaking in air. Better, actually, because their voices seemed to carry farther.

"We swim faster than the Jets could guess," Pigeon said. "But they're still faster than us. If we ambush them outside of Arcadeland, we'll be out of our element, and they'll be flying. Our chance was when the Hermit was in the water. We blew it. It's over."

"Are we sure they got it?" Mindy asked. She had been temporarily stunned when she was clobbered by the boom. Steven, the fourth Sub, had stayed behind to tend to her. She claimed to feel fine now.

"Sure as we can be," Pigeon replied. "The Jets were in the air, hot on his trail. The Hermit was unarmed. No way Nate blew an advantage like that."

"The Hermit might have had more tricks in his backpack," Steven said. "Like the sailboat."

"Possibly," Pigeon conceded. "Even if the Jets fail, it just means they'll lose their stamps along with us. Either way, the party is over."

"You're giving up too easily," Mindy complained. "Why not race back to Arcadeland and see if we can intercept it? One of the Jets got hurt. We'll probably outnumber the ones with the Gate."

"Sure, they can fly," Drew said. "But they'll have to enter through a door. Maybe they'll get sloppy."

"Worth a try," Pigeon said, trying to hide his lack of enthusiasm. He didn't want to beat the Jets. And he didn't think the Subs had much chance of doing so even if they tried their hardest. "Lead on."

Pigeon followed the others, trying to enjoy the swim. They should have explored big, open water before tonight. It was a whole different experience from the training room pool or the canal where they had sometimes practiced after hours. It felt amazing to zoom effortlessly through the water, breathing easily. He had no fear of colliding with obstacles or encountering danger because he could sense everything around him more clearly than with sight on a bright day. He could feel the textures of surfaces he was not touching. He could sense tiny particles in the water hundreds of yards away. When he lost his stamp, he would miss the experience of flying through water with his senses enhanced.

Drew backtracked toward Arcadeland at top speed. Pigeon tried not to worry about Nate and Lindy. The Hermit had run off into the trees at an unmatchable pace. After the Subs had lost him in the darkness, there had been nothing they could do to catch him.

Nate and Lindy had tranquilizer guns, they could fly, and they were smart. He had to trust that they would be all right.

As they glided through the water, the other Subs talked about what Arcadeland doors they would cover to try to intercept the Gate. Pigeon chimed in just enough to make it seem like he cared. He wasn't worried about the Subs stopping Nate. He doubted whether any amount of planning would make any difference.

When they finally exited the water, a car awaited to take them to Arcadeland. The ride had been prearranged through Todd, for a small fee. All of the Subs had chipped in.

Pigeon let Drew claim shotgun, content to sit in the back with Steven and Mindy. What would he do without any future stamps? For one thing, he could start working more closely with Mr. Stott and the Battiatos again. Also, once his latest sub stamp wore off, he should be able to use magical candy again.

The car came to a stop in the Arcadeland lot. The facility was closed. Todd and Cleon stood out front.

Drew and the other Subs hurried out of the car, but Cleon raised his hands calmingly. "No rush," he said. "The Jets beat you here with the Gate."

"It's over?" Mindy asked.

"This phase of the contest is done," Todd explained. "But your involvement hasn't ended yet. Mr. White wants to speak with you all about a special assignment."

"And take away our stamps," Pigeon said.

Cleon held up an objecting finger. "That's for him to decide." He opened one of the front doors.

Katie Sung awaited them inside, clipboard in hand. The arcade had only a fraction of its normal lights on. The games created a flickering twilight, mostly blues and reds. Katie smiled professionally.

"Welcome back, Subs," she said. "We all really appreciate your hard work and dedication. Rest assured, you won't leave without some impressive consolation prizes. Mr. White wants to meet personally with you all regarding a bonus assignment."

"Are we losing our stamps?" Drew asked unhappily. "I worked hard for my stamp."

"Mr. White is calling the shots," Katie said. "Let's go find out how he feels about the matter."

Pigeon wasn't sure he wanted to know how Jonas White felt.

They followed Katie through an EMPLOYEES ONLY door, then down a hall to a room they hadn't previously visited. Mr. White was not awaiting them. Instead, the four Subs waited together in the empty room with Katie.

"He's coming?" Pigeon asked.

"He'll just be a moment," Katie replied. "The Jets didn't beat you four by much. I expect that he's still congratulating them."

"And telling them that they'll get our stamps," Mindy grumbled.

"Don't be a sore loser," Katie chided. "You would have happily taken theirs."

"How is Risa?" Pigeon asked. "It looked like she got hurt."

"She'll be fine," Katie said. "She's already good as new. Mr. White can work wonders with healing if he has a simulacrum of you."

"Wait a minute," Steven said urgently. "What's going on? I can't move!"

"He can do other things too," Katie said. "Don't panic, or he'll render you incapable of speech as well."

"I can't move either," Mindy announced.

Pigeon flexed his fingers and toes. He still felt fine. Should he run?

Drew made a dash for the door, falling rigidly to the floor before he was halfway there. "What's happening?" he cried, lying in an unnatural pose.

"You should keep still," Katie advised. "There is no escaping this. You'll be more comfortable if you relax."

Pigeon was trying to decide what position would be least annoying when he felt his body lock up. He retained sensation in his limbs, but nothing would move. He couldn't turn his head. He couldn't even glance around—his eyeballs were frozen in place. He could breathe. He could swallow. He could blink.

"What's he doing?" Pigeon asked, fighting to keep the panic out of his voice. At least his lips and jaw could move. At least he could speak.

"I expect he's preparing you for unwelcome news," Katie answered. "We'll know shortly."

"Can I at least stand up?" Drew asked.

"You forfeited that right when you attempted to flee," Katie said.

Focusing all of his will to the task, Pigeon tried to twitch his thumb. Nothing happened. It was as if his extremities were no longer accepting messages from his brain. He tried to shift his glance, but his eyeballs remained fixed.

A door opened, and Jonas White toddled into the room. Unable to look directly at him, Pigeon had to content himself with monitoring the magician peripherally. Jonas wore slippers and a silky robe embroidered with a pattern of gold, purple, and black diamonds. He came to a stop facing them.

"My Subs," he said affectionately. "It would have been quite a coup had you brought home the Gate. But your presence was necessary. Without you there, the Hermit might have fled deep underwater and escaped. Your aquatic abilities may still play a role in upcoming challenges, but alas, those talents will be wielded by others."

"Why freeze us?" Mindy asked defiantly.

"Out of concern for your welfare," Jonas replied smoothly. "You may have reacted poorly to some of my news. Out of the water, you're as vulnerable as any ordinary schoolchildren, and I would hate to see any harm befall you."

"What news?" Pigeon asked.

Jonas placed his hands behind his back. "This treasure hunt is a very sensitive matter. Now that you have lost your stamps to the Jets, I cannot permit you to leave here until our competition is over."

"What?" Drew exclaimed.

"You never said anything about this!" Steven accused.

"My parents will freak out," Mindy warned.

Jonas shuffled over to Mindy and patted her shoulder. "I have seen to it that your parents will disregard your disappearances.

Nobody will even realize you're gone. At the end of all this, I'll deliver the four of you safe and sound."

"How long?" Pigeon asked.

"As long as it takes," Jonas answered. "Hopefully not more than a week."

"We'll be paralyzed like this the whole time?" Drew fretted.

Jonas furrowed his brow. "Nonsense. That would be tedious for me. Taxing. You'll remain inert until I deliver you to your cells."

"Cells?" Steven cried hysterically.

Jonas waved a hand. "I could call them guest rooms, but that would be an exaggeration. You will have food, shelter—the basic necessities. Not much more. Don't try to escape. Don't test me. Do not forget that I have your simulacra. I was gentle this time. You had not defied me. I am only holding you here as a necessary evil. But it is necessary." His voice hardened. "If you cross me, I will not be gentle."

Pigeon could feel himself sweating. Unable to move, he was more aware of his perspiration than usual. He was trapped in his own body. He had never felt so helpless. He tried to think of a way out of this. Nothing came to mind.

"How will we get to our cells?" Mindy asked.

"Don't worry about the logistics," Jonas said amiably. "I'll see to that. Try to relax and make the best of your situation. You will be amply rewarded upon release. That is all."

Jonas turned and shuffled toward the door. Pigeon realized he might not get another chance to ask questions, but no sensible inquiries came to mind. If he asked about John Dart or Mozag, it would only arouse suspicion of Nate and the others. His best chance to gain information might be to simply keep his eyes and ears open as a prisoner.

After Jonas left the room, Katie approached Pigeon. Her hands traveled over him probingly. She found his stamp and kept it. She disarmed him. But fortunately she missed the tracking button.

Todd and Cleon loaded Pigeon onto a dolly, and Todd wheeled him from the room. They passed along industrial halls, turning a couple of corners before reaching an elevator.

"Are we going underground?" Pigeon said.

"You'll see," Todd replied, pushing the call button.

"Will he really release us?" Pigeon asked.

"Be a good prisoner, and everything should work out fine," Todd replied.

When the elevator doors opened, Todd wheeled Pigeon inside. Pigeon was left facing the rear of the elevator. He heard the doors close, felt the elevator start descending, and then felt it stop. He heard the doors open, and Todd wheeled him out into a drab, concrete hall.

They traveled down the hall a considerable distance, passing few doorways or intersecting corridors. At last the hallway ended at a T-shaped intersection with another hall. Todd turned left, then made a few other turns before stopping outside a heavy wooden door. He unlocked it with a key and trundled Pigeon inside.

"Give it half an hour or so," Todd said, lifting Pigeon off the dolly and setting him on his feet. "Then do yourself a favor and sit tight."

Pigeon was left facing away from the door. The ceiling, walls, and floor were all bare concrete. A primitive toilet awaited in the corner. A flimsy cot paralleled one wall, blankets folded at the foot. Pigeon heard Todd wheel the dolly out, close the door, and lock it.

Standing still was not tiring, but whenever he attempted to

move, Pigeon found it infuriating. He tried to focus on the things he could do. He blinked. He breathed. He opened and closed his mouth.

Pigeon worried about his friends. He worried about himself. How could they fight a magician who could immobilize them like this? What chance did they have against this kind of power? He thought about the button in his pocket. Hopefully the Battiatos could use it to track him here. Jonas probably didn't have simulacra of them. Maybe they could mount a rescue. Unless these cells somehow muffled magical tracking. Lindy hadn't been able to see several parts of Arcadeland.

Pigeon didn't have many assets. He didn't have his tranquilizer pistol. He had doubted whether the weapon would survive extended submersion, so it was home in his bedroom. He had brought no magical candy because he couldn't use it with the sub stamp. Katie probably would have taken it from him anyway. All he had was his mind—and the button stuffed in his pocket.

Pigeon guessed it hadn't been more than ten minutes when he began to regain control of his body. It started slowly—his fingers could twitch, his eyeballs could shift, his toes could stretch. Then all at once the other frozen parts of his body abruptly thawed.

His limbs felt sore and rubbery, so Pigeon walked over to the cot and sat down. He removed the button from his pocket. The Battiatos had told him that in an emergency, he could break it and they would come running.

But shouldn't he wait? It seemed likely that if Jonas White held John and Mozag prisoner, they would be down here someplace. The underground holding area seemed plenty big and secure.

He held the button in both hands. What if he snapped it and

the Battiatos couldn't sense it? What if this underground complex was shielded against magical transmissions? Would the Battiatos at least have a sense of where and when the tracker had stopped sending a signal? It was all speculation because Pigeon had no clue how the button actually worked.

The button felt brittle in his hands. He was no Hercules, but he doubted whether he would have trouble breaking it. Wouldn't such a move be a little hasty, though? They had wanted to get inside to do reconnaissance. He could be a bigger help to the Battiatos if he found out more about this holding area before he called them. Presumably he would get to shower occasionally, or get some exercise. He might get a chance to learn the layout of the hallways. He could try to ascertain how well the place was defended. He could even try to discover where John and Mozag were imprisoned.

Pigeon placed the button back into his pocket. He wanted nothing more than to go home and sleep in his own bed. He didn't want to remain in this dingy cell, bored and uncomfortable. But he could always snap the button later. First he would see what information he could uncover from within this secret prison.

CHAPTER FOURTEEN

THE GRAYWATERS

As Nate followed Cleon through an EMPLOYEES ONLY door to get his stamp refreshed, he couldn't stop worrying about Pigeon. After bringing the Gate to Jonas the night before, Nate and Lindy had gone to Pigeon's house and waited for him to show up. But Pigeon had never made an appearance.

Today, none of the Subs had visited the training center. Nate supposed that might be expected if they had been stripped of their powers, but it still added to his unease. During their lunch break, Nate had returned to Pigeon's house, and Lindy had gone looking for the Battiatos.

After feeding Diego Brain Feed, Nate learned that the dog hadn't seen Pigeon since the day before. Lindy found that the Battiatos had also heard nothing from Pigeon, and that they were having trouble pinpointing his tracking button. She had set up another meeting with the Battiatos for the evening.

The purpose of spending time at Arcadeland, the point of

earning stamps, the idea behind joining the treasure hunt, had all been to find John and Mozag. Nate felt no closer to finding John than when they had started, and now they had lost a member of their rescue team.

When he returned to the training facility, Nate had filled in Summer and Trevor about Pigeon. They had kept the conversations short—it was getting hard to talk to each other at the training center as tensions increased between the rival clubs.

Then Todd and Cleon had shown up with a new assignment. As expected, this new challenge would pit the Racers against the Tanks. They were supposed to meet at the training center at five P.M. in order to go collect a map to an artifact called the Protector. Whichever club brought the map to Arcadeland first would retain their stamps and win the stamps belonging to the losing club.

Walking along a hall cluttered with pipes and wires, Nate felt like too much was happening too quickly. The challenge between the Tanks and Racers meant Summer and Trevor would miss the meeting with the Battiatos tonight. It also meant one or the other of them might go missing as well.

After rounding some corners, Cleon led the way to an elevator. He wore jeans, boots, and a creamy leather jacket with fringed sleeves. Cleon thumbed the button to call the elevator.

"This place has levels?" Risa asked. Jonas had already healed her by the time Nate arrived last night. The only remains of her arrow wound had been faint scars on the front and back of her thigh.

"You know when you hit a ball into the last hole out on the mini course?" Cleon asked.

"Sure," Risa said. "The one you don't get back."

Cleon gave a nod. "Those balls have to end up somewhere."

The elevator doors opened, and Cleon accompanied the Jets inside. He hit a button. Nate noticed that the elevator only had two levels. They were currently on 1, heading down to B. Either the elevator was very slow, or the basement was well below the ground level.

"You're about to make a new friend," Cleon announced as they exited the elevator. "She'll take care of refreshing your stamps from here on out."

"Who?" Lindy asked.

"A special guest," Cleon said. "Jonas brought her here because of her particular talents." He stopped in front of a door and knocked. "Her name is Tallah Brooks. You can call her Ms. Brooks."

The door was opened by a heavyset woman with mocha skin. She had a broad, kindly face and wore a lavender scarf bound in her graying hair.

"Seems I have visitors," Tallah said. "You may as well come inside."

The woman stepped aside, and Cleon led the Jets into the spacious room. A pair of sofas sat at right angles to each other near a large coffee table. Thick carpeting covered the floors, and wallpaper softened the walls. Shaded lamps gave the room a pleasant glow. Three doors led to other rooms. The contrast between the comfortably furnished apartment and the bare concrete of the hall outside was so extreme that Nate felt like he had walked onto a movie set rather than into an actual home.

"These four need your services," Cleon said.

"So young," Tallah said, looking them over and clucking her tongue. "How did you kids get mixed up with these folks?"

"Arcade games," Nate said.

Tallah rolled her eyes. "I don't expect to see the day when any good comes from video games." She gestured at the couches. "Have a seat, children. I'm Ms. Tallah Brooks. Call me Brooksie if you like. Or Tallah."

"Or Ms. Brooks," Cleon inserted.

"This is no schoolhouse, Cleon," Tallah scolded. "Let them call me what they like. Anybody hungry?"

"We're here for the stamps," Cleon said.

"Shush," Tallah said. "I know why you're here. Jonas White already had a talk with me about that. Doesn't mean an end to civility. Doesn't mean kids no longer get hungry. I have chocolate peanut butter brownies."

"That sounds good," Nate said.

"Sure," Chris chimed in.

Tallah smiled. "That's more like it. Give me a moment." She turned and bustled out of the room.

"She's a magician," Cleon murmured once Tallah had left. "Don't eat the brownies."

"She'd hurt us?" Chris asked.

"We have a specific arrangement with her," Cleon replied quietly. "She can't do anything harmful against your will. But if you eat something voluntarily . . . let's just say I won't be having one."

Tallah returned to the room bearing a plate of gooey brownies. "These are a specialty," she said warmly, offering the plate to Nate. He looked from the brownies to Tallah. He didn't accept one. "Lost your appetite?"

Cleon hooked his thumbs into his pockets. "Can you assure us the brownies will have no side effects?"

Placing the plate on the coffee table, Tallah shook her head and clucked her tongue. "Nobody trusts anybody these days. I suppose we should get down to business. What would you like blended?"

"Blended?" Lindy asked.

"I have a knack for reconciling different enchantments," Tallah said. "I can help diverse types of magic function simultaneously."

"She can make a jet stamp and a sub stamp work at the same time," Cleon said.

"Is it safe?" Nate asked.

"I've studied your stamps," Tallah replied. "The enchantment is complex. I should be able to coax any two of them to harmonize. Three would be too many."

"You don't have to blend your stamps," Cleon said. "But I would generally recommend it. The other clubs will have this option as well."

"We'll be going up against Racer Tanks?" Nate asked.

"That's the idea," Cleon replied.

"Me first," Lindy said. "Make me into a flying submarine."

"Give me your hand, child," Tallah said. She dipped a brush in a tube and spread a clear solution on the back of Lindy's hand. Then she applied the jet stamp, followed by the sub stamp, one atop the other. Eyes closed, Tallah held Lindy's hand and mumbled some words, then released her.

"Did it work?" Lindy asked.

"Success," Tallah said. "Who's next?"

Chris stepped forward. Nate got in line.

* * * * *

Trevor sat up front with the driver on the way to Devil's Shadow Mobile Home Park. He did not get shotgun because he was in charge—he was in front because he hadn't gelled with his group.

Paige, Hailey, and Claire sat behind him. The girls had all completed sixth grade, and they knew each other from going to the same Walnut Hills school. They had two other friends who had been gunning for stamps but had failed to earn enough tickets in time.

"How much farther?" Trevor asked the driver.

The swarthy man checked his GPS. "Five minutes tops."

Trevor was glad to be riding in a car. He and the Racers could move quickly, but with time slowed down from their point of view, they still had to run every step of wherever they went. The car would let them save their energy for when it mattered.

Trevor turned to face the girls in the back. "Do we have a strategy?"

Paige looked at him as though he had just asked the color of the sky. "Outrun them?"

"Right," Trevor said patiently. "But we also have to find the Graywater family and get the map from them. It could take time. Those Tanks are really strong. If they catch up, we could be in trouble."

"They won't catch up if we hurry," Paige replied.

"Even if they did, we just keep away from them," Hailey said. "You can't hurt what you can't catch."

"What if they corner us?" Trevor challenged. "How would we outrun them in a small room or narrow hall?"

"How about we don't let them corner us like that?" Claire said as if the solution were obvious. "We run away before they pin us down."

"Won't we need a lookout?" Trevor asked.

"Good idea," Paige said. "You can be the lookout."

Hailey and Claire giggled. Clearly they thought it would be a good way to keep him uninvolved.

Trevor faced front, fighting down his frustration. The girls were seldom openly mean to him. They were just dismissive. And not very bright. He was pretty sure that Paige and Claire came from wealthy families, and he suspected that they had won their tickets by spending lots of money rather than by having much skill.

"You want to keep your stamps, don't you?" Trevor asked.

"No, we want to give them away," Hailey responded sarcastically.

"Nobody can catch us," Claire said. "Stop stressing out so much."

"This might not be as easy as you girls think," Trevor insisted.

"Thanks for the twentieth warning," Paige said. "We're ready. Blabbing about it won't change anything. We find the Graywaters. We get the map. We outrun the Tanks. We bring it to Arcadeland."

"Whatever," Trevor said.

The driver had a small smile. He rubbed his oily moustache. Trevor looked away. Todd had assured them that the driver would convey them back and forth between Arcadeland and Devil's Shadow, no questions asked. They were free to speak about anything in front of him, but they shouldn't expect any extra assistance from him. Trevor didn't even know his name.

They turned onto a smooth dirt road and followed it across a field and around some oak trees. "Here we are," the driver announced. "Up ahead."

An arched sign reading DEVIL'S SHADOW formed the entrance to the trailer park. Beyond the entrance, Trevor could see a number of mobile homes in various states of disrepair. The driver pulled off to the side of the road just shy of the entrance.

Trevor looked back at the Tanks pulling over in their car as well. "The Tanks are right behind us," he warned.

"Not for long," Paige said, climbing out of the car. She and the other Racers took off at superhuman speed.

Trevor jumped out as well and followed. He shifted into race mode, an adjustment that had already become second nature, as simple as concentrating to read the words in a book. Everything around him slowed down. He glanced back at the Tanks getting out of the car with unnatural slowness, then sprinted to catch up with the girls.

Right now he was moving three or four times faster than everything else around him. He felt normal until he noticed a butterfly fluttering sluggishly. Running still made him tired, but no more tired than ordinary running. He could increase his speed again by entering the second altered state three or four times speedier than the first, but it would make him tire rapidly and could lead to a headache. He would save that secret weapon for emergencies.

The girls were not running too quickly, so he caught up to them just beyond the trailer park entrance.

"Shouldn't we slow down?" Trevor asked. "Won't it look weird to people?"

"Aren't you more worried about the Tanks?" Claire asked.

"We'll slow up if we see people," Paige said, still running hard.

Trevor had to agree that the trailer park didn't look very lively. The outdated mobile homes were arranged haphazardly. There couldn't have been more than thirty or forty total. Some appeared abandoned. Off to one side, a scrawny cat disappeared through a glassless window, the slow leap looking odd from Trevor's quickened perspective.

Paige slipped out of race mode, and the others followed her lead. It took Trevor a moment to realize why she had slowed. As they came around the nearest mobile home, a man had come into view.

He was in his fifties or sixties, with thinning hair, a white T-shirt, and a bulging round belly. He stood in front of a trailer watering the nearby dirt with a hose, his thumb over the nozzle to make the water fan out. Trevor didn't see any plants or grass. Maybe there were seeds in the ground, or maybe the man was just trying to reduce dust.

The girls jogged toward the man at a normal speed, and Trevor tagged along. The man looked up as the girls approached. "Evening," he said.

"Hi," Paige began in a bright, friendly voice. "We're looking for the Graywater family. Could you help us out?"

His eyes narrowed suspiciously. "What would you kids want with the Graywaters?"

"We have a present for them," Hailey invented.

"Were you invited?" the man asked. "How do you know them?"

"They're old friends of my family," Claire said. "We're bringing them a surprise."

The man shook his head. "The Graywaters don't like uninvited guests. I hope you kids know what you're doing."

"Are they mean?" Paige asked innocently.

"Not mean," the man responded. "Just private. They own the park. If your family knows them, I expect it'll go all right." He waved an arm to indicate a direction. "Last unit in the back. Green with white trim. Can't miss it."

"Thanks," the girls answered in chorus.

The man nodded, turning and flicking his wrist as he started dampening a new area. Trevor kept quiet and trotted away with the girls. Once they passed out of the man's view they sped up again.

Trevor had misgivings about their strategy. If the Tanks were hurrying, the pause talking to the man had given them a chance to catch up quite a bit. If he and the girls didn't get the map quickly, how long before the Tanks showed up and bullied their way to the prize?

Trevor did not want the Racers to lose. Summer was a Tank, but she had more capable people on her team. If they didn't want Jonas White to reach his goals, they needed Hailey, Paige, and Claire helping him rather than the Tanks.

The girls slowed back to a regular pace as the green trailer came into view. It was by far the nicest trailer in the park—larger, newer, and better appointed. It had a neat lawn with a tidy fence. A small satellite dish perched on the roof, aimed skyward. Flowers bloomed in the window boxes. A large porch with glider chairs and a swinging bench provided a shaded sitting area. Trevor had a great aunt who had retired to a trailer park, living in a nice little place similar to this one.

The Racers hurried over to the modest yard. Hailey opened the gate. Paige led the way up to the porch, opened the screen, rapped on the door, then stepped back. Trevor waited at the bottom porch step. He kept glancing over his shoulder so he could spot the inevitable arrival of the Tanks.

The door was opened by a tall Native American with an athletic build and high, hollow cheekbones. He wore a displeased scowl and remained behind the screen. "Who gave you permission to enter my yard?" he asked in a low voice devoid of humor.

"How were we supposed to knock?" Paige asked defiantly.

"Call from beyond the gate," he said.

"Are you Mr. Graywater?" Claire asked.

"This is the Graywater residence," he said. "I own this mobile home park. Strangers are unwelcome here. That includes solicitors. You kids are trespassing."

Trevor avoided making eye contact with Mr. Graywater. He didn't like the way the conversation was headed. There was still no sign of the Tanks.

"Of course we're strangers," Paige said lightly. "We haven't been introduced. I'm Paige. This is Claire, Hailey, and Trevor."

"William Graywater," he said. "Why are you here?"

"We need the map to the Protector," Paige said simply.

His eyes widened. He looked beyond the kids, as if expecting other enemies. "Who sent you?"

"Why would somebody have to send us?" Hailey asked.

"We need it for a school project," Claire improvised.

"Celia!" William called, his eyes on Paige. "Ted! Horace! Arrista! You know what to do!"

"We're not leaving without it," Paige said. "Make this easy on yourself and hand it over."

One of William's hands disappeared to the side of the door and reappeared with a sword. The long, silvery blade had a slight curve at the tip. From somewhere behind William, Trevor heard the double crunch of somebody working the action of a shotgun, and he took an involuntary step back. William glowered. "We're ready to protect the guidestone with lethal force. This is your last chance to leave."

"You're going to stab us over some map?" Claire asked, annoyed.

"Do you have any idea what I'm protecting?" William challenged incredulously.

"Uweya," Hailey said matter-of-factly.

"My family has guarded the guidestone for countless generations," William said. "We have sacrificed much to keep Uweya safe, for if it fell into the wrong hands—"

"Whatever," Paige said. "We'd rather be stabbed than bored to death."

William angrily slammed the door.

"Tanks," Trevor called as Summer, Roman, Derek, and Ruth rushed around the side of the nearest trailer.

"Now what?" Claire asked. "Did you hear the shotgun?"

"We let the Tanks do it," Trevor said. "Otherwise they could corner us in the trailer. We won't have much room to maneuver."

"And lose our stamps?" Paige scoffed. "As if!"

"We're fast," Trevor argued. "We can try to swipe it back."

The girls hesitated.

"Unless you plan to beat the door down, then dodge shotgun blasts with the Tanks on your tail. Do what you want—I'm backing off."

Trevor ran at his highest speed away from the trailer toward the nearest oak. He heard the girls following.

CHAPTER FIFTEEN

THE GUIDESTONE

Summer watched Trevor speed away from the trailer with the other Racers. They streaked to an oak tree and gathered behind it.

"They want us to do the dirty work," Roman said.

"I don't mind doing the work," Derek said. "But I don't want them stealing the prize."

"Did that guy have a sword?" Ruth asked. She had been the final addition to the Tanks. Soon to enter seventh grade, Ruth was thickset and tall for her age. She wore her reddish hair in two short pigtails.

"Looked like it," Summer said.

"Doesn't matter," Roman said. "We have to remember that. Swords, bullets, none of that matters anymore. But we'll have to watch the Racers. They're scary fast."

"Well, we're scary strong," Derek said. "Whoever gets the map holds it tight. The rest of us protect it."

"Sounds like the right idea," Roman said, striding toward the green and white trailer.

"We don't want to hurt anybody," Summer interjected.

"Not permanently," Roman agreed. "But Racers who don't want to get hurt shouldn't mess with Tanks."

They passed through the gate and walked up to the porch. Roman opened the screen and knocked.

"Go away," a voice called from inside. "I don't want to hurt a bunch of kids."

"We don't want to hurt a grown-up," Roman called back. "We're just here for the map. Open up or we'll bust the door down."

"Touch my door and you'll wish you hadn't," the man replied. "Walk away."

Roman kicked the door just below the handle. The wood splintered a little, but the door held. Roman kicked it again and the door tore open, ripping away part of the wall with it.

A grim Native American man stood beyond the door, a shiny sword held ready. Behind him was a comfortably furnished combined living room and dining room. Doors led away from the living area on both sides. "That door was reinforced," he said.

"Not enough," Roman replied, stepping inside. "Back off."

"Last warning," the man said, knuckles tight on his sword handle.

"Go for it," Derek invited. "Or don't. Either way, we're taking the map."

With a sigh, the man set the sword aside and quickly grabbed Roman. Squirming, Roman seized the man's arm with both hands, twisted, and hurled him to the ground. Derek pounced, putting him in a headlock.

"Who are you?" the man growled in surprise, grasping at the headlock but unable to wrench it loose.

"We already told you," Roman said. "We're the guys taking your map. Just tell us where it is. We don't want to tear up your house."

Summer felt sick. She knew they were after the map to try to help John and Mozag, but invading this man's home was wrong. He had set aside his sword because, regardless of his duty, he didn't want to chop up a bunch of kids. She had no doubt that he was the noble guardian of a secret that needed to stay hidden. Seeing him on the floor in a chokehold made her want to kick Derek in the face.

"Ease up," Summer demanded.

Derek looked at her like she was crazy. "Are you kidding? This guy is strong! I can barely hold him."

"Do it!" the man cried, his voice hoarse because of the stranglehold.

A loud blast sounded from an unseen room, followed by a rumble that Summer could feel through the floor. She and the others all jumped. Then came the unmistakable sound of a shotgun being reloaded.

"Shoot us, stab us," Roman said, "you can't stop us."

A second Native American man dashed into the room with a stun gun in one hand and a hinged club in the other. Wires launched from the stun gun and hit Roman. An instant later, Roman was flopping on the ground.

Ruth charged the man, who raised his padded club and swatted her. The blow glanced off the side of her head but did nothing to slow her as she tackled him to the floor.

Summer stood frozen. She didn't want to join the fight. The Graywaters weren't enemies. These were good people defending their home, trying to protect a dangerous secret.

Ruth straddled the man with the hinged club, sitting high on his chest, holding his wrists pinned beside his head. With the current no longer jolting him, Roman jerked the wires from his clothes.

"Are you all right?" Summer asked.

"I'm okay," he replied, leaning over the man in the headlock. "That didn't feel really great. Somebody tries something like that again, we start breaking bones."

The man in the chokehold was red in the face. Tendons stood out in his neck. "You're not children. You're demons in disguise."

Roman shrugged. "Whatever we are, you'd better cough up the map."

An older woman shuffled into the room using a cane. "You want the guidestone? Take it! You'll take it anyway." She held up a smooth stone sphere between her thumb and forefinger.

Roman crossed to her. "A marble?"

"Do you know so little?" the woman replied. "It will lead you to the Protector."

"Arrista, no!" the man in the chokehold protested.

"It's for the best, William," Arrista replied. "If we have lost the cover of our secrecy, we can no longer protect the map."

Roman took out a drawstring bag and withdrew a pinch of Finder's Dust. He let it fall, and the particles drifted away from the woman's hand, toward a doorway opposite from where she had emerged.

"You think you can fool us?" Roman accused.

The woman gave an apologetic smile. "It was worth a try."

The man Ruth straddled made a strangled sound. "Should we start really hurting them?" she asked with frightening casualness.

"Let's start with the old lady," Roman said.

Summer hoped he was bluffing. It was hard to tell.

"No," William said, the word weighted with despair. "We're defeated, I admit it. Don't make them suffer for my failings. You have Finder's Dust. It's only a matter of time before you claim your prize. Release me and I'll give you what you want."

Roman picked up the sword, then nodded at Derek, who released William. Derek positioned himself near Arrista. William stood, rubbing his neck.

"Any tricks, you let them have it," Roman told Derek and Ruth.

"What was with the big boom?" Derek asked.

"Warning shot," Arrista said.

"Then where is the gun?" Roman asked.

"I'll go check," Summer said.

She walked past Arrista into a narrow hall with a small bedroom on either side. In one of the bedrooms, acrid smoke hung in the air. Shattered crystal fragments rested on the charred carpeting. A shotgun leaned against the wall.

"I think they destroyed something in here!" Summer called.

Roman trotted over to look. "Great," he muttered. He turned and raised his voice. "Was that the map? Did you blow up the map?"

William gave a grim chuckle. "If we could destroy the map, our ancestors would have done so long ago."

"Then what's the mess in there?" Roman pressed.

"Something valuable," William replied glumly. "Something private. Something we did not want taken. Something that can never be replaced."

"We wouldn't have taken it," Roman said. "We just want the map. Take us to it. Or should I use the Finder's Dust?"

"Don't bother," William said, leading Roman and Summer to the other side of the living room, where a door gave access to a largish bedroom with a comfortable bathroom attached. William lifted the queen-sized bed, folding it up into the wall. Pulling a rug aside, he revealed a trapdoor.

"Down there?" Roman asked.

In reply, William produced a key, inserted it, and opened the trapdoor. He started down a ladder, then glanced up at Roman. "You coming?"

"Is this an ambush?" Roman asked.

"You have my mother and my brother," William said. "You are fortified by potent magic. Come on."

Roman and Summer followed William down the long wooden ladder into a secret cellar. Homemade shelves held canned food supplies. Numerous unmarked crates cluttered the dusty room. Sliding some cans aside, William pulled a loose block from the wall and produced a smooth stone marble like the one his mother had offered.

Roman sprinkled some dust, and almost every particle misted over to the little sphere, dissipating into smoke on contact. "It doesn't look like a map."

"That is not my concern," William said. "Search the house with your dust, if you choose."

Roman walked around the room, dropping pinches of dust. It all went toward the stone marble. Roman went and took the marble from William.

"Won't you reconsider?" William asked. "What can your employer offer that is worth granting him power to destroy the world?"

"The guy who sent us is really powerful," Roman said. "If he wanted to mess up the world, he could do it on his own."

William shook his head. "You're blind. You don't even know

what he's after. Whatever power your employer possesses is nothing next to Uweya."

Roman glanced at Summer. For the first time, he seemed a little indecisive.

"Maybe we should just let him go," Summer said. "Maybe we should let him take the guidestone. We might not get what we've gotten ourselves into."

"I've gathered that much," Roman said. "But he'll find it again. Our boss. He'll just send somebody else. Another club. New recruits. His own people."

"Just because other men would do evil does not mean you must participate," William said. "Help us stand against your employer."

Roman shook his head. "I don't think so. You stay down here. Don't bug us and we'll leave quietly."

"Are you sure?" Summer asked.

"I'm not sure about anything," Roman snapped. "How do we know this guy isn't lying? He could be the bad one."

"A bad guy would have tried to stab you with his sword," Summer pointed out.

"Maybe," Roman said. "Maybe not, if he'd already guessed there was no chance to win."

"Is being a Tank worth it?" Summer asked.

"He made those dolls of us," Roman said. "Those simu-whatevers. If we turn on him, we're toast. We just have to hope he wants Uweya for good reasons."

"Not likely," William grumbled. "The kind of power Uweya represents should never be unearthed. A wise person would know that."

Summer knew that Jonas White was a pretty bad guy. He had abducted Mozag and John. Just like his crazy sister, he was luring kids to do his dirty work and selling mind-altering food. But she couldn't trust Roman not to turn her in if she revealed her true purpose and shared all of her information. Without her, who would monitor the Tanks? "William might have a point," was all she said.

"Doesn't matter," Roman said. "We already chose sides. If Uweya is so powerful, we're smart to stay on the winning team. If you were going to wimp out, Summer, you shouldn't have accepted the stamp."

Sighing, Summer gave William an apologetic glance. "You're right, Roman. Let's get out of here."

Roman started up the ladder first. Summer looked at William intently. "I'm on your side," she mouthed. "I'll try to help."

She wasn't sure whether he could read her lips. She couldn't afford to make Roman suspicious by confirming that William understood. She followed Roman up through the trapdoor. He shut it and pulled the bed down over it.

They returned to the living room. Ruth remained atop the man who had fired the stun gun.

"Did you find it?" Derek asked, standing beside Arrista.

Roman held up the stone marble. "It's called a guidestone."

The screen door shifted, and everyone turned to look as a figure blurred into the room. Derek lunged toward the door, but the figure had already charged Roman, who held the guidestone between his thumb and forefinger. A little slow to react, Roman had barely begun to lower his arm by the time the Racer reached him. He had failed to enclose the guidestone in his fist, and the stone marble vanished before he could do so. He reached for the quick figure, but the thief was already beyond his grasp and heading for the door.

Derek, who was standing nearest to the door, had started for it as soon as the screen opened. He made it there just in time to become entangled with the Racer on her way out. Together they tumbled out onto the porch.

Summer ran to the door. Lying on the porch, Derek held Paige tightly. With a flick of her wrist, Paige tossed the guidestone into the yard, where Trevor quickly recovered it.

"Give it back!" Derek yelled. "Give it back now or she gets hurt!" He had one leg across Paige's shins and gripped both of her forearms.

"You're already hurting me!" Paige spat. "Get off."

"Not until we have the map," Derek insisted.

"Okay," Trevor said. "You win. Catch."

Trevor tossed the guidestone underhand to Derek. The stone marble traveled in a high, slow arc. When Derek reached up to catch it, Paige yanked her legs out from under him and darted away. Trevor blurred forward, catching his own throw before it reached Derek, then streaking away before Derek could grab him.

Claire and Hailey dashed forward as well. Whether they meant to intercept the thrown guidestone or help Paige was difficult to tell. But since Trevor had beaten them to the guidestone and Paige had managed to scramble away unaided, they arrived with nothing to do and tried to turn around. The two girls got tangled with each other on the porch steps, slowing them enough that Derek's desperate swipe at Trevor clipped Claire's leg.

Squealing and spinning, Claire tumbled down the porch steps, landing on the cement walkway that divided the grass yard. Derek pounced, grabbing her ankle with both hands before she recovered.

"No tricks!" Roman cried, pushing past Summer onto the porch. "No more games or you'll be sorry!"

"I think he broke my leg," Claire whimpered.

"Don't move," Derek warned.

Trevor looked closely at the guidestone. "What is this? The world's smallest globe? I don't see any markings."

"Give it back," Roman demanded. "Not to Derek. He'll keep hold of Claire. Give it to me, and you guys can leave."

"What do I care about Claire?" Trevor said, putting the guidestone in his pocket. "She's the worst. You can have her. Keep Paige, too, if you can catch her."

Paige and Hailey glared at him.

Roman looked furious. "If you don't give us the guidestone—"

"Do what you want to them," Trevor said. "That's your business. Mine is winning."

Before Roman could reply, Trevor turned and streaked away at top speed.

* * * * *

As Trevor sprinted away from the trailer, he hoped he had made a good choice. He doubted they would hurt Claire. The Tanks were strong, but they were kids. They weren't out for blood. If the guy with the stone they wanted ran off, there would be nobody to threaten and no reason to hold hostages.

As he dashed away, Trevor heard Roman shouting something, the words unintelligibly slow. It didn't matter what he said. By stopping to listen, he would give them a reason to keep harassing Claire. By pretending that he didn't care, he would decrease her value as a hostage and hopefully make her safer.

If he kept hurrying, the Racers should win, which was probably for the best. Trevor had taken some time to think it through while the Tanks were in the mobile home. He had firmly concluded that he would have more luck backstabbing the other Racers than Summer would have betraying the Tanks.

Using his maximum speed, Trevor ran past the trailers, distantly aware of how slowly the rest of the world was moving. Water leaked from a spigot, dripping as if gravity had almost ceased. A few small birds took flight in slow motion, startled by his rapid approach. Everything but him seemed restrained by some invisible force, while he was free to run like normal.

Except the running was making him much more tired than any natural sprint. As the arched DEVIL'S SHADOW entryway came into view, his head started to pound and his lungs burned. It felt as though he had sprinted ten times as far as he had actually run. The day had grown inexplicably hotter, and his mouth was suddenly parched.

Trevor shifted down to normal race mode and reduced his sprint to a jog. All he had to do was make it to the car. His burst of super speed meant he was well ahead of the Tanks.

Even in normal race mode, moving at a jog almost felt like too much. He knew through practice how much running at top speed sapped his energy. Adrenalized by the need to escape the Tanks, he had stayed at top speed for longer than ever before. He had known that overdoing it could wipe him out, but fear and excitement had driven him to push the limits.

Even at this slower pace, his legs felt rubbery, his head remained sore, and his heart was drumming like a hummingbird's. He began to get dizzy. Wouldn't that be great if he fainted?

Trevor slowed to a quick walk. In race mode, this would still be like a normal run, and his time at top speed had given him a huge head start. A glance back showed nobody following him yet—not Paige, Hailey, or any Tanks.

It was probably best if Paige and Hailey stayed with Claire. They could help her get back to Arcadeland and find the medical care she needed. Had she really broken her leg falling off the porch? It was possible. She had fallen hard.

All Trevor had to do was make it to the car. Then he could rest while the driver sped away. The Tanks would try to pursue him, but with his lead, hopefully they would never catch up. If they did, he would be rested and could escape on foot.

Trevor dropped to his knees and dry heaved. The need hit urgently, leaving him no chance to resist. He briefly wondered how this would look to an observer, watching somebody violently gag in fast motion.

Trevor staggered back to his feet. His muscles remained fatigued, his head woozy. Would it help if he left race mode altogether? But then his walk really would be just a walk. He couldn't risk the Tanks catching up. Race mode had never tired him much more than normal mode. It was the speediest mode that really drained him.

Beyond the arched entrance, Trevor stopped in his tracks. Both cars were still waiting out front. But his was upside down.

What had happened? The Tanks must have flipped it over before they followed the Racers into the trailer park. Was that allowed? He supposed there had been no rules against it.

His driver stood outside the flipped vehicle, leaning against it. He saw Trevor looking and shrugged, hands raised helplessly.

Would the other driver take him? It was worth a try. Motivated by desperation, Trevor picked up his pace and trotted to the car that had brought the Tanks. When he reached the driver's door, he shifted back into normal mode so they could converse.

The driver, a Middle-Eastern man with a scruffy beard, rolled down the window. "Yes?"

"Would you take me back to Arcadeland?" Trevor panted.

"I'm their driver," the man said. "Not yours. Overturning your car was a dirty trick, but so it goes."

"I could pay you," Trevor tried.

With his wrists still on the steering wheel, the driver raised his hands. "I've already been paid. I accepted the job. I'm sorry."

Trevor slumped. His body remained unusually exhausted. He wanted nothing more than to lie down and sleep.

What if he sabotaged this car? Let the air out of the tires or something? Would the driver prevent him? Maybe.

Trevor looked back at the trailer park to see all four of the Tanks racing into view, sprinting at their best speed. He shifted back into race mode. He could run off and try to lose them in the wilderness. But he had wrecked his endurance. The thought of running made bile rise in his throat. His head was throbbing a little less, but it still hurt.

Trevor knew from Summer that the Tanks tired slowly. They weren't fast like a Racer, but they would keep coming. Running at top speed was no longer an option. How long could he last in race mode? Could he get far enough ahead of the Tanks to lose them before he collapsed? If he got away, they'd try to head him off back at Arcadeland.

He turned and started running into the field beside the dirt road. It was worth a try. His legs gave out with no warning, and he sprawled in the brush. The ground swayed as if he were at sea. He lay still for a moment, spitting out dirt and smelling dry weeds.

He couldn't let them win. So what if his worthless teammates had stacked the odds against him? So what if the Tanks had sabotaged his car? He still had super speed. He would find a way to keep going.

Trevor got up and tried to run. His legs felt leaden. He shuffled along like an old guy who had lost his cane. Still, he kept moving.

Roman came alongside him on one side, Derek on the other. A strong hand clamped down on his shoulder. Only then did Trevor realize he was no longer in race mode. When had he slipped out of it? When he had fallen? It was hard to be sure.

Trevor stopped, his legs wobbly, and held out the guidestone on his palm. Roman claimed it and shoved him to the ground. Trevor felt no desire to rise.

CHAPTER SIXTEEN
THE RESISTANCE

Nate awoke to the sound of somebody tapping on his window with a coin. It took only a moment for him to realize that it must be an emergency. After kicking off his covers, Nate crossed to the window to find Summer outside.

He opened it. "What's up?"

"We got the map," Summer said. "The Racers lost. I'm worried about Trevor."

"What time is it?" Nate wondered.

"After midnight."

"Let me get dressed and I'll come down."

Summer nodded and walked carefully away from the window, shingles groaning and splitting under her augmented weight. She jumped off the roof and plummeted out of sight.

Nate changed into jeans and a T-shirt, then added a light jacket. He put on his shoes and glided out the window and down to Summer.

"What happened to Trevor?" he asked.

"I'm not sure," Summer said. "We were out at some trailer park getting the map to the Protector, which turned out to be a little round rock called the guidestone."

"Okay."

"Trevor had the stone," she said. "He almost beat us single-handedly, even though his teammates messed up. But I guess he ran at his top speed for too long and wiped himself out. We didn't get much chance to talk. Anyhow, we got the stone back from him. Both clubs had gone to the trailer park in cars. We had flipped the Racers' car upside down to mess them up, but then we flipped it back once we had the guidestone, so the driver could take them home. The car was busted up, but it still worked."

"Then what?"

"One of the Racers tried to steal the guidestone back, but Roman held tight, and she hurt her wrist. By the end, Paige had a sprained wrist and Claire had injured her leg pretty bad. It took the fight out of them. They went back in their car. But Trevor refused. He just took off into a field."

"Probably smart," Nate said. "Pigeon disappeared after his club lost."

"Right," Summer said. "But Trevor still hasn't shown up at his house."

"Wait, when did you guys turn in the guidestone?"

"Around eight o'clock. Afterward, I kept looking for Trevor. I just came here from his house. I'm worried he won't ever show up. And I'm worried that we're getting too deep into this without solving anything. I keep waiting for a chance to sneak into the secret parts of Arcadeland, and that chance keeps not coming. We lost Pigeon. We're no closer to finding John. We can't let Jonas White get Uweya."

Nate patted her shoulder. "Maybe we should go talk farther away. I don't want to wake up my parents."

She looked at him like he was being ridiculous. "Haven't you noticed?"

"What?"

"Our parents are all zombified. It's just like with Mrs. White. They can't get enough of that nacho cheese. He's been targeting them with taco carts—Arcadeland Taco Fiesta. My dad brought some of their food home tonight."

Nate thought about it. He'd been generally avoiding his family, partly because he'd been busy at the training center, and partly because he didn't want them placing limits on his excursions. Nobody had raised a complaint about the long hours he'd been away. When he had spoken with them, they had been calm and easygoing. "I should have known," he said.

"He's had my dad in a daze for a couple of days," Summer said. "Just one more reason we need to take him down."

Nate nodded. "You want to go look for Trevor? Or should we wait at his house? How far away were you?"

"It was a pretty far drive," Summer said. "Almost an hour. But as a Racer, he should have been back by now. I think we should talk to Mr. Stott."

"That's a good idea. We've gotten out of touch with him. So, you guys are going to be Racer Tanks?"

"Huh? Because we earned the racecar stamp?"

Nate held out his hand. "They have a lady who can blend two stamps so they work together. We're all Jet Subs now. I can hardly imagine going up against Racer Tanks."

Summer raised her eyebrows. "Don't let my teammates get ahold of you. They play rough."

"I believe you."

"Will they be able to blend all four stamps?" Summer wondered.

"The lady told us she could barely handle two," Nate replied. "I guess that's the limit. You'll find out about it when you go in to refresh your stamp."

"Tomorrow morning," Summer said. "Did you and Lindy meet with the Battiatos?"

"Yeah," Nate said. "There's no news on Pigeon. Nothing new at all, really."

They walked to the candy shop and went to the back door. A light was on, so Nate knocked gently. Mr. Stott answered a moment later, a steaming mug of hot chocolate in one hand, eyes anxious as he glanced beyond them into the night. "Come inside," he urged. "I'm glad you're here."

Mr. Stott closed the door behind them.

"We're worried about Trevor," Summer said.

Mr. Stott raised the mug. "I'm less worried now."

"He's here?" Nate asked.

Mr. Stott motioned with the mug for them to follow him. He led them up to the apartment, where Lindy greeted them. "This is turning into a party," she said.

"Where's Trevor?" Summer asked.

"He's in my sanctum," Mr. Stott said.

"Your sanctum?" Nate asked.

"The heart of my lair," Mr. Stott explained. "The most protected space. Magically, it's cut off from the rest of the universe. He may have to stay put for a while."

"Jonas White shouldn't be able to reach him there," Lindy added. "Even the simulacrum shouldn't work."

"Shouldn't or can't?" Nate checked.

Mr. Stott rubbed the side of his beard. "It would require a massive amount of skill and energy to overwhelm the barriers that protect my sanctum, but it is possible."

"Can we see him?" Summer asked.

"Sure," Mr. Stott said. He led them down a short hall to a modest room. Trevor sat on the edge of a futon.

"Hey, guys," Trevor said, brightening as Nate and Summer entered. "You're up late."

"How long have you been here?" Summer asked.

Trevor glanced over at a clock. "About four hours."

"You got here quickly," Summer said. "You ran?"

"Part of the way," Trevor said. "Not a lot. I took it easy at first. I needed some time to recover from pushing too hard back at the trailer park. Once I was feeling good, I used my speed to sneak into the back of a pickup truck."

"Couldn't you have just run the whole way?" Nate asked.

"In theory, I guess," Trevor said. "But even though to you guys I go super fast, to me I'm still moving at my normal speed. A long run is still tiring and boring. We must have been at least thirty miles from here. That's a long way to jog."

"So you used your speed to secretly hitch rides," Summer said.

"Pretty much," Trevor said. "Then I bailed when the cars went the wrong way. If I use my top speed, I'm faster than cars on the freeway. But I can only keep it up in short bursts, or it wipes me out."

"He took a risk," Mr. Stott said. "Until Trevor reached this sanctum, Jonas might have used the simulacrum to harm him at any time. Apparently Jonas didn't figure out that Trevor was on the run until after he found sanctuary here."

"So now he has to stay?" Nate asked.

"Or he risks magical retaliation," Mr. Stott said. "To exit this sanctum would leave him exposed."

"I'm worried that I'll get the rest of you in trouble," Trevor said. "If they track me here, it'll mean problems for Mr. Stott. And Jonas knows I was involved with Nate, Lindy, and Summer. He'll be watching all of us more carefully."

"It's a risk I'm happy to take," Mr. Stott said.

"Don't worry about it," Nate said. "I'd much rather take a little more heat than have you vanish like Pigeon."

"I worry about Pigeon too," Trevor said with frustration. "If I had let myself get caught, maybe I could have found him and helped him."

"More likely you'd just be in the same trouble as him," Lindy said.

"I'm worried about how far Jonas is getting in this search for Uweya," Summer said. "I helped take a map from a family that has guarded it for a long time. They seemed really worried about what would happen if Jonas found Uweya."

"I haven't been able to learn much about Uweya," Mr. Stott said. "I've consulted all of my usual resources, but there is almost no information about what it does or how it can be found. Jonas must have gone to great lengths to learn anything about it."

"I felt bad about taking the Gate from the Hermit," Nate said. "If all of this adds up to Jonas getting Uweya, I think we're doomed."

"What's your next mission?" Mr. Stott asked.

"Probably to get the Protector," Summer said. "The map we got will supposedly lead us to it."

"What is the Protector?" Mr. Stott inquired.

"I don't really know," Summer said.

"They'll tell us more when we get the mission," Nate guessed.

"Only two clubs left," Mr. Stott mused. "That would lead me to assume you are approaching the end of the treasure hunt."

"It feels that way," Summer said. "As far as we know, the next challenge after getting the Protector could be to find Uweya."

"Or you might just be gathering the tools Jonas needs," Mr. Stott speculated. "He may not involve the clubs in retrieving the actual prize."

"We need to start fighting back before it's too late," Nate said. "But how? With those wax statues, Jonas can take us down whenever he wants!"

"Watch for opportunities," Mr. Stott advised. "I'm working on a project that might be of service. I just hope I can finish it in time."

"New candy?" Nate said hopefully.

Mr. Stott nodded. "Something that might help you get around without Jonas using the simulacra against you."

"Has the Flatman seen anything useful?" Nate wondered, referring to the mutant that Mr. Stott kept floating in a shallow aquarium of formaldehyde. The Flatman had offered some useful predictions back when they were dealing with Belinda White.

"He has been silent of late," Mr. Stott said. "His activity has always been unpredictable. For now, your best bet is to keep playing along. I'll keep working on my new treat. But stay vigilant! Remember the Battiatos if you need backup. We need to find John and Mozag. And, at all cost, we need to keep Jonas White from obtaining Uweya."

* * * * *

Pigeon leapt to his feet when his cell door opened. Cleon looked in, wearing a red vest over a white shirt. "You want that shower?"

Pigeon had not yet left his cell. Living underground without windows, he found it tricky to judge how much time had passed. He estimated it had been more than a day. Whenever a meal was brought he asked for a shower. Until now, his keepers had not acknowledged his requests.

"Really?" Pigeon asked.

Cleon hooked a thumb in the front pocket of his jeans. "Nobody likes a smelly kid."

"Great," Pigeon said, wishing he felt less flustered by the opportunity. He was no fan of Cleon, but it was refreshing to see a familiar face. Pigeon had no prior association with either of the men who had brought his meals. "Do I have to wear handcuffs?"

Cleon chuckled. "That won't be necessary. Come on."

Pigeon walked out of the cell. So far, anxiety had been the worst part of his incarceration. The cell stayed at a livable temperature, the cot was reasonably comfortable, and the food tasted all right. Nothing was great, but nothing was horrible.

His biggest frustration had come from his inability to accomplish anything. He had hoped that becoming a prisoner might give him access to useful secrets, but so far all he had managed to do was sleep, eat, pace, and stew.

Cleon escorted him down the hall. Pigeon appreciated his ability to move his gaze around rather than having it fixed. He could not help noticing how far the hall extended in both directions, and how many cell doors it contained.

"Big prison," Pigeon said conversationally.

"Yeah," Cleon replied.

"Do you guys keep a lot of people here?"

"Not many," Cleon replied. "The boss doesn't do things halfway. There are whole wings that I doubt we'll ever use."

They turned a corner and Cleon led Pigeon to an unmarked door. "You'll have the whole place to yourself. I'll wait out here. I don't have all day. Make it snappy."

"I'll hurry," Pigeon promised. "Do I just put my same clothes back on?"

"For now, yeah," Cleon said. "We'll look into finding something else."

Pigeon passed through the door into a large locker room. Long fluorescent lights cast an even radiance onto the tile floor. He found soap, shampoo, conditioner, and a folded towel on a bench between rows of lockers. Proceeding to a large communal shower, Pigeon chose a nozzle and turned on the water. He checked the temperature with his hand and adjusted the knobs a couple of times, then stepped into the spray.

Despite the wide, eerily empty room and the guard waiting outside to return him to his cell, Pigeon felt his body relax as warm water gushed over him. With a small sniff, he tried to breathe the water and immediately began coughing. The sub stamp had worn off.

After a few moments wallowing in the relaxing sensation, he remembered his promise to Cleon and grabbed the soap. Pigeon hummed as he washed. Then he started singing. The echo off the bare walls helped his voice sound better than usual. He started getting into it, loudly singing the national anthem, until he imagined Cleon laughing at him out in the hall. Hopefully the door would serve to muffle his voice, but Pigeon decided not to take any chances.

When he finished, Pigeon shut off the water and grabbed his towel. The air felt cooler after the warm spray, so he hurried and pulled on his clothes while he was still too wet, causing his shirt and pants to stick uncomfortably to his skin. Once he was presentable, Pigeon exited the locker room to find Cleon waiting.

"How fast do you think you were?" Cleon asked.

"Pretty fast," Pigeon said.

"I thought you'd fallen asleep until you serenaded me," Cleon said.

"I liked the echo," Pigeon explained.

"I could tell," Cleon chuckled. "Let's get you back to that comfy cell. I bet you've got an echo in there, too. Have you tried it out?"

"I'm never singing again," Pigeon said, his cheeks hot.

"Don't squander your talent," Cleon said. "I think you've got a future! Next time you shower, I just might charge admission. Maybe we'll play a ball game afterward. Come on."

They began to retrace their steps to Pigeon's cell. When they reached Pigeon's hall, loud footfalls sounded behind them. Pigeon and Cleon turned at the same time.

A man charged down the hall toward them. A large man, with broad shoulders and a strong jaw. His shoes slapped the floor unapologetically. An unbuttoned overcoat flapped behind him like a cape. The man was not wearing his customary fedora, but it was definitely John Dart.

"Great," Cleon muttered. He gave Pigeon a shove that almost knocked him over. "Go to your cell."

Pigeon didn't obey. He wasn't about to miss a chance to see John.

Cleon stepped around the corner, out of John's view. Then Cleon suddenly teleported four feet to one side.

Pigeon blinked. "How'd you do that?"

Cleon waved him away. "Scram."

Pigeon could hear that John had almost caught up with them. He backed away a few paces.

John raced around the corner and without hesitation threw a hard punch at Cleon's face. The blow passed right through Cleon's head, as if he possessed no more substance than a hologram. The lack of contact left John off balance. Cleon lashed out with his leg, and even though the kick came nowhere near to striking John, the detective doubled over. A few feet to the side of John, Cleon punched. Without any visible impact, John staggered back.

John skipped several steps to one side and closed his eyes, knees bent, fists ready. "Go ahead, hit me again," John invited.

Cleon frowned. He stepped forward quietly, not directly toward John.

"He's coming," Pigeon said.

John shushed him. "I know."

"He's not where he seems to be," Pigeon said.

While John made a motion for Pigeon to keep silent, Cleon lunged forward and threw a punch that looked to have no chance of landing. John's head snapped back and he stumbled away, hands raised defensively.

"Keep talking, Pigeon," Cleon invited. "Stamp your feet. Sing us a song."

Pigeon realized that John had been relying on his ears to hear Cleon approach. Pigeon clamped both hands over his mouth.

John turned to face Cleon's voice, which originated from somewhere to the side of his visible mouth. As soon as Cleon stopped speaking, he slunk quietly to one side, stepping carefully.

John still had his eyes closed, apparently to avoid interaction with the distracting illusion. Pigeon felt tempted to explain where

Cleon was moving, but held his tongue. If John wanted to see, he could simply open his eyes.

"A little less bold this time," John said.

Cleon didn't respond. He was creeping forward, fists raised. Pigeon couldn't hear him.

Lunging to the left of John, Cleon threw another punch that didn't look like it could connect. John made a blocking motion and seemed to trap something invisible. He swung the invisible attacker into the wall, both men grunting with the impact.

The illusion of Cleon disappeared and his actual form became visible, his arm trapped by John. Cleon tried to twist away, but John landed a brutal punch that sent him sprawling. John flinched as he issued the blow, and blood began gushing from one nostril.

Pigeon winced. John had a huge disadvantage in any fight—he suffered any injury that he inflicted on another. If he broke some guy's arm, his arm broke as well. If John punched a guy, he received the same damage.

"If you wanted to hurt me, you should have just let me hit you," John said, wiping away blood with the back of his hand. "It would have saved us time."

A siren began to wail.

"He's on to you," Cleon said from the floor.

John kicked Cleon in the side, doubling over as he issued the blow. "This way, Pigeon," John grunted, running back the way he had come.

Pigeon followed as fast as he could. A hand to his side, John slowed his pace, allowing Pigeon to keep up.

"Hurry, Pigeon," John said. "We're both in danger."

"Where have you been?" Pigeon exclaimed.

"Here," John said. "Faster, Pigeon."

"This is my fastest."

Slowing, John scooped Pigeon up and heaved him over his shoulder. Then he sprinted down the hall, breathing hard, his footfalls echoing.

They turned a corner. Pigeon could hear angry shouts from behind. There were fewer doors in this hall, longer stretches of blank cement walls. John ran to an iron door, shoved it open, and staggered inside.

An old man closed the door. He was short, with bushy sideburns and a bald spot atop his head. It was Mozag.

John dumped Pigeon onto his feet, then slouched against the wall. Blood continued to drain from his nose, coming fast from one nostril and slow from the other.

"You cut it close," Mozag said. "I can feel it in the air. He's already working on your simulacrum."

"Close suffices," John said.

"What's going on?" Pigeon asked.

"Welcome to the resistance," Mozag said with a smile.

"The resistance?" Pigeon asked.

Mozag motioned at the surrounding apartment, which was much larger and better furnished than Pigeon's cell. "This is our special corner of Jonas White's prison. I've claimed it as my own."

Groaning, John pushed off the wall and walked out of the room. He returned with a washcloth held to his face. "Mozag made this an impromptu lair," John said with admiration. "A sanctum, actually. Few mages could have pulled it off. I don't think Jonas realized that such a feat was possible. No outside magic can touch us here. And nobody has managed to bother us. They learned quickly not to go up against a wizard like Mozag in his lair."

"They forgot about us," Mozag said. "Well, not completely. We haven't been aggressive lately. They stopped being careful—enough for John to make a foray and recover you."

"How did you know I was here?" Pigeon asked.

Mozag raised his eyebrows. "Wasn't easy. Once I cut this room off from outside magic, I couldn't reach out from here in most of the standard ways. Isolation was the price of security. But we have an ally here, an experienced magician named Tallah. She can blend incongruous magic like nobody else. She's a prisoner as well. Jonas let her establish her quarters as a provisional lair because he needs her magical expertise, but she has no sanctum."

"I haven't met her," Pigeon said.

"No," Mozag agreed. "One of her hobbies is creating tiny spies to prowl these halls. They look like mosquitoes or gnats. Delicate work. The barriers of my sanctum prevent her from reaching out to me directly, so she sends her miniscule spies to my door. They can't enter on their own, but we can bring them in ourselves. Crossing the barrier damages them, but once we have them inside, I'm able to revive them enough to experience what they've seen."

"Plus, the guy who brings our food is terrified of Mozag," John explained. "You have to understand, Mozag is both famous and infamous in the magical community. Nobody is eager to cross him. Our food guy delivers messages for us now and then to Tallah. Once we realized that you were here, we asked Tallah to monitor your specific door. She did, and a gnat made it here just in time for me to attempt a rescue."

"So when you came after me," Pigeon realized, "you'd left the safety of the sanctum behind."

"Temporarily, yes," John said. "Jonas no longer leaves guards on our door. We've found ways to harass them."

"We can open the door and throw things at them," Mozag chuckled.

"But Jonas monitors this hall, of course," John continued. "He just does it magically. He doesn't get around very fast. I was betting that I could snatch you and make it back here before Jonas arrived at my simulacrum."

"A very risky wager," Mozag mentioned. "If by chance Jonas had been close to John's simulacrum at the time, the rescue would have ended differently. After the trouble we've caused, given the chance, Jonas would probably just skip the lesser punishments and kill him."

"He could do that?" Pigeon asked in a small voice.

"Jonas White is a very gifted Simulcrist," Mozag said. "With simulacra of the quality that he possesses, not only could he kill us, he could probably reach out through us and harm the people we most love."

"Wow," Pigeon said. "Is there any way you could take him on?"

Mozag shook his head. "Not directly. Not here in his lair. Not with him in possession of our simulacra. That's why our strategy has been almost entirely defensive."

"Mozag can't leave this apartment or the sanctum would collapse," John said. "There is no permanence to it. This sanctum was created as an emergency measure without the necessary time, materials, or support. It is maintained more by his willpower than anything."

"Indirectly we might be able to serve a purpose," Mozag said. "Simulcry of the sort Jonas is performing with his wax figures requires a massive amount of magical power. Somewhere in his lair he is hiding a power source. If we could locate his Source, we would know how to break his hold on us."

"What about those gnats and mosquitoes?" Pigeon asked. "The little spies?"

"A good thought," Mozag said. "Tallah has tried. We're fairly certain Jonas keeps his Source in his sanctum. It's also where he keeps his wax figures. His waxworks factory is located here on this level, but no magic can penetrate it. To investigate, we would have to physically go there."

"Can we?" Pigeon wondered.

"In theory," Mozag said. "But the moment we set foot beyond this sanctum, we become vulnerable. The waxworks creation area is sealed by a stout door and protected by a monstrosity. It will not be an easy place to spy."

Pigeon sighed. "So for now there's not much we can do. We're trapped."

"For the present, yes," John agreed. He laid a large hand on Pigeon's shoulder. "Come sit down."

Pigeon noticed John wince, a faint tightening around his eyes. "You're still hurt."

"I'm all right. Part of the job. I might have overdone that kick to the side a little. It happens."

"You beat up Cleon pretty bad. He didn't chase us. How could you still run?"

John almost smiled. "I've been doing this for a long time, Pigeon. I've built up a high pain tolerance. I've learned to keep going despite my injuries. I know how much I can take, and I try not to dish out more than I can handle. I also have a physical advantage— even though I have to suffer any harm I inflict, I heal much faster than a normal person."

"You haven't healed yet," Pigeon noted, sitting down on a couch.

"Not yet," John agreed. "It'll pass."

"Would you care for some sunflower seeds?" Mozag asked.

"I'm all right," Pigeon said.

"Hummus?" Mozag tried. "Not the best, but edible. Or we could do popcorn. I have a microwave."

"Maybe later," Pigeon said. "How do you have all this food? Why doesn't Jonas starve you out?"

"He tried," John said. "He cut our power and water, didn't bring us food. Mozag can't work magic beyond this sanctum. But he can do a lot here. Mozag started shaking up the sanctum pretty hard. See the cracks in the walls? The magic didn't travel beyond the sanctum, but the physical shockwaves did. It felt like an earthquake through-out the building. Jonas couldn't have it interrupting business. So we struck a deal."

Mozag chuckled. "We got power, water, and food—and the tremors ceased."

"How did he catch you two in the first place?" Pigeon asked.

Mozag's face fell. "Don't remind me. It was a low point of my career."

"Mine too," John grumbled. "And it was my fault."

"I don't like to place blame," Mozag said. "John is an excellent operative. But if you demand that I speak candidly, yes, he's mostly to blame." Mozag winked at Pigeon.

"What happened?" Pigeon wondered.

"Jonas learned that I was here investigating him," John said. "He laid a trap. You remember Kyle Knowles?"

"Of course," Pigeon said. "He was one of the kids who helped Mrs. White. He got changed into an old man. You guys cured him."

"Kyle didn't set me up deliberately," John said. "He started visiting Arcadeland when it first opened. Jonas recognized that he had experienced some magical tampering. A trained eye could spot similar residual evidence on Nate. Jonas did some digging and suspected that Kyle had been connected to me and Mrs. White. He offered Kyle a job here—regular employment, no magic involved. Then he made a simulacrum of Kyle."

"Jonas really is an outstanding Simulcrist," Mozag inserted. "He can work some very nuanced enchantments."

"Tell me about it," John muttered. "He worked a subtle spell, using careful acupuncture on the simulacrum to put Kyle in a highly suggestible state. Sort of like hypnosis in the movies. He created a fictitious scenario that Kyle believed completely. Kyle unwittingly played right into his hands. He called me and asked for my help. He asked me to meet him in a vacant office not far from here. It was an ambush. They overwhelmed me, took my hat, and made a simulacrum of me."

"Tell him the rest," Mozag prompted.

"Jonas then did to me what he had done to Kyle," John grumbled. "In one of my greatest failures since I started working as a magical investigator, I lured Mozag here, and they trapped him."

"And they took my hat too!" Mozag complained, as if it were the biggest tragedy of all. "My Cubs hat! The one I magically reinforced to last indefinitely. They crafted a simulacrum of me. But before Jonas completed it, I freed John and turned this apartment into a sanctum. We've been here ever since."

"What was it like?" Pigeon asked John. "Being hypnotized?"

"I can hardly recall," John said. "It's like a half-forgotten dream. But the circumstances they planted in my mind felt completely authentic. I believed that I had escaped Jonas and was facing a desperate emergency where Mozag had to personally intervene. Trusting my judgment, Mozag came exactly where Jonas wanted him."

"And here we sit," Mozag said. "In some ways I'm glad to be here. I make it a point of knowing the different ways magic could obliterate the world. An unscrupulous magician gaining control of Uweya is one of the bleakest scenarios. I just wish I were in a better position to intervene."

"Nate, Summer, and Trevor are trying to help us," Pigeon said. "I'm glad you rescued me, John, but I'm worried that now Jonas will know for sure that we're all working against him."

"Will that be a problem?" John asked Mozag.

"Jonas does his homework," Mozag said. "He already knew Pigeon and the others had been involved with me, Sebastian, and John. He's using the four kids in spite of that knowledge. Who else is on our side, Pigeon?"

"Mr. Stott and Lindy are on the case as well, along with the Battiato brothers."

"Victor and Ziggy," Mozag said with a grin. "Not my most subtle operatives, but they can be quite effective."

"Do they know you're here?" John asked.

"I'm not sure," Pigeon said, pulling out his button. "They gave me this."

Mozag took it from him and held it up, examining it closely. "A very talented magician made this tracking beacon. Me. My sanctum is completely and unavoidably blocking the signal. The wards Jonas put in place would probably interfere with it as well. But I expect we could find a way to boost the transmission." Mozag closed his hand around the button. "Well done hanging on to this, Pigeon. It gives us hope."

"I'm glad," Pigeon said.

"Are you positive you don't want popcorn?" Mozag asked. "I have some real butter in the fridge."

Now that he was settling down, Pigeon already felt hungrier than he had before. "Sure, why not?"

CHAPTER SEVENTEEN

LIGHTHOUSE

Hovering in an upper corner of the room, Nate reflected that the training facility seemed much less busy when occupied by only two clubs. He kept catching the other Jets glancing nervously at the Tanks. It was one thing to watch the rival club sling around heavy weights and abuse punching bags, and another to see them perform the same workouts in fast-forward. The Jets knew they were in trouble. How were they supposed to match up against opponents who were both drastically stronger and considerably faster?

Nate hoped the next assignment would involve water. If not, their second stamp would be worthless. If so, by staying in the water and the sky, hopefully the Jets could partially negate the rival club's advantages.

"Nate!" Chris called. "Wake up!"

They were running a drill in which they practiced going from air to water and back to air again while retrieving rings. Nate stretched a fist ahead of himself and flew forward, curving near the wall to snatch a ring, then diving toward the pool. He broke the surface of the water, slowing only slightly as he skimmed the bottom to nab three more rings, then angled back up into the air, accelerating as he rose. His hair, skin, and clothes dried instantly, and he snagged a ring from the ceiling before joining the other Jets floating in the center of the room.

"Well done," Chris applauded. "You're getting the hang of this."

"I hope so," Nate said. "I don't envy those punching bags."

Derek currently thundered away at a heavy bag, his blurred fists attacking like machine-gun bullets. The bag jerked and jolted under the fierce onslaught.

"They can't fly," Risa reminded everyone. "And they can't torpedo through water."

"Hopefully that will matter," Nate said. "I don't want to be part of the next club that disappears."

"You guys still haven't seen Pigeon?" Chris asked.

"Not since his club lost," Nate said gloomily. He had started sharing some information about Pigeon's disappearance with Chris and Risa in hopes that they might eventually turn into true allies against Jonas. "His parents have no idea he's been gone. They've been eating Arcadeland tacos and nachos."

"I was paying more attention to my parents," Risa said. "You're right that they seem really distracted. I told them I was going to drive Dad's car to the mall and they told me to be careful. Mom even handed me the keys. It was like they had no idea how many years it'll be before I'm old enough to get a license."

"My parents are out of it too," Chris said. "Way more than usual."

"I tried to find the Racers this morning," Lindy said. "It was early, before dawn, and nobody was home."

"We need to keep our guard up on all sides," Nate said. "We know the Tanks will be gunning for us. But I'm not sure how much we can trust Jonas, either."

"You've worked with magicians like him before?" Risa asked.

Nate had only dropped some hints. He didn't want to risk telling them too much and having it get back to Jonas. "I have. Some are good, but I've met one who wanted to take over the world. To me, Jonas seems more like the scary kind."

"I definitely didn't like those wax statues," Risa admitted. "Truth? I almost bailed when I saw mine. I mean, how creepy is that?"

Cleon and Todd entered the building. The Jets gazed down at them, and the Tanks stopped exercising.

"Today?" Chris asked. "Already? These guys aren't messing around."

"Jonas wants his treasure," Nate murmured. "Let's go hear what they have to tell us."

Using their speed, the Tanks reached Cleon and Todd before the Jets, but not too far ahead. "What's up?" Roman asked.

"Mr. White wants to talk with both clubs," Cleon said. The whole area around his nose looked bruised.

"What happened to your face?" Chris asked.

Cleon tenderly rubbed his upper lip. "Basketball. I didn't see it coming until the last second."

"We shouldn't keep Mr. White waiting," Todd suggested.

They all followed Todd and Cleon out of the training facility and back to Arcadeland. They entered through a side door, and Todd led them to a conference room where Jonas White awaited, seated at the head of a long table. Katie Sung flanked him on one side, a muscular man with black spiky hair on the other.

Jonas gestured at the table. "Please, take a seat."

The Jets and Tanks sat on opposite sides of the table. The chairs were comfy and swiveled. Cleon and Todd remained in the room, standing near the door.

"Our competition is getting exciting," Jonas commented with a slow smile. "Two teams, both powered up more than ever. And the toughest mission yet lies ahead."

Jonas held up a smooth stone marble. "This is the guidestone the Tanks brought to me. Was it only yesterday? How can something so small change so much in such a short time? I have yearned to know the location of the Protector for ages, and now I do, thanks to this remarkable little wayfinder."

He placed the ball on the table, and it immediately rolled diagonally toward Katie Sung, who caught it as it fell off the edge. She handed it back to Jonas.

"Whenever we set the guidestone on a relatively flat surface," Jonas went on, "it rolls toward the Protector. Simple, elegant, and effective."

"Do we have to share it?" Roman asked, looking across the table at Chris.

"No," Jonas said. "The guidestone will go to the Jets."

"What?" Roman exclaimed, hopping to his feet. "How is that fair?" Derek had risen as well.

"I appreciate your competitive spirit," Jonas soothed. "However, I also appreciate order and decorum. Perhaps in the future you could allow me to offer a full explanation before issuing an objection."

Although Jonas remained calm and polite, Katie and the spiky-haired guy glared at Roman with naked disapproval. After glancing at Derek, Roman sat.

Jonas softly cleared his throat. "We have already used the guide-stone to trace a path to the Protector's hiding place. As I have long suspected, the location was not far from here. I have avidly studied these matters since well before your grandparents were born. Decades ago, I learned that the Protector resided within an ancient structure dubbed the Lodestar of the West, or the Great Western Pharos—a magnificent lighthouse somewhere on the western coast of North America. An ancient structure that had no business standing here, given all we know of the region's history."

"It's nearby?" Lindy asked.

"At first I was looking for ruins," Jonas said. "I found nothing. But then I realized a truth that the guidestone confirmed—the light-house is submerged."

Roman huffed, folding his arms, clearly frustrated. But he kept his mouth shut.

Jonas nodded at Roman. "As the Tanks recognize, this provides a certain advantage to the Jets, who now also share the attributes of the Subs. Please hold all complaints until after the full briefing. As you will see, the Tanks are not yet out of the running." Pushing against the arms of his chair, Jonas attempted to rise. He paused halfway up, trembling, and then managed to straighten. "Until now, your trials have been preparatory. I knew retrieving the Gate would provide a challenge, but I doubted that it would prove fatal. Same with the retrieval of the guidestone. That all changes with this assignment."

Nate leaned forward in his seat. All around him listened raptly.

"The Gate has changed hands many times over the centuries," Jonas related. "The Protector remains where it was first hidden, clev-erly guarded. Learning that the Graywater family held the secret to its location was the most difficult part of this entire puzzle. Through my research, I know some of the dangers that await. Having come this far, given the risk you will take, you ought to know some of what I have learned. But only if you mean to continue. Only if you are fully committed. This next assignment will be life-threatening. I do not make a habit of wasting my time. I believe you can succeed. But I will not compel any to proceed. If you wish to abandon the treasure hunt at this point, please let me know immediately."

Nate looked at Summer and Lindy. Many of the kids around the table exchanged wary glances. Nobody backed out.

"Very well," Jonas continued. "Once we have both the Gate and the Protector, we will be in position to go after Uweya itself. Claiming the Protector will be no easy matter. The Lodestar of the West is submerged off the coast of Yerba Buena Island in the San Francisco Bay. This is the island motorists encounter while traversing the Bay Bridge. It adjoins a man-made islet dubbed Treasure Island. Much of the area has been owned by the U.S. Navy, although naval operations there have decreased in recent years."

"How deep is the lighthouse?" Roman asked.

"The San Francisco Bay is not particularly deep," Jonas said. "At the same time, our lost monument must be fairly deep to have avoided discovery. The particulars are for the Jets to discover. They will let the guidestone lead them. Much about the guidestone remains a mystery to me. I know that the Graywater family has watched over it for generations. In my studies, I most often found it referenced as a map, but also as a key, a compass, a lodestone, and a simulacrum. Before this mission is over, the Jets will know more about the subject than I do."

"The first club to bring the Protector back to Arcadeland wins?" Nate checked.

"Correct," Jonas said. "But there is a catch. The Protector resides within an ancient chest. The chest is not light, and it will not open in close quarters. The Protector will be difficult to extract from the chest. I do not want the chest. I want the Protector."

"They won't be able to open the chest underwater?" Roman inquired.

"Very doubtful," Jonas said. "The chest is temperamental and dangerous. It was designed by Iwa Iza himself. According to legend, wherever it opens is where it will remain. I do not want it opened within ten miles of Arcadeland. I will provide a map to dispel any ignorance regarding that boundary. Failure to open the chest far enough away will result in disqualification. In addition, I want the chest opened in a remote area. The map also identifies areas I consider too close to civilization for opening the chest. Again, failure to comply will result in disqualification. Do we understand one another so far?"

Nobody dissented.

"The Jets begin with a decided advantage," Jonas said. "They get the guidestone, and they will enjoy a lack of competition retrieving the chest. To balance out this advantage, I have fashioned bracelets for the Jets to wear. Though unobtrusive, the bracelets will enable the Tanks to track their opponents."

"What?" Chris exclaimed.

"As if you get to whine," Roman snapped.

"Save it, Roman," Chris said. "The guidestone isn't an advantage. It just means the Jets have to do all the heavy lifting. How is it fair that after we salvage the chest from the lighthouse, you get to know where you can come to steal it?"

"Sounds about right to me," Derek said.

"How heavy is this chest?" Nate wondered. "Will we be able to move it far?"

"It will probably be heavy," Jonas said. "I don't know how far you'll be able to transport it."

"This is ridiculous," Chris muttered.

Roman shook his head. "You'll still have the advantage."

"Give me a break," Chris huffed. "Rested and ready, you get to swoop in and take something you couldn't have gotten yourselves."

"Enough debate," Jonas said. "These are the rules for this mission. There is no room for negotiation. Either participate or quit."

Silence followed the ultimatum.

"When do we start?" Nate finally asked.

"At nightfall," Jonas said. "Both clubs will set out from here tonight. The Tanks will have the same driver who took them to Devil's Shadow. He will go wherever they direct. They are free to abandon him at their discretion. The Jets will take to the sky. I'll wait for a winner to return with the prize."

"And if some of us die?" Summer asked.

"That's the risk," Jonas said. "Dismissed."

* * * * *

Around sunset, Summer cornered Roman outside of Arcadeland. Ruth and Derek had gone ahead to get dinner. She and Roman were supposed to catch up and eat with them, but Summer had failed to get him alone all afternoon and wasn't about to let the opportunity slip away. The Tanks looked to Roman for leadership, so she had to know where he stood regarding Jonas White.

"Roman, can we talk for a minute?" Summer asked.

"Can we do it over hamburgers?" he asked. "We're running out of time."

"Not really," she said. "It won't take long."

Roman leaned against the wall. "What's up?"

"How much do you trust Jonas White?" Summer asked bluntly.

Roman seemed at a loss for a moment. "Enough, I guess. He's held true to everything he's told us."

"You realize the Subs and the Racers didn't just lose," she said. "They disappeared."

"I asked about that," Roman said. "They're on special assignments. Prep work for those of us still in the game."

"Do you believe that?"

"Don't you?"

Summer realized that she was on dangerous ground. If she seemed too rebellious, and he doubted her loyalty, Roman might report her to Jonas. She could get left behind on the upcoming mission, unable to help anyone.

"I'm just worried," she said. "The Graywaters seemed sincere to me. I'm afraid that Jonas getting Uweya may not be a good thing."

"It's just some old treasure," Roman said.

"You know that isn't true," Summer countered. "You know magic is real. The things guarding Uweya are magical. Whatever Uweya is, it's powerful, and I'm not sure Jonas White has given us any reason to believe he's a very good person."

"You think he's the bad guy?" Roman said. "You think we're the evil henchmen?"

"I think we could accidentally end up helping the bad guys if we're not careful," Summer said. "Did you feel like one of the good guys back at the trailer park?"

"How do you know the Graywaters were so good?" Roman said. "What if Uweya could do a lot of good but they're keeping it hidden?"

"Well, I know they didn't send anybody to break down our doors and steal our stuff. And they didn't try to hurt us when they could have. They didn't make creepy statues that can control us, or send kids on life-threatening missions."

"Do you want out?" Roman asked with some heat in his tone. "Is that what this is about? Nobody is making you go, Summer. The three of us will be just fine."

"It isn't that," Summer said. "I'm just not sure we should deliver Uweya to Jonas."

"You think we should keep it?"

"Maybe nobody should have it," Summer said.

"Look," Roman said, "we wouldn't even know about Uweya if it weren't for Mr. White. If we don't get it for him, somebody else will. Which means somebody else will be Tank Racers, or maybe flying Tank Racers, and we'll be back to normal. I agreed to this treasure hunt, and I'm going to fulfill my agreement. Whatever else I think about Mr. White, one thing seems certain to me—he's not the kind of guy you double-cross."

"I guess you're right," Summer said, feeling nothing of the sort. "I'd hate to lose my stamps."

"I'm sure this will be intense," Roman said, "but what can happen to us? We're super fast and almost impossible to hurt. If we work together, we'll be fine."

"I hope so," Summer said. "Thanks for talking me through it. Part of my problem is that I'm nervous."

"No sweat, I get it. Should we grab those burgers before it gets too late?"

"Sure."

Summer had talked to Nate earlier. He felt confident that Chris and Risa were beginning to distrust Jonas. Plus he had a sure ally in Lindy. As she walked toward dinner with Roman, Summer determined that whatever else happened tonight, she needed to make sure the Tanks didn't win.

* * * * *

Nate flew beside Lindy above SR-24, gaining altitude over the hills where the freeway disappeared into the Caldecott Tunnel. He could hardly believe they were about to plunge into the San Francisco Bay in search of hidden treasure. He wondered if the Tanks were behind them on the road, heading toward Yerba Buena Island, or if they had some other strategy.

The Jets had consulted the map and decided that if the chest was too heavy to fly far, they would transport it to Angel Island. The Tanks had a driver, but getting to the island would surely prove problematic. Of course, if the chest was light enough, they would simply fly it an absurd distance into the wilderness.

Having studied the map, the Jets had no trouble following SR-24 until it met up with I-580, and then continuing to I-80 and the Bay Bridge. The Jets flew high over the water, staying well away from the bridge. Dressed in dark clothes, gliding far from any lights, Nate felt invisible. From his lofty vantage above the bay, the gleaming spires of the San Francisco skyline looked beautiful. A cool breeze filled his nostrils with the humid smell of the sea.

Some distance from Yerba Buena Island, the Jets joined together in a hovering huddle. Risa held a large bowl, and Chris put the guidestone inside. They watched the stone marble roll to a certain side of the bowl, then moved off in that direction. After they had checked several more times, the guidestone finally settled squarely in the bottom of the bowl.

"We should be right over it," Chris said.

"It feels like the stone is tugging downward," Risa said.

Nate looked down at the black water of the bay. "I guess we'll get a better sense of things once we're underwater."

"Too bad Jonas didn't have waterproof night vision gear," Risa said.

"We can perceive everything just fine underwater," Chris said.

"Right, I meant for after we come up," Risa explained.

"We have Lindy," Nate said. "She'll be enough."

"I see it," Lindy reported. "The top is barely poking above the floor of the bay."

"You see the lighthouse?" Chris asked dubiously.

"Remember how she tracked the Hermit?" Nate asked. "Just trust her. She sees really well. Even through water in the dark."

"Down we go," Chris muttered.

They flew down and plunged into the water. Suddenly Nate had a precise sense of the floor of the bay and the sea life swimming around him. So far, he had sampled his Sub abilities only in the training facility pool. The capacity to perceive the surrounding environment in open water was a totally different experience. The vivid sensory input was almost too much to process.

Gliding down through the water felt different from flying through the air. The basics remained the same, but everything was slowed down. Not only was his top speed reduced, but it was tougher to accelerate. At least he could make tighter turns.

The temperature seemed perfect. Breathing the water felt no

different from breathing air. His eyes saw less, but his perception of his surroundings remained effortlessly detailed.

The water here was neither terribly shallow nor shockingly deep. The bay floor was dozens of feet down, but not nearly a hundred. As Lindy had described, the top of the stone lighthouse protruded from the silt.

"It's big," Nate said, his voice carrying clearly through the water.

"Huge," Lindy said. "This is just the tip."

"It seems more like the roof of a building than the top of a tower," Chris said. "It's too big around."

"It's a tower," Lindy assured them. "It goes a long way down."

"Really?" Risa said. "You can see through sand?"

"Pretty much," Lindy replied.

"How do we get in?" Nate asked.

"We dig," Lindy said. "There are openings into the tower not far below."

"The guidestone is pulling me," Risa said. "I think the attraction is increasing as we get closer."

"Can you feel those sharks?" Chris asked.

"Yeah," Nate said. Several prowled the water near the edge of his perception, the largest around six or seven feet long. "They don't seem interested in us."

"If they come this way, I'm out of here," Risa said emphatically. "I won't mess with sharks. Not for any reason. I'll fly home and go to bed. I'm serious."

"Where do we dig?" Chris asked as they neared the exposed portion of the tower.

"This side," Lindy said, pointing. "It'll get us to an opening fastest."

Nate plunged his hands into the silt and began scooping it away. The others worked alongside him, sending up clouds of fine particles. At first their progress was hard to measure, but as they kept working, a definite hole began to form. As they burrowed deeper, a large quantity of sand collapsed inward through a gaping window.

"I guess we loosened it up," Nate said.

"Whoa," Chris said. "I can feel it now. The inside of the tower."

Nate instantly recognized that Chris was right. Now that the barrier of sand had been removed, Nate could sense the water extending down to the base of the tower. He could feel the stone stairs winding down the enormous tube.

"It's solid stone," Nate realized.

"Yeah," Chris agreed. "I don't feel blocks. No bricks or anything. No mortar. It's one big hollow rock."

"I don't want the guidestone anymore," Risa said. "It's tugging too hard. I don't trust it."

"I'll take it," Nate offered.

Risa handed it over. He noticed the pull immediately. Until this moment, Nate had never felt anything unusual while holding the stone. Now the tug was unmistakable.

"After you," Chris said.

Nate drifted into the lighthouse. "I don't sense anything alive," Nate said. "There's nothing moving,"

Chris agreed. "Stay ready for traps."

"Can you feel how the tower widens out down at the bottom?" Lindy asked. "Like it finally reaches a really large room."

"I feel it," Risa confirmed. "Really big. Lots of space."

"But no giant squids," Nate said. "No sea serpents."

"I don't feel anything like that," Lindy said.

Nate started gliding down the stairs at a gentle pace. They had a long way to go, but he didn't want to hurry too much and blunder into a trap.

"This is perfect darkness," Chris said. "It makes no difference whether my eyes are open or shut. I've never seen anything to match it."

"I almost can't appreciate it," Nate said. "I can tell that my eyes see only blackness, but I sense everything even better than when I have full sight. That sense almost becomes sight in my head, even though I see nothing."

"Not for me," Chris said. "I can feel everything, but it's way different from sight. It's more like touch. It's like my nerves extend into the water. I feel whatever the water feels."

"I can feel and see," Lindy remarked.

"No surprise there," Risa said. "You see better than Superman. Should we speed it up? The Tanks will be after us."

"We don't want to hit traps," Chris cautioned.

"What traps are we going to hit?" Risa argued. "We're not touching the floor or the walls. We'd feel tripwires coming long before we reached them."

"She has a point," Nate conceded. "I'll hurry more."

As they wound deeper into the lighthouse, the guidestone pulled harder than ever, not with overpowering force, but certainly insistent. Nate suspected that if he let it go, the stone would zoom directly to the Protector.

"Finding the Protector should be easy," Nate commented. "The stone will haul us straight there."

"I hope so," Chris said. "I don't want to stay here long. This would be a lonely place to die."

"Shut up, Chris," Risa said.

"Our bodies would be lost forever," he said.

"I'll leave," Risa warned. "Don't mess with me like that."

"The one who freaks out and leaves is usually the first to get taken," Chris assured her.

"Don't let him scare you," Nate said. "This is more cool than scary. Think how ancient this lighthouse must be. We're probably the first people to come here in thousands of years."

"It'll be cooler once it's a memory," Lindy said quietly.

They continued deeper. When the space widened out, it did so dramatically. The lighthouse must have had a huge building at the base. Nate could feel multiple large rooms. Trying to find the Protector would have felt really daunting had the guidestone not kept tugging him in an obvious direction. Soon it was dragging him along with enough force that he questioned whether he could bring himself to a standstill.

"You keep going faster," Chris noted.

"It's the guidestone," Nate explained.

"I think I feel the chest," Risa said. "Farther ahead on the path we're on."

"You're right," Nate realized. "We're almost there."

"I see it," Lindy said. "It's pretty. I can't see inside of it."

Nate felt the chest coming closer. It rested alone on a platform. As the stone pulled harder, Nate began to worry that his hand would get crushed if he kept hold of it. Just before he reached the chest, Nate let go of the stone. The guidestone thumped softly against the chest.

"It changed shape," Lindy said.

Nate could sense the transformation. He reached out and

grabbed the new incarnation of the guidestone. It no longer seemed drawn to the chest. It had grown somewhat. "It turned into a tiny replica of the chest," Nate said.

"The chest is pretty big," Chris observed.

"What's it made of?" Lindy asked.

"Wood, maybe?" Nate said. "Worn really smooth? With jewels in it?"

"Is it clay?" Chris wondered. "Some type of ceramic?"

"It's definitely smooth," Risa said. "I don't feel any cracks. It's shaped like a chest, but I can't tell where it opens."

"No hinges," Lindy agreed. "No keyhole. Not the tiniest crack. It's like it has no lid."

"The little replica has a lid," Nate said. "I can feel the lid."

"Right," Chris agreed. "Me too. It seems obvious on the guidestone."

Nate tried to open the replica. The lid wouldn't budge. "It's locked."

"Mr. White didn't think we could open it underwater," Chris reminded him. "We can give it a better try when we get it out of here. Should we see if we can move it?"

"Lindy?" Nate said. "Would you hold the replica?"

"Sure," she said, accepting the transformed guidestone.

Chris went to one side of the chest, Nate to the other.

"Moving the chest could set off a trap," Nate said.

"True," Chris acknowledged. "Everybody get ready for trouble."

"Go for it?" Nate asked.

"Why not?"

They lifted together. Nate found the chest a bit lighter than he expected. It had a fair amount of weight to it and was pretty bulky, but overall it felt manageable. Nothing indicated that lifting it had triggered any sort of trap.

"How is it?" Risa asked.

"Could be worse," Chris said. "Let's get out of here."

Advancing through the water, Nate and Chris carried the trunk back to the tower and started gliding up the stairs. Risa and Lindy followed.

Taking the chest up the tall tower didn't particularly fatigue Nate. Once they got some momentum going, the effort almost felt more mental than physical. They just kept toting the chest upward, keeping away from the stairs, walls, and ceiling.

At last they emerged from the lighthouse and brought the chest up to the surface of the bay. The air felt empty and dark after the vivid sensations available underwater.

Lindy and Risa surfaced nearby.

"So far, so good," Lindy said.

"Should we try to fly with it?" Chris asked.

"Sure," Nate said.

With the chest between them, Nate and Chris ascended out of the water. They hadn't risen more than ten feet before Nate's arms were trembling with exertion. The boys stopped rising, and Chris's side of the chest dipped. Nate lost his grip, as did Chris, and the chest splashed down into the water.

Nate dove down and stopped the chest from sinking clear to the bottom. Chris took hold of the other side. The girls gathered near.

"It's too heavy to go far," Nate said.

"It isn't bad underwater," Chris noted. "We could take it through the water to Angel Island. Then we would just have to fly it a little ways to a quiet spot."

"Alcatraz is closer," Lindy said, "but Jonas nixed that as a destination, along with Treasure Island and Yerba Buena."

"He left Angel Island as fair game," Chris said. "The Tanks will have a tough time getting there. Let's go see if we can open this thing."

CHAPTER EIGHTEEN

THE CHEST

Working together, with one of them at each corner, Nate, Chris, Lindy, and Risa managed to fly the chest a few hundred yards inland from the Angel Island shore, crossing a small road and struggling some distance up a brushy slope. When they reached their limit and let the chest thump down, it struck the ground with finality.

Risa rubbed her hands briskly. "I lost circulation to my fingers."

"That thing was heavy," Chris said, stretching his arms. "This spot seems as remote as anywhere."

Nate ran a hand over the top of the chest, then down the side. Unlike his body, the chest remained damp. "I still can't feel how to open it. I can't even tell whether it's wood or ceramic or what."

"I can sort of see it with the moonlight," Chris said. "The color is darker than I realized. But I had a much better sense of it back in the water."

"Let me get out the guidestone," Lindy offered. She had stashed it in her backpack so she could help carry the chest. "Maybe it has a key inside."

"The chest has no keyhole," Risa pointed out.

"Well, maybe there's something else in it," Lindy said, rummaging. "It seems suspicious that the guidestone turned into a miniature chest. At least the little replica has a lid."

Lindy produced the tiny chest and started prying at it with her fingers. "It's stuck, but the lid has some wiggle to it. Wait, here we go." She lifted the small lid, and simultaneously the top of the chest folded open as well. And then the chest kept unfolding in astonishing ways, as if lid after lid were opening in unpredictable directions. With a startled squeal, Lindy dropped the miniature chest as it transformed as well, mimicking the larger version.

"Whoa," Nate breathed, taking involuntary steps back as the chest grew and evolved with each new lid that lifted. The unfolding process sped up. Strange new shapes unfolded manically, expanding the chest to improbable proportions.

When the process ended, Nate found himself staring at the entrance to a stone building that extended back into the slope. The structure stood three times his height, with a triangular pediment supported by pillars. Because of how the building protruded from the slope, it looked as if it had been mostly buried in a landslide. A massive bronze door shielded the entrance.

"That was awesome," Chris said.

"More like freaky," Risa replied.

"I can't see inside," Lindy said. "Same as with the chest."

Nate crouched, pointing at the ground. "Look, the guidestone matches the chest's new shape. It's even partly buried."

"What's with the guidestone?" Chris asked.

"It must be some sort of simulacrum," Nate said. "I think touching it to the chest activated it."

"Opening the guidestone chest made the actual chest transform," Lindy said.

"So what happens if we open the little door?" Risa worried. "Will it change again? Will it turn it into a spaceship?"

"Let's try the actual door first," Chris suggested. He walked to the entrance of the building and tugged on the bronze door. It didn't budge. Planting himself firmly, he pulled hard but still got no result.

"It might take them some time, but the Tanks are coming," Nate said. "We should probably try the little door."

Lindy crouched and opened the door of the small building. The door to the large building opened in perfect synchronization. Nate was braced for something more, but nothing else happened.

Risa, Nate, and Lindy joined Chris at the entrance. Nate could see a long, shadowy hall with seamless stone walls. Light shimmered in the distance.

"Big chest," Chris said, the words gently echoing down the corridor.

Nate snorted softly. "A building in a box. It's kind of like the Hermit making a boat or a barn using some junk in his backpack. Weird magic."

"Let's go find the Protector," Lindy said.

"She's right," Chris agreed. "We should hurry." He bent down to grab the guidestone, only to find it solidly stuck in the ground. "It won't budge," he said.

"We'll have to leave it," Nate said.

"That means we can't keep the Tanks out," Chris said.

"Then, like you said, we should hurry." Rising off the ground,

Nate glided forward. The others followed his lead. The air was cool and still. Glancing back, Nate saw his fellow Jets hovering along the dark corridor, their feet dangling. They looked like phantoms. From up ahead, Nate heard a distant, steady pounding, supplemented by whirring murmurs and rhythmic squeals.

"Hear that?" Risa asked.

"Sounds like a big machine," Chris said.

"A machine?" Lindy questioned. "In here? This place looks pre-historic."

Nate increased his pace.

"Be ready for traps," Chris warned.

Nate slowed a little. He could no longer feel everything the way he had in the water. All it would take was him brushing up against a tripwire in the gloom to trigger some serious trouble.

Up ahead, the hallway elbowed left. Golden light reflected from beyond the turn. The pounding, swooshing, squeaking, whirring sounds grew louder. When Nate reached the corner he stopped, then looked back at the others. "I think I found the traps."

The hall stretched ahead of him, a chaos of moving parts, the scene lit by lamps embedded in the walls. Razor-sharp pendulums whisked back and forth at high speeds. Deadly blades whipped out of slots in the walls, ceiling, and floor, disappearing only to return, some alternating their vicious swipes, others twirling like propellers. Sharp spears erupted out of deep sockets, thrusting and retracting at a disheartening pace. Toward the far end of the corridor, large pillars pistoned up and down, pounding the floor with implacable force. The other Jets joined Nate, staring down the lethal corridor in despair.

"You've got to be kidding me," Chris muttered.

"It'll be like flying through a blender," Risa said.

"Like flying through fifty blenders," Nate said, surveying the lethal obstacles. "It doesn't matter that we can fly. There are as many traps up high as down low. If we don't get shredded into pasta, we'll get crushed into paste."

"There must be a pattern to it," Lindy said.

"There's a pattern," Chris agreed. "Look at any specific part of the corridor. That pillar just goes up and down, same every time. That spike pokes in and out, over and over. That huge blade swings side to side. But the pattern is designed not to let anything through. We might dodge the first few blades, but then what? It's the length of a football field!"

"Afterward we'd have to come back," Risa pointed out.

"Is there a path through it?" Nate asked. "Like if we start on the lower right, then fly along the upper left side, then in the center, that sort of thing?"

They considered the passage together. Light glinted off sharp points and slashing blades. Nate traced possible routes through the obstacle course.

"They covered everything," Chris said. "High and low, left and right, down the middle. The only hope would be to dodge and dodge and dodge perfectly for a really long time."

"No way," Risa said. "We'd have a better chance if we got flushed through a garbage disposal. Or caught under a lawn mower. Or sucked into a jet engine. Or—"

"We get it," Lindy interrupted. "You're not wrong. What do we do?"

"The Tanks would be suited for this," Nate realized. "They can move super fast, and, even if they messed up, they might survive the damage."

"Good for them," Chris said bitterly. "How does that help us?"

"Somebody has to get the Protector," Nate said. "If we go after it, we'll find out what our insides look like."

"You think we should let them have it?" Risa asked.

"I think we should let them *get* it," Nate said. "Kind of like how they let us bring the chest up from the lighthouse. I'm not saying we should let them keep it."

Chris shook his head. "They're too strong and fast. Once they have it, we'll never get it back."

"Our whole strategy is built around never letting them catch up," Lindy said.

"That was before we knew we'd have to go through a meat grinder," Nate said. "Killing ourselves isn't an option. Look at that hallway! We'd be lunch meat in seconds! But that doesn't mean we have to give up. On land, we'd never get the Protector from the Tanks. Our advantage is in the air and in the water. We're on an island. We'll have a chance when they leave."

"They might be in a boat," Chris said.

"Then we sabotage it," Nate said. "We sink it."

"They'd still be strong and fast in the water," Risa said.

"But they'll need to breathe," Nate said. He paused, aware that they were trying to recover the final object Jonas White would need to claim Uweya. Obviously they needed to beat the Tanks. But if they succeeded, what then? The time had come to find out whether Chris and Risa would assist with his real mission. "We need to talk about something."

"What?" Chris said.

"Jonas White is a bad guy," Nate said.

"Well," Chris replied uncomfortably, "he's kind of scary."

"Not just scary," Nate said. "Not just intimidating. Not just bossy. Evil. Jonas White is not the only magician in the world. Some are good, some are in between, and some are really bad. I fought a magician who was trying to take over everybody in Colson. It was Mr. White's sister."

"Does that make him evil?" Risa asked.

"She used a treat called white fudge to tame everyone," Nate said. "It was addictive and made them oblivious to her magic. With his nacho cheese, Jonas is using a similar trick to mess with our parents and many other people. There's a magical police force that protects the world from evil magicians. Jonas White captured their leader along with one of their best detectives and is holding them prisoner. I'm here undercover. I've been investigating the arcade to help them. Same with some of my friends."

"It's all true," Lindy said. "I know about it too. To make matters worse, Jonas White is also making the kids from the losing clubs disappear. His people may tell us they gave them special assignments, but what are nonmagical kids going to do? And why would the kids completely vanish?"

"What do you want us to do?" Chris asked.

"We need to stop Jonas from getting Uweya," Nate said. "He's a bad guy, and it's really powerful. If he succeeds, it won't just be bad for us. It'll be bad for the whole area. Maybe even the whole world."

"Mr. White has those simulacra of us," Risa said. "How could we fight him?"

"We'll have to worry about that later," Nate said. "First I need to know whether I can count on you. I haven't told you guys much about this yet because I couldn't risk you warning Mr. White. But I can't be careful anymore. We're running out of time. The powers

Jonas White gave us are fun, but once he has what he wants, he'll get rid of us. He's not our friend."

"I believe you, Nate," Chris said. "It makes a lot of things make sense. Is Lindy a magician too? Is that why she sees so well?"

Lindy shook her head. "I have a fake eye. The magician who Jonas captured gave it to me. It sees better than a normal eye."

"Risa?" Nate asked.

"I'll help," she said. "I was stressed he might be evil ever since I saw my wax twin."

"We have to get the Protector from the Tanks," Nate said. "Summer is on our side, but she doesn't think she can get the other Tanks to turn against Mr. White. Which means if we want to stop him, we first need to beat the Tanks."

"Do you have a plan?" Chris asked.

"I think so," Nate said. "It depends on what supplies we can find in time."

He started flying back toward the entrance of the magical structure. The others followed. They emerged onto the slope of Angel Island, with a prime view of the San Francisco skyline.

"Oh, no," Lindy said in a loud whisper. "We need to hide. The Tanks are on the island, coming straight toward us. They're almost here!"

* * * * *

"This way!" Roman said excitedly, his eyes on the little compass that pointed toward Nate's bracelet. "We have to catch up before they get it!"

Summer glanced at her compass, which was attuned to Lindy. As they ran along the slope, the needle swiveled more than ever, forcing more frequent course corrections, which meant they had to be close. She worried that Nate hadn't had enough time to get the Protector. Roman had made an educated guess, and it was about to pay off.

While studying the map before the challenge began, Roman had pointed out Angel Island almost immediately. "They know we're in a car. They like the water and we don't. It's not far from Yerba Buena Island. Jonas left it as an option. If I were them, and the chest was heavy, I'd go there."

"And if the chest isn't heavy?" Derek had challenged.

"We lose," Roman said. "They'll fly it someplace really far. We'll still try to track them down, but I bet we won't make it."

And so when the competition had started, Roman had directed the driver to head straight to Tiburon. The town of Tiburon occupied a peninsula that ended less than a mile from Angel Island. The Tanks had crossed the Bay Bridge, then passed over the Golden Gate Bridge, continuing until they reached Tiburon and drove to the end of the peninsula.

At the tip of the peninsula, their compasses had pointed toward Angel Island. Derek had talked about stealing a boat, but Roman had insisted they couldn't risk the attention. Instead they swam across the gap to Angel Island. As Tanks, they were heavier than normal, but between her increased speed and her enhanced strength, Summer had found that she could swim a little better than usual. The others had felt the same way. Even so, the crossing had been scary in the dark. But they had made it, and now, clothes dripping, they were closing in on the Jets.

"Whoa," Ruth said. "They're moving."

"My compass is going nuts too," Derek said.

"My needle is turning too quickly," Roman said. "They must be nearby, in the air." He frantically looked skyward.

Summer looked up as well. She saw no flying kids in the moonlight. They would probably be hard to see unless they crossed directly in front of the moon. "Do they have the Protector?" she asked.

"If they do, we lost," Roman growled, increasing to maximum speed.

Summer and the other Tanks sped up to stay with him. Being a Tank gave Summer extra strength and endurance, but she still felt the draining effects of running at top speed. She did not expect she could keep it up for more than a minute or two without getting totally wiped out.

Roman had stopped, and she came to a standstill beside him. He was facing a strange stone building that protruded from the slope. A miniature replica of the building jutted from the slope in front of the open bronze door. They shifted down to race mode.

"Looks like they came and went," said Summer, feeling huge relief at the thought that the Jets might be under way with the Protector in their care.

Roman looked down at his compass. "They didn't fly toward Arcadeland. At least not Nate. He went back toward Tiburon."

"Risa too," Ruth said.

"And Chris," Derek chimed in. "Maybe we scared them off. Maybe they're running."

"The Racers tried the same thing," Roman said. "Once they saw us coming, they let us do the hard part, then tried to steal the prize. Let's hope the Jets are equally stupid. Come on."

Roman led the way into the long hallway. Summer could see light glimmering toward the end of the passage.

"What is this place doing here?" Derek wondered.

"It must have something to do with the chest," Roman said. "Maybe the chest led them here. This building sure doesn't seem to belong."

"Hear that?" Summer asked.

"Are those drums?" Roman wondered.

"Not just drums," Derek said. "Listen."

"Let's check it out," Roman said.

They charged down the hall at top speed. By the time they reached the corner, Summer was breathing hard. Shifting down to race mode, she stared in amazement at the assortment of whirling blades, stabbing spikes, and pounding pillars.

"Could they have flown through this?" Derek wondered.

Roman glared at the deadly obstacles for a moment. "No way. Even at top speed, we'll have a tough time. If they had tried, they'd be splattered all over the walls."

"I think you're right," Summer said, trying to hide her disappointment. Even with everything three or four times slower than usual, some of the blades were moving quite fast. She couldn't see a route she would take to fly through the sharp-edged maze. Nate almost certainly didn't have the Protector. She would have to find a way to deliver it.

"Then we just need to claim our prize," Roman said.

"Might not be easy," Ruth remarked.

Roman grunted his agreement. "No point in all of us risking it. Should we draw straws?"

"I'll do it," Summer said. If she had possession of the Protector, she might find a chance to get it to Nate.

"Really," Roman said, impressed. "You're volunteering?"

Summer shrugged. "I've always liked a challenge. I'm a Tank. At worst I'll get pushed around a little."

Roman eyed the frenetic corridor. "I don't know, Summer. I wouldn't want to test myself against those mashers down at the end."

"Or some of those blades," Derek added. "They look sharp and they're swinging hard."

"I wouldn't ride through there in an actual tank," Ruth said.

"I get it," Summer said. "I'm not thrilled about the risk. But we need the Protector. At top speed I bet I can dodge everything."

"Okay," Roman said. "Be careful."

"Give me a second to recover," Summer said. "We shouldn't have run here so quickly."

"Take your time," Roman said. "Ruth, go watch the entrance. Make sure the Jets don't try to sneak up on us."

"Sure," Ruth said. Summer watched her walk away, her shoulders hunched. Ruth rarely spoke much. She always followed whatever Roman told her.

"I'll come help out if you get into trouble," Roman said, patting Summer's arm.

"We'll be watching your back," Derek pledged.

Summer stared down the deadly corridor. She felt like she had most of her energy back. When she switched into her fastest mode, the frenzy of blades and spears slowed. Nothing was terribly fast now, and many things were comically slow. Some stretches of the corridor still appeared dangerous, but now it seemed survivable.

She started forward. At first she advanced diagonally, zigzagging down the corridor, navigating from one side to the other while stepping over blades and dodging razor pendulums. Then she reached a portion of the hall riddled with holes. Spears thrust from the walls, ceiling, and floors fast enough to make her dance forward in a precarious rush. Twisting, sliding, and leaping, she narrowly avoided sharp points as they came up from below, down from above, and sideways from all heights.

The next stretch of the obstacle course became a mix of everything. Slow pendulum blades got in the way as other blades scythed out from the walls and floors. Jack-in-the-box spikes continued to poke at her in unpredictable rhythms. Axes swung back and forth menacingly.

At their seemingly reduced speed, any one of the obstacles would have been avoidable, but together they made Summer duck, jump, dodge, and contort as never before. The result felt like a wild game of hopscotch and dodge ball all at once. Breathing hard, Summer relied on instinct and reflex. She felt out of control as she spun, rolled, and lunged. Her progress slowed as the increasing onslaught of obstacles forced her to skip backward or focus on lateral movements rather than advance.

A blade nicked her shoulder, slicing her sleeve but not her skin. A spear grazed her leg, tearing her jeans. Staying at top speed was making her weary. After jumping a curved blade, she fell to one knee, and a spear poked her square in the shoulder, jolting her sideways into a sweeping blade that flung her forward.

Summer ended up on her hands and knees. Before she could recover, a spike from the wall hit her in the side of the head, rolling her onto her back. None of the blows had broken skin, but they felt like hard punches, and they left her unbalanced.

Summer could feel exhaustion setting in. She worried that if she remained at top speed, she might pass out. Rising to her feet, Summer shifted down into race mode.

Everything sped up around her. The formerly slow pendulums became a threat, and everything else became too quick to process. Summer skipped forward a couple of steps before she started getting hit from what seemed like all directions at once. Her body flopped around the corridor. It was like being caught in a stampede. There was no dodging anymore. She just closed her eyes and tucked her head as her body was mercilessly hammered. She was heaved forward and backward until she lost all sense of which direction was which.

Finally she came to a rest, flat on her back. Blades whirled above her. Spears protruded and retracted near her. But nothing was currently striking her.

Summer downshifted out of race mode, and everything sped up even more. Still nothing hit her. She had found a safe little pocket in the midst of all the chaos.

"Are you all right?" Roman called, his voice faint due to the surrounding commotion. "Want us to come after you?"

"I'm okay," Summer managed. She was over halfway through the inhospitable hallway. She wasn't bleeding. She felt pummeled and dizzy, but she didn't think anything was broken. "I found a quiet place. I need to rest for a minute."

Slowly her breathing returned to normal. Her clothes were tattered—her jeans had lost most of one leg, and both of her sleeves hung in shredded ribbons. At least her body was holding up.

Pressing her cheek to the floor, Summer closed her eyes. She needed to let herself fully recover from running at top speed or she would end up getting battered again. There was no big hurry. In fact, the delay was probably just what Nate needed. It would give him time to strategize how to steal the Protector from the Tanks.

Mostly unaware of the passing time, Summer paid attention to how her body was feeling. The dizziness passed. Her heart rate lowered. Her breathing slowed. Still she waited.

"Are you awake?" Derek asked. It was hard to hear him over the pounding pillars and noisy devices all around.

"If we hadn't run so much at top speed for no reason, I wouldn't need a break," Summer replied.

"We're just making sure you're all right," Roman said. She didn't think that was completely true. They were getting impatient.

"You're welcome to go get it," Summer said. "I can just come back."

"You're doing great," Roman said.

"Did it hurt?" Derek called.

"It was like getting punched and tackled a lot," Summer said. "I felt it, but I didn't get cut or break any bones. I'm not even very sore anymore."

"You were really getting thrown around," Roman said.

"I could tell," Summer replied. "I'm almost ready to try again."

She took deep breaths, trying to gauge how rested she felt. It seemed like she was mostly recovered. She was almost two-thirds of the way down the corridor. She figured she had enough energy to at least make it to the end.

Summer shifted into race mode. Everything slowed. She shifted up to her fastest state, and everything slowed again.

She rolled forward, then rose to her knees. After leaning back to avoid a spear, she regained her feet and dashed forward. Once again she skipped, hopped, ducked, and dodged her way onward, feeling slightly calmer with the knowledge that even if she got hit, she should survive the beating.

Up ahead, a brutal series of pillars pummeled the ground. Even at her top speed, they moved pretty fast. Each struck with tremendous force. Summer did not want to test her Tank stamp against a direct hit. The relentless pillars looked strong enough to squash anything into a pancake.

As Summer twisted, shuffled, and jumped, the mashing pillars drew closer. Four pillars wide and twenty pillars deep, the crushing section of the corridor never held still. It was hard to identify a pattern in the constant motion.

A blow that clipped her shoulder made Summer stagger when she reached the pillars. A heavy column of stone slammed down beside her. As it lifted up, she stepped underneath it, barely avoiding a pillar that boomed down onto her previous position.

Keeping her eyes up, Summer zigzagged forward, columns thundering down to the left and right, ahead and behind. Toward the end she dove, rolling out onto the stone floor beyond the reach of the pitiless columns.

No obstacles remained ahead of her. At the end of the corridor, a small statue awaited in an alcove. The floor vibrated each time a column crashed down behind her. She had survived. She returned to regular race mode.

Summer thought she could hear Roman or Derek yelling at her, but with the pounding pillars so close, she couldn't make out any words. Standing, she took a moment to examine the punctures and tears in her ragged clothing. Then she walked to the end of the hall.

In the alcove stood a statue of a shirtless warrior, less than a foot tall. Squat and broad, he had thick limbs, large feet, and a cartoonishly oversized head. His eyes lacked irises or pupils; his nose was broad, his ears small. He was slightly crouched, his legs together, and he held a club in each fist.

Summer looked around. The corridor ended here. "You must be the Protector," she said.

The statue offered no response. Behind her, the pillars continued to batter the floor.

She found the statue quite light. Of course, with the tank stamp, she was considerably stronger than usual, making it tricky to guess how much the statue might normally weigh.

Turning, she faced the booming columns. The thought of running back through the frantic gauntlet was disheartening. She would need to rest again before attempting the return trip.

As she watched the columns piston up and down, Summer realized how difficult it was to see Roman and Derek at the far end of the hall beyond all of those moving obstacles. Which meant they couldn't see her.

Summer looked down at the Protector. If she broke it, wouldn't that mess up Jonas White's plans? He needed it to access Uweya. She could pretend it had happened by accident.

With her stamp-enhanced strength, Summer flung the Protector to the floor. Nothing broke off. Upon closer examination, she failed to find a chip or a crack. She threw it down again. She bashed it against the wall. She threw it head first, then feet first. She hurled it end over end across the width of the corridor. None of the punishment even scratched it.

Summer supposed she should have known it wouldn't be so simple. If the Protector were easily destructible, somebody probably would have broken it long ago.

Then she considered the pillars. If anything could destroy the little statue, it would be them.

She carried the statue to the nearest row of pounding columns.

As she neared, the columns stopped ramming the ground. She continued forward, and the next row of pillars stopped functioning as well.

It was good news and bad news. She couldn't use the obstacles in the corridor to destroy the statue, but apparently the Protector was her free ticket out. The trend continued as she progressed along the hallway. When she passed beyond the pillars, the spears stopped stabbing, the blades quit whirring, and the pendulums halted. In no time she made it back to Derek and Roman.

"Nice work, Summer," Derek said, giving her a high five.

"Looks like you rescued your clothes from a pack of wild dogs," Roman joked.

"I'm starting a new trend," Summer declared. "Wet and mangled."

"Can I see the Protector?" Roman asked, holding out his hand.

Summer could think of no good reason to deny him, so she handed it over.

"It's light," he said, hefting it. "Small. We need to be ready for the Jets to try to swipe it. You've got to be tired, so I'll keep hold of it for now."

Once again, Summer could think of no plausible reason to disagree. She nodded woodenly.

Derek and Roman trotted ahead of her. She had to help Nate. When would he strike? In the water, if he had any sense. But he needed to be careful. She knew how ruthless Roman and the other Tanks could be. If they got hold of anybody, they would force Nate to back off with threats of violence.

Roman stepped warily out into the night. As he passed through the entrance, the stone building began to shudder.

Summer raced out the doorway as the hallway behind her began to collapse. As she watched in surprise, the stone building folded in on itself, promptly shrinking down to nothing. The miniature replica of the building did likewise. The hillside where the building had stood looked churned up, as if an excavation had caved in. Otherwise there was no indication the building had ever existed.

Roman studied the sky. "We have to be ready for an attack at any moment. When they come for us, grab them. If we show them we're in charge, they'll back off."

"Should we go straight across to the mainland?" Derek asked. "Or should we loop around wide, maybe avoid them."

"Subs can sense things in the water," Summer said, wanting to appear helpful. "They'll probably sense us wherever we go. Our best bet is to get across as fast as possible."

"Good thinking," Roman said. "I'll keep hold of the statue. You guys make a triangle around me."

They ran to the side of the island facing Tiburon without encountering any of the Jets. They dove into the water and started swimming. Summer kept her arms and legs thrashing, hoping the exertion would help her get over the shock of the cold water.

"Don't go top speed unless we get attacked," Roman huffed. He seemed to be having trouble keeping afloat with the statue cradled in one arm.

"You all right?" Summer asked.

"Isn't easy," Roman replied. "We're stronger, and we're moving faster than normal. But we're also heavier. I feel the Protector's weight more in the water. I'll make it. Don't worry about me. You guys keep an eye out for the Jets."

* * * * *

Nate floated motionlessly beside Lindy, Chris, and Risa as the Tanks swam away from Angel Island, arms and legs churning with inhuman speed. He couldn't see them with his eyes, but he could sense every stroke. Roman was barely keeping his head above water, flailing along with a small statue in the crook of one arm.

"We'll wait until they're out in the middle," Nate said. "They won't see us coming. Lindy and I will snag Roman."

Nate held one end of a rope they had stolen from a boathouse. Lindy clutched the other end. Chris and Risa had a rope as well. When you could fly, it was easy to forage.

"If you miss him, we move in," Risa confirmed.

"Right," Nate said. "Lindy and I will use the rope to drag Roman down away from the others. Once he hands over the Protector, we'll pull him back up."

"He's stubborn," Chris warned. "And he's still mad at us. He won't give it up easily."

"Stubborn or not," Nate said, "when you don't have air, nothing else matters."

"You won't let him get hurt," Risa checked.

"No way," Nate said. "The last thing I want to do is hurt anybody. I'm more worried about us. If those Tanks get hold of us, we could really get hurt. Especially if they're panicked."

"Like they will be if they're drowning," Chris said. "I don't like this. Somebody is going to get thrashed."

"I don't like it either," Nate said. "But we can't let them have the Protector. It's not an option. Somebody needs to mess up Mr.

White's plans. Unless we get the Protector, we'll be in no position to do it. Let's get ready."

Nate and the others drifted along about fifteen feet below the Tanks. As they approached the midpoint between the island and the peninsula, Nate gave a signal to Lindy. The two of them rose up through the water, moving with the ease of flight, until they were almost within reach of the Tanks' flailing limbs. Up close Nate had a better appreciation for how quickly they were moving.

Leaving Lindy on one side of Roman, Nate surged up out of the water, leaping over him and draping the wet rope across his back. They both swam down swiftly, allowing Roman no time to recover. By the time he twisted free, he was twenty feet below.

As Roman tried to stroke upward, Chris and Risa swept in with their rope stretched between them. The rope caught him around his midsection, and they dragged him almost to the bottom.

Moving in a frightening blur, Roman yanked on the rope with his free arm, trying to pull Chris closer. Chris and Risa released the rope and kept out of reach. Freed from the rope's pull, Roman had clearly gone into overdrive. He swam upward with three limbs, making only modest progress considering how fast his arms and legs were moving.

Above, the other Tanks were diving down, but they obviously could see nothing, and their futile search stayed confined to the ten feet nearest the surface. Nate stayed aware of them but didn't feel the need to worry.

Suddenly Roman was no longer moving in fast motion. Not at all. He shoved the statue aside and stroked pathetically for the surface. Nate sensed the abandoned statue sinking. At first Nate didn't understand the hasty surrender. Roman had barely been underwater for ten seconds. Then the realization hit.

"Roman used his fastest mode," Nate called, already swimming to help him. "Every second to us was like ten to him. That's a long time without breathing. He's drowning."

When Nate and Lindy snared Roman with their rope, he clung to it. They surged for the surface, angling away from the other Tanks.

* * * * *

"Where is he?" Derek shouted in frustration.

"I don't know," Summer replied. "I can't see anything."

After Roman was sucked under, Derek and Ruth had shifted into top speed. Summer had followed suit in order to avoid looking suspicious.

"He's been under a long time," Ruth fretted.

They were no longer diving down. Summer supposed you could only dive to look at blackness a certain number of times before it began to feel useless. The Jets could have dragged Roman away in any direction. And Ruth was right—he had been under a long time.

"Are they trying to kill him?" Derek asked angrily. He squinted at his compass in frustration.

"No," Summer realized. "It only seems like a long time to us. And if Roman is at top speed, it seems like a long time for him too. But the Jets might not know."

"They could drown him by accident," Ruth gasped.

"Let's go back to race mode," Summer said. Staying at top speed was starting to make her woozy.

Not long after she slipped out of her fastest state, Summer saw Nate and Lindy burst from the water twenty yards away. They left Roman behind, slowly gasping and flailing.

"Why is he moving so slowly?" Derek asked.

"He caught on," Summer realized, switching back to her fastest state and stroking over to him. "He slowed down to conserve oxygen."

Nate and Lindy were flying back toward the peninsula. Summer and the other Tanks reached Roman. They slowed back to race mode.

"Help him float," Summer ordered. She slowed down to regular speed. "Just rest," she told Roman. "We'll hold you up."

Between wheezing and coughing, Roman managed to speak. "I lost it. I lost the statue. I was drowning. They pulled me deep. It was heavy. I couldn't swim up . . . fast enough."

Chris and Risa burst out of the water ten yards away. They paused, hovering about ten yards in the air.

"You okay, Roman?" Chris called.

"Like you care," Roman spat.

"If we didn't care, we wouldn't ask," Risa shot back.

"Have you guys seen Nate and Lindy?" Chris wondered, looking around.

"We knocked them out," Roman said. "Give us the statue . . . and we'll tell you . . . where to find the bodies."

"Nice try," Chris said. "We know they flew up out of the water."

"They went back toward Tiburon," Summer said.

"Why that way?" Risa asked.

"Probably to help these guys," Chris said. "Sorry about almost drowning you, Rome. It took us a bit to realize you were spending more time underwater than it seemed thanks to your super speed."

"You guys are geniuses," Roman said darkly. "I don't need comfort. Either give us the Protector or get out of here."

"Suit yourself," Chris said.

He and Risa flew away.

"I hate them," Roman mumbled.

"It was nice of them to check on you," Summer said.

"It's easy to act nice after you've won," Roman griped.

"You're sounding better," Summer pointed out.

"Failure must agree with me," Roman replied. He struck the water with his fist. "I didn't think about them using tools to drag us down. Nets, ropes—I should have been ready for that!"

"Here," a voice called from above. It was Nate. He didn't pause. He and Lindy swooped over the Tanks, each dropping a boogie board.

Derek and Ruth retrieved the flotation devices.

"This will make it easier," Ruth said, giving hers to Roman.

"Or more pathetic," Roman said. "I hope they crash into a helicopter."

"You need to grow up," Summer said. "And you better start acting nicer to them. Soon they'll be flying Tanks."

CHAPTER NINETEEN

RESCUE

Trevor tossed the last of his six darts at the target across the room. The dartboard had two sides—one consisted of a circular grid with numbers around the perimeter; the other displayed a simple target of concentric rings with a bull's-eye at the center. The complicated side involved calculations to determine the score. This time Trevor had opted for the simple target.

His final dart missed the center circle by a finger width. Two of the previous darts had already hit the bull's-eye. Only one had strayed beyond the second innermost ring. After all the recent practice, his aim was getting reliable.

Trevor had not left the room since coming for help from Mr. Stott. The sanctum had a small bathroom, and Mr. Stott brought him meals. He slept fine and ate well, but he often felt bored. Tonight, although it was getting late, he couldn't settle down. The confinement was making him increasingly restless.

After a quick knock, the door to his room opened and Mr. Stott entered with the Battiato brothers. Victor and Ziggy nodded their greetings.

"What are you guys doing here?" Trevor asked happily. "I thought you steered away from lairs."

"We generally do," Victor agreed. "But any port in a storm. Jonas White has started actively targeting us. Some of his sideshow henchmen mixed it up with us earlier tonight. We had crossed paths with a few of them since our arrival, but it never came to blows. Any unspoken truce between us has officially expired. And now we have an opportunity that will leave one of us defenseless."

"They got a message from Pigeon," Mr. Stott said.

"His tracking button went dark after he disappeared," Ziggy reported. "But tonight the signal returned long enough for us to pinpoint a location. He's being held somewhere below Arcadeland."

"The tracker had been dark too long for it to suddenly function without a reason," Victor said. "We assume he got help from a fellow prisoner."

"Almost certainly Mozag," Ziggy added.

"Unless Jonas White is being sly," Mr. Stott murmured. "Could he be using Pigeon's tracker to lure you into a trap?"

"Possibly," Victor said. "But this late in the game, I don't think we can afford to ignore the signal."

"How do you get the signal?" Trevor asked.

Mr. Stott held up a stocking cap and a pair of mittens. "By wearing these. Mozag enchanted them."

"A single mitten is enough," Ziggy explained, "but wearing everything clarifies the signal."

"With one mitten, we can feel the direction of the various

trackers," Victor said. "With both mittens, we can feel the distance. Add the stocking cap, and we can almost see the location."

"Did Pigeon break the button?" Trevor wondered.

"I'm not sure," Victor said. "The signal didn't last long. The mittens vibrate a lot if the button gets broken. That didn't happen, but interference from the magical barriers around Arcadeland could have blocked the effect."

"What's the plan?" Trevor asked. "Are you going in?"

"The Battiatos came straight here after pinpointing the signal," Mr. Stott said. "Victor intends to go after Pigeon. Ziggy will rest here in his depleted state. But you might be able to accompany Victor."

"Really?" Trevor asked.

"Let me see the back of your hand," Mr. Stott said. Trevor extended his arm, and Mr. Stott took a close look at the stamp, probing the ink with his fingertips. "It's as I suspected. The stamp recently became inactive. When were you last stamped?"

Trevor considered the question. "About three days ago. Does this mean I can use candy?"

Mr. Stott produced a small box. "Bestial Biscuits," he said. "My latest invention. A blending of Brain Feed, Mrs. White's notes on Creature Crackers, and my general interest in shape-shifting."

"What do they do?" Trevor asked.

Mr. Stott shook a biscuit from the box. "I've wanted to attempt something like this for years. Mrs. White's notes together with this emergency provided me with the means and the motivation. Ideally, I'd like to produce a broader variety at some point. For now, six variations will have to suffice."

"Same question," Trevor said. Sometimes Mr. Stott could get a little long-winded.

Mr. Stott held out the biscuit to Trevor. "What does this look like?"

"A bear," Trevor said.

"Correct," Mr. Stott replied. "If you eat it, you will transform into a Kodiak bear, the largest of the brown bears."

"Awesome," Trevor approved.

Mr. Stott placed the bear cracker back inside the box. "Your bond to the simulacrum Jonas White produced corresponds directly to your physical form. While you remain in an altered shape, your simulacrum should prove useless. The transformation will only last for about half an hour. When you revert to your actual shape, you will become vulnerable again."

"What other animals do you have?" Trevor asked.

"I've cooked up a mountain gorilla, a golden eagle, a great white shark, a Siberian tiger, a gray wolf, and the Kodiak bear. I made two of each. The effort stretched me to my limits. I want to retain one set for whoever loses the next competition."

"So I get to go with Victor?" Trevor verified.

"It won't be a picnic," Victor warned.

"I bet," Trevor said. "You guys don't usually go after magicians in their lairs."

"Not ideally," Victor said. "However, this lair is more vulnerable than some. By taking prisoners and holding them in his lair, Jonas White has reduced his claim on the space, weakening his entitlement to protective magic. The more prisoners he holds, the more fragile his barriers become. Parts of Arcadeland are open to the public, which further weakens the lair. Plus, a Simulcrist needs to leave certain barriers down in order for his simulacra to stay connected with their targets."

"Still, Jonas White is an old magician with plenty of skill," Ziggy said. "He has help from several engineered apprentices, and we can count on him to have a number of other tricks up his sleeve."

"That means Victor will need help," Trevor said. "I'm coming. I have to help my friends."

"They could use all the help they can get," Ziggy said. "We haven't confronted a threat like Jonas White in quite some time. The world is in big trouble."

"Your clothes will be absorbed into the animal you become," Mr. Stott explained. "Small items on your person as well. After you spend half an hour as a tiger, for example, you'll revert to your true form, fully dressed with all of your gear."

"Definitely beats having to streak across town looking for clothes," Trevor said gratefully. "So I can keep extra crackers with me, and eat another as soon as I become human again?"

"That is exactly what I would suggest," Mr. Stott approved. "The longer you spend in your human form, the more opportunity you'll give Jonas to attack you with your simulacrum. Keep the Bestial Biscuits handy."

"Are we ready to go?" Trevor asked.

"I believe so," Mr. Stott said, looking to Victor.

Ziggy began to age, shrink, and droop. Victor swelled with new muscle, gaining several inches of stature. His face became more youthful and chiseled. His suit coat looked ready to burst. He rolled his head on his thick neck, producing snaps and pops.

"I'm ready now," Victor said.

Ziggy sagged into a chair, wiping sweat from his brow.

"You all right?" Victor asked.

Ziggy nodded sluggishly. "I figured you could use all that I could spare. I'll be fine. You're the one heading into the thick of it."

"You'll probably want to start as an animal that can ride in a car," Mr. Stott advised Trevor. "Victor can have a second biscuit ready for when you storm Arcadeland."

"Will I still feel like myself?" Trevor asked.

"Losing yourself in your new form is an inherent risk of shape-shifting," Mr. Stott said. "I've taken some measures to limit the risks. I modified the animals so that their senses will feel closer to what you're used to experiencing. The minds of the animals will react as if under the influence of Brain Feed, which should allow your mental processes to remain unclouded. The limited time you'll spend as each creature will also help you retain your self-possession."

"Okay, let's do it," Trevor said. "I guess I'll start as a wolf."

Mr. Stott rummaged in the box. "Let me find the right biscuit."

"Why call them biscuits?" Trevor wondered.

"Here in America, biscuits are fluffy," Mr. Stott said. "In Britain, biscuits are like cookies or crackers."

"Are you British?"

"Not particularly." He held out a cracker to Trevor. "I guess I liked the alliteration—Bestial Biscuits."

Trevor accepted the biscuit. "You want to give Victor the box?"

"I'll give you the box," Mr. Stott said. "It should disappear along with your clothes and remain with you. But let's give Victor the biscuit you want to use inside Arcadeland. Eat it the moment you change out of your wolf form."

"What should I use?" Trevor asked Victor.

"I'm no animal expert," Victor said. "Gorilla, bear, or tiger all sound good."

"I guess bear," Trevor said. "It seems big and heavy and strong. A tiger seems better outside. A bear could bulldoze through those halls. Hopefully I'll be able to help you knock down doors and intimidate the bad guys."

"I like it," Victor said, accepting the bear cracker from Mr. Stott. "Let's get rolling."

Trevor put the wolf biscuit in his mouth. It tasted like cinnamon shortbread, but it was a little too chalky for him to call it delicious. When he swallowed, his entire body burned and tingled. His arms and legs shortened as he fell forward. His nose and mouth elongated into a muzzle, his ears shifted higher up his head, a tail sprouted from his rear, and fur emerged all over his body.

By the time his front paws hit the ground, the rapid transformation felt complete. Trevor could feel new strength in his jaws. His eyesight seemed pretty much unchanged. He sensed a new spectrum of aromas rising from the carpet, as well as distinct odors coming from Mr. Stott and the Battiatos. Faint sounds that he hadn't noticed before came to him clearly, like the news on the TV in the family room. Trevor stretched his back and lifted his paws. The new form felt surprisingly natural.

"Quick change," Ziggy said.

"How do you feel?" Mr. Stott asked.

"Great," Trevor said. "My hearing is sharper. I'm picking up new smells. I want to run."

"I wouldn't mind being in motion myself," Victor said. "Follow me."

Victor led the way out of the room, down from the apartment, and out the back of the candy shop. The pungent aromas coming from the display cases of sweets were almost too much for Trevor, but he liked how smoothly he could move on all fours.

Trevor paused after exiting the candy shop. What if Mr. Stott was wrong? What if Jonas White managed to attack Trevor with his simulacrum while he was in wolf form? Trevor supposed it was possible, but he had to take the risk.

Victor opened the passenger door to the van, and Trevor hopped inside, reflecting that without fingers it would have been almost impossible for him to work the handle. Victor came around and slid in behind the wheel, moving the seat back a little to accommodate his larger physique.

"Do we have a strategy?" Trevor asked.

"I considered ramming the van through the front doors," Victor replied. "I decided that might be a little dramatic, plus we could needlessly injure ourselves. It's nearly eleven. Arcadeland will be closed. We'll go in on foot, probably through a side door. I'm not sure how we'll access the basement. We'll have to improvise. Plan to storm in and play rough."

This late there was only modest traffic on the roads. With every moment that passed, Trevor gained confidence that Jonas couldn't harm him. He felt eager to be in motion and squirmed restively as they made their way to the arcade. At length, Victor eased to a stop a block from Arcadeland.

"Now we wait?" Trevor asked.

"We get out of the van," Victor said, opening his door. "Then we wait for you to return to normal and instantly make you a bear."

Victor closed his door and walked around the van. He opened Trevor's door and let him jump down. They walked to a quiet alleyway.

Trevor could smell a discarded ketchup packet, old gum, and dozens of subtler scents. He followed Victor into the dark alley, aware of how the pads on his feet felt against the asphalt.

"How much longer?" Trevor asked.

Victor checked his watch. "If it lasts half an hour, we need to wait at least ten more minutes."

"If I eat the bear biscuit now I guess we risk mixing magic," Trevor said.

"Right. We have to hold off. No telling what would happen otherwise."

"And I guess we shouldn't get much closer," Trevor said.

"Smarter to wait," Victor said. "I could scout ahead and open the door, but I might get discovered and ruin our surprise. We'll go together, a guy and his bear."

The conversation died. Victor seemed content to stand with his hands in his pockets. Trevor paced back and forth, sniffing at the more interesting scents.

When Trevor finally transformed, there was little warning. His body became hot and tingly—then he was on his hands and knees, fully clothed, the box of animal crackers in his hand.

Victor was immediately at his side, the bear biscuit in hand. Trevor chomped it down, hoping Jonas White wouldn't sense his availability in time to work any magical mischief.

Again heat rushed through him as his body fleshed out and expanded. His muscles ballooned, covered by layers of fat and shaggy fur. Rising up on his hind legs, Trevor looked down at Victor, surprised to stand so much taller than the burly investigator.

"That's more like it," Victor said. "Feeling good?"

Trevor dropped down to all fours. "I feel big." He padded forward, heavy muscles bulging across his back. His hearing had lost some of its edge, but if anything his sense of smell was keener. "Jonas White better watch out."

"Don't get too cocky," Victor said, walking beside him. "The guy is a magician. We'll keep things quiet for as long as we can. When they come after us, don't be shy about letting them have it. Tonight we're playing for keeps. We have to find Mozag and get him out."

"What about John?" Trevor asked. "What about Pigeon?"

"On our priority list, they rank a distant second," Victor said. "I mean them no disrespect, but Pigeon and John probably can't stop Jonas White. Mozag probably can. We need him to fix this mess and save the others."

"Okay," Trevor agreed. "But if we can save all three?"

"We save all three. Don't get me wrong. John and Pigeon could help us fight our way out. I value them. I'd love to spring them as well. But we need to go in with our priorities straight. Once this gets started, I expect things will move quickly. We won't have lots of time to ponder our options."

"Got it," Trevor said.

"This way," Victor said, speeding up to a run.

Trevor increased his pace. He was not as light on his feet as before, but he could still move rapidly. He expected that at full speed he could easily outrace Victor.

They slowed as they reached Arcadeland. Producing a couple of tools, Victor went to work on a nondescript door. Trevor could hardly believe how quickly he opened it.

"Did you used to be a burglar?" Pigeon asked.

Victor shrugged. "You work as an investigator for almost a hundred years, you pick up a trick or two. Get in there."

Trevor squeezed through the doorway, brushing the frame on both sides. The main lights were off, leaving the flickering displays of various games to illuminate the room. Trevor smelled no people, but some delicious fragrances beckoned him toward the snack bar.

"Stay with me," Victor said, trotting past Trevor toward an EMPLOYEES ONLY door across the arcade. Upon arrival, Victor found the door locked, but he again used his tools to remedy the problem.

With the door open, they could hear an alarm blaring. "What did we do?"

"We're both magically altered," Victor said. "We probably tripped a warning system as soon as we entered. I bet Jonas didn't want that kind of alarm heard in the public areas."

"What now?" Trevor asked.

Victor withdrew a tranquilizer pistol. "We hurry."

Trevor pressed through the doorway and followed Victor down an industrial hall lined with pipes and wires. His ursine body almost felt too large for the relatively narrow passage.

"Any idea how to get down a level?" Victor asked.

"I've never been down there," Trevor said. "Nate mentioned an elevator."

Victor tried every door they passed. The first three were unlocked. He poked his head in, then proceeded down the hall. The fourth door was locked.

Tucking his pistol under his arm, Victor went to work with his tools. The door swung open and he leaned through the doorway. "Bingo."

"Elevator?" Trevor asked.

"Stairs."

Victor passed through the doorway. As Trevor started through, he paused, catching the distinct scent of a person other than Victor.

The odor came from the far corner of the landing, where nobody was standing.

"There's a guy in that corner," Trevor said. "I can smell him."

For a moment, the air in the corner shimmered, then Todd materialized, charging forward with an upraised baseball bat. Thanks to the warning from Trevor, Victor had already turned to confront the attacker. Stepping toward Todd, the beefy investigator caught the bat in his palm before the swing had reached full momentum. A measured blow from Victor's elbow sent the smaller, thinner man skidding to the floor. Bending over, Victor seized Todd by the front of his shirt and dragged him to his feet. Todd's eyes kept darting nervously at Trevor.

"You like my bear?" Victor asked, shaking him. "Bears are omnivorous. They'll eat just about anything. Even malnourished little twits like you."

"It sounds like a kid," Todd said, failing to keep his composure.

"It bites like a steel trap," Victor promised, still gripping Todd by the front of his shirt. "Who are you?"

"I just work here," Todd said.

Victor lifted Todd upward so he had to stand on his tiptoes. With his free hand, Victor messed up Todd's green faux hawk. "You just work here? What are you supposed to be? The invisible custodian who cleans the stairs with his baseball bat?"

"Not invisible," Todd corrected. "Unnoticed. I'm good at blending if people haven't seen me."

"Then you sneak up behind them and knock them out," Victor said. "You blew it, pal. I've seen you. And my sidekick can smell you. Take us to Mozag."

"Who's that?" Todd asked.

"He's the reason you can still walk and talk. Are you sure you want to take away my one motive for keeping you functional?"

"I've heard of him," Todd admitted.

"You feel fragile. I've always wanted to see my bear dance on a skinny little guy like you."

Trevor lumbered toward Todd and started sniffing him. Todd smelled strongly of beef jerky and potato chips. He tried to flinch away from Trevor, but Victor wouldn't let him. Trevor nuzzled him roughly.

"Don't waste one more second of my time, deadbeat," Victor threatened. "Now or never."

"I'll take you," Todd said. "But you have to make it look like you're dragging me there, or no deal. You won't get Mozag out, no matter how many steroids you take, no matter how big a bear you use as backup. This is Jonas White's lair, man."

Victor shifted his grip to Todd's upper arm. "Let's go. Double time."

Trevor trailed Victor and Todd down multiple flights of stairs until they reached a door at the bottom. Victor opened the door and yanked Todd through. As Trevor followed, a blur from the side streaked across his line of sight, striking Victor on the side of his shoulder and sending him sprawling.

The attacker was a muscular man with spiky black hair. He turned to face Trevor defiantly.

"Watch out," Victor warned. "He's a Combat Kinetic—a ComKin."

This concrete hallway was wider and taller than the one upstairs. Trevor reared up on his hind legs, towering over the man. Sneering, the ComKin jumped forward, kicking both legs into Trevor's furry chest with sudden ferocity. The blow landed before Trevor could react. It felt like he had been hit with a sledgehammer. Trevor stumbled back, slamming his head against the side of the doorway on his way to the floor.

"Nice, Conner," Todd said.

Trevor heard Victor start firing tranquilizer darts. Conner dodged from side to side, moving in quick, precise bursts, gradually worked his way down the hall toward Victor. Rolling over, Trevor saw Todd running off down the hall. Casting his pistol aside, Victor retreated from Conner, arms raised defensively.

Conner darted forward, his hands a blur as he issued blow after blow. Unable to divert the rapid onslaught, Victor staggered back like the victim of a machine gun, barely staying on his feet until Conner sent him flying with a vicious kick.

Roaring, Trevor tore down the hall. It felt good to get some speed behind his bulk. Turning, Conner looked alarmed. As Trevor reached out with his front claws, Conner jumped against the wall, then kicked off and sprang over the charging bear.

Trevor wheeled around just in time to receive a fierce kick to the head that knocked him onto his side. The stunning blow made a primal anger well up inside of him.

"Stay on him," Victor advised, charging forward. As he drew near to Conner, Victor twisted sideways just in time to avoid a supercharged flying kick. Having dodged the extended foot, Victor stuck out an arm in time to clothesline Conner and tackle him to the floor.

Grunting and scuffling, the two men wrestled until Trevor approached from behind and bit down hard on the top of Conner's shoulder. Trevor shook his head to the side, slamming Conner into the wall. The ComKin went limp in his jaws.

"Good work," Victor said, brushing off his suit. "It's all about timing with a ComKin. You have to anticipate and counter the attack before it comes. Otherwise they move too quickly and hit too hard."

"Are you all right?" Trevor asked.

"I'll have some bruises," Victor said, spitting blood onto the floor. "Todd ran off that way." He motioned down the hall.

"Do we follow him?" Trevor asked.

"I don't know," Victor said. "I doubt he was running to Mozag."

"We know they have at least one other ComKin," Trevor said.

"Katie Sung," Victor agreed, retrieving his tranquilizer pistol. He started reloading it. "This guy dodged a few darts, but I hit him a few times, too. He should have been out cold. He must have some kind of immunity. Or maybe Jonas White was somehow using a simulacrum to give him a boost."

Victor started running down the hall in the direction Todd had fled. Trevor ran along beside him.

"Where are we going?" Trevor asked.

"Not sure," Victor replied. "But I don't want to hold still and let them bring the fight to us."

Reaching an intersection, Victor turned left. Trevor rounded the corner a pace or two behind, letting Victor lead.

From up ahead, Trevor heard a strange clattering, like lumber being poured from a dump truck. "What's that?"

"Don't know," Victor replied, not breaking stride.

Though nothing was visible down the hall, the clacking tumult drew nearer. Then a strange monstrosity bounded around the corner and came galloping toward them. Fashioned from wood, wires, and steel cables, the jumbled construct had no clear form. Considerably larger than a bear, it alternated between running on five and six legs, depending how it tilted. The overall impression was that a bizarre piece of modern art built from scrap wood had savagely come to life.

"Don't back down," Victor growled. "We have to fight our way through it."

Trevor roared and increased to his full speed. The living lumber pile loomed larger than him, but a lot of it was empty space, and much of the wood looked rotted. Trevor bet that he had more mass.

The wooden monstrosity charged equally hard. They were playing chicken, and the enemy showed no sign of relenting. The gap between them closed quickly. Roaring and lunging, Trevor collided with the fearless construct. Wood snapped as Trevor collapsed the front end of the creature. The shock of impact sent Trevor reeling, and he and the construct tumbled end over end. Wires and cables tangled his limbs as Trevor thrashed against moving wooden segments. The more Trevor fought, the more the construct wrapped around him, caging him in wood and wires, tightening its hold rather than trading blows. His thick hide and fur protected him from feeling severe pain, but it was very frustrating to be so strong and yet feel so constrained.

Trevor could hear Victor beating against the wood. Trevor craned to see what was happening. The monstrosity shoved Victor with a wooden limb, sending the large investigator rolling to the floor.

"Go!" Trevor called. "We have each other tied up! This is your chance! Find Mozag."

Victor regained his feet. "I'll return for you." Then he dashed away.

* * * * *

Pigeon watched as John Dart opened the door and collected four mosquitoes. Sirens continued to wail. John shut the door quickly and rushed the mosquitoes over to the kitchen table, where Mozag spread his hands over them, eyes closed. One of the little bugs twitched.

"Victor," he said. "And a big bear."

Another mosquito fluttered.

"Nothing of interest."

A third bug spasmed.

Mozag opened his eyes. "Jonas sent his ungainly monstrosity to deal with the intruders. His sanctum is momentarily unguarded."

John Dart strode to the counter. He grabbed a pair of locators Mozag had devised, then rushed to the door. Pigeon followed.

"Stay with Mozag," John ordered as he opened the door.

"Don't activate the locators until you're inside the sanctum," Mozag warned, not for the first time. "Because of his simulcratic connections, his sanctum is imperfect. But the locators will work better if you smuggle them in while dormant."

"I'll wait until after I cross the threshold," John said.

"Let me come!" Pigeon demanded. "You might need help! What if you get pinned down? While you fight them off, I can find the Source!"

"Too dangerous," John said. "Jonas White will probably kill us when he finds out we've left our sanctum."

"Not if we get the Source," Pigeon said.

"Take him," Mozag said. "This may be our only shot. Hurry."

John tossed one of the locators to Pigeon, who dropped it but retrieved it quickly. John was already out the door. Pigeon hurried to catch up. Out in the hall, John raced ahead, lengthening his lead with every stride. Pigeon resisted calling to him to slow down. He knew that speed was essential. The commotion from the intrusion and the resultant alarm might temporarily prevent Jonas from realizing Pigeon and John had abandoned their sanctuary. But as soon as Jonas became aware, he could turn both of them into living statues—or worse.

John disappeared around a corner. Pigeon ran his fastest, worried about not getting to the corner in time to see John's next turn. When Pigeon reached the corner, he saw John racing down the hall. A man lay on the ground in the distance. When John reached the fallen figure, he paused, searching his pockets, giving Pigeon a chance to gain ground.

"Sure you want to stay with me, Pigeon?" John asked without looking up.

"I'm sure," Pigeon said.

"Ah-ha!"

"What?" Pigeon asked.

"Access card," John said, holding up what looked like a credit card. "This is Conner Grady, one of Jonas White's most trusted bodyguards."

"I'm coming," Pigeon said resolutely. He wanted to help John. He also wanted to run back to Mozag. He definitely didn't want the wax figure used against him. But if this escape failed, would they get another chance? If they had to take down Jonas White now or never, shouldn't he lend his help, even if he was underqualified?

"I can't protect you," John said. "I have to reach the Source at all cost. I have to find it and destroy it."

"I won't do any good back with Mozag," Pigeon said.

John started running again, crouching to pick up a baseball bat near a doorway. "Try to stay with me."

At the next intersection John kept running straight. Looking down the hall as he crossed it, Pigeon saw a bear tangled in some sort of trap made of wood and wire. The shaggy animal was wrestling fiercely, making the trap flop and writhe, the wood clattering and splitting.

Once again, John turned a small lead into a long one. Panting heavily, Pigeon tried to ignore the sharp pain in his side. Up ahead, John turned a corner. Pigeon tucked his head and kept pumping his arms and legs. Despite his best efforts, he could not stay at a full sprint.

Pigeon made it past the corner in time to see John disappearing around another one. He hustled, worried about losing him. When he rounded the next corner, he found John receding down a long hall.

Breathing hard, Pigeon kept running, motivated by thoughts of running into enemies without John to help him. John turned again. It took Pigeon more than thirty paces to reach that intersection. When he got there, Pigeon found John standing before a large iron door at the end of the hall, looking back over his shoulder.

As soon as Pigeon came into view, John swiped the card he had taken from the unconscious bodyguard. Then he hauled open the door.

Pigeon glanced down at the locator in his hand. It looked suspiciously like a plastic Easter egg. But Mozag had explained that the tiny bubbles inside would work like Finder's Dust. The bubbles would remain inert until activated by contact with oxygen. Once active, the bubbles would be drawn to the most potent source of magical power in the area. If the bubbles were activated before entering Jonas White's sanctum, they could lose potency upon crossing the threshold.

"John Dart!" a strident voice warned, and Katie Sung sprang into view, wearing a black turtleneck and gray slacks. Through the doorway, beyond John and Katie, Pigeon saw a multitude of wax figures.

Katie blocked John from progressing into the room. For a moment they faced each other motionlessly. Then Katie pounced. John raised his bat to block her punch, and her fist broke it in half. Ducking, Katie spun and delivered a low, sweeping kick with impossible speed. John's feet were whipped out from under him so hard that he landed almost upside down.

Pigeon charged through the doorway and crushed the eggshell in his hand. Tiny bubbles floated free, no larger than peas. The air in the sanctum was much cooler than the air out in the corridor. Pigeon recognized many of the wax figures—he saw himself, his friends, and also figures of Katie, Cleon, Todd, and some of the other henchmen. Jonas White stood at the far side of the room. He looked enraged by the intrusion.

From his position on the ground, John kicked at Katie's legs, but she nimbly sprang away. He started to rise.

Katie pointed to Pigeon. "It's our lost Sub!"

"I can see," Jonas White said as he toddled toward a life-sized wax replica of John Dart. "Jeanine, if you will."

A slight, youngish girl whom Pigeon had never noticed before stepped forward, palms facing him. Suddenly Pigeon was falling upward. Desperately twisting to avoid smashing his head, Pigeon slammed sideways against the ceiling; then gravity went back to normal, and he fell to the floor, landing hard, the breath crushed out of him.

John Dart was back on his feet. Jeanine held her palm toward him. John flipped as he fell upward, landing in a crouch on the ceiling, then flipped again, landing smoothly on the floor.

Scowling, Jeanine extended both palms at John. He hunched as if under the weight of an invisible burden. He took a couple of shaky steps to one side, his knees quivering unsteadily. "She's a Crusher," John panted. "Very rare. Can manipulate gravitational fields."

John fell upward again, landing roughly against the ceiling. When he dropped back to the ground, he hit hard.

Pigeon looked to where his bubbles were collecting against a jade urn upon a recessed shelf on the far side of the room. There appeared to be more bubbles than had come from his egg, which led him to conclude John must have released his bubbles as well.

Jonas White reached the wax figure of John Dart and inserted a needle at the back of the neck. John instantly went rigid.

Katie Sung relaxed, turning her attention to Pigeon. "You sided with the wrong team," she said.

Victor Battiato burst into the room and skidded to a halt. "What the devil?" he asked, taking in the scene.

"The urn is his power source," Pigeon blurted, pointing. "The green one in the niche. We're up against a ComKin and a Crusher."

Victor aimed his tranquilizer pistol but fell upward before he fired. He smacked against the ceiling on his side. As he dropped back toward the floor, Katie interrupted his fall with a brutal flying kick that made him land in a painful tumble. His pistol clattered to the floor.

The bear Pigeon had glimpsed earlier loped into the room, its shaggy fur matted in some places, ruffled in others. Katie dove to recover the tranquilizer pistol. She rapidly unloaded the gun into the bear.

The bulky bear staggered. "Uh-oh," it said in a very humanlike voice.

"The urn in the niche," Victor urged, rising and pointing.

Katie attacked, kicking the bear in the side hard enough to knock it over. After skidding to a stop, the bear flew up to the ceiling, then flopped back to the floor.

Pigeon crawled toward the urn. Everybody seemed distracted by the fight. He worried that if he got up and ran he might draw attention. He was getting close. Behind him, Victor was fighting Katie. The bear no longer moved. Jeanine sat down, rubbing her temples, her brow glistening with perspiration.

Slowly but steadily, Pigeon kept crawling. He was almost there. The jade urn was less than five yards away. He rose to his feet and charged. His body abruptly went rigid and he fell onto his side, landing just shy of the niche. As he went down, out of the corner of his eye, Pigeon glimpsed Jonas White near a wax figure of an eleven-year-old boy in a black leather jacket.

Trapped on his side, Pigeon couldn't move his eyes. He couldn't move his lips. He found himself staring at the paralyzed form of John Dart. Behind John, Katie had subdued Victor Battiato.

The attempt to destroy the Source was over. They had failed. Immobilized and utterly helpless, Pigeon dreaded what might come next.

CHAPTER TWENTY
DESPERATE MEASURES

A hundred feet above Arcadeland, Nate pulled up beside Lindy. As they hovered together in the darkness, a lone car motored along the dark street. A few other vehicles hibernated in the parking lot below.

They had not caught up with Chris and Risa on the way back from the bay. Nate assumed the other Jets had been flying at full throttle to ensure the Protector would make it back safely.

"See any Tanks?" Nate asked.

"All clear," Lindy confirmed, eyes sweeping the area. "Chris and Risa are waiting for us inside, just beyond the main doors. I would guess they only beat us here by a minute or two. They're with Katie Sung and Cleon."

"Can you see anyone else?"

"No. Some people are probably in the basement or the other rooms and halls that I can't perceive."

"Chris and Risa have the Protector? We won?"

"Right."

Nate sighed. Jonas White now had everything he needed to go after Uweya. If he and Lindy wanted to trip him up, they needed to act now. Nate worried that he might have already waited too long.

"We need to start putting up more of a fight," Nate said. "We keep waiting for the right opportunity, and it never comes. Jonas has what he wanted. He might send us to go after Uweya, and then again he might not. What if he quits using us? What if he tries to keep us here?"

"You think he might send his own people after Uweya?"

"Maybe," Nate said. "Or he might hold us here until he sends us. He's so close to winning, he won't want to risk blowing it. We can't get stuck here. Jonas has already proven that he doesn't mind making kids disappear. I should probably take off. I need to try to get a plan together. We're the last line of defense."

"Should I come with you?" Lindy asked.

Nate hesitated, trying to think through the best strategy. "Somebody should stay at Arcadeland," he decided. "There's a chance Jonas will go after Uweya right away. Just like we can't afford to get trapped at Arcadeland, we also can't afford to leave Jonas or the other Jets alone."

"How do I explain your absence?"

"Tell him I got hurt," Nate suggested, his mind racing to find better excuses. "Tell him I was stressed that we almost drowned Roman. Tell him I wanted to see Mr. Stott about it."

"What if he sends us after Uweya while you're gone?"

"Break your button," Nate said. "We'll need all the help we can get. Try to convince Chris and Risa to help us. Jonas has the Gate and the Protector. We can't let them get used."

"What are you going to do? Are you really going to Mr. Stott?"

"I'll go there first," Nate said. "That will help your story check out. Hopefully Mr. Stott can help me get rid of this tracking bracelet. I really can use whatever advice I can get. Once we make a plan, I'll do whatever it takes. Maybe I'll end up attacking Arcadeland with the Battiatos. If so, we'll probably be glad to have you inside. Stay ready to help."

"Okay."

"I'm not ditching you," Nate pledged. "I just don't know what else to do."

"It's all right," Lindy assured him, trying to fake a brave smile. "I get it. We need to take action, and we can't leave Arcadeland unwatched. I agree. One of us should stay and one should go. I'll do what I can until you come with the cavalry."

"I should get out of here."

"Go," she urged. "We're out of time. You're right—it's now or never."

"Be careful."

"You too."

Nate flew away.

As he cruised at his top speed, buildings and streets streaked by beneath him, and cool air washed over him. It didn't take long to reach the Sweet Tooth Ice Cream and Candy Shoppe. Landing in the back, Nate rapped on the door. After a prolonged pause, he knocked again. The door opened a moment later.

"Come inside," Mr. Stott said, alert eyes gazing beyond Nate into the night.

Nate entered hastily. "We got the Protector," he said. "It's the last thing Jonas White needs to go after Uweya."

"You delivered it to him?" Mr. Stott exclaimed.

"The other Jets handed it over, along with Lindy. I wasn't sure what else to do. Jonas has simulacra of us, and the Tanks could track us. If we had tried to run, we wouldn't have made it far. I guess the next step will be to track down the Battiatos."

"They've already been here," Mr. Stott said. "Ziggy is upstairs taking refuge in my sanctum. Trevor and Victor went after Pigeon and Mozag a few hours ago."

"What?" Nate cried. "How'd it go?"

"Not well," Mr. Stott grumbled. "John Dart and Pigeon got out of their cells and tried to help, but they were captured along with Victor and Trevor."

"Wait," Nate said. "If they were all captured, how could you know what happened?"

"Victor recently regained consciousness," Mr. Stott explained. "He was out for some time. When he revived, he transferred much of his strength back to Ziggy. In the process, he managed to also transmit a great deal of information."

"Like what?"

Mr. Stott glanced toward his apartment. "It might be safer to let Ziggy explain. Jonas White shouldn't be able to eavesdrop on us in my lair, but he certainly won't be able to overhear us in my sanctum. You look haggard. Would you care for a refreshment?"

"Sure," Nate said, realizing it had been some time since he had a bite.

"Something sweet and nutritious?"

"I'd take that."

"Go on up. Get filled in. The treat will take me a minute or two."

Nate flew up the stairs. Flight required less energy than walking, and he was feeling pretty weary. Now that he had reached the relative safety of the candy shop, it was like his body knew it could unwind.

Nate entered the apartment, glided to the sanctum, and knocked.

"Come in," Ziggy called.

Nate opened the door. Ziggy looked young and bloated with muscle. Nate raised his eyebrows. "Dude, you're a beast."

Ziggy smirked. "Wish I wasn't. It's a reminder that Victor ran into more trouble than he could handle. What's the latest?"

"Jonas White has the Protector. The other Jets brought it to him tonight. He can go after Uweya whenever he wants."

Tilting his head back, Ziggy closed his eyes. His thick neck bulged. "This keeps getting stickier. We're up against the ropes getting pummeled, and Jonas shows no hint of letting up."

"I heard that Victor and Trevor got caught."

Ziggy let out a defeated sigh. "Without freeing anyone. We're running out of allies. And Jonas has some heavy hitters working for him."

"Mr. Stott told me you got some info from Victor?"

"Might be our one ray of hope," Ziggy said. "We've always shared a strong connection. Victor managed to send a lot of information when he transferred his vitality to me. Poor guy must be in lousy shape." Ziggy rolled one of his shoulders and rubbed his chest. "I felt how brutally he got hammered. I'm still achy all over."

"What did he learn?"

"Victor and Trevor made it to Jonas White's sanctum. John and Pigeon beat them there. John was going for the throat. He wanted to take out the Source."

"The Source?"

"A Simulcrist needs a steady stream of magical power to energize his many connections. This power source is both his strength and his weakness. With it, he can manipulate many complicated enchantments at once. Without it, the connections would unravel. Jonas keeps his Source in his sanctum. It's a jade vase."

"I take it they didn't destroy the Source?" Nate checked.

"They got into the room," Ziggy said. "Impressive, since it was locked with a keycard. John must have lifted it off a guard. They almost succeeded, but the sanctum was well defended. Jonas used his simulacra to paralyze John and Pigeon. Katie Sung and a Crusher dealt with Victor and Trevor."

"A Crusher?"

"They can manipulate gravity—reverse it, decrease it, increase it. I don't know where Jonas found her. Maybe he helped create her. It's a very rare ability."

"Did Victor free Pidge and John?"

"I don't know how they got free," Ziggy said. "I only know that they beat Trevor and Victor to the sanctum, then got recaptured. Victor never encountered Mozag."

Mr. Stott entered the room, balancing three smoothies on a tray. "Berry colada," he announced. "Fortified with protein, quality carbs, and an herbal assortment of pick-me-ups. Try it."

Nate accepted a tall glass and sucked the pink liquid through a thick straw. Coconut dominated the flavor, sweet and strong, accented by the berries. Only a faint graininess hinted at the protein and other additives.

"It's amazing," Nate said. "Thanks."

"Did you show him the map?" Mr. Stott asked Ziggy, offering him a glass.

Ziggy claimed a smoothie, then leaned over and picked up a sheet of graph paper off a small table. "I saw what Victor saw. This should be close to the actual layout. It's incomplete, but better than a poke in the eye."

Sipping his smoothie, Nate studied the paper. Half of the sheet was labeled LEVEL ONE, the other half BASEMENT. Nate recognized the main arcade room at Arcadeland, then a single hall that led to a stairway. The basement diagram displayed several intersecting corridors. Most of the hallways ran some distance and then stopped, not at a wall, but open-ended, as if the mapmaker hadn't known where they went. The halls that were intact led from the stairway to a room labeled SANCTUM.

"If we destroy the Source, Jonas goes down?" Nate verified.

"It would pull the plug on his simulcry," Mr. Stott said around his straw. "He'd still have his engineered apprentices and whatever other magic he knows."

Nate stared at the graph paper. "If Jonas knows I'm coming, he could freeze me like he did to Pigeon and John."

"Freeze you or worse," Mr. Stott agreed. "He'll be on his guard after tonight. The sanctum will be locked. His henchmen will be on high alert. Not only did Jonas just repel a potentially devastating assault, but he has also just acquired the object he needs to ensure his success. He'll be protecting his interests with every asset at his disposal."

"What do you think, Ziggy?" Nate inquired.

"If the two of us charge in fully loaded, we'll promptly be escorted to private cells of our own. I'd never tell him this, but Victor is at least as competent as I am in combat. So is Dart. Your friend Trevor went in as a Kodiak bear."

"He was using a new treat I invented," Mr. Stott interjected.

Ziggy rubbed his big hands together. "No bologna? If they failed to win through with twice our numbers and surprise on their side, our chances of pulling off a direct assault are less than zero."

Nate turned to Mr. Stott. "Any other new surprises up your sleeve?"

"I wish," Mr. Stott sighed. "Ziggy is right. A frontal assault doesn't sound promising. I have more of my Bestial Biscuits, but you can't risk changing into an animal while your stamp remains active. I don't have another Sands of Time. I would require a team of assistants and a long, arduous retreat to produce another."

"I've called for backup," Ziggy mentioned. "Highest priority alert. But our closest available operatives won't get here until tomorrow afternoon."

"Which might be too late," Nate said. "We have Lindy. She stayed behind to keep watch. She could help. Both of us can fly."

"And both of you can be petrified or worse at the whim of Jonas White," Mr. Stott reminded him. "He really has engineered an extremely advantageous scenario."

"Maybe I could go to the Hermit," Nate proposed. "He had some amulet that protected him from simulcry."

"Think he would hook you up?" Ziggy snorted. "A talisman like that could take years to produce. No way would he surrender his."

"What if I took it?" Nate asked. "I've kept a couple canisters of pepper spray in reserve, just in case. I mean, we're desperate. I'd give it back."

"Take it by force?" Mr. Stott mused. "Such an item might be uniquely attuned to the Hermit himself. It might not shield another."

"But if it happened to work, we could sure use it," Ziggy said. "Can you find the Hermit?"

"I think I know where he'll be," Nate said. "I told him I would try to return the Gate to him. He told me where to find him. It would be a pretty big betrayal if I showed up and swiped his amulet. I guess I could ask first."

Ziggy chuckled. "Right. Feel free to write the request on my personal stationery. I'm sure he'll be anxious to comply."

Mr. Stott suddenly sat up straight. "Someone is at the back door." He hurried out of the room. Nate flew after him.

Mr. Stott rushed down the stairs and answered the door. Summer stepped into the candy shop.

"You got away!" Nate cried, giving her an enthusiastic hug. She hugged him in return, tilting back to lift him off the ground with her embrace. Her clothes were mangled. She felt a little damp. "Put me down," he complained.

"Everything feels so light," she replied, setting him on his feet.

"Maybe I was flying," Nate said.

"Maybe I'm a Tank."

"What happened?" Mr. Stott asked.

"I ditched the other Tanks on my way back to Arcadeland. I told Roman that I was done with all of this. I acted hysterical. He tried to tell me that I didn't need to leave, that our part was already finished, but I wouldn't listen to him. I think they all bought that I had been pushed over the edge. It probably helped that I wasn't completely faking it."

"Get to the sanctum," Mr. Stott ordered. "It's the guest bedroom. Otherwise, Jonas White could use your simulacrum at any moment to—"

He stopped speaking as Summer streaked away, dashing up the stairs in a blur of speed. Nate and Mr. Stott returned to the apartment to find her waiting in the sanctum with Ziggy.

Summer had questions, so they filled her in regarding all that had happened. She looked as dismayed as Nate felt.

"Summer has tank and racecar stamps working together," Nate pointed out. "Would her help make a direct attack more possible?"

"More possible than without her," Ziggy allowed. "But success would remain highly unlikely. Summer shares the same vulnerability that limits you and Lindy—once Mr. White realizes that she has turned on him, he'll go after her with her simulacrum."

"I probably shouldn't have left Lindy at Arcadeland," Nate worried. "Jonas knows that me, Lindy, Pigeon, Trevor, and Summer are all friends, and that we're all involved with you, Mr. Stott. Pigeon and Trevor attacked. Summer has run away. What if he retaliates against Lindy?"

"He might," Mr. Stott observed grimly.

"Could he use her simulacrum to restore her memory?" Summer asked quietly.

"Not by any means known to me," Mr. Stott said. "But I'm unwilling to rule out anything. Jonas White has proven himself disturbingly resourceful."

Bowing his head, Nate covered his eyes with his hands. "This is a giant mess. Jonas has to suspect I'm up to something. He could use my simulacrum at any time."

Summer scowled thoughtfully. "But if we all stay hidden in this sanctum, who'll stop him from getting Uweya? That could make him invincible, right?"

"I wish we knew more about the true nature of Uweya," Mr. Stott murmured.

Summer brightened. "William Graywater seemed to know a lot about it. More than he told us. Maybe if we went back to him and explained everything, he could give us some pointers. He definitely doesn't want Uweya found."

Ziggy gave a heavy shrug. "Might be worth a shot. Want me to head over there? Jonas has no simulacrum of me."

"I'm not sure he'd open up to an engineered apprentice," Mr. Stott said.

Ziggy straightened his tie. "Technically, I'm not engineered. I'm cursed."

"Whatever the distinction," Mr. Stott clarified, "you've been permanently altered and you work for Mozag. I can't imagine the Graywaters dealing with you."

"I'll go," Nate offered. "The Jets won the contest. Jonas might suspect me, but he has no official grounds to come after me."

"That might not stop him," Summer warned. "You bailed. There's no telling what he might do. What if he freezes you while you're flying?"

"I'll hope I'm over water," Nate mumbled. "I'm not sure what else we can do. Jonas is in a strong position. Seems like the surest way to get steamrolled by him would be to do nothing."

"Kid's got a point," Ziggy said. "Whatever measures we take will be risky. Gathering info about Uweya could be our best chance."

Mr. Stott leveled his gaze at Nate. "Are you sure you're up for this?"

"I'm willing," Nate said. "We have to try something." He held up a hand. "But I need to lose this bracelet. Otherwise Jonas will be able to track my movements easily."

"I can take care of that." Mr. Stott shifted his gaze to Summer. "Can you show Nate how to reach the Graywater home?"

"Can you get me a map?" Summer asked.

* * * * *

Air whistled past Nate as he rocketed through the night at his maximum speed. He had paused only once to consult the map. Ahead, light shone from just a few of the windows at the Devil's Shadow Mobile Home Park.

Nate had decided to visit the Graywater family first. A trip to the Hermit would also be important, but information about Uweya seemed like his most urgent need. Another hour or two of vulnerability would hopefully make little difference. If Jonas White had meant to incapacitate Nate with his simulacrum, he probably would have already done so.

Nate easily spotted the nice trailer with the tidy yard at the far side of the park. He landed on the front porch, feet pounding heavily against the artificial turf. Although light glowed from the windows, Nate could hear no activity inside. He pulled open the screen and knocked.

William answered, wearing a snug black T-shirt and faded jeans. "Who are you?"

"I'm your last hope of protecting Uweya."

William closed his eyes, his mouth tightening. For a moment, Nate got the impression that he was restraining harsh emotions. When his eyes opened, William appeared calm. "What do you want from me?"

"I want to know how I can help," Nate said. "Jonas White has the Protector."

The muscles at the sides of William's jaw bulged conspicuously. "So it was Jonas." He stepped aside. "Come in."

Nate entered the trailer, mildly surprised by how much it looked like a regular house on the inside. "You alone?" Nate asked.

"The others left," William said. "Probably wise. Not that there will be anyplace to hide if Jonas succeeds."

"Why'd you stay?"

Moving with an easy grace, William slumped into an armchair. "Maybe I'm punishing myself. Maybe I think ground zero is the best place to face an atomic blast. Maybe I still harbor a shred of hope. One of the girls who stole the guidestone seemed torn. It seemed as though she wanted to help. Maybe I wanted her to be able to find me."

"Summer," Nate said. "She sent me. She couldn't come because her club lost the assignment to retrieve the Protector. Jonas has a simulacrum of her. She has to stay in a shielded place."

"I take it your club won?"

Nate tried to think of an evasive reply. He failed. "We did."

William shook his head. "How does it feel?"

"What do you mean?"

"Changing the course of human history. Making the whole planet slaves to the whims of a maniacal mage."

"It isn't over yet," Nate said firmly.

"What can you do? Are you super strong? Super quick?"

"I can fly," Nate said. "Through air or water."

"You need to work on your landings," William advised. "It sounded like you dropped a bowling ball out there. Was the Protector underwater?"

Nate nodded.

"Thought so."

An uncomfortable silence ensued.

"We need to learn about Uweya," Nate finally said.

"We?" William taunted. "You and Jonas? Did he send you?" William regarded Nate intently.

"No. I'm working with a magician called Sebastian Stott. I've been against Jonas White from the start. He kidnapped some of my friends."

"Go on," William invited.

Nate related all that had happened. He told how Mozag and John Dart were abducted. He shared how he and his friends became involved with the clubs in order to spy on the operation. He explained about the Battiatos. William said little. He listened impassively, occasionally asking clarifying questions.

After Nate finished, William leaned forward in his chair, palms together, thick veins visible on the backs of his long hands. "Quite a story. Of course, you may not have spoken a word of truth. You might have cooked up that tale to help Jonas White learn more about Uweya before he goes after it."

"I guess I could have," Nate admitted. "But I didn't."

"Maybe," William said. "I need to be sure. Would you submit to a test? It involves an ancient tribal ritual. It's basically a magical lie detector."

"Sure," Nate said, relieved. A test like that would allow him to prove his honesty. "How do we do it?"

"It never fails," William warned.

"Perfect," Nate said.

William nodded pensively. "I have no such test. But you seemed willing—happy, even. Either you're a master deceiver, or you're telling the truth."

"You'll help me?"

William rubbed the arms of his chair. "When will Jonas go after Uweya?"

"I'm not sure," Nate said. "Soon, I expect. I'll probably be sent to help, along with the other kids in my club."

"Where do the other kids stand?" William asked.

"One has helped me since the start," Nate said. "I think the other two are on my side as well."

"You aren't sure?"

"Sure enough to risk my life."

William narrowed his eyes. "You truly mean to thwart him?"

"No way will I let him get Uweya. I was hoping that if I understood more about Uweya, I'd be in a better position to mess up his plans."

William folded his hands and stared at them for a moment. "You haven't stopped Jonas yet. Why didn't you act earlier? What makes you think you can stop him now?"

"I don't know that I can!" Nate cried. "I kept waiting for a good opportunity." He took a shuddering breath, trying to get a grip on his frustration. "I wanted some clue to where the prisoners were held. I wanted to get below Arcadeland unobserved. The chance never came. So I'm out of options. It's now or never, and I'm not okay with never."

"Just because you need to stop him doesn't mean you'll be able to."

"But I have to try," Nate replied. "He has a simulacrum of me. That has been hanging over my head since just after I became a Jet, but I might have found a way to break that hold. If I'm invited to go after Uweya, the others in my club will help me sabotage the mission. Even if I'm not invited, I'll go anyhow. Even without your help, I'll still try. But I'd rather have what help I can scrounge."

Inhaling loudly through his nose, William rubbed his thighs. "I'm not going to fill you in about Uweya. Even if you are sincerely working against Jonas, if he has a simulacrum of you, he may have ways of extracting that information."

"I'm on my own?" Nate asked.

William shook his head. "I'll help in every way that I can." Rooting in his pocket, he withdrew a keychain attached to a short strand of beads and a few wispy feathers. "This token is given voluntarily." He held it out to Nate.

"What's this?"

"The invisible keys to Uweya."

"Really?"

"No, not really. This token confirms you a friend of the Graywater family. There is a carwash in Fresno where it can get you half off. Also, if you can reach Uweya ahead of the others, it may help you get assistance."

"Seriously?"

William gave a nod.

"I should try to get to Uweya first? Ahead of the others?"

William settled back in his chair. "If Jonas claims Uweya, he will become the most powerful man on Earth. No exaggeration. But if you get there ahead of his people, with this token in hand, you might be able to use Uweya against him."

"You won't tell me how?"

"It won't be easy," William warned. "Use the token. This is the best I can do. I won't tell you more."

"Would you come with me?" Nate asked. "Maybe follow us in secret?"

William rubbed his mouth, perhaps covering a grin. "I know some secrets about the way to Uweya. Without an enhancement like yours, I could never get close. It's all up to you."

"Is it underwater?" Nate asked.

"I don't believe water will be an issue."

"Okay," Nate said. "Thanks for the keychain."

"Thanks for trying. It's more than many would do."

"You can't give me a better clue about Uweya?"

"I sent my family away in case your employer came to me and tried to use them as leverage to get me to reveal all I know. I've told you all that should be told." William extended a hand toward the door.

"'Bye," Nate said as he exited.

"Good hunting."

* * * * *

Nate soared through the darkness, rising and falling, using the wind of his speed and occasional acrobatic maneuvers to keep his mind alert. It was late. He was feeling the effects of a long, taxing, uncertain day. And there was still more to accomplish.

Upon reaching the *Striker,* he veered north, watching for the three hills of equal height where the Hermit was supposedly hiding. He found them as described, and on the north side of the farthest hill, he discovered the mouth of a cave.

With a canister of pepper spray in hand, Nate alighted just beyond the cave entrance. The cave appeared dark and still. He wished he had Lindy with him to reveal who or what might be hiding inside.

"Hello?" Nate called. "I'm back!"

"Why bring the inflammatory agent?" a scholarly voice responded from the blackness. "Have you the Gate?"

"No Gate," Nate confessed.

"Then why have you come? To rob me again? To take me hostage? To gloat about the end of the world?"

One of the questions made Nate particularly uncomfortable. He *had* come prepared to rob the Hermit again. He hoped it wouldn't come to that.

"I need your help," Nate said.

"The magic words we victims hope to one day hear from our attackers."

"It's an emergency," Nate said.

"I do owe you a lot of favors," the Hermit said sarcastically. "You drove me from my home, assaulted me, scalded me, and robbed me. I've been praying I could find some way to repay your generosity. How can I be of service?"

"It isn't just for me," Nate said. "Everyone needs your help. Including you. Jonas White has the Protector."

Still unseen in the darkness, the Hermit sighed wearily. "Of course he does."

"He'll be going after Uweya. I'll probably be involved."

"That certainly fits your profile."

"We have to stop him."

The Hermit laughed wildly. "You are turning understatement into an art form."

"He has a simulacrum of me," Nate explained.

"Now we're talking," the Hermit said with relish. "I'd love to get my hands on that!"

"His simulacrum of me would make it impossible for me to beat him."

"Many things will make it impossible to beat him," the Hermit scoffed. "If Jonas has the Gate and the Protector, his quest is essentially complete. You've already handed him victory. He need only claim his prize."

"Jonas hasn't won yet," Nate protested. "William Graywater told me that if I reach Uweya first, I may be able to use it against Jonas."

"You?" the Hermit mocked. "What do you know of Uweya? Now I know you're telling tall tales. As if William Graywater would trust you!"

"His idea, not mine," Nate insisted, digging in his pocket for the keychain. "He gave me this." Nate held up the totem.

The Hermit offered no reply. After a long pause, he stepped out of the darkness of the cave, his skin ghastly pale beneath the moonlight.

"How did you get that?" the Hermit asked slowly.

"William gave it to me."

"Yes," the Hermit marveled. "It was freely given. How did you convince him?"

"I told him the truth."

The Hermit rubbed the back of his arm roughly. He glanced around, then took a long look back at his cave. He seemed torn. "Very well. What aid do you seek?"

"I need protection from my simulacrum," Nate said.

The Hermit stared flatly. A membrane briefly shimmered over his eyeballs. "You wish to strip me of protection?"

"I'll bring it back," Nate said uncomfortably.

"Like you brought the Gate back?" the Hermit erupted. "If I refuse to hand it over, do you plan to hurt me again?"

"I'm trying to save the world," Nate sighed.

"A Simulcrist needs protection. Especially a homeless, friendless Simulcrist. I don't have much. I don't ask for much. I did not cause this problem. You've wronged me in the past. Why should I take a risk for you?"

"It won't just be bad for me if Jonas wins," Nate said. "It'll be bad for you. Bad for everyone."

The Hermit shook his head. "I've always been adept at avoiding attention. I keep to myself. I no longer have anything that Jonas wants."

"Would your amulet work on me?" Nate asked.

The Hermit considered him in silence. "If freely given, I could make it work."

"You don't want Jonas to get Uweya," Nate said.

"Correct. There are many people I don't want to get Uweya. In fact, I don't want anyone to get it. Including you. That's why I kept the Gate with me! Then you came along and stole it! For all I know, you delivered Jonas the Protector as well."

"I kind of did," Nate admitted. "It wasn't what I wanted, but he has the simulacrum of me."

The Hermit folded his arms. "This is preposterous! You're a hoodlum!"

Nate struggled to think of a way to convince the Hermit. He didn't seem very concerned about others, but at least he acted interested in himself. "You're a Simulcrist. No matter how good you are at hiding, that makes you a target. Jonas is too careful and too paranoid. He won't rest until you're captured or killed. With Uweya, he'll find you no matter what necklaces you hide behind."

The Hermit held very still. Nate held his breath. On the hillside around them, insects chirped.

"You're right," the Hermit finally said. "Unfair though it may be, you're absolutely correct. Very well, I'll lend you my charm. I lack a better option. A long shot is better than no shot."

Nate couldn't resist a relieved smile.

"Don't look at me like that! This is no victory for you. My charm has been yours since I saw what William gave you. You're in serious trouble. We all are!"

"At least we'll have a chance," Nate said.

The Hermit gave a halfhearted shrug. He slipped the twine over his bald head. The metallic figure eight swung gently. "Come here."

Nate approached.

Muttering mysterious words, the Hermit looped the amulet around Nate's neck. His breath reeked of fish. "This will shield you from simulcry. It will be virtually impossible for a Simulcrist to perceive unless he actively works simulcry against you."

"Thanks," Nate said.

"Don't thank me," the Hermit said. "I don't like you. It was foolish of you to take the Gate. I have zero tolerance for fools. But you happen to be the least terrible of several terrible options. If you're willing to risk yourself to stop Jonas, I'm willing to let you assume that risk."

"All right."

"Don't try to find me to return my charm. I won't be here. If you succeed, I'll find you. If you fail, you'll have bigger problems than returning borrowed enchantments. Don't fail."

"Is there anything—"

"This is all I can do for you," the Hermit interrupted. "I'm now unshielded. There are measures I must take. Go."

The Hermit turned and ran off down the slope. Nate waited for a minute, listening to him crunching through the brush, then took flight.

* * * * *

When Nate reached his house, he landed gently on the roof near his window. He had been concerned about falling asleep in midair, but now he was home. Body and mind ached for sleep. All he currently desired was to crawl into bed.

Nate had stopped by Arcadeland on his way home. It had appeared closed and quiet. There was no sign of Lindy or the other Jets. Either Jonas had let them go home or he was keeping them there. Either way, Nate had decided there was not much he could do at the moment. Exhausted, he had chosen not to worry about Jonas until morning.

Nate slid open his window, climbed through, and found Lindy waiting on his bed. She sat primly, hands folded on her lap.

"Are you all right?" she asked.

"You freaked me out," Nate said, a hand on his chest. "I'm okay. What's up?"

"Why didn't you tell me?" she asked in a small voice.

Nate froze. "Tell you what?" His mind raced to consider all the possible meanings of her question. She sounded hurt and upset.

"That I'm Belinda White."

Nate sagged. He felt a turbulent mix of guilt, regret, frustration, and disbelief. He wiped his tired eyes with his hands. Weren't things bad enough? How could everything keep getting worse?

"Who told you?"

"Who do you think, Nate?"

Nate sat down on the floor. How was he supposed to handle this? "What now?"

"Jonas wants me to spy on you," Lindy said. "I told him that I would."

"Isn't the first rule of spying to keep it a secret?"

"Only if you're actually going to do it."

"Right," Nate said sheepishly. "So you're not here to kill me?"

"Nate!"

"What? Belinda wasn't very nice. We tried not to mention her too much when you were around. It seemed wrong to talk about you behind your back right in front of you."

"Thanks for being so considerate," Lindy said with an edge to her voice.

Nate studied her. She didn't look any more evil than before. "How are you feeling?"

"I don't know. Angry. Confused. Ashamed. It's a pretty big list. At first I was really mad at you guys for hiding who I am. Then I cooled down and started thinking more clearly. Now I can't understand why you guys have been so nice to me. Didn't I almost wreck your lives?"

"In a way, it wasn't you," Nate said. "You don't act like her. You seem like an entirely different person."

"Really?" she asked eagerly, as if she desperately wanted to believe his words.

"How much did he tell you?" Nate wondered.

"You used a Clean Slate to wipe my mind. I created it and entrusted it to you. Then you used it against me. Is that true?"

Nate nodded. "Do you know who you wanted me to use it on?"

She shook her head.

"Mr. Stott."

"Dad?"

"That's right."

"Why?" Lindy whispered.

"He was competition," Nate said. "You wanted the Fountain of

Youth. Magic works better on the young. You would have become very powerful. You were trying to take over the town."

"I wanted Uweya," Lindy murmured numbly. "Jonas told me that was my ultimate goal."

"We never knew about that," Nate said. "We knew we had to stop you. Putting the Clean Slate into the water from the Fountain of Youth seemed like the only way. You became young, but you also lost your identity. I gave you some of your own medicine."

Tears glistened in her eyes, even the false one. "You did the right thing."

Nate got to his feet. "Lindy—"

"No. I'm not looking for sympathy. You did what you had to do. I'm glad you did it. Jonas told me that you stole my life. He promised to help me finish what I started. He said he would help me regain what I lost. But I see it a different way. You gave me a second chance, Nate. A chance to change. A chance to be better." Her brow furrowed. "Or maybe I'm kidding myself. Maybe it's just a matter of time."

"Before you become evil again?"

She let out a nervous laugh. "I guess. I don't feel any wicked urges. I don't *want* to become whoever I was. I like who I am now. Everyone has been lying to me, but they had a good reason. They were kind lies. Protective lies. It's hard to know the truth, but I'm glad I do. Everything fits now. Why dad was so worried about Arcadeland. Why you guys were so evasive about my past. I knew you guys cared about me. I knew you were my friends. But I also felt sure you were hiding something. All the little inconsistencies that nagged at me have fallen into place. At least it all makes sense now."

Nate could not keep eye contact with her. "Sorry you found out from him."

"He did me a favor," Lindy said. "It probably had to be him. You guys cared about me too much. You were trying to protect me from my past. But I'm glad I know. I'm relieved the truth came out. It's hard to face, but I needed to hear it."

Nate felt relieved by her reaction. He wanted to give her a hug. She seemed to need one. He approached where she sat on his bed and placed a hand on her arm. "Are you okay?"

Her chin quivered. "Not really. How would you feel if you found out you used to be somebody horrible? I was afraid it would be something like this. I was afraid maybe my parents had been bad people. But the truth of it tops all of my worst fears."

"You don't have to go down the same path," Nate said. "You don't have to become who you used to be."

Standing, Lindy threw her arms around him. Tears flowed freely. "I hope not! I hate Jonas! I hate Belinda! I don't want to be like them!"

Nate hugged her back. "It's okay. It's all right."

Lindy sniffed and ran her sleeve across her eyes. "I'm supposed to tempt you. My assignment is to test your loyalty to Jonas. I'm supposed to tell you that I learned how we can take him down. I'm supposed to lead you into a trap tonight."

"You agreed to it?" Nate asked.

She nodded. "I agreed so I could misinform him. I acted angry that you guys had hidden my past from me. I explained that I had felt something was wrong, that you were all lying to me, that I couldn't trust any of you. I told him I wanted to learn about my real past. He promised to help me. He promised that after obtaining Uweya he would raise me like a father."

"What now?" Nate asked.

Lindy backed away from the embrace. "I'll tell him that you wouldn't take the bait. That you passed the test. I'll tell him you decided the best way to help your friends would be to make sure you were on the winning side. I'll tell him you warned me that we can't beat him. I'll tell him you want to go after Uweya."

"Will he believe you?"

She shrugged. "I think so. We'll see. We're supposed to meet to go after Uweya in the morning. What do we do, Nate? I'm honestly not sure we can stop him. Did you know the others tried some sort of jailbreak tonight?"

"Yeah, I found out from Mr. Stott."

"How is he doing?" Lindy asked.

"He's fine. He's worried. Jonas added Trevor and Victor to his other prisoners. He's all geared up to repel another assault."

"He's definitely paying more attention to security."

Nate debated how much he should reveal about his plan. Lindy seemed to be truly on his side, but it was still hard to place full confidence in her. "We have a new strategy. We need to go after Uweya. I need to get there first. If I do, there are some things I might be able to do to stop Jonas."

"What things?"

"I talked to William Graywater. He told me that I'd figure it out when I get there. He made it sound like this is basically our last chance."

"We won't be going in alone," Lindy warned. "Jonas will be sending some of his people to secure Uweya. We'll learn more in the morning. We're supposed to be there early, like five-thirty. Tallah will refresh our powers. You need rest. You're worn out. Just show up tomorrow. I'll go convince Jonas that you're with us."

"I doubt he'll believe you."

"I'll make him believe enough to let you come. I don't think he trusts any of us. We'll be chaperoned. Who knows what he might do to us with our simulacra? There might not be much we can do. But we'll try. I should go."

As she started toward the window, Nate gripped her upper arm. "Lindy, be careful."

"I'll be fine," she said. "Let me handle my brother. Get some sleep. We'll both need to be at our best tomorrow."

Lindy went and flew out the window. Nate closed it. He started pacing. Maybe it was good that Lindy had learned about her past. Or maybe the whole conversation had been an act. Maybe the trap was already closing in around him.

She had been right about one thing. He needed sleep. He could hardly think straight. He carefully set his alarm for five, then crawled into bed. His mattress and pillow had never felt more inviting. Before he could stress about anything else, he fell asleep.

CHAPTER TWENTY-ONE

THE GATE

The approaching sunrise was beginning to bleach the horizon as Nate landed in a stumbling rush near a side door to Arcadeland. The jolt helped rouse him more than the flying had. He wiped sleep from his eyes as he knocked. Chris opened the door. He was dressed in the same clothes as yesterday.

"Hey," Nate said. "Am I the last to arrive?"

"You could say that," Chris replied. "Where'd you go last night? Jonas didn't seem happy that you skipped coming back here."

"I was freaked out," Nate said, unsure who else might be listening to his response. "I mean, we almost drowned Roman. I needed some time to get my head right. But now I'm good. I'm ready."

Nate stepped through the door. Chris leaned close. "Can you believe we're going after Uweya so soon?"

Nate kept his voice low. "Yep. It leaves nobody time to react. Pretty smart." Nate stopped whispering. "Did you sleep here?"

"It was late," Chris said, as if making an excuse for a misdeed.

"We were exhausted. Mr. White thought it would be better than to have us go home only to come back so early."

They were walking toward an EMPLOYEES ONLY door. Cleon stood beside it. He gave a casual, two-fingered salute. He wore tinted sunglasses and had a toothpick between his lips. Nate waved.

"Long night?" Cleon asked.

"Short night," Nate replied. "I slept like a rock."

Using a key, Cleon opened the door, then followed them through. He escorted them to the elevator, and from there to Tallah's door. He knocked.

Nate scanned up and down the hall, searching for signs of a fight. No evidence of the showdown with Victor and Trevor was apparent.

Tallah answered the door. She wore long, beaded earrings and an embroidered wrap over her purple top. "Welcome," she said to Nate. "So nice to see you again."

"Thanks," Nate said, entering with the others as she stepped aside.

"Hey," Lindy greeted. "Nice of you to rejoin us." She sat on a sofa beside Risa.

"I needed alone time," Nate said. "I was feeling overwhelmed. I had to go crash."

"Now that you're all here, we can begin," Tallah said. "Who would care for oatmeal with cinnamon apples?"

"They're not here for tainted snacks," Cleon snapped.

"Mind your tongue, Mr. Cleon," Tallah chided. "No need for unpleasantness. You kids want to get down to business?"

"Yes, please," Risa said.

"There we go," Tallah said. "Ask politely and I'm happy to accommodate. First things first. We need to wash your stamps away. Mr. Jonas insisted that we start from scratch. Hold out your hands."

Nate extended his stamped hand. Tallah brushed a clear fluid onto the back of his fist. The pungent solution stung a little and felt very cold, as if it were evaporating rapidly. He turned his head away from the smell.

Once they had all been brushed with the solution, Tallah came by with a coarse cloth and scrubbed their hands briskly. Nate studied the back of his hand after she finished. His skin was red and raw. No trace of ink remained.

"You can choose two stamps," Tallah said. "Jonas urged me to attempt three, but I swore I could make no three of his stamps stable, and he believed me. Good thing, too, else you kids might have suffered damage without remedy. Mr. Jonas informed me that due to the nature of your upcoming task, one stamp must enable you to fly. Each of you is free to choose whichever second stamp you wish."

"For the record," Cleon interjected, "you'd be wise to make sure various abilities are represented. This promises to be your toughest assignment yet."

"I want to be a flying tank," Chris said. "I've always thought that would be the best combo."

"Fine with me," Nate said.

"I think a racer jet would be best," Risa said. "Do you guys mind if I do that?"

"Go for it," Lindy encouraged. She turned to Cleon. "Think we'll need to go underwater?"

"Not as far as I know," Cleon said. "We can't guarantee anything, but it seems unlikely."

"Then maybe I'll be a flying tank also," Lindy replied.

"What about you, Nate?" Cleon asked.

Nate dug a piece of Peak Performance gum from his pocket. "What about this?" Nate asked, holding the stick of gum out to Tallah. "Could you blend this with two stamps?"

Furrowing her brow, Tallah accepted the gum. She unwrapped it and sniffed it. She tested the corner with her tongue. After scowling thoughtfully, she gave it another tiny lick. Then she passed the gum back to Nate.

"No way could I blend this with two stamps. It is very potent magic, premium work. I could, however, modify the gum so it would harmonize with a single stamp."

Nate nodded. "Okay. Then I want flight and this gum. I have two other sticks. The effect doesn't last very long. Could you set up all three to work with a jet stamp?"

"I believe I could," Tallah said. "You'd want to use the gum one stick at a time, of course. Are we all resolved? Should I get to work?" She looked to Cleon.

"Why the gum, Nate?" Cleon asked. "You sure it beats tank strength and racer speed?"

"I'm not sure," Nate said. "But you saw it in action in the arcade. We already have a flying racer and two flying tanks. This gives us a different weapon. You suggested variety."

Cleon shrugged. "Fair enough. It's your hide. I won't object."

Tallah set about her work. She applied dual stamps to Chris, Risa, and Lindy. After some time fussing with Nate's three sticks of Peak Performance, she mixed a new solution, then applied a jet stamp to Nate and sealed it with her new concoction.

"There we go," Tallah pronounced. "All four of your little soldiers are geared up as requested."

"Pleasure as always," Cleon said.

"If you say so, Mr. Cleon," Tallah replied. Her expression sobered. "You kids take care what you bring out of the Devil's Mountain."

"And you be careful what spews from that mouth of yours," Cleon cautioned. "Come on, Jets. You have appointments to keep."

While Tallah looked on, Cleon ushered the kids into the hall. Nate watched Tallah as he walked out. She appeared worried. She looked like she wanted to cry out a warning. But she didn't, and the door closed.

"Are we out of here?" Chris asked.

"Not so fast," Cleon said. "Three of you had the opportunity to meet with Mr. White. But not Nate. The boss wants to have words with him before you all depart."

"Okay," Nate said, hoping he sounded casual. "No problem."

"I'm relieved to have your permission," Cleon drawled. "Come on, Mr. Gum Jet. The boss is this way."

Cleon led the four Jets down a hall and around a corner. They found the muscular guy with black spiky hair coming toward them.

"Hey there, Conner," Cleon said.

"I'll take Nate from here," Conner said stonily. "You get the others to the vehicle."

"Sure thing," Cleon said. "Come on, you three."

Cleon did an about-face and led the others back the way they had come. Without acknowledging Nate, Conner reversed his direction as well. Nate followed.

Nate had seen Conner before but had never spoken to him. "You guys have a lovely underground base here," he tried.

Conner said nothing.

"I love what you've done with the concrete. Very parking garage."

Conner kept strutting down the hall without a backward glance. They passed an intersection. Nate felt tempted to take a side hall, just to make Conner react. But he didn't want to stir things up too much. If he got dropped from the mission to recover Uweya, his last chance to stop Jonas White would be gone. He had reason to hope he would be included. Tallah had stamped him. They wouldn't restamp him just to drop him from the mission, right?

"Have you worked here long?" Nate asked.

Again Conner neglected to respond. Nate decided not to press him further.

After more walking, Conner stopped to open a sturdy door. He motioned for Nate to go through, then followed, pushing the door closed.

They had entered a rather bare room divided by a thick, clear wall with small clusters of holes in it. On the far side of the wall, Jonas White sat in a high-backed armchair. Conner took up a position behind Nate.

"Kind of you to join us," Jonas said silkily. "We missed you last night. You had other engagements, I take it?"

"I was tired," Nate said. "It was a long day."

"Too long to join your fellow Jets when they returned the Protector? Too long to confirm your victory?"

"It was already confirmed," Nate said. "Chris and Risa went ahead with the Protector. We left the Tanks treading water. It was a rough day. People almost died."

"I noticed that you removed your tracking bracelet," Jonas said.

"The task was finished," Nate replied. "It was uncomfortable."

"I don't like children, Nate. I never have."

"I can tell," Nate said. "Hole eight on your western course is practically impossible. I was putting on it with Chris and Risa the other day, and—"

Jonas held up a weary hand, motioning for him to stop. "Children have underdeveloped judgment. They say foolish things. They do foolish things. They bore me. They disappoint me."

"If it's any consolation, I sometimes feel the same way about adults."

"I expect you do," Jonas said. He gestured at the clear wall. "Please forgive the inconvenience of this barrier. Recent events have inspired me to take additional precautions. What little faith I had in you is fading."

"I keep delivering what you want."

"You have a vital task ahead of you. A hazardous task. Dangerous for you, dangerous for the other Jets. This task means a lot to me, Nate. It means everything. And I don't trust you."

"Then why send me?"

"For the assignment to recover the Protector, the Tanks had the advantage. If I were to have gambled on the outcome, I would have bet on them. Given the variables involved, their speed and strength should have outclassed your aeronautic and aquatic abilities. You had the means to raise the trunk from the tower, but they had the means to extract the Protector and keep it from you. I need capable people, Nate, and you have proven yourself the most capable."

"We almost killed Roman taking the Protector from him," Nate said. "It was a close one."

"I may not like children," Jonas said, "but I can admire ruthless dedication to victory. You will open the way to Uweya for me."

"Count on it."

"I know that you are not my ally. But you should be. Do not tangle with a man who has a simulacrum of you. Foolish child or not, you ought to learn that lesson before it is too late."

"Fighting you would be crazy," Nate said.

"It would be futile," Jonas assured him. "The other Jets look to you for leadership. They expect you to join them on this mission. I want you to join them as well. But I want you to understand what will happen should you attempt to cross me."

"I'm listening."

"I have simulacra of them, too," Jonas reminded him. "And you know I currently hold Trevor here, and Pigeon, as well as Victor Battiato, John Dart, and the illustrious Mozag. Cross me, and they all perish, Nate. I've killed before. I won't hesitate. Are we clear?"

Nate felt stunned by the man's bluntness. He nodded weakly.

"Serve me well and you'll be rewarded," Jonas said. "Do I keep my promises, Conner?"

"Yes, sir."

Jonas gave a sickly smile. "It's important to keep your promises when dealing with mercenaries. My word matters to me for many reasons. For example, I set rules to the contest between the clubs. The Jets won the contest, therefore the Jets will retrieve Uweya."

"Makes sense," Nate said.

"Once I have Uweya," Jonas continued, "you and your friends will no longer be threats to me. Serve me well, and you will all go free. Your families will be spared. Even though you never had my best interests at heart, I'll reward you. Defy me, and it's not just your own life you're gambling with, Nate."

"I get it," Nate said. "I'm not crazy."

Jonas wagged a finger. "Yet children sometimes do crazy things." He waved a dismissive hand. "Very well, Nate. Off you go. Serve me well. Fetch Uweya. Your friends are depending on you."

"I understand."

Conner opened the door.

Nate jerked a thumb at Conner. "In the interest of employee feedback, this guy needs to work on his people skills."

"Conner wasn't hired to do customer service," Jonas said around a smirk.

Nate followed Conner out of the room.

* * * * *

The SUV climbed a steep, rutted dirt road that made Nate cling to the door for support. Cleon drove. A small woman named Jeanine rode shotgun. Seat belts fastened, Nate, Lindy, and Risa sat on the bench behind them. Chris reclined in the far back.

The SUV rocked and reared over the challenging road. A couple of times Nate thought they were going to tip over. In her middle position on the bench, Lindy flopped from one side to the other with all of the jostling.

"Are you sure we're going the right way?" Nate asked.

"Don't tell me you can't handle a little bump or two," Cleon replied.

"What happened to the regular drivers?" Lindy asked. "The guys you used to cart around the other clubs?"

"This mission is too sensitive for anyone but family," Cleon said with a grin.

A particularly strong jolt sent a shockwave through Nate's spine.

"We might have a hard time getting Uweya if we're paralyzed," he complained.

"This is nothing," Cleon said. "You're just used to driving like city kids. You need more off-roading in your life. It's good for the soul."

"But not the spine," Nate muttered.

They continued to climb the shoulder of Mt. Diablo. The sun was now well above the horizon. Cleon had said that due to the daylight, he was under orders to escort everyone to their destination instead of letting them fly.

"You guys found a tunnel last night?" Nate asked. Cleon had not yet fully explained.

Cleon yawned, his fillings visible in the rearview mirror. "I deserve a big, fat nap after all of this is done. So does Jeanine. Those in the know have searched for an entrance to Mt. Diablo for years. Several of the mines in the region secretly had that as a goal. But everybody dug too low."

"Are we going to the top?" Lindy wondered.

"Closer to the top than you might have guessed. See, if you drop the Protector, he always falls facing the direction to Uweya. We spent much of the night fumbling in the dark. In the end, we found the entrance."

"Where are the Gate and the Protector now?" Nate asked. "We'll still need them, won't we?"

"They're up ahead, ready and waiting," Cleon said. "We left them there last night. Figured it beat losing them in a hijacking today. Mr. White likes to play it safe."

The SUV continued up the mountainside. From time to time, with a rough shake and the grinding of metal, the SUV would get high centered and become immobile. Cleon would look over at Jeanine, who would close her eyes and make the SUV wobble until the wheels got traction. Nate assumed she must be the Crusher Ziggy had mentioned.

At length they reached a steep, rocky point where the SUV could proceed no farther. Cleon killed the engine and got out of the vehicle. The others climbed out as well.

Cleon stood with his hands on his hips, teeth bared as he glared up the slope. "We're not too far from the entrance. A little hike might do us some good."

Nate levitated a few inches off the ground. "Do *you* some good," he corrected. "Daylight or not, I don't see anyone around, so I'm saving my strength."

"Kid has a point," Jeanine said, her voice a bit huskier than Nate would have predicted. She rose half a foot off the ground. "It'll cost me less exertion to float there than to walk."

"How about floating me?" Cleon suggested.

Jeanine arched an eyebrow. "Drop a few pounds and we'll talk."

Cleon pressed his lips together, as if biting back a sharp reply. He nodded, rubbed his lips, and started plodding up the long slope. The others hovered around him like a flock of ghosts.

Risa drifted over to Jeanine. "You can fly?"

Jeanine considered her coolly, but answered. "In a sense. I can do tricks with gravity that enable me to float."

"Why not fly Cleon?" Chris asked. "Is he really too heavy?"

"Messing with gravity takes finesse," Jeanine said. "I've learned to float myself efficiently through lots of practice. Floating others requires more energy and concentration."

"You were making the car float back there?" Lindy inquired.

"I was shifting gravity enough to let us get traction," Jeanine explained. "Lifting the entire SUV would wipe me out before long."

"Do you really want to specify your limits?" Cleon huffed.

"Are you really out of breath already? You need to slow down on the ribs and nachos."

Nate tried to choke back his laughter. Muffled giggles surrounded him.

"Yuck it up," Cleon complained. "We'll see how funny old Cleon is once the trouble starts under the mountain."

"If we're attacked by corn dogs," Jeanine said with a straight face, "our enemies will be doomed."

As they progressed up the slope, the observation tower atop Mt. Diablo came into view above them. Nate had once enjoyed the view from the solid structure on a day trip with his family. It had never crossed his mind that he might be close to an ancient magical treasure.

Cleon paused, staring up at the observation tower and wiping sweat from his brow. "Folks might be able to see us. You freaks might want to get back down on the ground."

"That building is still a long ways off," Jeanine protested. "No way can anyone see the six inches between my toes and the ground. I know misery loves company, Cleon, but we're going to keep hovering. Pick up the pace if you can. Boss wanted this accomplished today."

Grumbling angry words under his breath, Cleon sped up a little. He kept his eyes on the ground in front of his feet.

At last they arrived at a dark cleft in the ground sheltered by a boulder. The cavity didn't look like much of a cave. Nate wouldn't have expected it to extend back more than a few feet out of view.

"We had to excavate this," Cleon said, his lungs working hard. "Jeanine didn't pitch in. She sat back and watched. Everybody who wants to criticize my hiking should keep in mind that I was up most of the night uncovering this entrance."

"We're very proud of you," Jeanine consoled. "It's a majestic hole."

Cleon gestured at the cleft with both hands. "In we go."

Chris ducked inside.

"Watch out for that first step," Cleon called, one hand beside his mouth. "It's a doozy."

"The kid can fly," Jeanine pointed out.

"It's an expression," Cleon growled.

"Watch your tone," Jeanine said. "You'll need my help before long."

Cleon gave a little nod and tipped an imaginary hat. "No disrespect intended."

Risa hesitated, crouching at the entrance of the cleft.

Cleon waved for her to enter. "Go on, girl. You'll be fine."

"They left light in here," Chris called from inside. His voice already sounded kind of distant.

Risa entered. Nate followed, squirming through the narrow opening. He wondered how a big guy like Cleon could fit. He probably couldn't squeeze through without getting scraped up.

The deeper Nate progressed into the cleft, the more it opened up, until he was no longer squirming and could walk comfortably. The air smelled of minerals. Up ahead he saw Chris silhouetted against an electric lantern.

"Come here," Chris called, waving.

Lifting off the ground, Nate flew along the cave to where Chris stood by the lantern. Nate caught up to Risa, and they reached Chris together.

Where Chris waited beside the lantern, the cave widened considerably, forming a large, craggy chamber. A massive hole dominated the floor. Chris lingered a few paces from the brink of the yawning crater.

"Looks like we go down from here," Chris said.

"I don't see any other openings," Risa agreed.

Nate drifted out over the void. "Hello," he called, tilted downward, hands cupped around his mouth. The acoustics of the echoes suggested that the hole was extremely deep.

"How can you hover over all that emptiness?" Risa asked with a shiver.

"I don't know," Nate replied. "The same way I can swim in deep water, I guess. It's a long way down, but I can fly."

"I can't," Cleon remarked, striding toward them. "That's why I need Gravity Girl."

"And why you had better be nice to her," Jeanine reminded him.

Lindy glided out over the void to hover beside Nate. "Wow," she murmured. "Now, *that* is a deep hole. It's like staring down the throat of a volcano."

Jeanine cracked a chemical light stick, then shook it until it emitted an even, green radiance. She tossed it underhand into the crater. Nate watched as it fell and fell, shrinking to a faint green spark before vanishing entirely.

"It has a bottom, right?" Nate asked.

"I can't confirm," Lindy said. "It extends a long way and then elbows a little to the side. I can't see through the rocks here."

"It has a bottom, all right," Cleon said. "The Gate and the Protector are down there right now."

"How'd they get down there?" Risa asked.

"We had a busy night," Jeanine said.

"Are we ready?" Cleon asked.

Jeanine cracked more chemical light sticks, distributing one to each of them. Then Jeanine and Cleon floated out over the pit. Cleon wobbled and waved his arms for balance.

"Keep still," Jeanine advised. "You're messing up my concentration."

Cleon obeyed without comment.

"I'll lead the way," Lindy offered.

They started downward. Nate regretted his lack of opportunity to strategize with the others. Somebody employed by Jonas was always present to overhear. He hoped that when the time came, Chris and Risa would help hold back Jeanine and Cleon so he could race ahead to Uweya. He would have to pick his moment with care. If he failed today, Jonas would win.

Nate stole glances at Cleon and Jeanine. If he made it to Uweya ahead of everyone, what would he do? How much time would he have before others caught up? This was not the sort of situation where he wanted to trust to luck and improvisation. But what else could he do, considering how little he really knew about Uweya? What else could he expect, with so little time to collaborate and plan? A nervous, fluttery feeling persisted in his belly.

The air grew cooler as they descended. The gentle glow of their light sticks seemed a feeble weapon against the thick darkness above and below. They didn't rush—the ominous obscurity around them forbade haste. Nate felt like a deep-sea explorer sinking into an oceanic trench.

The profound shaft elbowed once, then again. After the second bend, the bottom of the pit came into view, illuminated by various electric lanterns.

"Katie Sung is waiting for us," Lindy announced.

"Jonas wanted his best people along," Cleon said.

"Is that why you're here?" Jeanine said, straining to resist laughter. "Don't make me crack up, Cleon. I wouldn't want one of his best people to fall."

"You calling me minor league?" Cleon challenged.

"We'll let your performance today do the talking," she replied. "Now let me concentrate."

"Welcome," Katie greeted warmly as Nate touched down between a pair of lanterns. Her form-fitting outfit emphasized her athletic build. Nate noticed the cot where she must have slept. "Turns out the Jets were the top squad after all. A few of us employed by Mr. White lost some money on that outcome."

"Don't remind me," Cleon grumbled.

"You bet against us?" Chris exclaimed.

"Nothing personal," Cleon said as his feet reached the ground. "I figured that racer plus tank equaled domination."

"Don't bet against the delinquents," Katie said. "Nate and especially Lindy earned their stamps through suspicious means. The kind of person who beats the system once is likely to do so again. I have my eyes on them."

Nate didn't miss the message—Katie was there to ensure that Nate and Lindy would perform as expected. When he tried to make his move, she would be there to stop him.

"What now?" Risa asked.

"You'll see," Katie promised. "This way."

They followed her down a passage away from the base of the

shaft. The passage opened into a cavernous room, lit by glowing crystals in the walls and ceiling. A colossal stone gate dominated most of one wall.

"It looks exactly like the Gate," Lindy realized. "The one we took from the Hermit."

"The Gate is a simulacrum," Katie said. "As is the Protector. No doubt the Gate will open the way once placed on the pedestal. How the Protector will be employed remains to be seen."

A pedestal composed of white stone flecked with gold projected up from the floor in the center of the room. The Gate and the Protector rested on the ground near the base of the pedestal.

"We use the little gate to open the big one?" Chris verified.

"Presumably," Katie said. "Sadly, we don't know what to expect once the gate opens. Mr. White suspects we will face some stiff opposition. Enough that it could spell the end for all of us."

"Unacceptable," Cleon said. "My team's playing tonight. I have a date with my TV."

Jeanine elbowed him.

"I brought some weapons," Katie announced. She motioned toward a large canvas bag. "Take what you want."

Risa made it to the bag first and pulled open the mouth. "Lots of baseball bats."

"Bats, hammers, shields, a few axes," Katie recited. "Mr. White suspects we'll want blunt instruments."

"Not for smashing giant Protectors," Nate hoped.

Katie shrugged. "We'll know when the gate opens."

"What about machine guns?" Chris asked. "What about a bazooka?"

Katie scowled. "Mr. White warned that an accomplished mage

like Iwa Iza would have installed powerful defenses against magical attacks. Since Iwa Iza lived long before the invention of gunpowder, firearms would probably register as magical attacks and engage those formidable defenses. This place is mage-proof, and consequently gun-proof."

"But we're all using magic," Risa said, confused.

"We're magically enhanced," Katie explained. "We're not wielding magic ourselves. None of us are mages. We're just employing our enhanced skills."

"We're using gifts bestowed by mages," Jeanine added. "We're originating nothing. It makes a difference."

"Go on," Cleon said, shooing the Jets toward the bag. "Cowboy up. Those who can fly and are bulletproof get to bear the brunt of the attacks."

The first bat Nate tried felt too heavy. The next was made of wood and seemed about right—light enough to swing fast, but heavy enough to do some damage. He chose a small mallet as a backup weapon.

Nate edged over to Lindy, who was testing the weight of a much larger bat than he had selected. Having a tank stamp had some advantages when it came to strength, although her practice swings lacked expertise.

"You don't see anything, do you?" Nate checked quietly.

"Not through the rock," Lindy murmured. "Not through the gate. This place is impermeable."

"Nice Pigeon word."

"It means—"

"I get that it means you can't see through it."

"We good?" Cleon asked. "All set?" He held a baseball bat over

345

his head with both hands, pivoting at the waist and reaching high to stretch. "Let's see what lies behind door number one."

Risa zipped up into the air at an amazing speed. She zoomed to different positions around the room in quick bursts, darting like a dragonfly.

"Flying in race mode is cool," Risa crowed. "You guys seem so slow."

"Use the ability to good advantage when the gate opens," Katie admonished.

"Will we need the Protector when the gate opens?" Nate wondered. "Should we have it ready?"

"I'm not sure," Katie admitted. "We'll need it at some point up ahead."

"I'll watch over it," Chris offered. "I can take some punishment."

"Are you going to chew a Peak Performance?" Lindy asked Nate.

"I'll wait and see what we're dealing with," Nate replied. "I have a limited supply." He held up the stick of gum in his hand.

"Who wants to do the honors?" Katie asked.

"I'll open it," Lindy offered.

Katie gestured for her to go ahead.

Lindy flew over to the pedestal. She picked up the Gate and set it on the pedestal. The Gate took on a faint glow, as if a light source within the stone had been ignited.

Chris took up a position near the little warrior statue. Nate and Risa hovered together. Nate rubbed his stick of Peak Performance with his thumb. He tried to keep calm.

"Open it?" Lindy checked.

"Everyone ready?" Katie asked, looking around.

"I'm past ready and halfway to bored," Cleon said, taking a practice swing with his bat.

Nobody offered opposition.

"Do it," Katie said.

Lindy pulled open the miniature gate.

Nate braced for the Gate to start morphing into a bizarre new form. Instead, the gate merely swung open, as did the enormous gate in the wall.

Beyond the open gate, Nate could see another large chamber populated by a horde of figures of varying size. Some were the height of children, some matched up with adults, and a few were larger than man-sized. The figures wore primitive, painted masks of extensive diversity. Some masks represented animals like snakes, wolves, bears, hawks, or seals. Other masks were grotesque caricatures of people. Still others bulged with inexplicable shapes, abstract and unsettling. None of the figures moved. They were composed of a grayish ceramic material.

"Are they made of clay?" Risa asked.

"There are hundreds of them," Katie observed, her voice hushed.

"Are they just going to stand there?" Cleon asked.

"Maybe they're out of batteries," Nate said wishfully.

The remark drew a few uneasy chuckles.

The ceramic host remained stationary.

"They have weapons," Risa observed.

Most bore simple armaments—stone hammers, wooden clubs, stout rods, crude spears. A few carried primitive bows. Some lacked obvious weapons.

"Are they just for effect?" Chris asked.

"I'm a fairly lucky guy," Cleon said. "But I can't believe I'm *that* lucky."

"Should I fly in there and look around?" Risa asked. "We can't see the whole room. I could use my fastest speed."

"If you're volunteering, I won't stop you," Katie said.

"Wait," Risa hedged. "You think it could be dangerous? Even flying?"

"It shouldn't be too dangerous if you use your top speed," Katie replied smoothly. Nate questioned how much she believed her words.

"All right," Risa said with a trace of hesitation. "I'll take a peek."

Quick as a blink, Risa sped away, hardly even visible as a blur. Nate realized that, even under normal conditions, the kids could fly much faster than any person could run. If Risa was going around ten times her normal flight speed, she had to be moving at hundreds of miles per hour.

The instant the half-glimpsed blur of Risa's speedy form passed through the gate, the ceramic warriors attacked. Brandishing their weapons, the figures sprang into action, flooding through the gate as if their petrified poses had been an elaborate hoax. They raised no voices, but arrows launched into the air, stones were propelled from slings, and countless ceramic feet trampled over the stone floor.

After his initial jolt of surprise, Nate realized that several of the archers were targeting him. Flying higher, he popped the stick of Peak Performance into his mouth and started vigorously chewing.

His perception of the oncoming threat was instantly clarified. His attention first went to the twenty-two warriors within his field of view armed with projectiles. Avoiding arrows and stones would be essential to surviving the battle. But survival alone would not suffice—he had to help the other Jets!

Ranks of soldiers descended on Chris and Lindy. Katie Sung sprang to aid Chris, probably because it would help guard the

Protector. She joined the fray with jaw-dropping ferocity, shattering foes with explosive kicks and vicious blows from the pair of mallets she wielded.

Chris had a large bat, and he swung it recklessly. Spears jabbed him, stone axes chopped him, and clubs slammed against him. The strongest blows made him stumble a little. Otherwise, he absorbed each impact and kept on swinging. Stroke after stroke pulverized warrior after warrior.

Despite the fierce defense from Katie and Chris, the ceramic warriors pressed forward undaunted, showing no regard for their survival. None hesitated. None retreated. Unlike Chris, Katie could not afford to take blows. She danced wildly to avoid endless attacks, retaliating whenever possible. Given the overwhelming quantity of assailants, Nate wondered how long she could last.

Lindy was faring much worse than Chris. She got knocked off her feet, and a gang of ceramic figures surrounded her, issuing blows at will.

Cleon rushed to her aid. His body kept passing through ceramic figures, as if he had no substance. Their weapons swished through him as though he were a hologram.

A few feet to one side of Cleon, ceramic heads were bursting and limbs were getting bashed to pieces in time with his swings. With his heightened senses, Nate quickly recognized that Cleon had somehow projected an image of himself a short distance away from his actual position.

Cleon was making slow progress toward Lindy, so Nate flew to help. Since he was the lone target above the combat, stones and arrows kept streaking his way, but he dodged them with casual effort, twisting and curving to avoid the projectiles. Swooping down, using the speed of his flight to boost the force of his blow, Nate obliterated a ceramic head with his baseball bat. Staying low, bobbing up and down just above the heads of the inhuman soldiers, Nate started thumping them with precise forehands and backhands. Whether time had decayed their ceramic forms and masks, or whether they had never been particularly sturdy to begin with, they crumbled beneath his swings.

A group of ten warriors suddenly rose twenty feet into the air, then fell back to the ground, shattering on impact. Another group of attackers flew skyward, and another.

Nate helped Lindy to her feet while Cleon covered them. "You okay?" Nate asked.

Lindy looked up at him gratefully. "I'm unhurt. A little freaked, though. I wish I had spent more time practicing baseball."

Katie Sung and Chris fell back to them. Katie was breathing hard. Jeanine levitated more groups of warriors and sent them crashing down atop others. No matter how many ceramic figures they incapacitated, more kept streaming through the gate, swarming fearlessly.

"They break easily," Nate commented.

"True," Chris agreed.

"There are too many," Katie gasped, sweat running down the sides of her face. "Jeanine will get worn down before long. So will I. Fragile or not, they'll overwhelm us with sheer numbers."

More soldiers poured into the room, spreading out to approach from all sides. Nate took to the air again, narrowly dodging weapons while issuing perfect blows. Katie fought with manic intensity, moving in measured bursts from one enemy to the next, smashing them to dust with stunning power. Chris fought methodically, absorbing blows so he could focus on offense.

Risa returned abruptly. When she slowed to normal speed, her face was flushed, and she was panting. "There's an even larger room beyond the gate!" she called. "If you can get through it, there's a pedestal in there, and a big statue just like the Protector."

A rock glanced off her arm. Temporarily speeding up, she flew higher.

"Are you all right?" Nate asked, flying up to her. He used his bat to deflect a stone that would have struck her in the back.

"Going at top speed wore me out really quickly," Risa said. "Much faster than Trevor described. Even after I slowed to race mode, I got so woozy that I almost passed out. Everybody was shooting at me. I got spooked, climbed high, and slowed down. I came back as soon as I felt I could handle race mode again. I still don't feel great."

Nate yanked Risa to one side to help her avoid an arrow. "Can you keep flying in race mode?"

"I think so," Risa said shakily.

"You better try," Nate said. "If you hold still, they'll pick you off."

Down below, the illusionary Cleon flickered, and his actual self came into view. One of his arms hung limp at his side. Blood sheeted from a gash on his forehead. He fought on, one-handed.

Protector in hand, Chris took to the air, racing toward the gate. An arrow hit him, bouncing away harmlessly.

"Nate!" Katie cried from below. "Help guard the Protector!"

Risa started flying around at a higher speed, and Nate zoomed to help Chris. Apparently they were hoping that placing the Protector on the pedestal Risa had found might help the situation. Nate hoped it wouldn't make everything worse.

CHAPTER TWENTY-TWO

THE PROTECTOR

Chris led the way through the open gate and into the neighboring chamber. The vast room had a high ceiling. A third of the spacious floor remained covered by warriors pressing toward the gate. The pedestal in the center of the room was unguarded.

On the far side of the room, a monumental statue stood against the wall. In form and stance, it matched the Protector perfectly—stocky, thick-limbed, with a large club in each hand.

Chris landed beside the pedestal and slammed the Protector down on top of it. The Protector took on a faint inner glow. Nothing else happened.

Most of the ceramic soldiers continued to surge toward the gate, but those toward the rear turned and headed for Chris. Several archers targeted Nate all at once, forcing him to dive and contort himself to avoid the volley of arrows. Despite his maneuvering, two arrows breezed close enough that he felt the wind of their passage.

In frustration, Chris jostled the Protector, evidently hoping that by shaking it enough he might make something happen. His actions caused one of the Protector's arms to stretch out to one side. The arm of the larger statue extended in precisely the same way.

"Use the statue!" Nate called. "Use the big statue to fight the others!"

Chris tried to pick up the Protector, but failed. Gripping the legs, he made one of them step forward, then the other. The imposing statue took two steps away from the wall. Nate noticed a small door behind where it had stood.

Nate arrived at the pedestal, landing nimbly. "Cover me," Nate blurted. "With the gum I'm better at this."

Chris relinquished the Protector, and Nate began using the small statue to make the large one come bounding to their aid. As the first ceramic warrior reached the pedestal, Chris destroyed it with his bat. Chris waded forward resolutely. Spear tips snapped against his chest as each swing spewed ceramic chips into the air.

Lindy flew in to lend support. She landed roughly, and although she failed to bash soldiers as efficiently as Chris, she diverted the attention of many.

Nate only needed a few seconds. Under the influence of Peak Performance, he could visualize perfectly how to manipulate the Protector in order to make the big statue move exactly how he wanted.

Chris and Lindy hastily flew out of the way as the big statue stomped forward. A mighty swipe of one club blasted several ceramic warriors into confetti.

Nate swiveled the statue to attack in multiple directions. Swinging liberally, it shattered soldiers in droves. The tallest of the ceramic warriors failed to stand higher than the waist of the stout stone guardian.

Weapons struck the massive statue harmlessly, as if the ceramic warriors were attempting to kill a mountain. Unfortunately for them, the mountain was fighting back.

Despite his elation at his success, Nate controlled the gigantic statue calmly. Lindy and Chris dealt with the warriors that slipped by, freeing Nate to concentrate on his demolition work. Risa zoomed by a couple of times in race mode, lending extra assistance.

The ceramic soldiers that had marched into the other room had now reversed their course. Nate made the giant statue plod forward until it stood at the gate to receive them. The ceramic forces advanced recklessly, and the big statue mowed them down until the air filled with dust and the area around the gateway became heaped with rubble.

Toward the end, Nate felt the effects of the Peak Performance dwindling. His hands began to feel a little clumsier, and the ways he needed to manipulate the small statue became less intuitive. But by then, the battle was essentially over. As he swiped at the remaining soldiers with less precise swings, Nate trusted the others to dismantle the stragglers. He decided to save his other two sticks of Peak Performance for whatever dangers might lie ahead.

Led by Katie Sung and Chris, the others pounded the remaining warriors until they lay broken and inert. Nate let go of the Protector and backed away from the pedestal. The huge statue stood motionless once more.

Cleon came limping through the gate, using an ancient spear as a crutch. He seemed to have use of both arms. Dried blood stained his face, neck, and shoulder, but no fresh blood was flowing. Jeanine strolled beside him, apparently unhurt.

"You all right?" Nate called as Cleon approached.

"Mr. White patched me up as best he could using my simulacrum," Cleon said. "My leg took an ugly blow. I'm lucky I can walk at all."

Risa leaned against the pedestal. "I'm dizzy and tired," she said, head bowed. "Near the end, I was sure I would pass out."

"What now?" Chris asked. Scars and dents marred his heavy baseball bat. His clothes were punctured and torn.

Katie motioned to the location where the statue had originally stood. Recessed into the wall was a small door, intricately carved with concentric circles and swirling patterns.

"It's for short people," Lindy noted.

"It's too small for the big statue to fit," Nate realized. "Whoever designed this place didn't want us using the Protector beyond this room."

"You're probably right," Katie acknowledged.

"Any idea what comes next?" Chris asked, bat resting on his shoulder.

"My guess?" Cleon said. "Something beyond that door will try to kill us."

"Mind if we rest for a minute?" Risa asked. "The high-speed flying wore me out."

"Take a load off," Katie said. "We can't proceed until we get this next door open." She started toward the door.

Grunting and squatting, Cleon sat down on the floor. Risa sat down as well, leaning her back against the pedestal. Chris and Jeanine followed Katie.

Lindy sidled over to Nate. "No keyhole," she whispered. "No seams. I can't see through it, but I can see into it a little. It's at least three feet thick."

Nate sat down with his legs crossed. Lindy knelt beside him.

Katie stood nearly a head taller than the carved door. She ran her hands over it high and low, tracing some of the curvy lines etched into the surface. She applied pressure in certain places. Finally she backed away, hands on her hips, and asked generally, "Any theories?"

Nobody responded. Jeanine and Chris moved forward to take a closer look.

Katie turned to Nate. "Use the statue to break it down."

"Worth a try," Nate said. The Protector remained on the pedestal. As Nate used the little model to march the statue over to the door, he could feel that his gum had fully worn off. Still, guiding the statue while under the influence of Peak Performance had given him experience, so he managed to jerkily maneuver the statue into position and kick the door. The foot struck with a dull thud. The door showed no sign of weakening.

"Use a club," Katie recommended.

Nate shifted the position of the statue so he could swing a club low. A pair of blows accomplished nothing.

"Hit it hard!" Katie demanded.

Nate shifted the position again and took a big swing. The top half of the club broke off. The door appeared undamaged.

"Perfect," Cleon spat.

"Contact Jonas," Jeanine suggested.

Katie produced a small seashell and spoke into it quietly. She held it to her ear as if receiving a response. She spoke and listened several more times.

"Nate," Katie called. "Remove the Protector from the pedestal."

When Nate tried to lift the entire Protector, it felt glued to the top of the pedestal, which was strange because he had managed to lift individual legs with little problem. He had more luck as he tried to tip it with both hands. He found that constant effort slowly caused it to lean. As he tipped and lifted, he fought against what felt like a powerful magnetic attraction. With a final yank, the Protector came free. The big statue remained frozen in place. The small, thick door slid upward until it disappeared entirely.

"Bingo!" Cleon chuckled. "Boss knows his stuff."

Katie murmured something into the seashell. She listened, nodded, then put it away. "Is everyone recuperated?"

Cleon used the spear to help himself rise. "I'm about as ready to die as I'll ever be."

The others got up as well. They gathered near the small doorway. Peering inside, Nate saw a long, narrow corridor.

"A Tank should lead the way," Katie prompted.

"Out of the road," Chris said, stepping through the doorway. "You guys back me up."

Nate got another stick of gum ready. He dreaded to think what might await beyond the confining hallway. Lindy followed Chris, Nate tailed Lindy, and Katie entered behind Nate. The hall was no higher than the doorway. Chris was almost tall enough for the top of his head to brush the ceiling. Katie had to advance in a stooped position.

"I don't see any enemies," Lindy told Nate. "But the way ahead won't be easy."

Nate saw what she meant when he exited the cramped corridor. The hall opened into yet another large chamber. To the right, an enormous corridor led away from the cavernous room. The massive corridor was essentially a bigger, longer hallway full of moving obstacles like the passage that had guarded the Protector. Beyond the spinning blades, scything pendulums, jabbing spikes, twirling axes, and crushing pillars, Nate caught fleeting glimpses of a large, distant door.

"No way," Chris said. "This is worse than Angel Island."

"Much worse," Lindy agreed. "It's denser—more blades, bigger blades, more spikes. Many are faster than anything we saw in the other corridor. Some of the pillars are mashing together horizontally. I see evidence of trapdoors in the floor. Some of the holes in the wall have arrows and darts ready to fire. Plus it's more than twice as long."

Behind them, Nate noticed Katie speaking into the seashell. She regarded the frantic obstacle course with trepidation.

Risa approached the other Jets. "This isn't fair! Is every hidden treasure guarded by a hall like this?"

"Iwa Iza hid the Protector," Nate reminded her. "He also hid Uweya. Same designer."

Risa shook her head in despair. "Do we seriously have to—"

Her words cut off without explanation. Nate looked over and saw that Risa was holding perfectly still. Chris was motionless as well. And Lindy. He decided he had better freeze himself.

"Please don't panic," Katie said. "Jonas has temporarily immobilized the four of you for security reasons. He expected something like this final gauntlet. Our prize should lie just beyond. We needed you against those warriors, and we thank you for your fine service. The good news is, you won't have to make it through that deadly tangle up ahead. Jonas will use my simulacrum to boost me as he has never boosted anyone before, and the task of retrieving Uweya will be mine alone."

"I've never heard them so quiet," Cleon said.

"Can't they speak?" Jeanine asked.

"Jonas wanted to paralyze you four quickly," Katie explained. "As a consequence, he had no time for finesse. He'll go back and make you a little more comfortable if you behave well. Free up your mouths and eyes, for example. Then, once Uweya is secure, he'll release you entirely, and you can fly out of here, free to enjoy the fruit of your efforts."

Nate remained motionless, although keeping completely still was turning out to be harder than he might have guessed. He was worried that he might sway a little, or move his arm, or shift his glance, or somehow give away the fact that he remained in complete control of his body. The other Jets remained as immobile as wax figures.

Nate was positioned so he could see Katie. Her brow crinkled, and she lifted the seashell to her ear. Her alarmed eyes went to Nate. "Is somebody playing possum?"

The moment had arrived. It was now or never. The other Jets were out of commission. He knew where he needed to go. The amulet around his neck had obviously worked, preventing Jonas from freezing him, and now Jonas had noticed that something was interfering with his simulcry.

Nate still had the stick of Peak Performance in his hand. Shoving the gum into his mouth, he took to the air, rising quickly. Cleon, Jeanine, and Katie all shouted in dismay. Katie hurled her mallets at him with superhuman force, but the gum was already kicking in, and Nate narrowly dodged them. Gravity suddenly increased around him, dragging him down, but Nate found that if he angled down diagonally, he could slip away from the weighty pull. Each time he escaped, a moment later gravity would increase again as Jeanine refocused her power. But every time he slipped away from her increased gravity field, he climbed as much as possible before the downward tug hit him again. Overall, he kept gaining altitude instead of losing. After her seventh attempt to drag him down, Jeanine collapsed.

Nate took that opportunity as his cue and arrowed toward the deadly hall. He could fly, and his senses and coordination were enhanced, but his body was as vulnerable as ever. One wrong move and he would get shredded to ribbons. Even fully under the influence of Peak Performance, navigating the lethal hallway looked virtually impossible. He could see a way in, but even with his senses enhanced, Nate could not chart a complete route through from his current vantage. He hoped that he would somehow find ways to keep moving forward, yard by yard, foot by foot, without getting decapitated, flattened, or impaled. Gritting his teeth, he prayed that he and Peak Performance would be up to the challenge.

Nate entered the hall near the upper left corner. All of his senses were focused on survival. He tried not to get overwhelmed by the abundant lethal threats. He attempted to focus on the most immediate dangers, on how to survive one second to the next while still advancing. There was no time to plan, only to react. With desperate faith, he entrusted his life to his enhanced reflexes.

A huge blade swished by close enough that the metallic smell registered distinctly. Nate curved his body to avoid a thrusting spear, then ducked to barely dodge a pair of axes. He began to spin wildly, eyes roving, because it was the only way to see everything around him and avoid getting blindsided. He not only looked but listened.

Peak Performance offered no sense of security—even with the enhancement, he was stretched to his limits. Too much was coming at him too fast. He flew in strange new ways. Sometimes he flew feet first. Sometimes he flew spread-eagle. Sometimes he would drop or rise suddenly. He flew tucked into a tiny ball, he flew with his body ramrod straight, he flew in bizarre poses to dodge simultaneous slashes and stabs.

Nate didn't think about reaching the end of the obstacles. There was no opportunity to examine how far he had come or how much farther he had to go. He only had time to twirl and tuck, to climb and fall, to flip and swoop and twist.

He made dozens of split-second decisions. He chose to let a blade graze his back to avoid having an arrow plunge through his neck. He permitted a spear to nick his thigh to keep a speeding column from crushing his arm. When two ways to proceed presented themselves, he tried to estimate which was the lesser evil. There was no time to choose well.

Flying had never felt so exhausting. Nothing had ever felt so exhausting. He scantly avoided death over and over and over and over. How many near misses could a person survive? How many scrapes and scratches could one accept to avoid getting maimed or worse? There was no place to pause, no chance to regroup, only a host of fatal threats, followed by another barrage, and then another.

When he emerged from the far side of the obstacle course, it came as a shock. Nate flew to the ground and spread out his arms to embrace the floor. He had never felt so happy to be at rest. Little cuts and scrapes stung all over his body. He was truly stunned to be alive. Somewhere deep down, he had known that eventually he would reach a place where no amount of clever contortion would avoid a certain combination of threats. And that would have been the end.

Except he had survived. Would he have to fly back through the obstacles after reaching Uweya? Probably. He didn't want to think about that yet. For now, the frenetic corridor separated him from his enemies. Maybe not for long, though. Katie would be coming after him. How long would it take for Jonas to empower her? Even with additional enhancements, would she be able to navigate the lethal corridor? He had to assume she would survive. He had to keep moving.

Instead of standing up, Nate flew to the door. It was more than three times his height. A metallic lever to one side of the doorway seemed the obvious way to open it. Nate pulled the lever. The door opened.

CHAPTER TWENTY-THREE

UWEYA

Nate decided to walk through the doorway rather than fly. A short hall led into a circular room with a high, domed ceiling. The shape made Nate think of an observatory he had once visited. Thanks to his enhanced state, he took in many details, but his attention was not drawn to the tightly fitted stone blocks of the walls or ceiling, or the worktables positioned around the room, or the stacks of supplies against some of the walls. He found himself entranced by the familiar sphere floating in the center of the room.

Nate had seen globes, and he had seen pictures of Earth from space, so it was easy to recognize that the ball hovering above the floor was his home planet, rendered in breathtaking detail. From his present vantage, he could see most of the Atlantic Ocean, along with much of North and South America and part of Europe and Africa.

At least twelve feet in diameter, the sphere hung inexplicably suspended, slightly tilted on an invisible axis. Even from a distance, mountains stood out in clear relief, islands poked up out of the sea, and icecaps covered the poles. The color was so true to life that Nate imagined he could splash his hand in the ocean. Unlike with photos from space, no clouds obscured his view of the planet.

Fortunately Nate was still chewing his gum, which allowed him to dodge the two arrows that hissed toward him. Although the attack surprised him, after the obstacles in the corridor, the effort to evade the arrows felt minimal.

"What was that?" Nate complained loudly, now flying again. He swiftly gained altitude.

A young man and a young woman emerged from hiding, each armed with a bow, each nocking another arrow. They both appeared to be Native American, and they wore modern clothes. "You don't belong here!" the young man called.

"So you're just going to shoot me?" Nate asked incredulously.

They both fired again. Nate avoided the arrows.

"Wait!" Nate cried, fishing out the keychain William had given him. "I have permission to be here!"

They paused in the act of setting new arrows to their bowstrings.

"Where'd you get that?" the young woman accused.

"William Graywater gave it to me," Nate explained. "I'm here to protect Uweya. William told me I have to use Uweya to keep Jonas White from stealing it. There are others right behind me who work for him."

The young man set his bow aside. "Come here so I can have a closer look."

Keeping hold of her bow, the young woman shook her head. "It's a trick."

"I wasn't expecting to find people here," Nate said, unsure whether it was safe to approach.

"Yeah, well, surprise," the young woman said, aiming her bow at him.

The young man laid a hand on her shoulder. "Celia, nobody outside our family knew about the token. Uncle William must have really given it to him."

Celia gave a little nod and lowered the bow. "Others are coming?"

"No joke," Nate said. "A ComKin, meaning a Combat Kinetic. A tough magical mercenary. Jonas is boosting her power using a simulacrum."

"This could be the opportunity we wanted," the young man said.

Nodding, Celia set her bow aside. Nate swooped down to them.

"I'm Ted Graywater," the young man said. "This is my sister Celia."

"Nate."

Ted held out his hand. "Mind if I see the token?"

Nate handed it over.

Celia touched Nate's arm. "You're bleeding."

"Just scratches. Could have been much worse."

"This wasn't taken by force," Ted said. "William trusts you."

"How did you make it through that hallway?" Celia asked.

"I have an enhancer that boosts my reflexes," Nate replied. "I was going to ask you two the same thing."

"We didn't come through the hallway," Ted said. "We had a unique gateway that led right to this room. It was fairly small and made of crystal. We kept it in our trailer. When our trailer was attacked by super-powered kids, Celia and I went through the gateway. Things must have gone badly, because Grandma destroyed it behind us."

"We're trapped here now," Celia said.

"It was an emergency tactic," Ted said.

"You could come here whenever you wanted?" Nate asked.

"It was the fate of the Graywater family," Celia said. "We guard Uweya. We care for it. But if any of us touches any part of it, we all die."

"For generations we had a private way in and out of here," Ted said. "Right up until Grandma blasted it with her shotgun."

Nate nodded at the huge globe. "Is that Uweya?"

"You got it on your first guess," Ted said. "It's kind of hard to miss. It's a simulacrum of the whole planet."

"*Uweya* means 'Second Earth,'" Celia supplied.

Nate regarded the globe with new respect. "You mean, if I do something to the simulacrum, it happens to Earth."

Ted nodded solemnly. "You could flatten a mountain with your thumb, cause a tsunami with a flick of your wrist, or bash a country into oblivion with your fist."

Nate swallowed. His throat felt dry. "Are you serious?"

"I'm as serious as a nuclear holocaust," Ted said. "Serious as the sun going supernova. Serious as the end of the world."

"The simulacrum has no real atmosphere," Celia explained. "Wind and clouds aren't depicted. There are no satellites or moon or sun or stars. No living matter is represented, either. No living people, animals, insects, or plants. Once something dies, it's a different story. Dead trees are there, pressed flowers, fallen leaves, fingernail clippings, stuffed hunting trophies, bodies in coffins in the cemeteries. All nonliving matter is represented. This includes buildings, bridges, ships, planes, motorcycles, televisions—everything. It all moves around just how it is currently moving on the planet. Empty cars driving down congested freeways. Empty submarines patrolling below the surface of the ocean. It's miraculous."

"How can I use it to stop Jonas White?"

Ted shrugged. "It would be hard to stop him directly. In theory, you could find his clothes walking around and knock a building onto him. Clothes are visible. Hair isn't until it gets cut free from the body. But it would be almost impossible to single out a person from outside of Uweya."

"So what can I do?" Nate asked.

"William gave you the token," Celia said. "It probably means he thinks you're the one who should destroy Uweya."

"Destroy Uweya?" Nate exclaimed. "Won't that destroy the world?"

"Not if you do it the proper way," Ted said. "Not if you enter Uweya."

"What do you mean?" Nate asked, glancing over at the entrance to the room. Katie could barge in at any moment.

Celia rushed over to a workbench and returned with a stone coin. It had a hole in the center and fine markings on both sides. "You can use a coin like this one to enter Uweya. You look at the surface of Uweya through the hole in the coin, speak the command, and then you shrink down and are transported to the spot you were examining. You can then interact with Uweya as if you were a person standing on the Earth."

"Weird," Nate said.

"The nonliving material of Uweya differs from Earth in one vital way," Ted said. "If, while on Uweya, you journey to the location of Uweya, instead of finding another Uweya, you will find the power source that keeps Uweya active. Throw your coin into the power source, and you will terminate the connection between Uweya and Earth."

"Uweya becomes a regular globe," Nate said.

"Essentially," Celia agreed.

"What happens to me?" Nate asked.

Ted and Celia shared a glance. "The coin gets you in and out of Uweya," Celia said. "You look through the coin, aim it at the sky, speak the command, and you will exit Uweya. You can use the coin as many times as you want, but a person can only bring a single coin into Uweya."

Nate frowned. "If I destroy the power source while I'm still on Uweya, won't that leave me stranded there?"

"Destroying the power source will almost certainly destroy Uweya as well," Ted said. "You might get ejected from Uweya when you do it. Then again, maybe not. Depends how Iwa Iza set it up."

"You can't take matter from Uweya," Celia said. "Nor can you add foreign material to Uweya—it can only visit. You can only bring out what you bring in, and nothing you bring in becomes truly part of the simulacrum. That might mean that if Uweya ends, you would be expelled."

"Or it could be a suicide mission," Nate said.

"Possibly," Ted said. "We have no way of knowing for sure."

"Why can't I bring two coins?" Nate asked. "If I have to use a coin to destroy the power source, I'd feel better if I had an extra to at least attempt an escape."

"Only the coin you're looking through will come with you," Celia explained. "Any others you try to bring will be left behind."

"You should be able to use one of the coins you find there," Ted said. "There will be simulcratic versions of the coins in this room inside of Uweya. Just use one of the simulcratic coins to destroy the power source."

"That should work," Celia agreed.

"If it doesn't work?" Nate asked.

"Then you'll have to use the coin you brought with you," Ted said.

"And if I don't automatically get kicked out of Uweya?"

Ted and Celia shared a glance. "You'll probably die," Celia said.

Nate folded his arms and stared at the floor. Were there any alternatives? What if Katie got killed when she tried to get through the hallway? Jonas would just send somebody else. He would get somebody here eventually.

"You guys have known how to destroy Uweya all along?" Nate asked.

"Our family has known since the duty was entrusted to us," Ted said.

"The Graywaters have guarded Uweya for many centuries," Celia added.

"Then why didn't you end it forever ago?" Nate wondered.

"Think about it," Celia said. "We Graywaters can't touch Uweya. We can't use the coins. If we so much as poke Uweya with a stick from across the room, we all drop dead."

"We knew how to unmake it," Ted said. "We even had access. But we needed to find somebody we trusted completely—somebody we knew would destroy Uweya instead of abuse it. Think about the temptation! Anyone who controlled Uweya would literally control the world! In the end, generation after generation, we concluded it was safer simply to keep it secret."

"But now the secret is out," Nate said.

"Exactly," Ted said. "If this weren't an emergency, I can't imagine William would have bestowed the token upon you. But apparently he thought his chances were better with you than with Jonas White. What do you say?"

Nate's stomach felt knotted. His perspiration felt cold. "I'm not super eager to die."

"If Uweya falls into the wrong hands, we all die," Celia pointed out.

"You could theoretically survive destroying it," Ted encouraged.

Nate nodded neutrally. Was there another option? There had to be! But what? "Give me a minute to think."

Ted glanced at the doorway. "What are the chances this ComKin can make it through the hallway?"

"I honestly don't know," Nate replied. "It's so brutal. But Jonas seems to have planned for everything. It's definitely possible."

They all stared at the doorway in silence.

"I'll go have a look," Celia offered.

Nobody tried to dissuade her.

Nate looked at Ted. "So I'll have to go into Uweya, then go through that hall again to get to the power source?"

"It's the only remaining way to access this room," Ted said.

Nate still had one stick of Peak Performance. The thought of flying through the hall again was not exciting. "Will I still be able to fly if I enter Uweya?"

"Your magic should work the same," Ted said.

"Will I be able to breathe? You mentioned there's no wind. Is there air?"

"I'm not sure exactly how it works," Ted confessed. "Maybe you breathe the same air you're breathing now. Maybe there is a special layer of breathable air around Uweya. All I know is that in the distant past, Iwa Iza and his apprentices entered Uweya, and they didn't die."

"She's coming," Celia called from the door. "She's more than halfway through."

Ted stared at Nate expectantly.

"All right," Nate said. "Let's get ready. If she makes it through, I'll go in."

Ted hurried over to a workbench and returned with a coin. He gave it to Nate.

"How many coins are there?" Nate wondered.

"Dozens," Ted said. "Were you hoping to hide them to keep her from following you?"

"It had crossed my mind."

"There's too many," Ted said. "I don't know where we could stash them. Hopefully she doesn't know about the coins. We'll try to stop her."

"Don't try too hard," Nate said. "If she makes it through that hallway, you won't stand a chance. I've seen her fight. She probably knows about the coins. Jonas seemed to know everything about this place."

"We'll do our best to delay her," Ted vowed. "It's our sworn duty."

"I'd appreciate that. What now?"

"Normally you would lie on a levitating tablet to get into position," Ted said. "We have many of them. But you can fly, so you can probably get into position easier yourself. Be careful. Accidentally bumping Uweya with your elbow could kill millions. Look through the coin, then say 'utcha.' You'll enter Uweya where you're looking when you speak. Point the coin skyward and say 'utcha' to get out."

"Utcha?"

"Utcha."

"Will people be able to see me?" Nate asked.

"The people of Earth? No. You'll see their clothes and their cars, things like that, but they won't see you or anything you bring. Nor will they be able to touch you. Not directly. But all of the nonliving components of Uweya can interact with you. If a car runs you down, you'll feel it."

"It'll kill me?"

"Just like a normal car. Take care."

"She's almost here!" Celia cried. "She's unstoppable!" Celia heaved the door closed.

"Thanks," Nate said. "Good luck."

"Save all your luck for yourself," Ted said. "Take mine too!"

Nate glided over to Uweya. He approached slowly. It was easy to find the California coastline, easy to find the distinctive inlet of the San Francisco Bay. The Peak Performance remained active in his system, keeping his senses keen.

Holding the coin to his eye, Nate found that with a small effort, he could zoom his vision in closer to the surface, as if the coin were a magical telescope. He zoomed in and out at will, marveling at the details. There was San Francisco. There was the Golden Gate Bridge. He could see the vehicles crossing it. He found vessels in the bay.

Nate could not help thinking how much Pigeon would have enjoyed all the detail. Pigeon loved maps and geography, and this put every map in existence to shame. But if Nate accomplished his goal, Pigeon would never get a chance to see it.

There was Alcatraz. There was Yerba Buena Island.

Nate zoomed out. He needed to find Mt. Diablo.

But wait.

If he went to Mt. Diablo and destroyed Uweya's power source, Jonas White would still be holding his friends prisoner. Jonas would still have simulacra of Pigeon, Trevor, Summer, Lindy, and the others. If Nate took out Uweya, Jonas could retaliate by killing most of the people he cared about. Unless he went after another power source first.

The door opened. Nate saw that Celia and Ted had taken up hidden positions. Nate peered through the coin. With Peak Performance still augmenting his senses, locating Arcadeland was no big trick.

"Utcha," he said softly.

Nate felt like he was getting turned inside out. His head seemed to retract down into his belly, and his legs seemed to withdraw up into his head. Quickly, painlessly, he collapsed down to a single point.

When he expanded back to his regular size, Nate was standing on a curb, part of the way down the block from Arcadeland. He felt proud that he had landed so close to his destination. The buildings looked how they should, and the street, and the cars. But the planter boxes were empty except for dirt and some snarled, dead vegetable matter. A closer look revealed that the cars were empty as well. A combination of denim shorts, a T-shirt, a baseball hat, a wristwatch, sneakers, and socks strolled along the sidewalk, holding a leash attached to an empty collar, as though both dog and owner were invisible.

The sky was the oddest part. Instead of clouds, or a sun, or blueness, or starry black, the sky looked like part of the domed chamber that housed Uweya. Nate was not staring up from the Earth toward the immensity of space. He was staring up from a large globe in a well-lit room.

Nate slipped the stone coin into his pocket. He was relieved to find that he really could still fly. He soared over to Arcadeland, alighting near the front doors. A few sets of clothes pushed the doors open from inside, then walked toward the parking lot.

Nate pulled a door open. It felt no different from interacting with a normal door. He walked into the arcade.

Clothes stood playing arcade games. Clothes manned the food counter. Clothes threw basketballs for points. Clothes aimed the guns at the shooting gallery. The scene was very eerie, as if everyone in the world had obliviously become invisible.

Nate watched a set of clothes at a table lift a hamburger. A bite of the hamburger disappeared. The food was not visible as it was chewed or swallowed. Once ingested, it vanished.

Nate took out the simple map Ziggy had drawn. He studied it for a moment, comparing it to his surroundings, then flew to the appropriate EMPLOYEES ONLY door. He found it locked.

Of course it was locked! Now what?

Nate looked around for something he might use to break it down. Then again, maybe there was a subtler way. After all, nobody could see him.

He knocked softly. He knocked harder. Then he knocked really hard. He started beating the door with both hands. He kicked it with the sole of his shoe, making it shudder.

A set of clothes came hustling over. Nate scooted out of the way. A key came out and was inserted into the lock, and the door opened. Obviously the employee thought that somebody was stuck on the far side. Nate recognized that just as he could see no people, he could also hear no voices. He wondered if the employee was speaking, perhaps calling to the person who had battered the door. The set of clothes passed through the door, checking down the hallway beyond.

Nate used the opportunity to slip through the doorway, flying over the clothes of the employee. Leaving the clothes behind, Nate soared down the hall. He could feel the effects of Peak Performance wearing thin. He would have to be careful with his last stick. It was his only hope of making it through the obstacle course within Mt. Diablo.

Keeping an eye on his map, Nate found his way to the stairway door. Again, it was locked. Nate tried the same routine. He knocked softly at first, then harder, then he pounded it relentlessly.

This time a set of clothes opened the door from the far side. Nate recognized the clothes from that morning. It was Conner! That made sense. Conner had probably been posted to watch the stairway. When he heard the commotion, he had come to investigate.

Straightening his body, Nate flew over Conner though the top of the doorway. Conner passed beyond the doorway, turning to look up and down the hall. Then he hurried back through the door, shut it, and locked it. He rushed down the stairs. Nate followed.

Conner used a key on the door at the bottom of the stairs. Nate wondered whether they had kept all of these doors locked before last night's intrusion. When Conner opened the door, Nate darted through the top of it.

Below him, Conner paused, apparently conversing with another person. Nate didn't recognize the second person's clothes. After a moment, Conner started down the hall, striding briskly. He was going the same direction Nate wanted to travel.

Nate felt an excited flutter of hope. He had considered trying to blindside Conner with a heavy object in order to take his keycard to Jonas White's sanctum. But what if Conner was voluntarily heading to the sanctum to report the strange disturbance? Nate kept checking his map as Conner kept making the correct turns.

Sure enough, Nate found himself drifting above and behind Conner as he made his way down the hall toward a sturdy metal door. The metal door matched up with the location of the sanctum on the graph-paper map.

"Keep going, you brainless gorilla," Nate mouthed, not daring to speak the words even though he felt sure Conner wouldn't be able to hear them.

Conner paused at the door, looking back down the hall as his wallet came out of his back pocket. A plastic card was removed. Conner swiped the card, then tugged the heavy door open.

Just as Nate was about to slip over Conner and into the sanctum, he heard footfalls from behind. The rhythm was strange. Although each step sounded abnormally loud, there was too much time between them.

Swiveling in the air, Nate saw Katie come tearing around the corner at the end of the hall. Her eyes locked on Nate as she came bounding forward, devouring nearly twenty feet per stride. Her normally immaculate hair was disheveled, with part of it slashed away parallel to a clotted gash along her cheek. Scratches crisscrossed her face, the tip of her nose was gone, and it looked like wild animals had savaged her bodysuit. Her left arm was missing at the elbow. Despite her many injuries, no fresh blood flowed.

Apparently responding to a signal from within the sanctum, Conner moved to close the door. Nate knifed through just before it slammed shut.

Conner had shut himself and Katie out of the sanctum. For the moment, Nate was alone with a crowd of wax figures and a fancy black robe with gold embroidery that could only belong to Jonas White. The black robe stood near the wax figure of Katie Sung. The wax figure had injuries to match Katie's, including the scratches on her face and the missing forearm. Needles of varying size protruded all over the wax figure, and Jonas continued to insert more.

Nate saw the jade urn in the recess on the far side of the room. It was the only object that fit the description. He flew to the recessed shelf, grabbed the top of the vase, and yanked.

It didn't budge.

Behind Nate, the door to the sanctum opened. Katie sprang through before Conner heaved it closed. Although she had entered, he remained outside. Evidently Conner realized he was defending Jonas from invisible intruders, but he didn't understand that they kept slipping by him. Nate wondered how much Katie had communicated to Jonas via seashell.

Instead of yanking, Nate gave the urn a steady pull and felt it begin to tip. It was apparently held in place similarly to how the Protector had been anchored to its pedestal, as if by unseen magnets.

With a shrieking battle cry, Katie came flying at Nate, one foot outstretched. Nate had to soar away or she would have demolished him. Her foot hit the wall instead of his head. She landed nimbly. The urn remained upright.

Nate flew away from her as she gave pursuit. Katie leapt around the room almost as if she could fly as well. Nate made no effort to engage her. He had seen how hard she could kick and punch. One blow might be all she needed to finish him.

He tried to swerve back toward the urn, but she knew what he wanted and kept cutting him off. Gradually she herded Nate toward a corner.

Jonas toddled away from Katie's wax figure toward the figure of Nate. A knife emerged from his robe.

Nate realized that if things didn't change quickly, Katie would corner him and take him down. He crammed his final stick of Peak Performance into his mouth.

Jonas stabbed the figure of Nate in the back of the head. Slashing the throat, he removed the wax head from the body. Nate winced but felt no effect from the attack.

As the Peak Performance entered his system, Nate saw the room more clearly. He knew what he had to do.

Nate flew back into the wall as if he didn't know it was there. With triumph in her damaged features, Katie sprang at him, her foot snapping forward with a vicious kick. But Nate anticipated the move based on the pattern of her offense and swooped under her attack, his nose inches from the floor.

If he went for the urn, Nate knew Katie would get to him before he could overturn it. So instead he flew at her wax figure. First he kicked the figure in the stomach with everything he had. The wax figure toppled.

Behind him, Katie collapsed, vomiting violently.

Nate crouched and began stripping away the acupuncture needles all over the wax figure. Behind him, Katie went into wild convulsions.

Nate noticed the robe making its way toward the wax

representation of Mozag, knife upraised. Again, Nate doubted whether he could tip the urn in time. Instead he flew to the robe, grabbed the back of it, and jerked it hard. Jonas had always appeared unsteady. Sure enough, the robe fell to the ground and the knife skidded free. The sleeves of the robe reached toward one of the invisible legs, as if grasping an injury.

Nate flew to the urn. Bracing a foot against the wall, he seized the top with both hands and pulled steadily. The urn tipped a little at first. As Nate kept straining, and the urn tipped more, it began to lean easier. The urn came free, and Nate carried it away from the niche.

Raising the urn over his head, Nate crashed it down to the tile floor with all of his might. It burst into countless fragments, great and small. For an instant the light in the room dimmed and an indefinable energy throbbed through Nate, making him a little queasy. Then the moment passed, and all seemed as it had before.

Nate took no time to celebrate. He was chewing his last stick of gum, and he had a simulacrum to destroy. First he took out his stone coin, looked through it, aimed it upward, and said, "Utcha."

Nothing happened.

Apparently he needed to actually be looking at the sky.

Nate flew to where Katie lay inert. Noticing a telltale bulge in a zippered pocket on her side, he removed a keycard and a small set of keys. Nate flew to the sanctum door, swiped the card, and shoved it open.

Conner's clothes waited outside. Nate flew down the hall faster than he would have dared without Peak Performance. He swooped around corners and sped down halls until he reached the staircase door. He unlocked it with the second key he tried, sailed up the stairs, then unlocked the door at the top with the same key. Nate flew to an EMPLOYEES ONLY door that he remembered led outside, unlocked it, and flew out.

Flying to Mt. Diablo from here would consume too much valuable time. Removing the coin from his pocket, Nate peered through it, looked up, and said, "Utcha."

Nate shrank down to a point and unfolded hovering above Uweya. Without pausing, without looking at his surroundings, Nate peered through the coin, found Mt. Diablo, zoomed in close, found the SUV abandoned on the slope, then traced the path they had taken up the slope to the cavity they had entered. Enhanced as he was by Peak Performance, the task felt simple.

"Utcha," Nate said again.

He folded into himself and was suddenly standing on the slope not far from the little opening. Nate flew to the entrance and slithered through. He soared through the cave at a high speed. He snatched the electric lantern near the lip of the crater and dove into the enormous hole. Earlier he had descended slowly. Now he rocketed straight down, faster than he would have fallen had he simply jumped off the edge. The speed was essential. If his Peak Performance ran out before he reached the deadly obstacle course, he would get mutilated.

Nate slowed so he could make the turns where the shaft elbowed, then raced to the room with the Gate, through the next room, through the cramped hallway, and into the chamber that led to the obstacle course. He noticed the clothes of Lindy, Chris, and Risa flying around. Destroying Jonas White's Source had freed them. He also noticed the clothes belonging to Cleon and Jeanine.

The Peak Performance still felt fully operational. Nate paused for a moment in front of the churning corridor of blades, spears, and columns. He had been in such a hurry to get here that he hadn't stopped to consider whether he still needed to be here.

Did he still need to destroy Uweya?

Jonas White was in trouble. All of his simulacra were now useless. Some of his top people were down for the count. Jonas was probably not in a position to come get Uweya at this point.

But what if Jonas escaped? He knew where to look now. It would only be a matter of time before he tried again.

Even if Jonas was captured, how many of his people knew about Uweya? The secret was out. The way was now open. If Nate left Uweya unguarded, somebody would come and claim it.

As much as he hated the thought of passing through the deadly corridor again, he could not leave a voodoo Earth lying around for any wacko to come and claim. The Hermit and the Graywaters had been right—Uweya was too powerful to entrust to anyone. For the safety of the whole planet, Uweya had to be destroyed.

Nate knew he couldn't wait. If his Peak Performance started to wear off, he would never survive the obstacles ahead. So he zoomed forward.

Dodging through the brutal obstacles was no easier the second time. Nate took a similar route as he had the first time, with many minor variations. Once again, he progressed gradually, his body spinning and flipping into strange positions to avoid the endless dangers. He received nicks and scratches and plenty of close shaves, but he emerged alive at the other end.

This time the door beyond the obstacles was already open. Nate flew into the domed chamber. He saw the clothes belonging to Ted and Celia in motion, and felt relieved to see that Katie hadn't incapacitated them.

A large sphere hung in the center of the room, roughly twelve feet in diameter. Unlike the appearance of Uweya in the real world, this Uweya glowed brightly, its vivid surface an ever-changing palette of swirling color. Amid the dynamic hues, the forms of the oceans and continents remained visible, although the shapes undulated and blurred as diverse colors migrated across the globe.

Nate flew over to the worktable where Ted had gotten him a coin. Several coins lay in plain view, and he claimed one. It seemed identical to the coin in his pocket. Flying close to the brilliant sphere, Nate held the coin in his palm. When he threw in the coin, would Uweya be destroyed instantly? Or might he have a chance to try to fly out and look at the sky using the coin in his pocket?

Iwa Iza was supposed to be an amazing magician. Nate hoped he wouldn't have designed Uweya so that whoever unmade it would be killed.

Bracing himself, Nate searched for the courage to proceed. Throwing the coin might be the last thing he ever did. But it would make his family safe from the threat of Uweya. His friends would also be safer. In thousands of years, nobody had been in a position to remove this danger from the world. Even though he might die, he had to take the chance. He focused on the hope that he would live.

Nate flipped the simulcratic coin with his thumb toward the glowing sphere. After spinning through the air, it disappeared inside the globe. For a moment the sphere swelled and became blinding, then Nate experienced a sensation as if he and everything around him were being drawn into the globe and imploding down to a singularity. As he shrank, an instinctive terror of death rose within him. This could be it. There might not even be a body left to recover.

* * * * *

When Nate expanded out of that point where all of Uweya had united, he found himself back in the room with Ted and Celia. They stood gaping at him. Looking up, Nate saw that he was sitting below where Uweya had previously hovered. Except Uweya was gone. Dust swirled in the air and was spread on the floor. Glancing over his shoulder, Nate saw Katie Sung lying motionless.

"You did it," Celia gasped, her gaze fixed on him.

"It's gone," Ted said, astonished. "You survived."

The ground rumbled threateningly.

"Guys?" Nate asked.

A second rumbling was accompanied by some heavy quaking. A few blocks fell from the ceiling, streaming trails of dust.

"This place is old," Celia said. "It might not hold together without the power source."

"It might be deliberately rigged to fall apart without the power source," Ted added.

"Time to go?" Nate asked.

A stronger quake hit. Ted and Celia were already running for the door. Nate glanced at Katie. She had fought against him, but he couldn't just leave her to die. He went to her and slapped her cheek. Her eyelids twitched. He slapped her harder. "Get up!"

Katie groaned.

Nate shook her shoulder. "Get up or you're dead!"

Her eyes opened. "You?" Katie asked, disoriented.

"I trashed Jonas White's power source and also demolished Uweya," Nate explained hastily. "This place is coming down."

The strongest, longest quake yet made Nate fly into the air to avoid the shaking. Stone blocks and dirt cascaded from the ceiling, some landing nearby. Fragments skittered across the vibrating floor.

Katie sat up, eyes closed, legs crossed, her remaining hand in her lap. She breathed deeply, as if meditating. Her posture became more erect.

Nate realized she must be trying to recharge her batteries. "We need to hurry," he said.

There was a lull in the shaking. "You go," she said. "I'll be along."

Nate zoomed for the doorway. He could feel his Peak Performance wearing off. The obstacles in the corridor beyond the doorway no longer functioned. The blades had stopped swiping, the spikes had stopped stabbing, and the pendulums no longer scythed back and forth. Nate caught up with Ted and Celia as they made their way through the stalled traps.

Chris and Lindy came flying toward them. Their appearance surprised Nate—he had assumed they would already be headed for the exit.

"Nate!" Chris called. "You're alive!"

"We have to get out of here!" Nate yelled. "I wrecked Uweya! This place is falling apart!"

Another round of heavy quaking added emphasis to his warning. One of the heavy pendulums dropped to the floor, leaned into the wall, and came to rest against several inert blades.

"Who are you with?" Chris asked as he reached Nate.

"Ted and Celia Graywater," Nate said. "They're on our side."

"Lindy, get the girl," Chris ordered. "Nate, help me with the guy."

Nate was surprised to see Lindy scoop Celia into her arms and fly off down the corridor with only a little extra difficulty. Celia was fairly short and slender, but it was still impressive.

"As flying tanks you can handle more weight?" Nate asked.

"Quite a bit more," Chris said. "But I may need help with the guy."

Nate grabbed one of Ted's legs. Chris grabbed the rest of him. Nate wasn't sure how much he was helping, since Chris bore most of the weight, but together they shuttled Ted from the corridor.

Looking back, Nate saw Katie rushing through the corridor. Occasionally she would make a larger leap than seemed possible, but she was far from using the impressive bounding stride he had witnessed in Arcadeland on Uweya. Judging by her pained expression, her current effort was requiring all of her energy and concentration.

The quaking was getting more severe, and the pauses were becoming less frequent. Risa flew to greet Nate and Chris in the room beyond the cluttered corridor.

"Where's Jeanine?" Nate asked.

"She ran back toward the entrance with Cleon," Risa said.

"Stop her," Nate said to Chris. "We'll need her help to get everyone out."

"I'm on it," Chris said, setting Ted down. Extending a fist, Chris shot ahead.

Lindy put Celia down as well.

"Come on," Nate urged. "You can run. The ground is smoother from here on out. This way."

Nate led the way at a pace that allowed the others to keep up. In the next room, Nate noticed the Protector back on the pedestal. He suspected that Jeanine and Cleon had probably tried to seal them in. Fortunately, without Uweya functioning, the Protector was no longer operational.

They hurried through the gate and into the next room. Glancing back, Nate saw Katie trip on her way through the gate. She didn't get up.

The quaking worsened. Nate kept his eyes up to avoid falling blocks and stones. Here and there, boulder-sized chunks of stonework crashed down to the floor.

"Lindy," Nate shouted, flying back toward Katie.

Lindy grabbed one arm, and Nate seized what remained of the other. Katie was a fairly large woman. Carrying her between them, they soon found they could make better time if they let her legs drag.

Stone thundered down around them. The floor began to fracture dramatically. Gritty dust filled the air. Nate narrowly avoided a falling chunk of masonry the size of a microwave oven.

When they reached the enormous shaft, Chris awaited them with Jeanine and Cleon. Jeanine looked disgruntled. Cleon looked pale and exhausted.

"Get us out of here," Nate shouted over the seismic commotion.

"Too many people," Jeanine replied loudly. "I can't raise so many. I'm almost out of juice."

"We'll help," Nate said. "Just make them lighter."

Jeanine shrugged. "I'll try."

"Try now!" Chris yelled angrily.

Chris grabbed Ted, Lindy took Cleon, Risa claimed Celia, and Nate kept hold of Katie. Jeanine began to rise, and Katie became much lighter. Nate found that he could fly with her, although it wasn't easy.

"Stay near me!" Jeanine shouted. "That will help!"

Crowding close, they rose together. They passed the two bends. The rumbling began to recede. The shaft trembled, but not so violently as down below.

The higher they went, the heavier Katie seemed. With the top in sight, Nate could no longer make progress. He barely managed to hover. He exerted himself with everything he had, but instead of rising, he started to sink. He had draped Katie over his shoulder, so he wasn't losing hold of her, but he lacked the power to fly her any higher.

"A little help?" Nate asked.

"I'm giving it all I've got," Jeanine growled through clenched teeth.

Chris came down. Ted was riding him piggyback. Chris grabbed Nate's hand, and together they managed to haul Katie beyond the top of the shaft. As soon as they touched down, Jeanine slumped to the ground, and Nate felt Katie's full weight. He set her down as gently as he could. Which wasn't very gently.

The rumbling was now distant. This part of the cave seemed to be in no danger of collapse.

"Let's get outside," Nate said. "You know, just in case."

Jeanine got to her feet, Chris carried Katie, and the group made their way out through the cave mouth. Nate felt relieved to see the blue sky and to breathe air that didn't smell of dust and minerals.

"I thought I was a goner," Cleon said. "You kids are all right."

"You did it, Nate," Lindy said. "I can hardly believe it."

"We're not finished yet," Nate said. "We have to make sure

Trevor, Pigeon, and the others at Arcadeland are all right. Jonas can't use his simulacra anymore, but I'm sure he has other powers. And he has henchmen. I don't care if people see me flying, I'm going straight there."

"We're with you," Chris said.

"Lead the way," Risa seconded.

"Go on," Ted said. "We can't fly."

Nate looked at Cleon and Jeanine. "You guys will play nice?"

"I'm spent," Jeanine said wearily.

Cleon scrunched his face. "Jonas blew it, man. This is over."

Nate glanced at the other Jets. "Over or not, we can't trust them. Any volunteers to stay and keep an eye on things?"

Lindy looked worried by the prospect.

"Chris?" Nate asked. "Would you mind?"

"Go on," Chris said, waving Nate away. "I've got this."

"Great." Nate turned to Risa and Lindy. "Follow me."

CHAPTER TWENTY-FOUR

MOPPING UP

Pigeon sat with his back to the wall, gently tapping his head against the concrete. He tried not to envision the hot buttered popcorn that had been available whenever he wanted during his stay in Mozag's cell. He tried not to dwell on his failure to knock the urn off the shelf. If only he had been a little faster!

His stomach grumbled. It had been a long while since they had fed him. Had they forgotten about him? What if Jonas White had already gotten Uweya? What if the evil mage and his underlings had simply abandoned Arcadeland? Pigeon stroked his stomach. What if he and his friends were doomed to slowly starve in their cells?

The lock jiggled. Pigeon sat up straight. Was it mealtime? At least that would help take the edge off his misery.

The door opened. Mozag entered, wearing his Cubs hat.

"Mozag!" Pigeon exclaimed, standing up.

One of the Battiatos loomed behind him, looking beefy as a bull. A glance at the neck told Pigeon that it was Ziggy.

"Pigeon, good to see you!" Mozag said. "Your friends came through. Jonas White has been neutralized. I paid him a visit to be sure. Some of his people haven't gotten the memo yet, but this affair is basically over. Want to help us get out of here? Ziggy brought some treats."

"What do you have?" Pigeon asked.

"Let's see," Ziggy said. "I have a biscuit that would make you a shark. Or Shock Bits. Or Moon Rocks. Or Peak—"

"I'll do Shock Bits," Pigeon said. "They're good in close quarters. Do you have lots?"

"Plenty," Ziggy said, handing over the candy.

Pigeon followed them out into the hall. Trevor came up to Pigeon. He was the same color and texture as the concrete floors and walls—his face, his hair, even his clothes.

"What happened to you?" Pigeon exclaimed.

"Tallah gave me a couple of sweets she cooked up," Trevor explained. "Camouflage Caramels and Spider Bites."

"I guess the caramels make you like a chameleon," Pigeon said.

"And the Spider Bites let me climb walls and spit webs," Trevor said. "They make my throat feel kind of phlegmy, though."

Ziggy and Mozag unlocked a neighboring door. Ziggy went in. When he came out, he had shrunk back to his regular size and was accompanied by his twin brother.

"Where's John?" Pigeon asked.

"He went ahead with Tallah to clear the way," Mozag said. "I almost feel bad for any hirelings who resist. It has been a long while since I've seen John in a mood like this."

"Should we blow this joint?" Victor asked.

Mozag gave a nod. "It's time."

* * * * *

When Nate reached Arcadeland, the first person he noticed was Summer flying above one of the miniature golf courses. Nate glided over to her, and she paused in midair to greet him.

"You're here!" he exclaimed. "You're flying!"

Summer grinned. "Tallah escaped with jet and racer stamps. She's double stamping anybody who shows interest. She's over by the Eiffel Tower."

"How are Pigeon, Trevor, and everyone?"

"All free. Mozag, John, Victor, Roman, the Tanks, the Racers, the Subs."

"What about Jonas?"

"Mozag took care of him," Summer said. "We're just finishing up with his employees."

"And the regular customers?"

"Most of them have been blinded by the cheese. I guess alarms were going off, and people assumed it meant a fire. There are some folks out front in the parking lot. Otherwise we're all clear." Summer looked past Nate to Lindy and Risa. "Where's Chris?"

"He's making sure the bad guys at Mt. Diablo don't cause any more trouble," Nate said.

"I see my dad," Lindy said.

Nate looked to where an ice cream truck had rammed through one of the side fences. It currently sat idle near the Taj Mahal hole on the miniature golf course. Mr. Stott was behind the wheel.

"Go," Summer said. "He's been worried."

Lindy sped off in that direction.

Nate turned to Risa. "Can you help Summer? I'm out of Peak

Performance, so I might as well go add a racer stamp."

"Go for it," Risa said.

Summer nodded toward the ice cream truck. "Mr. Stott insisted on coming. He seemed especially anxious about Lindy."

Nate watched as Lindy reached the ice cream truck. She flew inside, and Mr. Stott clasped her to him. The old mage's eyes were closed as he held her. Even at a distance Nate could read the relief in his expression.

"I guess I should go get that stamp," Nate said.

"There may not be much else to do," Summer said. "This is over."

Nate smiled. "Then I'll get it for fun."

BREAKFAST FOR DINNER

ater that evening, everyone gathered at the Sweet Tooth Ice Cream and Candy Shoppe. With the store closed, they had pushed the furniture together to form a single massive table where they could all sit and converse. Nate sat toward the center of the long table. Summer, Pigeon, Trevor, and Lindy occupied seats nearby. Chris and Risa had joined the meal as well. They had tried to talk Roman into coming, but he had chosen to sulk instead. The Battiatos were present, as was John Dart. Ted and Celia Graywater had agreed to attend, and although William had declined his invitation, he sent along his gratitude to Nate.

Mr. Stott and Mozag had spent all afternoon whipping up food for the meal. Nate could hardly believe the variety of treats—banana pancakes, caramel waffles, ebleskivers, toasted bagels, English muffins, omelets, scrambled eggs, hash browns, bacon, sausage, fruit smoothies, hot chocolate, milk, juice, various syrups and preserves, margarine, butter, honey, dulce de leche, and fresh whipped cream all vied for attention.

Standing at the head of the table, Mr. Stott tapped a fork against a glass to summon attention. "I'd like to welcome everyone out to our impromptu victory feast."

The statement drew a noisy cheer.

Mr. Stott held up his hands. "When a crisis is averted, it is indeed cause for celebration. I'm profoundly impressed with your efforts to keep our world safe. I believe Mozag would like to share some words with you." Motioning to Mozag, Mr. Stott sat down.

Mozag stood. He wore his Cubs hat and munched on a fat, crisp strip of bacon. "I have been a mage for a very long time. Only an extremely large birthday cake would accommodate the necessary candles. On occasion, I have been asked the secret of my success. My automatic reply is, 'Surround yourself with good people.'" He gestured around the room. "Tonight I am surrounded by good people. Thank you for rescuing me, and thank you for protecting all of humanity from Jonas White."

They all applauded enthusiastically.

"I'm grateful to Sebastian Stott for hosting this gathering," Mozag continued. "He is not only a fine mage but also a fine cook. Tonight we will feast as the kings of old could only have dreamed, although I'm a little disappointed that some of you neglected to take me up on my more exotic offerings."

"We want it all," Victor said. "The stuffed figs taste amazing. The huevos rancheros look perfect."

"I can't wait for the Salmon Benedict," Ziggy said.

"I found some truly fine smoked salmon," Mozag confided.

"With you as our employer, we would work for food," Victor gushed.

"It was a rough week, but after tonight we'll call it even," Ziggy enthused.

Mozag gave them a grateful nod. "Always helps to bring your own cheering section. In all seriousness, the people at this table, especially the children, went above and beyond to keep our world safe from harm. You all deserve my protection, my gratitude, and my goodwill. Call upon me for favors and you will not be refused. But one of you deserves special recognition. Would Nathan Sutter please come forward?"

Nate looked up and down the table. He hadn't expected this. "Everyone helped," he said. "Trevor, Summer, and Pigeon all took huge risks. Chris, Risa, and Lindy came with me after Uweya."

"And they all have my thanks," Mozag said. "Particularly Lindy, who handled the revelation about her past with grace and maturity. Like some of the best people I employ, she understands that she need not be defined by her past. We are who we choose to become."

Lindy wore a faltering smile. Nate felt bad for her. She had been quieter than usual since they had left Arcadeland. Right now it looked like she wished she could crawl under the table and hide.

Mozag was still talking. "Many contributed in valuable ways, but I've pieced together all you did, Nate, and it merits extra recognition. Come stand beside me."

"Get up there," John Dart ordered.

Feeling self-conscious, Nate pushed his chair back and walked over to Mozag. The old magician shook his hand. "Nate not only destroyed Jonas White's Source, making our revolt possible, but he also dismantled the most powerful simulacrum on the planet, which happened to be a simulacrum of the planet. We owe Nate our lives, and the world owes Nate for salvation from a long-buried threat."

Everyone applauded.

Nate wasn't sure how to react. He smiled and gave a little wave.

Mozag cleared his throat before continuing. He held up a gold medal with a black ribbon. The Battiato brothers gasped in unison. John Dart leaned forward with a small smile and a twinkle in his eyes. "In recognition of your extraordinary courage in protecting the world from the forces of magic, I induct you into the Order of the Unseen and offer you our highest commendation, the Medal of Valor."

"Impossible," Mr. Stott murmured.

Victor and Ziggy looked thunderstruck.

Mozag patted Nate on the arm. "The Medal of Valor can only be awarded after a unanimous vote by the Unseen Magi. It has been awarded a mere three other times in the past hundred years. The existence of Uweya has long troubled the Magi, and this medal is a token of their sincerest gratitude." Mozag pinned it on Nate, muttering strange words as he did so. "In the magical community, you now have friends in very high places."

As everyone clapped again, Nate returned to his seat, trying not to blush. His friends patted him on the back and crowded around to see his medal.

Mozag held up both hands. "With that bit of ceremony behind us, I would also like to mention that you're all free to sleep well tonight and for many nights to come. Some of your loved ones will experience withdrawals from the cheese Jonas shared, but they will be back to their old ways before long. Jonas White and all of his major apprentices and assistants have been taken into custody. Thanks to Ziggy Battiato's communication skills, I now have several of my other operatives in town. While they deal with unpleasant matters such as holding areas, trials, and sentencing, we get to feast! Dig in!"

Before long, Nate had too much syrup on his hands, so he got up to use the restroom. While he washed off the stickiness, he admired his medal in the mirror. On the way out, Mr. Stott was standing there.

"A word, Nate?" he asked.

"Sure," Nate said, pausing as he wiped his damp palms against his shirt.

"I need to ask a favor."

"Anything."

"Keep an eye on Lindy for me over the coming days."

"No problem."

Mr. Stott looked a little uncomfortable. "Mozag has expressed some concerns. She reacted admirably when confronted with her true identity, but Mozag fears this may not be the kind of matter that can be resolved in a moment, and I tend to agree. Lindy will be dealing with that knowledge during the coming days, weeks, months, and even years. She'll probably be coping with it to some degree for the rest of her life. I just want to make sure she gets the support she needs."

"I'll do everything I can," Nate promised.

"Mozag shared one other unsettling tidbit," Mr. Stott said, stroking his beard. "There is a third White sibling—Camilla, the youngest, and undoubtedly the wildest. He's had her under surveillance. She recently left her lair in Brazil to visit a lair in Italy, and then went on to a lair in Portugal. Could mean nothing. But Mozag promised to pay special attention to Camilla and to keep me posted."

"Thanks for telling me," Nate said. "I'll watch for anything suspicious."

"I'll keep you informed as I learn more," Mr. Stott said. "I wish I could promise that your troubles are over forever, but I've been around a long time. Not as long as Mozag, but long enough to know that once you get involved in the magical community, it's hard to break away completely."

"I don't want to break away," Nate said.

"Nor do I," Mr. Stott said, "which is probably part of the problem. You did well, Nate. You're an outstanding young man. Keep your wits about you and you'll go far. Shall we return to the feast?"

"Definitely."

Nate soon got lost in the joyful atmosphere and the delicious food. In between chatting and joking, he managed to eat until he felt ready to burst. When the meal finally ended, full and happy, he reflected on the power of good food and good company to wash away trauma and injuries, and even wondered whether there might have been a touch of magic involved.

NOTE ON LOCATIONS

I used to live in the San Francisco area. Many of the locations in this book are real, including Yerba Buena Island, Angel Island, and Mt. Diablo. From fourth to seventh grade, I lived in Clayton, California, not far from Walnut Creek. In the Candy Shop War books, Colson is a modified version of Clayton, and Walnut Hills is a fictionalized mix of Walnut Creek and Concord. Many details are not accurate, but some features are probably recognizable. The destroyer where the Hermit lived was inspired by the reserve fleet of mothballed ships in Suisun Bay, although the USS *Striker* was not deliberately based on an actual vessel.

Arcadeland is not based on any single arcade. I visited several different arcades in Utah and Arizona to do research (I know, my life is hard) and incorporated elements from many of the places I visited along with some details that came entirely from my imagination.

ACKNOWLEDGMENTS

I wrote this book because people asked for it. To be more specific, lots of kids (and adults) who had read *Candy Shop War* kept expressing interest in a sequel. When I wrote *Candy Shop War*, I expected it to be a single novel. But as people kept requesting more, my wheels started turning, and I found an idea that I liked. I'm glad readers asked, because I feel good about how the book turned out, and I'm excited to share it with them.

I had a good time dreaming up another adventure for Nate, Trevor, Summer, and Pigeon, along with their new pal Lindy and some of their grown-up friends.

There are some people I should thank. Chris Schoebinger and Emily Watts played the heaviest roles in editing this one. They were fun to work with, as always, and did a great job tightening the story, plugging holes, and generally helping me make it better. I also got help from Cherie Mull, Bryson Mull, Pamela Mull, Sadie Mull, Tucker Davis, and Kim Richards. Thanks also to the rest of the team at Shadow Mountain, especially Richard Erickson and Sheryl Dickert Smith, who created the book's design, and Tonya Facemyer, who handled the typography.

I also owe thanks to Simon & Schuster for relaunching The Candy Shop War books in paperback. Many thanks to the people who are helping this book reach new readers!

Once again, Brandon Dorman created the cover and all other illustrations. This is my ninth book that he has illustrated. He's so talented.

I'd like to give a special nod to my cousin Mike Walton. As kids, we used to play that he tasted what I ate and I tasted what he ate, which helped me come up with the magical side of the Battiato brothers.

I also have to thank my wife, Mary. She not only helps edit all of my books, she also keeps me on task when deadlines get tight. Deadlines were super tight on this project, but Mary helped me make time to get it done. I should thank my kids as well, for being patient with their busy, daydreamy dad. I love you guys!

Finally, thanks to you, my reader. If you enjoyed this book, check out my Five Kingdoms and Fablehaven series. ANd if you ever want to see the latest books I have coming, go to brandonmull.com, "like" my Facebook page, or follow me on Twitter: @brandonmull.

READING GUIDE

1. At the start of the story, Mr. Stott had hidden the fact that John was in trouble, and he hadn't told the kids about the trouble brewing in Walnut Hills. Why do you think he withheld that information? Do you think it was a good choice? Explain.

2. Nate, Trevor, Summer, and Pigeon chose to get involved with Arcadeland even though they knew it might be dangerous. Would you take a risk like that to help a friend? Why or why not?

3. As the story went on, the kids did some things they might not have normally done in order to remain undercover working for Jonas White. Why do you think they did those things? What alternatives did they have?

4. Jonas White claimed not to mind that Nate had helped take down his sister. Were you convinced? Why do you think Jonas was willing to let Nate and his friends work for him even though he didn't really trust them? How did this hurt him in the end?

5. Belinda White had been an enemy to Nate, Trevor, Summer, and Pigeon, but after her identity was wiped and she became a kid, they turned into friends. Do you think you could become friends with a former enemy under those circumstances? Why or why not?

6. Mr. Stott and the Blue Falcons kept Lindy's true identity from her. Do you think they were right to withhold that information from her? What would you have done if you were making that choice?

7. Diego and Pigeon wondered whether Belinda had originally become evil due to her nature or because of her upbringing. What do you think?

8. When talking about Lindy, Mozag said, "We are who we choose to become." Does that statement seem true to you? Why or why not?

9. If you could have any stamp from this book, which would you choose? Why? If you could blend any two stamps, which would you choose? Why? If you could blend any two candies or stamps from this series, which would you choose? Why?

10. Uweya was an amazingly powerful simulacrum. How could it be used to do good? How could it be used to cause harm? If you had access to Uweya, would you use it or destroy it? Why?

11. If you could create magical stamps, what new stamps would you invent, and what powers would they have?

12. Which of Jonas White's helpers would you least want as an enemy? Why?

13. Who would you rather have on your side—John Dart, Mozag, Mr. Stott, or the Battiatos? Explain why. Who would you most want as a friend—Nate, Trevor, Summer, Pigeon, Chris, Risa, Roman, or Lindy? Explain.

14. Do you have a favorite arcade that you visit? What is your favorite game to play in an arcade? What is your favorite video game to play at home? Describe a video game or arcade game that you wish existed.

ABOUT THE AUTHOR

Brandon Mull is the author of the *New York Times, USA Today,* and *Wall Street Journal* bestselling Beyonders and Fablehaven series. He resides in Utah, in a happy little valley near the mouth of a canyon, with his wife and four children. Brandon's greatest regret is that he has but one life to give for Gondor.

Turn the page for a peek at *Sky Raiders*,
Book One in Brandon Mull's new
Five Kingdoms series!

Weaving down the hall, Cole avoided a ninja, a witch, a pirate, and a zombie bride. He paused when a sad clown in a trench coat and fedora waved at him. "Dalton?"

His friend nodded and smiled, which looked weird since his mouth was painted into a frown. "I wondered if you'd recognize me."

"It wasn't easy," Cole replied, relieved to see that his best friend had worn an elaborate costume. He had worried that his own outfit was too much.

They met up in the middle of the hall. Kids streamed by on either side; some dressed for Halloween, some not.

"Ready to score some candy tonight?" Dalton asked.

Cole hesitated. Now that they were sixth graders, he was a little nervous that people would think they were too old to go door to door. He didn't want to look like a kindergartener. "Have you heard about the haunted house on Wilson?"

"The spook alley house?" Dalton clarified. "I heard it has live rats and snakes."

Cole nodded. "The guy who moved in there is supposed to be a special-effects expert. I guess he worked on some big movies. It might just be hype, but I keep hearing amazing things. We should check it out."

"Yeah, sure, I'm curious," Dalton said. "But I don't want to skip the candy."

Cole thought for a minute. He *had* noticed some sixth graders trick-or-treating in his neighborhood last year. A few kids had looked even older. Besides, did it matter what anyone else thought? If people were handing out free candy, why not take advantage? They already had the costumes. "Okay. We can start early."

"That'll work."

The first bell rang. Class would start soon. "See you," Cole said.

"Later."

Cole walked into his classroom, noticing that Jenna Hunt was already at her desk. Cole tried not to care. He liked her, but not in *that* way. Sure, in the past he might have felt excited and scared whenever she was around, but now she was just a friend.

At least that was what he kept telling himself as he tried to take his seat behind her. He was dressed up as a scarecrow that had been used for archery practice. The feathered shafts protruding from his chest and side made it tricky to sit down.

Had he ever had a crush on Jenna? Maybe, when he was younger. During second grade, the girls went through a phase when they ran around trying to kiss the boys at recess. It had been disgusting. Like tag, except with cooties involved. The teachers had been against it. Cole had been against it too—except when it was with Jenna. When she was chasing him, a secret part of him wanted to get caught.

It wasn't his fault he kept noticing Jenna during third, fourth, and fifth grades. She was too pretty. He wasn't the only one who thought so. She had modeled in some catalogs. Her dark hair had just the right amount of curl, and her thick eyelashes made her eyes look made-up, even when she wasn't wearing makeup.

He sometimes used to daydream about older jerks picking on Jenna. In his imagination, he would come along and save the day with a burst of bravery and action-movie karate skills. Afterward, he would be forced to suffer through her tearful thanks.

But everything had changed at the start of sixth grade. Jenna had not only ended up in his class, but by pure chance the seating chart had placed him directly behind her. They had worked together on group projects. He had learned to relax around her, and they had started to talk regularly and make jokes. She had turned out to be cooler than he had hoped. They were actually becoming friends. So there was no reason for his heart to pound just because she was dressed up like Cleopatra.

A graded test sat on top of his test, a circled 96 in red ink proclaiming his success. Tests waited on the other empty desks as well. Cole tried not to spy on the other scores, but he couldn't help noticing that his neighbors got a 72 and an 88.

Jenna turned and looked at him. She wore a wig of limp black hair with ruler-straight bangs. Dramatic makeup accentuated her eyes. A golden circlet with a snake at the front served as her crown. "What are you?" she asked. "A dead scarecrow?"

"Close," Cole replied. "I'm a scarecrow that got used for target practice."

"Are those real arrows?"

"Yeah, but I broke off the tips. Halloween or not, I figured they would send me home if I brought sharp arrows to school."

"You aced another test. I thought scarecrows weren't supposed to have brains."

"I wasn't a scarecrow yesterday. I like your costume."

"Do you know who I am?"

Cole scrunched his face, as if she had stumped him. "A ghost?"

Jenna rolled her eyes. "You know, right?"

He nodded. "You're one of the most famous ladies in history. Queen Elizabeth."

"Wrong country."

"I'm kidding. Cleopatra."

"Wrong again. Are you even trying?"

"Seriously? I thought I knew it for sure."

"I'm Cleopatra's twin sister."

"You got me."

"Maybe I should have come as Dorothy all shot up with arrows," Jenna said. "Then we would have matched."

"We could have been the sadder ending to *The Wizard of Oz*."

"The ending where the wizard turns out to be Robin Hood."

Laini Palmer sat in the desk next to Jenna's. She was

dressed as the Statue of Liberty. Jenna turned and started talking to her.

Cole glanced at the clock. There were still a few minutes before class would begin. Jenna had a habit of arriving by the first bell, and Cole had coincidentally developed the same habit. More kids were coming in: a zombie, a vampire fairy, a rock star, an army guy. Kevin Murdock wore no costume. Neither did Sheila Jones.

When Jenna had finished talking to Laini, Cole tapped her shoulder. "Have you heard about that new haunted house?"

"On Wilson Avenue?" Jenna asked. "People keep talking about it. I've never really been scared by Halloween decorations. I always know they're fake."

"The guy who just moved in there supposedly did effects for Hollywood," Cole replied. "I heard that some of the stuff in his spook alley is real. Like, live bats and tarantulas and amputated body parts from hospitals."

"I guess that might be freaky," Jenna admitted. "I'd have to see it to believe it."

"It's supposed to be free. Are you going trick-or-treating?"

"Yeah, with Lacie and Sarah. You?"

"I was planning to go around with Dalton." He was relieved she would be out hunting candy as well.

"Do you know the address?" Jenna asked.

"For the haunted house? I wrote it down."

"We should check it out. Want to meet up around seven?"

Cole tried to keep his expression casual. "Where?"

"Do you know that old guy's house on the corner, with the huge flagpole?"

"Sure." Everybody in the area knew that house. It was one story, but the flagpole was basically a skyscraper. The old guy looked like a veteran. He raised and lowered the flag every morning and night. "Meet there?"

"Bring the address."

Cole retrieved a notebook from his backpack and opened it. While he looked for his homework, his mind strayed. He had never hung out with Jenna after school, but it wasn't like they were going on a date. They would just be part of a group of kids checking to see if a spook alley was actually cool.

Mr. Brock started class a few moments later. He was dressed as a cowboy with chaps, a big hat, and a sheriff's badge. The outfit made it tough to take him seriously.

Cole walked along the street beside Dalton, one foot on the curb, the other in the gutter. He was still a scarecrow bristling with arrows. The straw poking out from his neck kept tickling the bottom of his chin. Dalton remained a gloomy clown.

"She wanted to meet at the flagpole?" Dalton verified.

"Just near the house," Cole said. "Not on his lawn."

Dalton pulled back the sleeve of his coat and checked his watch. "We're going to be early."

"Only a little."

"Are you nervous?"

Cole shot him a scowl. "I'm not afraid of haunted houses."

"I don't mean the spook alley," Dalton clarified. "Haven't you always sort of liked—"

"No, Dalton, come on," Cole interrupted. "Be serious. It isn't like that. We're friends."

Dalton bobbed his eyebrows up and down. "My parents say they started out as friends."

"Gross, knock it off." Cole couldn't let Dalton say or do anything that might make Jenna suspect he thought she was cute. "I should have never told you I used to like her. That was forever ago. We're just doing this for fun."

Dalton squinted up ahead. "Looks like a big group."

He was right. They found Jenna waiting with seven other kids—three of them boys. She was still dressed like Cleopatra.

"Here they are," Jenna announced. "We can go now."

"I have the address," Cole offered.

"I know where it is," Blake said. "I went by earlier tonight."

"What's it like?" Dalton asked.

"I didn't go inside," Blake replied. "I just live nearby."

Cole knew Blake from school. He was the kind of guy who liked to take charge and talked a lot. He always wanted to be goalie at recess, even though he wasn't that good.

As they started walking, Blake took the lead. Cole fell in beside Jenna. "So what's your name?" Cole asked.

"Huh?" she replied. "Cleopatra?"

"No, you're her twin."

"Right. Want to guess?"

"Irma?"

"That doesn't sound very Egyptian."

"Queen Tut?"

"Sure, let's go with that." Jenna laughed lightly, then strayed over to her friend Sarah and started talking. Cole fell back to walk with Dalton.

"Do you think the spook alley will actually be freaky?" Dalton asked.

"It better be," Cole said. "I have my hopes up."

Blake set a quick pace. They marched briskly, passing a herd of little kids with plastic superhero faces. Most of the houses had halfhearted decorations. Some had none. A few had really elaborate jack-o'-lanterns that must have been carved using patterns.

Dalton elbowed Cole and nodded toward a doorway. A portly witch was handing out full-size Twix bars to a group of little kids.

"It's okay," Cole said, hefting his pillowcase. "We already made a good haul."

"Not much full-size candy," Dalton pointed out.

"A few little Twixes are just as good," Cole said, unsure about whether he had any in his bag.

"I heard they have some real cadavers," Blake was explaining. "Dead bodies donated to science but stolen to use as decorations."

"Think that's true?" Dalton wondered.

"I doubt it," Cole replied. "The guy would end up in jail."

"What do you know about it?" Blake challenged. "Have you been stealing corpses?"

"Nope," Cole said. "Your mom was too broke to hire me."

Everyone laughed at that one, and Blake had no reply. Cole had always been good at comebacks. It was his best defense mechanism and usually kept other kids from bothering him.

As they continued down the street, Cole tried to think

of an excuse to walk alongside Jenna. Unfortunately, she now had Lacie on one side and Sarah on the other. Cole had spoken with Jenna enough to feel fairly natural around her. Sarah and Lacie were a different story. He couldn't work up the nerve to barge in and hijack their conversation. Every possible comment that came to mind seemed clumsy and forced. At least Dalton was getting plenty of proof that he and Jenna were only friends.

Cole paid attention to the route. Part of him hoped Blake would lead them the wrong way, but he made no mistakes. When the spook alley house came into view, Blake displayed it to the others as if he had decorated it personally.

The house looked decent on the outside. Much better than average. A few fake ravens perched on the roof. Webby curtains hung from the rain gutters. One of the jack-o'-lanterns puked seeds and pulp all over the sidewalk. The lawn had lots of cardboard headstones, with an occasional plastic hand or leg poking up through the grass.

"Pretty good," Dalton conceded.

"I don't know," Cole said. "After all the buildup, I was expecting granite tombstones with actual human skeletons. Maybe some ghost holograms."

"The best stuff might be inside," Dalton said.

"We'll see," Cole replied. He paused, studying the details. Why did he feel so disappointed? Why did he care about the impressiveness of the decorations? Because he had talked Jenna into coming here. If the haunted house was cool, he might get some reflected glory. If it was weak, she would have gone out of her way for nothing. Was that really it?

Maybe he was just frustrated that he had hardly talked to her.

Blake led the way to the door. He knocked while the other nine kids mobbed the porch. A guy with long hair and a stubbly beard answered. He had a cleaver through his head, with plenty of blood draining from the wound.

"He must be the special-effects pro," Dalton murmured.

"I don't know," Cole said. "It's pretty gory, but not the ultimate."

The fatally injured man stepped away from the door to invite them in. A strobe light flashed nonstop. Dry-ice smoke drifted across the floor. Tinfoil coated the walls, reflecting the pulsing light. There were webs and skulls and candelabras. A knight in full armor came toward them, raising a huge sword. The strobe light made his movements jerky. A couple of the girls screamed.

The knight lowered his sword. He moved around a little more, mostly from side to side, trying to milk the moment, but he was less menacing because he had failed to pursue his attack. Seeming to realize he was no longer very threatening, the knight started doing robotic dance moves. A few of the kids laughed.

Cole frowned, feeling even more disappointed. "Why did everyone build this up so much?" he asked Dalton.

"What were you expecting?" Dalton replied.

Cole shrugged. "Rabid wolves fighting to the death."

"It's not bad," Dalton consoled.

"Too much hype," Cole replied. "My expectations were through the roof." Turning, he found Jenna beside him. "Are you terrified?"

"Not really," she said, looking around appraisingly. "I don't see any body parts. They did a good job, though."

The clunky knight was retreating to his hiding place. The cleaver guy started distributing candy—miniatures, but he gave everybody two or three.

Then an older kid with messy hair wandered into the hall. He was skinny, probably around college age. He wore jeans and an orange T-shirt that said BOO in huge black letters. Otherwise he had no costume.

"Was this scary enough?" he asked nonchalantly.

A couple of the girls said yes. Most of the kids were silent. Cole felt like it would be rude to tell the truth.

The Boo guy folded his skinny arms across his chest. "Some of you don't look very frightened. Anybody want to see the really scary part?"

He acted serious, but it also could have been a setup for some corny joke.

"Sure," Cole volunteered. Jenna and a bunch of the others chimed in as well.

The Boo guy stared at them like he was a general and this new batch of troops might not be up to his standards. "All right, if you say so. Fair warning: If any of this other stuff was freaky at all, don't come."

Two of the girls started shaking their heads and backing toward the door. One of them turned and buried her head against Stuart Fulsom. Stu left with them.

"Check out Stu," Cole muttered to Dalton. "He thinks he's Dr. Love."

"Why would those girls have come in the first place if

they didn't want to get freaked out?" Dalton complained.

Cole shrugged. If Jenna had wanted to bail, would he have left with her? Maybe if she had buried her head against his chest, trembling with worry . . .

The remaining seven kids followed the Boo guy. He led them through a regular kitchen to a white door with a plain brass knob. "It's down in the basement. I won't be coming. You sure you want to go? It's really messed up."

Blake opened the door and led the way down. Cole and Dalton shared a glance. They had come this far. No way were they wimping out now. None of the others chickened out either.

BEYONDERS

"Brandon Mull is a wizard with words.
With Beyonders, he has conjured one of the most
original fantasies I've read in years—an irresistible
mix of adventure, humor, and magic."
—RICK RIORDAN, *author of*
the Percy Jackson and the Olympians series

BRANDONMULL·COM